W9-AOA-911

THE THIRD WIFE

Also available from MIRA Books and
JASMINE CRESSWELL

THE CONSPIRACY
THE REFUGE
THE INHERITANCE
THE DISAPPEARANCE
THE DAUGHTER
SECRET SINS
NO SIN TOO GREAT
DESIRES & DECEPTIONS

JASMINE CRESSWELL

THE THIRD WIFE

ISBN: 0-7394-2880-2

THE THIRD WIFE

Printed in U.S.A.

To Fiona,
with love and admiration for all you've achieved.

One

Southwestern Colorado, June 1987

Brushing away sentimental tears, Betty Jean gave a final tweak to her daughter's wedding veil, fluffing air into it so that it fell in a puffy cloud around Anna's bouffant hairdo.

''You look real pretty,'' Betty Jean said, urging her daughter to turn around so that she could look at herself in the mirror hung on the back of the bedroom door. ''Aunt Debbie did a fine job with your dress, didn't she? She's so talented with her sewing now she's got that lovely new machine Ray bought for her birthday.''

Anna heard worry in her mom's voice, barely hidden beneath the note of forced cheerfulness. Betty Jean might not be too smart in terms of book-learning, but she had a streak of shrewdness that surfaced when you least expected it, and she sensed something seriously off-key in her daughter's meekness, even though she probably couldn't pin a name on her worry.

For a moment Anna considered giving up her pretense and just appealing flat out for her mom's help, but she quickly gave up on that idea. Relying on her mom would be dangerous. Real dangerous. If Betty Jean let her down—and she almost certainly would—then all the careful playacting Anna had done for the past six weeks would be wasted. Six weeks of pretending that she was looking forward to marrying Caleb Welks, her stepfather's brother. Six weeks of pretending that she was ready to submit, humbly and dutifully, to God's will.

God's will as interpreted by Ray and Caleb Welks, that was. In this house, there was no need to waste time praying, or reading the Bible to try to find out what God might want for you to do. Here, all you had to do was ask Ray. Sometimes it seemed like Ray just about had a speed-dial phone line direct to God, he was so sure he knew exactly what the Lord wanted.

Anna never doubted that her mom loved her, but love wasn't enough to ensure that Betty Jean would be on her side, much less stand up for her. Ray had her mom so much under his thumb that she mostly didn't have a mind of her own anymore. The truth was, Betty Jean was so crazy mixed-up right now that she couldn't see what a crock of shit Ray Welks was passing off on her, pretending it was something real good and sweet-smelling.

Anna wished her mom could be stronger, but that was like wishing the moon would shine over the cow barn in the middle of the day. Betty Jean had gone to pieces when Anna's dad died way back in 1979, when Anna was only in the third grade. Ray had been the person who'd helped glue her mom back together again, Anna had to admit that much. But what Betty Jean didn't seem to realize was that Ray had stuck the pieces together according to his own messed-up pattern, so that instead of being nice and smooth and confident, her mom was all cracked and rackety. The fragile person Betty Jean had become couldn't function without Ray to tell her what she must do and how she must think. And, of course, Ray always told Betty Jean it was her God-given duty to think just like him.

Anna hated to see how her mom had lost all confidence in herself. In the old days, Betty Jean had been pretty good at stuff like cooking and keeping house and reading fun bedtime stories. Anna remembered how they'd baked cookies after school every Friday, and how her mom always kept a jug of flowers on the table, although they had no money after her dad died and the bank was threatening to take back their house. But nowadays, Betty Jean was so beaten down that even caring for five-year-old Billy and three-year-old Susan would be way beyond her if it weren't for all the help she got from Aunt Debbie and Aunt Patsy.

Which left Anna pretty much on her own when it came to taking care of herself. That was okay, though, because she had her plans for the future all worked out. She just had to submit to this dumb wedding ceremony, and then she'd be free. Well, almost free. A little bubble of nausea formed in the pit of Anna's stomach, but she ignored it. No need to think about what would happen after the wedding ceremony, when she would be expected to climb into bed with Caleb Welks. Thinking about having sex with Caleb wouldn't change the need to go through with it, so there was no point in getting roiled up about it. Right now, what she needed to do was concentrate on keeping everyone in Ray's house convinced that she was happy as a songbird with a belly full of juicy worms.

When Ray first delivered his announcement that God wanted her to be sealed in marriage with his brother, Caleb, shock had made Anna stupid. Otherwise she'd never have made the fatal error of screaming out she'd kill herself before she agreed to marry Caleb Welks. He was old, only a year short of forty, and he was going bald, and he had a look in his eyes that scared her. Not exactly a mean look, but something that scared her even more than plain old mean.

Her stepfather never tolerated any opposition, but at least he'd never given her the sort of hot, squirmy look she got from Caleb. Besides, Ray wasn't physically violent. Well, not unless you counted him dragging her up the stairs to lock her in her room when she screamed that she wasn't going to be married off before she finished high school. But Caleb Welks…well, that was another story. Anna had heard rumors, whispers among the women when they thought Anna wasn't paying attention. After watching Caleb and his family closely in church every Sunday for the past six weeks, Anna believed the whispers. She was sure her soon-to-be husband used his leather belt for a lot more than holding up his fancy, bought-in-Denver pants.

Anna had kept up her defiance for three days after Ray's original pronouncement, even though she'd been locked in her room, with her clothes and shoes taken away, forbidden to go to school for the final week of the semester. At the end of the three days, she finally realized how brainless she was being. What did she think she would achieve with her protests? Even if she managed to stave off marriage to

Caleb—which was about as likely as her pig Polly learning to fly around the farmyard—she would simply be betrothed to someone else. Now that she'd finished her junior year of high school, Ray was going to make sure she was married off before she could complete her senior year and graduate. Educated women with diplomas and dreams of attending college didn't fit well into the Alana Springs community.

Three days of despair concentrated her mind enough that Anna finally got smart. She realized that pretending submission to Ray's wishes was the only way she would ever be able to escape from his clutches. She sent one of her stepsisters to Ray with a message, begging for forgiveness. Then, when he unlocked the door, she fell down on her knees in front of him, sobbing. God had spoken to her, she informed Ray and her anxiously hovering mother. She realized now that it was part of the Divine Plan for her to marry Caleb, and she looked forward to having the ceremony as soon as possible.

Ray announced that the ceremony would take place on Anna's seventeenth birthday, only six weeks away. He sent her a sidelong glance as he made the suggestion, clearly expecting opposition. Anna, newly wise, smiled and told him the date was a perfect choice. It would make for a lovely double celebration to have her birthday and her wedding anniversary on the same day each year. Visibly gratified, Ray said he'd worried that she wasn't ready for marriage, but now he was hopeful she was going to make his brother a loving and obedient wife.

Not in this lifetime, Anna swore to herself. Besides, if Ray harbored so many doubts about whether she was ready for marriage, why was he going ahead and insisting on marrying her off to his brother? She didn't ask, of course. Demands for logical explanations didn't fit well into her new role of mindless obedience.

After her dramatic display of contrition, she'd hoped that Ray would relax his vigilance, giving her a chance to run away, but her stepfather was much too smart to accept her sudden compliance at face value. The door to her room had been unlocked, but she was still a prisoner, watched every minute of every day. Gradually, as the wedding date loomed relentlessly closer, Anna was forced to accept that she had no hope of escaping until after the ceremony.

Refusing to give up hope, she spent every minute she could spare from her chores perfecting her escape plan. Her husband-to-be had two cars, one of them a new Ford Taurus. If she disabled his old station wagon and stole the Taurus, she would probably be able to make it out of the county before he could catch her. Depending on how much gas was in the tank of the Taurus, she'd need at least another twenty bucks to get as far as Denver, where she figured she ought to be able to hide away pretty good.

The fact that Anna had money for gas was her secret weapon. Nobody knew that she had worked for the school principal during her lunch hour for most of the last two semesters, doing clerical jobs and filing in the back office. The principal had paid her fifteen dollars a week and she'd saved every cent of her earnings. Last night, when Joy, Brenda and Margaret had finally fallen asleep after hours of excited chatter about the wedding, Anna had hidden in the closet and, by flashlight, stitched $420 into a muslin band tacked onto the inside of the ruffled petticoat made specially to wear under her wedding gown. She had no illusions about how far that money would stretch. She knew four hundred bucks wasn't enough to rent an apartment in a big city like Denver, not by the time you paid a security deposit and everything, but it was enough to buy her food and she could wash in public rest rooms and sleep in the car until she got a job. Anything was better than getting trapped in a celestial marriage, endlessly pregnant with Caleb's babies.

"Anna, honey, what's the matter?" She'd been lost in thought much too long, and her mother's voice had taken on a new layer of worry. "Why don't you want to turn around so you can see how pretty you look in your lovely dress?"

Anna satisfied her mother by swiveling around and staring at herself in the mirror. An overweight, auburn-haired teenager stared back, reflected against a background of four bunk beds crowded into the bedroom she shared with Ray's three oldest daughters. Many of the women in Alana Springs were overweight, not only because they ate a lot of cheap, starchy food in an effort to stretch the grocery money as far as possible, but also because baking cakes and inviting each other to little in-home parties was one of the few ways they had to entertain themselves.

Her mom and Aunt Debbie were both looking at her with real concern, and even Aunt Patsy—the Queen of Mean—appeared a bit anxious. Since Anna had spent the past six weeks chirping and squealing with fake delight over the wedding plans, it was only to be expected that her sudden attack of silence would make everyone nervous.

The need to lull their suspicions gave Anna the strength to force her mouth into a smile, as if she were thrilled by the sight of her hideous, calf-length white wedding dress, with its frilled collar and bloated, elbow-length sleeves, trimmed with scratchy lace bought on sale from Wal-Mart. Panty hose and toeless white sandals completed a bridal outfit that was so far beyond tacky that Anna couldn't find words to describe its full awfulness even in the privacy of her own thoughts.

Still, she understood the need to appear both grateful and excited. She was carrying a bouquet of pink carnations and baby's breath, picked up yesterday afternoon from the supermarket in Cortez, and she held the bouquet out to one side, twirling around so that her skirt billowed out just a little. Her mom and Aunt Debbie both applauded.

Aunt Patsy wasn't willing to go that far, even if getting rid of Anna had been her main objective for the past three years at least. Instead of clapping, she started to deliver another of her rambling lectures about the sanctity of marriage, and a wife's duty to submit to her husband in all things. Anna was so close to exploding that she was actually relieved when Ray knocked on the bedroom door, asking if they were ready, and telling them they needed to hurry.

His words produced an immediate flurry of activity. Once Ray Welks spoke, the women of his household sprang into instant action. Her mom picked up the suitcase containing all Anna's worldly possessions, and she was rushed downstairs to say goodbye to her stepbrothers and sisters. The little ones looked bewildered, not understanding what was going on, but Brenda and Margaret, her two oldest stepsisters, hugged her fiercely, even though they expected to see her in church tomorrow. Anna felt a sharp pang.

Brenda and Margaret were only a little younger than she was, and the three of them had been almost inseparable for the past six years. She loved Billy and Susan, her half brother and sister, but she loved Brenda and Margaret, Aunt Patsy's daughters, even more. It was real hard to bear in her heart the secret knowledge that she would probably never see them again in her whole entire life.

His arm linked with his stepdaughter's, Ray hustled his three wives out of the house and into the waiting car. In honor of the special occasion, he'd taken the toddler car seats out of his 1982 Chevy Impala and cleaned off the exterior with the hose. As the bride-to-be, Anna got the position of honor next to Ray, while her mom sat in the back seat, along with Debbie and Patsy, Ray's two other wives. None of her brothers and sisters were allowed to attend the wedding because, according to Ray, it was necessary to keep the guest list small. It would be risky to draw too much attention to the day's activities.

That was why her wedding ceremony would take place in Caleb's house, not in the church meeting house. As far as Anna knew, nobody in Alana Springs had ever been prosecuted for bigamy, but apparently a couple of nosy reporters had gotten in touch with some wicked women who'd fled the protection of their families in the polygamous community that flourished in Colorado City, Arizona. The surge of outside interest had renewed fears of interference by the state in matters that the True Life Latter Day Saints considered private between God and his church.

According to Ray, reporters didn't care about sacred beliefs, they only cared about creating scandals, and even though everyone in Alana Springs knew that their lifestyle was part of God's Divine Plan, they were being extra careful these days to keep a low profile. At breakfast time this morning, Ray had solemnly reported on the warning he'd received during the night from God. A little prevention was worth a lot of cure, God had said, and Ray for sure wasn't going to ignore a direct warning from God.

Anna had noticed over the years that God had an annoying tendency to express Himself in clichés that were notable chiefly for their utter triteness. Besides, neither God nor Ray Welks needed to worry much about stirring up the wrath of the local authorities, however much trouble the folks in Utah and Arizona might be facing. The law was administered in Alana Springs by a sheriff and two deputies who were both practicing believers in celestial marriage, so it didn't seem very likely that they were going to invade Caleb Welks's home and cart him off to jail, even if they did get wind of the ceremony that was about to take place. The fact that Sheriff Betz was a practicing member of the True Life Latter Day Saints was the very reason Anna hadn't gone to him for help when Ray announced that she was to be sealed in marriage with Caleb Welks.

Anna had only a fuzzy idea of United States law, but she was fairly sure that a seventeen-year-old couldn't be forced to marry anyone she didn't want to, even if she was a minor and—according to Ray—subject to the will of her parents, under God. Still, all that was irrelevant now. She was going through with the marriage, because then she'd be free.

Her husband-to-be was the president of a bank in Cortez and the only member of the Alana Springs community who had money to spare. His house was bigger than most and in an excellent state of repair, eliciting little murmurs of appreciation from Betty Jean, Debbie and Patsy, even though they'd visited many times before.

"My, what a lovely home you're coming to," Patsy said, with a touch of genuine warmth. With Anna finally out of the house, she apparently felt able to be generous. "You're lucky that God and your stepfather have arranged such a wonderful marriage for you."

"It's a nice house," Anna agreed, scanning the facade of the two-story building, and noting with relief that Caleb's Ford Taurus was in the carport, along with the big Oldsmobile station wagon that was used by his other two wives and their six children, five of whom still lived at home. Anna strove to keep all trace of irony from her voice. "I know I'm very lucky to be marrying Caleb."

"My brother is a devoted servant of the Lord," Ray said as they drew up at the end of the dirt driveway. He parked the Chevy on a patch of gravel in front of the stoop, then unlocked the car doors so that the four women could get out. "He will make you a good husband."

They trooped up the steps, Anna's hand hooked through Ray's arm and his three wives ranged behind her. Anna realized it was getting easier and easier to act obedient now that she could count down the hours to the moment of her liberation. After all, this marriage wasn't legal and she didn't believe it was God's will, either. She could think of it as a piece of meaningless playacting. Which, in fact, was what it was in the eyes of most of the world.

Caleb opened the door in answer to Ray's knock. At thirty-nine, he was six years younger than Ray and about twenty pounds heavier, with all of the extra weight carried in a roll of flesh around his middle. In honor of the occasion, he was dressed in one of his banker's suits of dark blue pinstripes, and he wore a white starched shirt along with a sober blue paisley tie. His jowls hung slightly over his tight collar, making his small ears appear conspicuous. His gaze flicked toward Anna and she saw the usual hot flare of lust in his eyes before he turned toward his brother, adjusting his face into a mask of heavy solemnity.

"Ray, great to see you, come on in." He shook his brother's hand, then nodded to the three wives standing just a step behind Ray. "Ladies, thank you for coming. We've got everything ready in the living room. The children are all very excited."

"They do love a party, don't they?" Aunt Patsy gave her brother-in-law a friendly smile. "We'll take your children home with us, Caleb, and bring them to church with us in the morning. That way you and Anna can have a few hours to yourselves."

"That's thoughtful of you. I appreciate the offer." Caleb's gaze flicked toward Anna again, but this time she met his eyes and faked a shy smile. However difficult it was not to puke, not to scream, not to run, she had to play along. She couldn't blow it now, or her chance might be gone forever. Eventually she'd be able to escape, of course, since she couldn't be kept confined to Caleb's house indefinitely. But if they kept her under surveillance, she might be pregnant by the time she managed to make her getaway, and that would spell disaster because she knew she could never abandon a baby of hers, even one who had Caleb for its father. In the long run, Anna suspected it was the children that often kept the women of Alana Springs tied to their husbands, even when all the other bonds started to chafe.

Caleb led the visitors into his living room, where his two existing wives were waiting. Pamela, his first wife, was only thirty-seven, but she looked matronly, almost middle-aged. She'd been married to Caleb for nineteen years, and she had three children, a son who was eighteen and had already left home, and two daughters who were sixteen and fourteen.

Darlene, Caleb's second wife, was still in her twenties and the mother of two sons and a daughter who had all been born within three years of each other. Darlene's last pregnancy had been difficult, and she was known to have various unspecified female complaints. Anna thought cynically that a desire to avoid having any more children might well be the major female problem that she suffered from. Birth control was against the religious beliefs of the True Life Latter Day Saints, and sex was normally timed to provide the maximum chance of successful impregnation, so ill health was the only refuge for wives who wanted to escape the burden of too many pregnancies in too short a time.

Caleb's two wives rose to their feet as soon as Caleb and the bridal party entered the living room, children clustering near their mothers. Everybody already knew everybody else, and there were greetings all around, with much nervous laughter and many self-conscious smiles. Darlene told Anna that she looked beautiful, although it appeared as if it nearly choked her to utter the words. She might not want any more babies, but she didn't want another wife vying for Caleb's attention either.

Pamela, on the other hand, seemed almost gleeful in her welcome and Anna—well versed in the politics of polygamous households—quickly realized that Pamela was spitefully delighted that pretty young Darlene was about to face competition from a wife who was a decade younger, even if not quite so pretty.

Nobody else seemed to notice anything amiss with the welcome Anna was getting. She wondered if she could possibly be the only person who felt the tension prickling in the air. Or maybe it was just in her mind, and not in the air at all. There were lots of days when Anna was quite sure all the wives in Alana Springs knew their polygamous lifestyle was freaky. Other times, she felt a gut-wrenching fear that the women were as happy as they claimed to be and that she was the weirdo, the odd person out who was so corrupt and sinful that she couldn't see the beauty of the polygamous way of life. Her stepsisters, Brenda and Margaret, had no doubts that celestial marriage was God's will, so why did Anna have this pesky little voice deep inside that kept popping up with snide comments, making her feel as if she were always standing at the edge of the group, an observer at the events of her own life?

Ray was acting as priest for the wedding ceremony and he was clearly anxious to get things moving. Perhaps he still harbored a fear that Anna might change her mind if she was given too much time to think about it. He positioned himself in front of the room's largest window and quickly got the women and children lined up on either side of Caleb and Anna, according to which family they belonged to.

With everyone in place, Ray opened his Bible and read one of his favorite passages, where Paul the Apostle tells the women of Ephesus that they are duty-bound to submit to their husbands. Ray skipped over the verses in which Paul admonishes husbands to love their wives and took up again at the point where the apostle sternly advises children that they are always to obey their parents.

He then led her and Caleb through a short version of the wedding service. The men of the True Life Latter Day Saints wore only one wedding band to indicate their marital status, but husbands pledged their fidelity to their multiple wives by giving each of them a ring. So Caleb slipped a narrow gold band onto Anna's ring finger as he made his vows to love and cherish her for all eternity, but when it came time for her to give Caleb a ring, he slipped off the wedding band he was already wearing, and she gave it back to him, promising to love and obey him for all eternity.

Like that was going to happen in this or any other lifetime, Anna thought with silent defiance. It wasn't enough that she should promise to obey him in this life. She had to promise to obey him for ever and ever, amen. Yuk, and double yuk. Besides, when her thoughts were wandering during an especially boring sermon in church a couple of weeks ago, she'd decided that she believed in reincarnation, which made the whole idea of eternal marriage even more screwy. If that was possible.

Beaming with a relief he couldn't entirely hide, Ray pronounced that Anna and Caleb were now sealed in marriage for all eternity. ''Congratulations,'' he said, shaking his brother's hand. ''You can kiss your new bride.''

Caleb put his arms on Anna's shoulders and dropped a quick, chaste kiss on her forehead. Anna hadn't expected anything more passionate. It was one of the odder aspects of living in a polygamous community that all the residents of Alana Springs were majorly repressed about demonstrating physical affection in public. Not that she was complaining. The fewer slobbery kisses from Caleb that she had to endure, the better.

Caleb turned to face his two other wives. ''Pamela, Darlene. Come and kiss your new sister-wife.'' His tone was commanding rather than amiable.

The two women trooped to Anna's side and dutifully kissed her on the cheek, although she noticed that they both avoided meeting her gaze. Obviously Caleb's wives had even less thought of disobeying their husband than Ray's wives had of disobeying him. Then Anna had to kiss each of Caleb's children on the forehead and promise to love them as her own.

That final ritual over, Pamela clapped her hands and announced with every appearance of genuine merriment that it was now time to begin the party. The children raced out to the kitchen and returned bearing platters of food, and Pamela herself carried in a two-tiered wedding cake frosted with pale-pink roses.

The wedding party followed a predictable course, with everyone except Anna eating heartily and downing quantities of the homemade, sickly sweet lemonade that was a staple of social life in Alana Springs. Then it was time to cut the wedding cake, propose toasts—in lemonade, of course—and deliver speeches. Unlike the speeches at most weddings, there was absolutely no reference to the honeymoon, the wedding night, or anything that even remotely hinted that sex was a normal part of married life. Fortunately, Anna wasn't expected to do anything more during all of this than smile and blush modestly.

The party continued until dark, which was almost nine o'clock at this time of year. With great efficiency—polygamy tended to lead to competition for the title of best housekeeper—the women put away the food, washed the dishes, and generally tidied up, while Ray made the arrangements for escorting his brother's children back to the farm, where they would sleep over.

Despite the fact that she knew the children were being taken away in order to give her and Caleb more privacy for the consummation of their marriage, Anna felt the day's first spark of optimism as she listened to the two brothers plan transportation. There wasn't room in Ray's car to accommodate all five of Caleb's children, so Aunt Patsy was designated to drive the three girls back to the ranch in Caleb's Oldsmobile, while Ray planned to take the boys in the Chevy, along with his other two wives.

Her escape had just been made one giant step easier, Anna realized. Now there would be no second car of Caleb's that she needed to disable. If she could steal the Taurus—and she'd already located the car keys hanging on a hook in the kitchen under the pretense of getting a drink of water—then Caleb would be helpless to follow her. He could phone for help, but surely she could count on getting a minimum twenty-minute head start? And in the middle of the night, with no traffic on the roads, she could be twenty-five miles away from Alana Springs in that amount of time. The recent attention paid to the polygamous community in Colorado City, Arizona made her escape plan all the more likely to succeed, because she was sure Caleb wouldn't inform the legal authorities that she'd run off, so the state police weren't going to be looking for her. All she needed to do was escape the jurisdiction of the local sheriff and she'd be free.

In keeping with the near obsessive need to pretend that plural marriages had nothing to do with sex, the bedrooms in a polygamous household were off-limits to outsiders. Despite Anna's six Sunday visits to Caleb's house since her official betrothal, neither he nor his wives had ever taken her upstairs, so she had no idea where she would be sleeping and no idea how difficult it would be to make her getaway. The possibility that she and Caleb's other wives might all be expected to sleep together was too dreadful to contemplate, so she just didn't think about it.

She seemed to be doing a lot of not thinking about things today, Anna reflected wryly. Maybe that was how wives in plural marriages managed to get by. They developed the art of not thinking.

Her ignorance about the sleeping arrangements was rectified as soon as Ray left. Almost the moment the front door closed behind the visitors, Caleb announced that it was time for bed, and that Pamela should show her new sister-wife where she would be sleeping, while Darlene was instructed to finish the cleanup from the wedding party.

Anna meekly followed Pamela upstairs, although her stomach had started to churn with such sickening speed that her legs felt shaky. Her throat was so dry her tongue kept sticking to the roof of her mouth, and she couldn't produce enough spit to swallow.

It turned out that the upstairs had five bedrooms and two bathrooms, spacious accommodations by the standards of Alana Springs. Caleb's three daughters slept in one bedroom, the two boys had another, and all five children shared the bathroom located between their two bedrooms. She and Darlene each had their own room, Pamela explained, and they shared the master bedroom with their husband.

"But there's no bedroom for me," Anna said, genuinely puzzled. "Where am I going to sleep?"

Pamela gave her a look of mingled pity and envy. "You're the new wife. You'll be sleeping with Caleb, at least until there's a baby on the way."

Anna swallowed hard. "Oh. I see." She didn't ask what would happen when she got pregnant and Caleb wanted her out of his bed. With only five bedrooms, two of the wives would have to share a bedroom, just as her mom and Aunt Debbie did in Ray's house.

She was never going to subject herself to that humiliation, Anna vowed. She wasn't going to lie in bed, pregnant with Caleb's child, and stay there quietly waiting for one of the other wives to come back after having had sex with the lord and master. She would be out of here tonight or die in the attempt. Literally.

"Darlene and I always come into Caleb's bedroom each night for family prayers," Pamela explained, talking quickly to overcome a mutual embarrassment that was turning both of their cheeks red.

"Even tonight?" Anna found the prospect of praying in the company of Caleb and two other women who had all had sex with each other almost more than she could tolerate. In fact, it *was* more than she could tolerate. Her stomach gave a final protesting heave, and she ran into the communal master bathroom just in time to throw up into the toilet bowl.

Pamela followed her into the bathroom without waiting to be asked. In polygamous households, the concept of personal privacy was almost nonexistent and Anna felt no surprise at the intrusion. Pamela ran a washcloth under the faucet and knelt down beside Anna, wiping her face, her expression halfway between scornful and sympathetic. Emotions among polygamous wives tended to be ambiguous, and Pamela didn't seem to know quite how she felt about having a new contender for Caleb's time and attention.

"Thank you." Anna leaned back against the bathtub, her insides still queasy.

"You're welcome." Pamela looked away, jealousy and sympathy struggling for dominance. Sympathy won. "I know you must be scared," she said. "You're young, like I was."

"Did you want to marry Caleb?" Anna asked, getting up so that she could run her wrists under cold water.

"It was a good match," Pamela said, her gaze still averted. "You don't have to worry about tonight," she said hurriedly. "Caleb will take care of everything. Guide you in what has to be done—"

"Yes, I know." The prospect of discussing Caleb and sex with one of his other wives was about the only thing that could have brought Anna to her feet right at that moment. Galvanized, she jumped up. "I never saw my suitcase after Ray brought it into the house. Do you know what happened to it? I need to get out of this dress and find my nightgown…."

Her voice died away at the realization of what would happen when she was finally undressed. The trouble was, she thought, that the more you tried to avoid talking about sex, the more it seemed to intrude, until it swelled to the size of the elephant in the room that everybody insisted on pretending wasn't there. At least she could console herself with the bitter knowledge that Caleb must be pretty experienced in deflowering virgins by now.

Pamela knew exactly why Anna's voice had skittered into silence, but she didn't make any more references to what was about to happen. She could ignore an elephant with the best of them.

"Darlene brought your case up earlier on," she said, gesturing to the corner of the master bedroom, where Anna's suitcase was standing. "Would you like me to help you unpack?"

"No, but thanks for offering." Anna had her nightgown and toilet articles stacked right on the top of the case. She was hoping against hope that she'd be able to leave everything else undisturbed. That way, if she could sneak the case downstairs and out of the house, she'd have clothes to wear once she got to Denver. She knew from trips into the local town of Cortez that her homemade dresses were old-fashioned to the point of being conspicuous, but until she got a job, she couldn't afford to buy a replacement wardrobe. If she could sneak her case out of the house, at least she'd have clean underwear.

"We…er…say family prayers in our nightclothes." Pamela flushed again. "I thought you'd want to know," she said, then hurried on. "Darlene and I will use the children's bathroom tonight. That will give you more time. Caleb always says family prayers at ten."

"Thank you." Anna fought against a fresh wave of nausea. "I appreciate your help, Pamela."

Pamela hesitated for a moment, as if she might say something else, but in the end she simply nodded and left the room. As soon as she was alone, Anna removed her nightgown from the suitcase, then ran into the bathroom and pulled off her petticoat, ripping out the tacked stitches that held the muslin money pouch attached to the ruffled hem. Folding the pouch into thirds, she tucked it under the plastic liner of her new toilet bag.

She barely had time to brush her teeth and get changed into her ankle-length white cotton nightgown before she heard Caleb's voice outside the bathroom door. "Anna, it's time for family prayers. Are you ready?"

"Yes, Caleb. I'm coming." She opened the door, unexpectedly relieved to find Pamela and Darlene already kneeling on one side of Caleb's bed, both garbed in nightclothes very similar to her own. She went to join them, and Caleb smiled at them all approvingly. Like a father who's pleased with his small children, Anna thought with a spark of silent rage. In Alana Springs, children and wives were equally subservient to the male head of the household.

Caleb's prayers were short. Unexpectedly short, Anna gathered, if the expressions of her sister-wives were anything to go by. Dismissed by their husband, Pamela and Darlene both kissed her once again, then left the room.

She was alone with Caleb, and the gleam in his eyes made sweat break out along her spine. Anna found herself reciting an incoherent prayer to any god who might be listening, pleading for a miracle bolt of lightning that would strike Caleb dead.

Unfortunately, the gods were not in the mood for committing ritual murder. In the event, though, Caleb's taking of her virginity was clumsy rather than brutal, and had he not insisted on penetrating her a second time, she thought the physical pain might have been bearable. As it was, she was sore, bloody and aching by the time he rolled off her for the second time and fell asleep.

Anna wanted to take a shower and wash every last trace of Caleb's touch from her skin. Instead she had to lie next to him in the bed, forcing herself to wait for a full hour until his heavy breathing indicated he was deeply asleep. Inching out of the bed, grimacing at the soreness between her thighs, she retrieved her precious toilet bag from the bathroom, then returned to the bedroom to pick up her suitcase. She'd wait until she'd put a few miles between herself and Caleb's house before she wasted valuable minutes putting on day clothes.

Caleb slept soundly, the sleep of a man with an easy conscience and a sexually satisfied body. Anna looked at him with a mixture of contempt and loathing, then crept barefoot across the bedroom, her heart beating so loud and fast she would have thought even Darlene and Pamela would be able to hear it, let alone Caleb. But nobody stirred.

Anna inched down the stairs, her case held in her left hand, far away from the wall so that there was no risk of making a banging noise. Once downstairs, she made a beeline for the kitchen, grabbed the keys for the Taurus from the hook by the back door, and carefully—so carefully—eased back the bolt and opened the door.

Her momentary elation transformed to instant despair. Pamela was sitting on the back stoop, her arms hugged around her nightgown-covered knees, her gaze fixed on a distant star. She turned without speaking and her gaze locked with Anna's.

Tears welled up in Anna's eyes and overflowed down her cheeks, running in a hot, painful stream. "Let me go," she pleaded. "Please, Pamela, I don't belong here. Let me go before he makes me pregnant."

Pamela stared at her for a long, silent moment. Then, still without speaking, she stood up and walked over to the side of the yard, her back toward Anna.

Anna didn't stop to say thank you. She certainly didn't bother to inquire why Pamela was offering her tacit support. She simply fled across the narrow concrete apron to the carport and wrenched open the door of the Taurus, flinging her suitcase onto the passenger seat at the same time as she stuck the key into the ignition and turned on the engine.

The car hummed smoothly into action and she backed out of the carport. Thank heaven there turned out to be nothing obstructing her exit because she wouldn't have seen anything smaller than a jumbo jet for sheer, blinding panic. She swung quickly from reverse to drive and the Taurus roared down the driveway.

She stepped on the accelerator, her speed inching up toward eighty. The rear wheels skidded and gravel spewed up on either side of the car. The noise of her hasty leavetaking must have been loud enough to wake Caleb, for as she hit the county road, vaguely in the distance she heard the sounds of his angry shouting from an upstairs window.

Anna gripped the steering wheel and brought the car back under control, but she didn't slow down. Death or freedom. She would have one or the other tonight.

And right now, she didn't much care which.

Two

Denver, Colorado, March 2002

March was always a difficult month for Anna; it was too full of painful anniversaries and doubts about choices she'd made that couldn't be changed. This morning, the last Monday of the month, the weather was doing its best to add an extra layer of gloom to her annual attack of self-pity. Snow had been falling thick and fast since dawn, even though the TV weather forecasters last night had promised sunshine and mild temperatures.

Anna had nothing against snow—provided it was midwinter and she was going skiing. But right now, the snow was making her grumpy. She was done with winter. Had been done for at least two weeks, in fact. She was ready for tulips and chirping birds and mild spring breezes drifting through open windows. Instead, what she'd gotten during this morning's drive to work had been slippery roads, grouchy drivers acting as if they'd never before seen a snowflake, and traffic backed up from Fort Collins to Colorado Springs.

As if the spring snow and the lousy drivers weren't enough, right before Anna left the house Ferdinand had thrown up on her favorite cushion, leaving bits of furball inextricably tangled in the silk tassels. The cat-puking incident seemed the last straw, following as it did on top of last night's humiliating scene when she'd paid an unexpected visit to Pete's condo and found him bouncing around on his leather couch with a woman whose sleek ebony hair was only a tad less artificial-looking than the grapefruit-size implants bobbing in her naked breasts.

On her personal disaster scale, Anna rated the cat's puking on her new cushion at around a four. Finding Pete in the arms of a raven-haired bimbo came in at no more than a two, which either suggested that she had an unhealthy obsession with designer cushions, or revealed something sad about the state of her love life. Anna suspected it was the latter.

She could hardly claim to be shocked that Pete had opted out of a relationship that started out tepid and had been cooling off ever since. She'd recognized at least a month ago that sex with Pete had finally slipped from uninspired all the way down to terminally boring. But they shared a lot of interests even if they didn't strike sexual sparks, and she'd been content to let their relationship drift. Finding someone who shared her enjoyment of the great outdoors had struck her as a reasonable substitute for romance, especially since her capacity for romantic passion seemed to have vanished in the terrible months following her escape from Caleb Welks.

Pete obviously hadn't shared her contentment with their easygoing relationship, and Anna's pride smarted a little from the knowledge that he hadn't cared enough about their friendship to warn her before he moved on to another woman. She wished he could have found a way to break up that hadn't left her feeling like quite such a…dork. For a woman who had a master's degree in family counseling, it seemed she had been humiliatingly out of touch with the true state of Pete's feelings.

Still, Pete was now in her past—last night had made that pretty obvious—and she'd learned years ago that the past wasn't a healthy place to live. Keeping focused on the present avoided the danger of getting mired in might-have-beens and made for a lot less emotional pain.

Trudging through the parking lot, head bent against the wind, Anna told herself she was lucky that her heart had escaped Pete's betrayal without severe injury. As for her pride…well, it would soon heal.

A welcome blast of hot air enveloped her as she walked into the Denver Federal Building and took the elevator to the fourth floor. She exchanged greetings with a couple of fellow workers and hurried to the cramped, particleboard cubicle that some sadistic government official had jokingly designated as her private office.

"Hi, Matt. You're in early." She smiled in passing to the parole officer who worked in the "office" next to hers, then turned back and stopped in the doorway of his cubicle. "Hey, I almost forgot. This was the weekend you were going to Albuquerque for your dad's wedding. So how was it?"

"Okay, I guess." Matt Jorgenson leaned back from his computer and gave her a rueful smile, pushing his glasses up onto his forehead. "Dad found a minister who managed to keep a straight face while the bridal couple exchanged their vows of eternal devotion. That's a miracle in itself. Plus the food at the reception was great, and nobody got drunk. Best of all, not a single stepbrother punched out another stepbrother. That's as good as it gets when the bride is going for marriage number three, and the groom is working on his fourth.''

Anna gave him a thumbs-up. ''Fourth time's a charm, Matt. This is the marriage that's going to stick.''

''Sure. All the way to the divorce court.'' Matt gave a shrug, his smile fading. ''My dad's fifty-seven. Around the time he hit fifty and ditched wife number three, I stopped wondering when he was going to grow up. Obviously the answer is never. He likes the fun of getting married a heck of a lot more than the daily grind of waking up each morning with the same woman.''

Matt's phone rang and Anna gave him a quick wave as he bent forward to take the call. Turning into her own office, she hung up her coat, stuffing her gloves into the pockets. The unexpected thought popped into her head that if Ray and Caleb Welks heard about Matt's dad, they would claim he was practicing a form of legalized polygamy. Much as she hated to agree with any view endorsed by her pseudo-husband and stepfather, she wasn't at all sure the Welks brothers would be wrong. Last week, when she and Matt were sharing a coffee break, he'd counted up all the stepsiblings he'd acquired at one point or another during his father's marital adventures. They came to a grand total of nineteen, the younger ones shuttling back and forth among so many different parents and stepparents that they would probably have led more stable lives if they'd been officially abandoned and taken into foster care.

Anna shook her head to get rid of melting snowflakes clinging to her hair, then ran her fingers through the damp strands, which were already twisting into curls in defiance of this morning's fifteen-minute session with the blow-dryer and a can of styling spray. She glanced into the tiny wall mirror next to the coatrack and sighed. Yep, she was Little Orphan Annie again. One of her favorite fantasies involved waking up and discovering that her mop of auburn curls had turned overnight into smooth, blond Grace Kelly elegance. In pursuit of her dream, she sometimes managed to mousse, spritz and gel her hair into four or five hours of sleekness. But apparently not today. Another black mark to chalk up to the weather, she thought grouchily.

Giving up on sleekness, at least until the snow stopped, she crossed to her desk, her stomach knotting when she saw the voice mail light blinking on her phone. It was barely eight-fifteen, forty-five minutes before the offices officially opened, and she already had three new messages waiting for her attention. Her first appointment was scheduled right at nine, and she had a pile of paperwork that had to be completed before the end of the day. No need to check her horoscope in order to foresee another late night in her immediate future.

The number of prison inmates had recently passed the two million mark, confirming the United States's position as world leader in the percentage of its citizens kept behind bars. Almost all convicts got released sooner or later, so it was no surprise that three-quarters of a million former prisoners were currently serving some type of parole. Despite those hair-raising statistics, the budget for parole officers, halfway houses and counseling programs kept getting cut by politicians eager to prove they were tough on crime. Since Anna had started work as a federal parole officer four years ago, her client load had increased twenty percent. Judging by the numbers, there was no relief anywhere in sight.

At a certain point, Anna knew the overburdened system was simply going to collapse under its own bloated weight. In the meantime, she was running hard to stay in place, constantly feeling that she was shortchanging everyone. Not just the public, who expected her to keep track of potentially dangerous criminals, but the parolees, too. Even those ex-cons who were genuinely trying to make a go of it ended up getting beaten down by the very system that was supposed to support them.

Still, there was nothing she could do right now to make things better except keep on top of the demands of her job as best she could. Taking a fortifying sip of double espresso from the thermal mug she'd brought in from the car, Anna eased her Glock .45 from her shoulder holster, checking the safety before locking it into her desk drawer. Unlike probation officers, parole officers were trained in weapons management and carried guns. Fortunately, she'd never yet had occasion to fire her gun except on the practice range, although she'd drawn it several times to face down offenders who'd violated the terms of their parole and were actively resistant to the idea of returning to prison.

Leaning across the desk, she hit the play button on her voice mail, the knot in her stomach pulling tighter as she listened to her messages. All three were disasters in the making, starting with Stanley Swann, whose wife had left him over the weekend, taking their two young kids with her.

''She's mos' likely gone to her mother's house in Kansas City.'' Stan's voice throbbed with rage, and with a pain that he'd never learned how to express except as swaggering anger. ''The bitch knows I ain't supposed to follow her, so she thinks she can get away with fuckin' me over. You gotta help, Miz Langtry. Because if you cain't do nothin' to get my kids back, I'm gonna go after them myself. She ain't got no right to take off with my kids. She's doin' this to mess with my head. Ain't no other reason for her to take off like this. Fuckin' bitch.''

He slammed down the phone, but not quite soon enough to cut off the sob that broke up his tirade. Stan's image of how men should behave was strictly macho street corner, and didn't include the possibility of tears, but Anna knew his love for his two children was real and deep. The desire to do right by his kids had been the primary motivator keeping him out of trouble over the past ten months.

It would be tragic if he screwed up now, when he was only a couple of months away from completing his year of parole. Coffee and tension swirled in her stomach, sending a burning sensation up into her throat. Anna shook out a handful of antacid tablets from the giant tub she kept in her desk drawer and tossed the tablets into her mouth, crunching down on them as if they were candy. Still crunching, she reached for her Rolodex, flipping through until she found Stan's listing.

She dialed his number and he snatched the phone at the first ring, sounding halfway between relieved and disappointed when Anna identified herself. His voice combative, he repeated his threat that if she didn't get his kids back today, he was going after them and to hell with the parole board.

Anna tried to navigate a path between cool authority and sympathy. Anything to calm him down. ''Chill out, Stan, and don't make stupid threats. Right now, you have the law on your side—''

''Ha! Cain't tell you how happy that makes me.'' Stan's voice dripped sarcasm.

''Well, it should make you happy, because the law can help you, or it can grind you up. If you go chasing after LaToya and violate parole by crossing state lines, you know what's going to happen. You'll be arrested—''

''So that bitch-woman I was dumb enough to marry kidnaps my kids and I get my ass tossed in prison. What's that supposed to be? Justice?''

''No, Stan, it's not justice. It's the law, which is something altogether different. And if you go after your wife, you'll definitely be on the wrong side of the law—''

''Gee. Now I'm *real* scared.''

''You should be. If you're back in prison, your wife can take the kids wherever the hell she wants and there won't be a damn thing you can do about it. Because you'll be on floor-scrubbing duty, eating lousy food with a plastic spoon when the workday's over, and trying to get the public defender's office to return your phone calls. So for once in your life, Stan, act smart. Stay in Denver.''

''I cain't sit around on my ass, waiting for that bitch to bring back my kids—''

''No, but you can go to work. That's why you called, isn't it? To hear me tell you that you can do this. You go to work, report in here tomorrow like you're supposed to, and let me take care of finding your kids."

"Ain't got no car. She took it. Fuckin' bitch. How'm I supposed to get to work?"

"Take the bus. Call a cab if you have to. Don't let her get the better of you. If she's messing with your head, don't let her win." Anna waited to let that piece of advice sink in. "Have you called your mother-in-law's house? Are you sure that's where your wife has gone?"

"Ain't sure about nothin'. I done called that number a hunnert times. Ain't nobody pickin' up the phone on the other end."

"It was Sunday yesterday. Maybe they went to church. Maybe they went to the movies. You can't assume they're avoiding talking to you just because nobody answers the phone. So listen up, Stan. I need to ask you a few questions before I can help you—"

Stan let rip with a string of obscenities, then calmed down enough to answer Anna's questions. He confirmed that he and LaToya were still legally married, and there was no custody agreement or court order that gave his wife the right to take the children out of the state without his permission. Stan gave Anna the address and phone number for his mother-in-law's home in Kansas City, and after another five minutes of cajoling, she managed to extract a promise from him that he would go to work today and call her for news about his kids when his shift ended. She gave him her cell phone number so that he could reach her after hours.

Whether Stan would stick to his promise was another story altogether. Patience and delayed gratification weren't concepts that he handled too well. No surprise, since his childhood had been so chaotic that sheer survival had required him to grab what he needed, any way he could, whenever he could. However, neither his children nor society at large would be better off if Stan were returned to prison, so Anna was determined to do whatever she could to prevent his wife turning a domestic dispute into the lever that thrust Stan back behind bars.

Trying to convey the urgency of the situation, she phoned the police precinct closest to his mother-in-law's house, and managed to persuade a cop to swing by the address Stan had given her. The cop, a sympathetic old-timer, promised to report back by five local time, which would only be four o'clock in Denver. If she could report back to Stan before the end of the day, there was a slight hope he'd keep everything together.

Anna's next message was from Antwan Jepson, letting her know he couldn't keep his scheduled appointment this morning because he was sick with the stomach flu and couldn't leave his apartment. Antwan didn't sound sick, he sounded high, and she suspected he was simply inventing excuses to avoid taking the drug test that was a mandatory part of his weekly appointment.

Anna called Antwan's apartment, and when he didn't respond, she pulled his file and found the phone number for the pet food factory where he worked. Sure enough, Antwan hadn't turned up for work since the previous Tuesday.

Anna was depressed but not surprised to discover that Antwan had probably fallen back into his bad old heroin-injecting habits. After four years on the job, she was pretty good at assessing who was likely to make it through their parole and who wasn't. Antwan, superficially streetwise but internally fragile, had always struck her as high risk. He'd been abused as a kid, abandoned by his alcoholic mother more than once, and life hadn't given him too many chances. Anna hoped like hell her suspicions were wrong, but she wasn't holding her breath.

Antwan's name had been on the waiting list for a residential drug treatment facility in Boulder since the day he got out of prison, but it was still at least another five months before he had any chance of being admitted to the program. Five months might as well have been never, because if Antwan could survive five months drug free, he would never have ended up in prison in the first place.

Anna made a note to remind herself to make a few calls on Antwan's behalf as soon as she could grab a spare moment. She would do her best to beg and plead Antwan into some form of rehab, but she knew she was basically whistling into the wind. Effective residential rehab programs all had waiting lists out the wazoo, and most applicants were at least as desperate as Antwan.

So much for rehabilitation as a cheaper, more effective alternative to incarceration. Antwan seemed likely to be heading back to prison some time very soon. Anna suppressed a spurt of anger and chugged another handful of antacids, washing the too sweet taste away with another shot of espresso. It was a good thing caffeine wasn't a controlled substance, she reflected wryly, or she'd be serving a life sentence right alongside some of her former clients.

The final message was from a cop who gave his

name as Bob Gifford. Detective Gifford was calling to inform her that Raul Estevan had been arrested over the weekend for attempted murder. Raul was currently hospitalized with multiple bullet wounds to the stomach and shoulder. If he survived long enough to be discharged—which seemed highly unlikely—the D.A.'s office would arrange for him to be returned immediately to prison while waiting trial on the new charges.

Anna clicked off the answering machine and put down her coffee mug, slamming her right fist into the palm of her other hand. *You stupid dickhead, Raul. What have you gotten yourself into this time?*

She played Detective Gifford's message again, feeling a familiar mixture of rage, hurt and resignation. She'd always nurtured doubts about Antwan's chances of making it, but she'd really thought that Raul Estevan was going to be one of her success stories.

Raul was smart, good-looking, with a wry sense of humor that often had her laughing out loud even when she tried to keep their encounters strictly professional. She'd told him just last week that if he applied half the talent and energy to a legitimate business that he'd applied to his previous illegal enterprises, he'd soon be a lawful millionaire.

Raul wasn't yet thirty and he'd already served six years in federal prison for his role in running a sophisticated cocaine distribution network that spanned three Rocky Mountain states. In spite of his shady past, Raul had seemed a model parolee. He arrived on time for his appointments. He attended mass on Sunday, and carried around ultrasound pictures of the baby his wife was expecting. The randomly administered drug tests that were a compulsory part of his parole always came up clean.

He'd recently inherited a small family restaurant that featured Central American specialities, and he'd brought in the books last week so that he could show Anna how he'd tripled the profits since he got out of prison. He'd claimed to have big plans for expanding his business as a franchise. According to Raul, his restaurant on the outskirts of Littleton was just the first in a chain that would one day do for *porco assado* what Taco Bell had done for burritos and enchiladas.

Anna had believed him, in part because she badly wanted him to achieve every one of his grand boasts. The occasional success story was what kept her going and made the failures and disappointments of her job bearable. She wasn't naive. Six months in this job was enough to scuff the shine off even the most starry-eyed idealist, and she'd never been starry-eyed. When you arrived in Denver driving a stolen car, with four hundred bucks in your purse, with no friends, no family, no job, and nowhere to live, you might start out naive, but you got smart real fast or you got to be dead. Still, there was a difference between being naive and being an optimist and, despite everything, Anna remained an optimist.

Which was why she wasn't willing to give up on Raul Estevan without checking further into the arresting officer's story. Maybe Raul had just been in the wrong place at the wrong time, she thought, booting up her computer in preparation for the day. When you were an ex-con, you often had friends and family who were more likely to cause you problems than to offer you support. She would talk to the arresting officer before she accepted that Raul had really been dealing drugs at the time of the shooting.

With a harried glance at her watch, Anna called the precinct and, by a miracle, managed to track down Detective Gifford without too much delay. His verbal report killed any hope of a mistake. Raul, it seemed, had been under surveillance by DEA agents for more than two months, ever since local police arrested a street dealer who had fingered Raul as his supplier. The only reason Raul hadn't been taken into custody weeks ago was the hope that he would lead detectives to *his* supplier, an Arizona businessman who had so far managed to stay out of reach of the law, even though DEA agents had been ninety-nine percent sure he was shipping Colombian cocaine into the States via the border town of Nogales, fifty miles south of Tucson.

The DEA's suspicions had now been confirmed. After Raul was shot on Saturday night, agents had executed a search warrant at his restaurant. They'd found ample proof that Raul had been using the place to launder profits from his drug-trafficking operation. Better yet from the point of view of law enforcement, an expert search of Raul's computer system over the weekend had uncovered enough e-mail correspondence between Raul and the dealer in Arizona to form the basis of an indictment.

So much for cooperation between law enforcement agencies. Anna didn't even bother to protest the fact that neither the local cops nor the DEA agents had taken five minutes to clue her in about what was happening with one of her parolees. She knew they would claim that the security of their ongoing operations had made it impossible to warn her that Raul was under suspicion.

It worried Anna a lot that she hadn't picked up on Raul's duplicity. His smiles and jokes had obviously been calculated to deceive her but that was no excuse. She should have realized that the camaraderie developing between the two of them existed only in her mind. As it was, he'd played her for the ultimate sucker, leaving her to write up glowing reports in his file while he cynically re-established his old drug connections and once again got himself tied into the network of Colombian cocaine traffickers.

According to Detective Gifford, Raul had been making a tidy profit as chief coke distributor for the greater Denver metro area—until he once again started snorting his own product. Since then, his control over his network of street dealers had slipped dangerously. This past weekend he'd ended up in a drug-fueled argument with two of his runners. The argument had escalated. Weapons had been drawn and shots fired.

As Detective Gifford explained, Raul would right now be looking at first-degree murder charges if not for the fact that he'd been so high at the time of the dispute that he unloaded an entire clip of bullets without managing to inflict fatal wounds on anyone. Quite a feat, Gifford said sarcastically, given that he was six feet from his intended victims. Still, under mandatory sentencing guidelines, charges of attempted murder and narcotics trafficking while on parole would be more than enough to put Raul away for the next quarter century. His intended victims were already locked up in the county jail, waiting trial on similar charges.

Anna thanked Bob Gifford for his report and hung up the phone, ruthlessly cutting off all regrets. She couldn't keep up with the demands of her job if she allowed betrayals and disappointments to become personal. From now on, Raul Estevan would simply serve as a warning to her that charm, intelligence and even a beguiling sense of humor were no proof of innocence, much less the intent to use time on parole as a chance for genuine lifestyle reform.

Determined to be practical, she made yet another note to herself. She needed to check out how Raul had managed to pass his frequent drug tests despite the fact that the cops claimed he'd been snorting serious amounts of coke for the past two months. There was only one way he could have avoided a positive urine test when he was using so intensively. Obviously, he'd been paying off someone inside the department. But who?

A quick scan of Raul's file showed that his drug tests had allegedly all been administered by different officials. In the circumstances, finding out who had been bought off was too big an issue to try to squeeze into the thirty seconds remaining before her first appointment. Anna knew she couldn't afford to get behind this early in the morning or her entire schedule for the day would collapse.

She leaned back in her chair, massaging her forehead. This was sure shaping up to be a stellar Monday. Barely 9:00 a.m. and already Raul was either dead or on his way back to prison. Antwan was almost certainly heading in the same direction, and Stan Swann—not a man known for his patience under pressure—was perched right on the edge of a major explosion if she didn't get him some positive news about his kids very soon.

There had to be good reasons why she'd chosen this particular profession, Anna thought, gulping the last of her coffee. Right now, though, she couldn't for the life of her remember what they were. Raul's arrest was making it harder than usual to keep hold of her belief that most convicted criminals were people who had made bad choices in the past but could always learn to make better choices in the future.

Move on. Don't dwell on what can't be changed. Anna repeated her personal mantra, then pulled the file for her nine o'clock appointment. She worked steadily for three hours and was about to take a walk to the soda machine—more for the break than the soda—when her phone rang again. She picked up the phone.

"Anna Langtry."

"Hi, Ms. Langtry. This is Father Patrick Olson. I'm the parish priest at Our Lady of the Assumption, which is the church Raul Estevan and his wife attend. I'm calling from the prison ward of Denver General Hospital. I assume you've been informed that Raul has been shot?"

Anna's heart lurched. "Yes, I heard about the incident from Detective Gifford this morning. How—how is Raul?"

"Not good," the priest said. "The doctors tell me he's not going to last the night."

"I'm sorry. Really sorry." And that was the truth.

"He's asking to see you, Ms. Langtry. Could you come? It looks like a visit from you would mean a lot to him."

"He's asking for *me?*"

"You're his parole officer, right?"

"Yes, I am."

"Then you're the Anna Langtry he's asking for."

Anna realized she'd twisted a rubber band around her thumb so many times that it was cutting off her circulation. She released the band, snapping it restlessly. "I would come, Father, but I have appointments scheduled all afternoon. It's almost impossible for me to get away. I'm sorry but I have to say no—"

"Raul really wants to see you, Ms. Langtry. It would be a very generous act on your part if you could somehow find a way to make the time."

Anna glanced from her watch to her desk calendar. It was a few minutes past noon. Her next appointment wasn't until three, when she was scheduled to meet with a prisoner released that morning from the Federal Correctional Facility in West Denver. If she skipped lunch, and if the roads had been cleared of snow, she could probably make it downtown to Denver General and back again by two, which gave her an hour to play catch-up before she interviewed her new parolee.

"All right, Father. I'll come. You can expect me in forty minutes, snow and traffic permitting."

"Thank you. I appreciate you making the time."

She found Raul in Intensive Care, buried under tubes and drips and electronic monitors. Normally a uniformed cop would be assigned to make sure that he didn't flee the jurisdiction, but Raul clearly posed no risk of flight and the room was empty except for an elderly man wearing a clerical collar and a young pregnant woman whose face was blotched with tears.

The priest stepped forward and spoke softly. "You

must be Ms. Langtry. I'm Father Pat and this is Guillermina Estevan. Raul's wife.''

She shook the priest's hand before turning to the sobbing Guillermina. ''I'm very sorry about what's happened, Mrs. Estevan. Raul deserved a better end than this.''

''Thank you for coming, *señora.*'' Guillermina's reply ended on a choked sob and she turned away, burying her face in a wad of tissues.

Anna crossed to the bed where Raul lay unconscious and gently curved her fingers over the needles and tubes feeding into his hand. He gave no sign that he was aware of her presence, or that of his wife, who came to take a seat on the other side of the bed, her tears dripping onto his cheek, her expression one of utter weariness and dull resignation.

''Has he been unconscious for long?'' Anna asked the priest.

''About an hour this time. He's slipping in and out. Hopefully, he'll come around again in a moment or two. For the brief moments when he's awake, he's surprisingly lucid.''

''Do you know why he wanted to see me?''

''He said you were the only person who ever made him feel that maybe he was worth something. Before they gave him his last shot of painkiller, he asked me to tell you that each week when he came to your office, he wanted to become the person you saw, and not the person he knew he was.''

Anna drew in a tight, hard breath. ''I wish he'd told me what was really going on in his life, instead of feeding me the *Fantasy Island* version.''

''You can't wish that any more strongly than I do. He didn't clue me in, either.''

Anna shook her head. "What happened, do you think? I would have sworn he wanted to make a fresh start."

"From what his wife's been confiding over the past few hours, Raul seems to have been doomed pretty much from the moment he walked out of prison. His old colleagues came calling before he'd had time to drink so much as a cup of coffee, and they were determined to bring him into the drug distribution network again. He's smart, and they needed his expertise to straighten out a turf war that was developing in Denver. According to Guillermina, they threatened her and her unborn baby when Raul refused to cooperate." The priest bowed his head for a moment. "I wish I understood why this had to be. For some people, life seems destined to be very hard."

Anna's stomach was churning. It had been bad enough to believe that Raul had deliberately deceived her. It was worse to discover that his family had been threatened and he'd been left with only rotten choices and nowhere to turn for help. Could she have saved him if he'd told her the truth? Maybe, but only if she could have bargained him into the Federal Witness Protection program, and that was by no means guaranteed. In the circumstances, how could she blame him for not wanting to expose Guillermina and their unborn child to the risk of retribution from the Colombians? The money and resources a major drug cartel could deploy left the forces of law and order scrambling in the dust, and Raul would be all too aware of that.

"What a waste of a life," she said bitterly. "Raul was so smart. Imagine what he could have achieved if he'd somehow found a way to stick to legitimate business dealings.''

The priest looked sad and unsure of himself. ''You're right. This is one of those days when I have to remind myself that God has a plan for each and every one of us, and nobody's life is ever wasted. I can only pray that everything will work out better for Raul in eternity than it did here on earth.''

Right at this moment, bliss in heaven didn't strike Anna as adequate reward for the suffering Raul had endured on earth. She was still searching for a polite reply to give Father Pat when Raul groaned. His eyelids flickered, then his eyes opened and his gaze fixed blankly on Anna.

She leaned closer to him. ''Hi, Raul. It's Anna Langtry.''

Recognition dawned. ''You...came.''

He sounded surprised and shockingly grateful. Anna had to swallow over a lump in her throat before she could speak. ''Yes, I came. How are you doing, Raul?''

His lips were cracked and swollen, but he twisted them in a parody of his familiar grin. ''Like shit, thanks. How 'bout you?''

''I've been better. I'm worried about you. Don't give up, Raul. You're a fighter, and this is a terrific hospital. The doctors here have worked miracles—''

Not surprisingly, he ignored her attempt at a pep talk. ''If I lived, I'd spend the next twenty years behind bars. It's better this way.''

Emotion spiraled deep inside Anna's gut. Not sorrow, she realized, but rage because what Raul said was essentially true. With lots of help from his so-called friends in the drug trade, he'd screwed up his life to the point where death was possibly a better option than any of the alternatives. She wasn't sure what to say, and her gaze roamed to the side of the room, where Father Pat was trying to offer comfort to Guillermina. She wondered what would become of Raul's unborn baby. Only good things, she hoped. Although, if you believed the statistics, the child's future was likely to be bleak in the extreme.

Anna was gripped by an uncharacteristic wave of despair. There had to be some way to break the endless cycle of abused and deprived children growing up into criminal adults, but right now she had no idea—none—what that way might be.

''You look sad,'' Raul said.

''I am sad. You're a great guy, Raul, and I had such high hopes that you were going to make it.''

''I know you did. Each week when I came to see you, I thought, shit, man, she really thinks you're somebody.''

''You *are* somebody, Raul. You're smart. You're too handsome for your own good. You have a great sense of humor—''

''Yeah, sure.'' His voice faded, and his mouth contorted into bitterness. ''I'm a father for my baby to be real proud of.''

She wished there was a response she could give that was both honest and encouraging. Not a damn thing came to mind. She could only fall back on useless platitudes. ''I'm sorry it turned out this way, Raul. I'm really sorry.''

He looked over at his wife, his gaze softening as it drifted down to her rounded belly. ''Yeah, so am I.''

Three

Traffic was light and Anna made surprisingly good time from the hospital back to the federal building. Even so, lunch consisted of a granola bar eaten at her desk as she scrambled to catch up on her e-mail, all the while juggling phone calls and trying to snatch a few moments to trace which officer had supervised Raul's drug tests and who, therefore, might have been paid off to lie about the results. That was one of the worst things about the illegal drug business, Anna reflected. It generated so damn much money that the corrupting tentacles of the trade stretched into every nook and cranny of the penal system.

A few minutes before three, a phone call finally brought her something that could almost be considered good news in a day notoriously short on cheer. Gerald Leary, the cop in Kansas City, had swung by the address Stan had provided for his mother-in-law. Miracle of miracles, the address was correct, and Stan's wife, LaToya, was at the apartment when Leary arrived. Even better, LaToya's mother was furious with her daughter for leaving Stan, and was making no bones about the fact that LaToya should get herself and her two kids back to Denver and her lawful husband as soon as possible.

At first, LaToya had been sulky and defensive but,

after some discussion, she grudgingly conceded that she'd only taken the kids because Stan was mad at her for spending money on a new giant-screen TV set they couldn't afford. After a little strong-arming from Officer Leary, she agreed she would consider driving back to Denver in a couple of days, once she and the kids had a chance to rest up. Best of all, she promised that the kids would be allowed to phone their dad that night, so Stan would be able to hear for himself that they were all right and having a good time playing with their Kansas City cousins.

Anna thanked the cop profusely, grateful to him for providing the one bright spot in a day that was otherwise relentlessly gray. She called Stan's boss, and was even more relieved when she discovered that Stan had followed her advice and was actually at work. She left word that his wife and kids had been found, that they were well and safe, and that he should phone his mother-in-law's house if he wanted to speak to them. She put down the receiver and drew in a deep breath, thankful that one major crisis seemed to have been averted, at least until the next time Stan and LaToya got into a fight.

Now all she had to worry about was making sure Stan's wife drove home as promised. Plus she still had to find Antwan Jepson and complete the grim wait for the phone call that would tell her Raul Estevan was dead. All this, quite apart from how late she'd have to stay at her desk in order to finish the pile of documentation that was threatening to explode out of her in-tray any minute now. As days went, she had no hesitation in certifying that this one pretty much sucked.

She was already ten minutes late for her three

o'clock appointment, and she still had prep work she needed to finish before she would be ready to meet her new parolee, a man named Joseph Mackenzie, who had been scheduled for release from the federal correctional institution in West Denver early that morning.

Anna buzzed the receptionist in the outer room where parolees completed preliminary paperwork and waited to be interviewed by their case officers. ''Hi, Gina. Has Joseph Mackenzie arrived yet for his three o'clock appointment? He's a new release.''

''Yes, he's been here a while. Do you want me to send him in?''

''Not quite. I'm still running behind. Too many crises today and nowhere near enough time to handle them all. Give me five minutes, then send him in.''

''Okay, will do.''

''Thanks.'' Anna leaned back in her chair and read quickly through the information that had already been forwarded to her from the prison. Joseph Alexander Mackenzie had been an officer of the Colorado Bank of Trade and Commerce, working as a senior vice president at the branch in Durango until he was convicted of fraud and embezzlement, and sentenced to serve two to six years in federal prison.

Mackenzie was thirty-two years old, six feet and half an inch tall, and weighed 180 pounds. His mug shot showed a man with regular features, light-brown hair, and eyes that were probably dark gray. He was rather good-looking in a quiet sort of way, although his face wasn't especially memorable.

He'd been paroled after serving four years of his sentence. A first-time offender, Mackenzie had missed two earlier chances for parole when the board decided he showed no signs of remorse for his crime. When he, in fact, stubbornly insisted that he was innocent, concocting some absurd story about being the fall guy for a vast, ill-defined conspiracy centered on the Durango branch of the bank he worked for.

Despite the rotten day she'd had so far, Anna almost laughed out loud at that one. She knew Durango fairly well, since Alana Springs was located barely a hundred miles to the northwest. A peaceful college and retirement community in a lovely setting, it was hard to imagine many towns in the continental United States that were less likely to be breeding grounds for a massive criminal conspiracy. Especially a conspiracy centered on one of the state's oldest and most conservative banks.

The parole board obviously felt the same way as Anna about Mackenzie's claims of innocence. They had agreed to Mackenzie's release only when he finally acknowledged his guilt, and promised to do his best to make restitution to his victims. Under the terms of his parole, he was forbidden to work in a bank, or in any position where he would be handling other people's money. During his stay in prison, he'd been assigned to the kitchens and, with the experience he'd gained there handling commercial ovens and cooking equipment, a prisoner's aid society had been able to find him a job as a prep cook in a major downtown Denver hotel.

For the next several months, the man with an MBA in finance from the Wharton Business School in Philadelphia was going to earn his living peeling carrots and chopping onions. He was scheduled to start work in the hotel kitchen tonight.

Anna was in no mood to consider the ironies of

that particular career change. Frankly, she wasn't too sympathetic toward a man who'd had every chance to succeed in life and who'd still chosen to steal from clients who trusted him. Contrary to the myth that federal prisons were full of highly intelligent white-collar criminals, Anna's experience had been that eighty-five percent of her clients came from under-privileged backgrounds and were serving time for crimes that had their roots deeply planted in dysfunctional childhoods and a generational downward spiral involving the abuse of drugs and alcohol. From her perspective, a guy who'd been privileged to attend the Wharton Business School and still managed to screw up wouldn't have elicited an overflow of sympathy even on a good day. Right now, he was provoking not even a twinge of compassion.

Still, she wasn't supposed to judge the moral worth of her parolees, merely the likelihood of their being able to support themselves without falling back into a life of crime. Anna took the stack of forms she was required to fill out during her initial interview with new parolees, and buzzed the receptionist again. ''Okay, Gina, I'm ready. Send in Mr. Mackenzie, will you?''

The man who presented himself in the door of her cubicle a couple of minutes later bore only a superficial resemblance to his police photo. His features might once have been blandly regular, but now they were transformed into disturbing hardness by the taut, contained line of his mouth and the impenetrable blankness of his eyes. His body was solid muscle, presumably bulked up by hours of exercise in the prison weight room, and he looked taller than the scant six feet his record attributed to him. In his mug shot, he'd worn a white business shirt and a conservative striped tie. Now he wore washed-out jeans and a baggy T-shirt bearing the faded logo of National Concrete Suppliers.

He carried a padded nylon winter jacket slung over his arm, and the chip on his shoulder was almost as clearly visible as the jagged scar that slashed diagonally across the back of his left hand, the flesh ridged where it had healed after being clumsily stitched. Almost certainly a prison wound, tended by an indifferent or incompetent prison doctor. The federal corrections center in West Denver was well run, but the inmates had an alarming tendency to slice each other up at the least provocation, the weapon of choice being razor blades lashed to the handle of a toothbrush. Joseph Mackenzie had apparently been the loser in at least one such encounter.

Anna had to draw in a deep breath before she could speak. She leaned back in her chair, surprised by the intensity of her reaction to the man's physical presence. "Come in, Mr. Mackenzie. I'm sorry to have kept you waiting."

"Yes, ma'am."

He stepped just inside the door of her office, then waited, hands clasped loosely in front of him, jacket dangling from his forefinger, gaze fixed straight ahead. It was the stance of a man who had spent the past several years moving only when given permission by his jailers, and Anna had seen it many times before. Usually it meant that the man had been beaten down by the strict discipline of his years in prison. But where Joseph Mackenzie was concerned, she suspected that his appearance of humility had nothing at all to do with fear and submission. Instead, she would lay odds she was looking at a man who'd learned to mask every trace of what he was really feeling so that he could glide unobserved and unmolested between the opposing hazards of the prison gangs and the prison guards.

Anna studied Mackenzie for another moment, but he studiously avoided her gaze, staring at his clasped hands without a twitch of bodily movement, or a glimmer of facial expression.

This one was going to be trouble, Anna thought. He might have fooled the prison authorities and the parole board, but he didn't fool her for a second. She could almost smell the tightly controlled rage that boiled beneath his passive exterior. Joseph Mackenzie hated the fact that he was standing in her office, a supplicant for her approval. He hated the fact that he was still essentially powerless, locked in the jowls of the penal system even if he was no longer behind bars. White-collar criminals often had borderline personality disorders that left them seething with resentment because they hadn't been smart enough to outwit the forces of law and order. Joseph Mackenzie probably carried a festering grudge against the society that had put him away, and she would bet he was more than willing to extend that generalized grudge into a personal one against her.

Anna had a reputation among her fellow parole officers for demonstrating a lot of patience with prisoners who had an attitude. But not today. Her experiences with Raul left her emotions rubbed raw, and she was in no mood to extend the milk of human kindness to a man quite likely to throw it back in her face, with a dash of acid added for good measure.

Joseph Mackenzie would have to learn to deal with his anger on his own. Or not. The choice was his.

She spoke more formally than was her habit with new parolees. "There's no need to loom in the doorway like that, Mr. Mackenzie. Come inside. Do you have the results of your drug screening test?"

"Yes, ma'am." He walked just close enough to the desk to hand the slip of paper to her. Then he stepped back and waited again in the same controlled silence.

The drug test was negative. Not a foregone conclusion, even though he'd been out of jail less than twelve hours. Some parolees walked through the prison gates and took their first hit in the car driving them away, courtesy of some idiot "friend."

She put the slip of pink paper into his file. "Sit down, Mr. Mackenzie. We have quite a lot of paperwork to get through, so you might as well make yourself comfortable."

"Thank you, ma'am." His voice was low, well-educated, and still without a trace of expression. What she sensed emanating from him wasn't wariness, Anna realized, but absolute control. Her immediate reaction was to wonder what he was hiding that he needed to exercise such rigid self-discipline.

She watched as he settled into the plastic chair drawn up to the other side of her desk. He leaned back, jacket still dangling from his fingers, his body curved into the contours of the chair. Despite the appearance of relaxation, Anna could feel the tension that encased him like an electronic force field. Normally she would have gone out of her way to break through the tension, but something about Joseph Mackenzie set up all her hackles.

Instead of offering him a friendly smile, she simply

took a form from the top of the pile on her desk. "Okay, let's get started. Practical details first, Mr. Mackenzie. I know you have a job at the Westwood Hotel that starts tonight. Is that correct?"

"Yes, ma'am."

"You're working the midnight shift?"

"Yes, ma'am."

"It's great that you have a job already. Getting employment is often a difficult task for people on parole."

"Yes, ma'am. I was sure lucky."

She detected irony in his comment, but chose to ignore it. "Have you managed to find yourself accommodation, Mr. Mackenzie? I see that you haven't been assigned to any of the halfway houses in the metro area. Is that because you have family here in town?"

"No, ma'am. I've taken a room at a residential hotel. The prisoner's aid society paid the first week's rent for me."

Knowing how scarce space was in halfway housing, Anna wasn't surprised that the prison authorities had decided a man with a college degree, convicted of a nonviolent offence, with no history of drug abuse, was a good candidate for independent living. "Can you give me the address of the hotel and your phone number?"

"There's no phone in my room, ma'am. The address is 1425 Poplar. Hotel Algonquin." He paused for a beat. "It's just off Colfax."

Anna knew the hotel all too well. In fact, it was the same place that Antwan Jepson was living in. A run-down relic from the 1940s, it was populated nowadays almost exclusively by prostitutes and parolees, with a few resident drunks thrown in for good measure. A volatile mix that resulted in regular Saturday night mayhem.

"Just a reminder, Mr. Mackenzie, necessary in view of your place of residence. Consuming alcoholic beverages, or availing yourself of the services of a prostitute is in contravention of the terms of your parole. The police raid that hotel regularly, especially at night and on weekends, so here's a friendly warning. Don't get caught with your pants down."

His voice became even more devoid of expression, a feat Anna would have thought impossible. He looked past her. "No, ma'am, I won't."

The warning about avoiding alcohol and prostitutes was standard, and she'd delivered it a hundred times before, but the air between them was suddenly charged. With sexual tension, Anna recognized to her astonishment. She looked up and found her gaze locked with his.

Deeply embarrassed, she realized that—just for an instant—she was imagining how Joseph Mackenzie might look when he was stripped naked, all hard muscle and lean flesh, with a tan burned deep into his skin from exercising in the prison yard under a hot Colorado sun.

She broke eye contact and bent her head, scribbling a meaningless note in his file just so that she would have a legitimate excuse to drop her gaze. She had never before felt even a twinge of sexual attraction to the parolees who marched through her office, even though many of them were good-looking, with the buffed-up bodies that came from aimless hours spent doing push-ups and sit-ups in their cells. She couldn't understand how Mackenzie had managed to get under her guard, provoking a primitive physical awareness right from the moment he appeared in her doorway.

Primitive physical awareness wasn't high on Anna's list of desired responses, even to the men she dated. In relation to one of her parolees, it was totally unacceptable. With cool efficiency, she repressed the unwelcome sensation.

It took only a few seconds to get herself back on an even keel, and when she looked up from her fake note taking, she spoke briskly. ''Once you've saved some money, you'll probably want to move into a regular apartment building where the surroundings are more congenial. Don't forget that you're required to notify me of any new address and phone number within twenty-four hours of making the change.''

''Yes, ma'am.''

''Do you have transportation to your place of employment, Mr. Mackenzie?''

''There's bus service, but I plan to walk most of the time.''

She wondered if that was from choice or by necessity. ''Do you have sufficient money for bus fare and food until you receive your first paycheck? Be truthful, please. I can direct you to a charity that will provide some financial aid if you need it.''

''Thank you, ma'am. I have sufficient money for my needs.''

''How is that? I see that you claim the money you stole was all spent, even before you were arrested. To get through almost a million bucks in six months, you must have been living pretty high on the hog.''

''Yes, ma'am. It sure was a lot of money to spend.''

''So how do you think you're going to handle living on minimum wage? Based on past behavior, I'd have to conclude that you don't do too well with the concepts of self-denial and surviving on a tight budget."

"It's not going to be a problem, ma'am." His voice remained wooden. "I went a little crazy for a while, but I'm back on track now. The counseling sessions in prison helped a lot."

At least he wasn't claiming that Jesus had turned his life around, which was a definite plus as far as Anna was concerned, although she tried not to let her own religious experiences as a teenager color her reaction to clients who found strength and comfort in their faith.

"Let's be really clear about this, Mr. Mackenzie, because it's important if you want to stay out of trouble. If you try to access any stolen funds you may have squirreled away, you will be in violation of the terms of your parole and you will be sent back to prison. Immediately, without a hearing, without any second chances."

"Yes, I understand that, ma'am. But I have no stolen funds waiting to be accessed."

Anna decided it was time for her to assume that at least some of his statements were truthful. "It isn't easy to make it through parole, Mr. Mackenzie, and it's even more difficult to be successful without family members to help you. Where does your family live? Would you like me to make an application for you to have your parole transferred to some other state? It can be done with a recommendation from your parole officer, you know, and I'd be happy to take care of the necessary paperwork."

"Thank you, ma'am, but I don't have any family."

"None at all? Not even foster parents, or brothers and sisters?"

"No, ma'am."

"I'm sorry. That must be hard for you."

"Yes, ma'am."

It must have been even harder during the years he'd been incarcerated. Without relatives to send him the occasional care package, life on the inside would have been almost unbearably bleak. Anna flipped through the information sheets forwarded by the prison, discreetly checking to see how many sets of foster parents had been involved in raising Joseph Mackenzie. Instead of finding a list of foster parents, she discovered that he had been raised by his birth parents, who were farmers in Kansas, according to the official record.

She looked up from his file. "It says here that you grew up in a two-parent home, Mr. Mackenzie, in a small town not far from Topeka. Are you estranged from your family? Is that why you don't want your parole transferred to Kansas?"

"No, ma'am, that isn't it. My parents are dead."

"You must miss them," she said. "How old were you when they died?"

"I was eighteen. They died in a car accident."

"Together?"

"Yes, ma'am."

A tiny prickle ran down Anna's spine. Not of sympathy, she realized, but a return of her previous disbelief. Something about Mackenzie's manner made her doubt almost everything he said, although she'd be damned if she could identify precisely what was making her so suspicious. She tried to probe a little, to find out if there was definitely something he wanted to conceal about his background or if it was just one more thing that she was imagining.

"That's a terrible way to lose your parents. It must have been very difficult for you."

"Yes, ma'am, it was."

"You already said you don't have brothers or sisters. What about cousins? Aunts? Uncles? Grandparents?"

"I have a big extended family, but they're scattered all over the States and we've never had the chance to get to know each other too well. Except for my grandparents. They were very kind to me after my mom and dad died. My parents' farm was in hock, so there was no money after the farm was sold and the debts paid off, but my grandparents helped me raise the money for college and they encouraged me to go on to graduate school."

"Since they did so much to help you, wouldn't you like to have your parole transferred so that you can be near your grandparents?"

He shook his head. "Unfortunately, my granddad died while I was in prison, and my grandma is in a nursing home. She had a stroke and wouldn't recognize me even if I went to see her."

These were the two longest answers he'd given yet, and his voice took on a hint of warmth as he spoke of his grandparents, followed by definite sadness as he mentioned his grandmother's stroke. Anna felt a pang of remorse. She'd been much too suspicious, she decided. What was the matter with her today? She had to learn not to impose disappointment with her other clients on new parolees or she couldn't hope to be effective in her job.

She spoke with more friendliness than she'd shown

so far. ‘‘Well, since you don’t have any family to help out, your finances are going to be tight for a while. Pride is a good thing, but not if it prevents you letting me know when you need assistance. If you find yourself getting into a financial jam, let me know and I’ll see what can be done. There are a few resources we can tap.’’

‘‘Yes, ma’am. Thank you.’’

‘‘Did you earn any money while you were incarcerated, Mr. Mackenzie?’’

‘‘Yes, ma’am.’’

‘‘Could you try to be a little more forthcoming with your replies, do you think? It would make it a lot easier on both of us. How much money did you earn, Mr. Mackenzie?’’

‘‘It was $3,423.50.’’

‘‘And you’re planning to put that money into a bank account so that it will be safe?’’ Anna felt her cheeks turn pink as she realized that might not be the most tactful of remarks to make to a prisoner convicted of bank embezzlement. She cleared her throat. ‘‘Anyway, it’s a decent nest egg. It should help tide you over the first few weeks of getting settled.’’

‘‘It would, but I don’t have most of the money I earned. The warden sent three thousand dollars to the bank where I used to work, as partial recompense for what I’d stolen. I was only allowed to keep the remaining $423.’’

‘‘What happened to the fifty cents?’’

‘‘It seems to have gotten lost in the accounting process.’’

She detected definite mockery in his response and almost smiled at him. Then she remembered how she and Raul had slipped into an easy camaraderie that ultimately hadn't been in anyone's best interests, and she decided that the more formal her relationship with Joseph Mackenzie, the better it would be for both of them. Every training session she'd attended had emphasized that maintaining a professional distance between case officer and parolee was essential. In retrospect, it was painfully clear that if she hadn't liked Raul so much, she might have been quicker to notice the subtle signs of renewed drug use. She wasn't about to repeat her mistake with Joseph Mackenzie, just because he had a high IQ and a sexy body.

"How long did it take you to earn that $3,400, Mr. Mackenzie?"

"It took me four years," he said flatly. "Forty hours a week working in the prison kitchens. For the last two years, I was earning fifty cents an hour."

Wages started at twenty cents an hour in federal prisons, so Joseph Mackenzie had been at the upper end of the pay scale. "Fifty cents an hour is quite a lot for a kitchen worker," Anna said.

"Yes, ma'am. But for the last two years I was allowed to do all the ordering of supplies, and I kept the accounts for the commissary. That's why I earned so much." His mouth twisted into a self-mocking line. "*So much* being a relative term."

Mackenzie had been fortunate in getting assigned to a job that made at least token use of his business training. Still, his generous rate of pay made no difference in the end, given that the warden had taken most of it away. He'd need to have the conscience of a saint if he didn't feel some resentment at the warden's garnishment of his wages. Even a man with no criminal tendencies might find it frustrating to work hard for almost four years and end up with less than

450 bucks to show for it. Given Mackenzie's past record of theft and embezzlement, it seemed a fair guess that he was mad as hell.

"In your opinion, was the warden justified in taking your hard-earned money and giving it to the bank where you used to work?"

If she'd hoped to provoke him into an unrehearsed response, she was disappointed. "Yes, ma'am, it was fair. I stole almost a million dollars from clients of the bank who trusted me with their money. A lot of the bank's customers in Durango were retired, and the money I embezzled was their life savings. It was a terrible thing that I did, and I have to make recompense any way I can. I don't mind giving up my wages. I only wish it had been more."

Right. And if she believed that, he had a nice collection of oceanfront properties in Arizona to sell her. Anna was fairly sure she was being treated to a repeat performance of the charade Mackenzie had enacted for the parole board. At his first two parole hearings, he had protested that he was innocent and that he'd been wrongly convicted. After four years in the pen, he would have learned enough from the old cons to realize that confessing your sins was the only way to get paroled.

She would lay odds that as soon as Mackenzie understood that repentance was the key to getting the lock on his cell door sprung, he had transformed himself into the most repentant prisoner in the state of Colorado.

Except she wasn't buying his repentance.

Anna leaned across the desk, her gaze narrowing. "Stop playing me for a fool, Mackenzie. You're beginning to annoy me."

He met her gaze. His gray eyes revealed nothing, but his voice was insolently mocking almost by virtue of its total blandness. ''Yes, ma'am. I'm real sorry, ma'am. How exactly did I offend you, ma'am?''

Anna pushed back from her desk, shocked by her sudden urge to grab him and shake him into being honest. She was acutely aware that her anger was out of all proportion to Joseph Mackenzie's misdeeds. What had he done, after all, except walk into her office and demonstrate scrupulous courtesy and appropriate remorse for his crime? So what if the courtesy and the remorse were both fake? Provided he didn't break any of the provisions of his parole, why did she care? It wasn't his fault that Raul Estevan was on his deathbed in the prison ward of Denver General. It wasn't his fault that Antwan had been unreachable for the entire day. It wasn't his fault that she had to work late tonight, and for sure it wasn't his fault that her body had reacted to his presence with a primitive, uncomfortable sensation of sexual awareness. A sexual awareness that, come to think of it, probably owed as much to the fact that she was smarting over Pete's betrayal as it did to any physical qualities Joseph Mackenzie might possess.

For some reason, it was reassuring to conclude that the debacle with Pete was the chief cause of her physical response to Joseph Mackenzie. Anna drew in a deep breath, getting her world back into a more normal perspective and withdrawing into the protection of her official position.

''Never mind. It's been a long day.'' She paused. ''Well, taking everything into account, you seem to have your affairs pretty much in order, Mr. Mackenzie. I wish you the best of luck in holding down your job and complying with all the terms of your parole. Let's take a few minutes to go over the remainder of these forms. I want to make sure you understand the conditions of your parole in every last detail, and that you're aware of exactly what will happen if you're found to be in contravention of any of these terms."

"Yes, ma'am. Thank you."

She went through the standard forms, obtained his signature in the appropriate places, the procedure moving swiftly since Mackenzie needed no clarification of the dense, official language, or the obscure vocabulary.

With the last form signed, she stood up, signaling the end of the interview. "Mr. Mackenzie, you understand that you are required to report back to these offices next Monday, and that if you miss that appointment for any reason at all, other than incapacitating illness, a warrant will be issued for your arrest and you will be returned to prison."

"Yes, ma'am, I understand."

"Then I'll see you next week. Goodbye, Mr. Mackenzie. Good luck."

Four

Joe managed to hold it together until he left Anna Langtry's office. As soon as he was outside in the corridor, he collapsed against the wall, fighting to draw steady, even breaths.

Long before he had himself back under control, she stuck her head around the door, her hair glowing like a summer sunset under the neon strip lights of the corridor. "Mr. Mackenzie, I need you to—" She broke off. "What's the matter, Mr. Mackenzie? Are you feeling all right?"

Of all the damn stupid questions she'd asked this afternoon, that had to rank right up there as the most stupid. Of course he wasn't all right. He was damn near dying of suppressed lust, sucker punched by the intensity and unexpectedness of his desire. He'd spent the past four years convincing himself that he had his sexual urges disciplined to a monklike state of control. Apparently he'd fooled himself about that, along with many other vital aspects of his life and his relationships.

Joe pulled together the battered dregs of his willpower and pushed away from the wall, so that he was standing pillar-straight in front of her. In front of his *parole officer.* He needed to drum into his thick, prison-stupid brain that this woman was an officer of the court and a threat to everything he planned to do over the next few weeks.

''Yes, ma'am, thank you. I'm just fine.'' He not only sounded like a nineteenth century village yokel, ready to tug his forelock in the presence of the master's wife, he felt that way, too.

''You appeared a little pale just now.''

''No, I'm fine.'' His monosyllabic responses had originally been part of a calculated determination not to get trapped into revealing a single damn thing that might get him noticed or make him memorable. By the time he'd been subjected to a couple of direct glances from Anna Langtry's sky-blue eyes, monosyllables had been all he was capable of producing. In fact, right at this moment, a three-word sentence pushed at the absolute limits of his available vocabulary.

''Well, good. I was afraid you might be feeling unwell. I know that prison health care isn't the best, to put it mildly.'' She sounded genuinely relieved that he was okay, although she didn't smile.

He would really like to see her smile, Joe thought.

He cleared his throat. ''Fortunately, I don't get sick easily. I rarely need medical attention.'' Jeez, what do you know? He'd produced two coherent, multiword sentences for the first time since he'd trotted out the well-worn lies about his parents. Things were definitely looking up.

Her gaze flicked for a second to the scar on his hand, an occasion when he'd obviously needed a doctor, and her mouth tightened. If she could see the monster slash across his stomach, she'd really flip, Joe thought. Or maybe not. As a parole officer, she would be well aware that plenty of convicts relieved the boredom of incarceration by picking fights with any inmate who seemed vulnerable. Joe had made damn sure that his appearance of vulnerability lasted for as short a time as possible, which still meant that he'd made two trips to the prison hospital within the first month of arriving at the West Denver facility.

He realized she was speaking again. "The reason I came chasing after you is that I need another signature from you, Mr. Mackenzie. Sorry, I overlooked this one last form you're required to sign."

She held out a clipboard with a small card attached. When he didn't move, she walked along the corridor until she was standing less than a foot away from him. Her scent invaded his senses, overwhelming him after four years of inhaling no smell more seductive than pine disinfectant. She wasn't wearing a sophisticated hundred-dollar perfume of the sort Sophie had always chosen, but her skin gave off a tantalizing fragrance that combined shampoo, soap and clean clothes that had never gone anywhere near the horrors of a prison laundry system.

Essence of woman, Joe thought, and although he wanted to laugh at his whimsy, his control was so fragile that he couldn't smile any more than he could lift his hand to take the clipboard she was extending toward him. Not unless he wanted to risk doing or saying something that at best would be humiliating and at worst would have him clapped back in jail.

"It's just a confirmation that you've received the departmental handbook for parolees, Mr. Mackenzie. I'd appreciate your signature some time before the twenty-second century."

Her sarcasm enabled him to snap out of his fugue and scribble a signature in the place she indicated. It was a mark of how totally befuddled he was by her nearness that, for the first time since he'd been arrested, he didn't read what it was that he'd signed. Was the presence of a sexy woman all it took to negate the lessons he'd learned at such high cost, Joe wondered. He sure as hell hoped not, or he was never going to survive long enough to fulfill the goals that had kept him going through 1,491 days of incarceration.

He handed her back the pen, and the tips of his fingers brushed against hers. Desire pierced him, painful as a knife wound. "I have to go now," he said, as if she'd been pressing him to stay, for Chrissake. "Goodbye." He turned abruptly and walked to the elevator, absurdly grateful when he discovered it waiting on this floor.

The doors swooshed closed behind him. Alone in a confined space—reassuringly reminiscent of his cell—he was finally able to relax, and by the time the elevator reached the ground floor his body began to function more or less like a normal person's. Still, he considered his assignment to Anna Langtry's caseload as another sign that Fate was not yet ready to smile on him. Why else did he have the bad luck to draw a beautiful, sexy, intelligent woman as a parole officer?

From his point of view, intelligent was even more troublesome than sexy. Sexual urges could be controlled. He'd proven that over the past four years. But he absolutely didn't need a parole officer who was going to take more than a minimal interest in his activities. He'd been hoping to draw someone incompetent or lazy. Better yet, someone both incompetent *and* lazy. God knows, the prison system had enough of that sort of employee to go around.

Shrugging into his cheap nylon ski jacket, Joe emerged into the chill of late afternoon. The sky was still low and sullen and the wind keen. As he trudged toward the main road, he was grateful for the hood on his jacket, and for the deep pockets, since the prisoner's aid society hadn't sprung for gloves, seeing as how it was supposedly almost spring.

He hadn't eaten since his breakfast of fake orange juice and Cream of Wheat before leaving prison this morning, so he stopped at the nearest McDonald's for a Big Mac and an order of fries. The taste of the food was nowhere near as wonderful as he'd remembered, but he liked sitting in the warm, clean, brightly lit restaurant, watching the kids clamber over the equipment in the play area and pretending he was a regular guy who didn't wonder between every bite of hamburger when a hand was going to clamp down onto his shoulder and whisk him back to his cell.

When he'd lingered as long as he could without becoming conspicuous, Joe caught a bus down Colfax Avenue and arrived back at his hotel forty-five minutes later. By car, the journey would have taken twenty minutes, or less. Still, he didn't waste any time bemoaning the unfairness of his former employers impounding his possessions to pay off his supposed thefts from the bank. He was too busy planning how he was going to find the sons of bitches who'd set him up—and what he'd do to them once he found them.

He had several satisfying scenarios worked out for that splendid moment, all of them involving fists, blood, and hot, pounding violence.

Who said prison didn't teach you anything useful, Joe thought cynically. Before society locked him away for the purposes of rehabilitation and repentance, he'd never raised a finger against another human being. Not even his father, despite the many occasions when he'd longed to drag the belt out of the bastard's hands and batter him to a pulp. Now, courtesy of the federal government, he had both the strength and the knowledge to kill a man with his bare hands.

Joe took the dirty elevator to the third floor of the hotel and unlocked the door to his room. He stepped inside, bolted the door after him, and allowed himself a small sigh of satisfaction as he looked around the space that was all his own. For $19.99 a night, plus tax, minus a five percent discount since the prisoner's aid society had paid a week in advance, he'd been given a ten-by-twelve room, with a worn linoleum floor and a plastic roller blind that hung drunkenly over the single barred window.

The furniture consisted of a bed covered by a hideous mustard-yellow chenille spread, a chest of drawers, and a metal pole equipped with a few misshapen wire hangers, currently holding his two other pairs of jeans and a couple of sweatshirts picked up from the Goodwill store. He had filled only one drawer in the chest with socks and underwear, and the shelf on the wall opposite his bed contained all his personal possessions other than clothes: an enlarged snapshot of his grandparents taken shortly before he was arrested, a leather-bound, gold-edged journal in which he had never written, and half a dozen books. There was no chair.

Four years ago, he would have viewed a room like

this with unmitigated horror. Now all he saw was the blissful opportunity for solitude, and the fact that there was an attached bathroom. The luxury of taking a shower or using the toilet in absolute privacy was enough to compensate for the fact that the towels were threadbare, and the sink so covered in rust stains that it would never come clean, however hard he scrubbed.

Joe crossed to the bed and tossed off his jacket, pausing a moment to admire the new pillow he'd bought before he left to sign on with his parole officer. The pillow had cost him six bucks at Wal-Mart, and another $2.99 for the zippered cover. Add in toothpaste, on sale with a free toothbrush, disposable razors, shaving cream, deodorant and the cheapest bottle of shampoo he could find, and he'd spent seventeen bucks. Seventeen bucks was more than he'd earned in four days of prison labor. It was also a frighteningly large chunk of the money he had left, given how soon next week's rent would fall due. He considered it worth every penny of the seventeen bucks to go to bed spanking clean, and to sleep for the first time in four years on something that didn't smell of other men's stale urine.

Joe was optimistic that some time soon he'd start to shed the layer of prison grime that felt as if it were indelibly pounded into his skin. He'd been allowed to shower and shave before leaving prison at six this morning. He'd showered again as soon as he took possession of this hotel room. Now he decided to take yet another shower before getting into bed, just to celebrate the fact that there wasn't a damn soul to tell him he couldn't. One surprisingly good thing you could say for this certified fleabag hotel—it had a plentiful supply of hot water.

He was showered and dressed again in boxers and a T-shirt, ready to catch a couple of hours' sleep before leaving for the night shift at his new job, when he heard the sounds of a commotion on the landing outside his room. Joe ignored it. One of the first lessons he'd learned in prison was that only idiots—total, unredeemably stupid assholes—got themselves involved in any disturbance that wasn't directly related to their own business.

The altercation seemed to be taking place right outside his room. A man was shouting, his words slurred, the occasional obscenity coming through loud and clear. Either he was high, or he'd been drinking. Maybe both. Joe gave a mental shrug. He'd learned to sleep through worse disturbances than this. Much worse. He rolled over onto his stomach, keeping his eyes closed.

He was actually drifting off to sleep, soothed by the fresh pillow, when he heard Anna Langtry's voice, breathless and breaking in midword, followed by a dull thud that sounded very much like a semi-conscious body hitting the floor.

Unreedemably stupid asshole that he was, Joe sprang out of bed, tugged on his jeans and opened the door, still zipping up his pants.

Anna toppled backward into his room the moment he opened his door. A tall, skinny black guy with dreadlocks lunged after her, screaming obscenities, fumbling under her jacket in the region of her left breast.

Christ, he was going for her gun.

Joe grabbed a handful of dreadlocks, dragging the

man's head up just enough to deliver a swift uppercut to his jaw. Momentarily stunned, the man's head snapped back and Joe was able to move between him and Anna's inert body before throwing another solid punch to the man's stomach. Effective, if somewhat basic. The man's eyes crossed, and he slid to the floor, landing in a boneless heap a couple of feet away from Anna.

A door banged shut at the end of the corridor. Joe glanced up. Another hotel resident, someone a lot smarter than Joe, was retreating into the safety of her room. It didn't take much brainpower to figure out that it was significantly better to be inside your room rather than outside when the cops arrived to take care of this latest disturbance.

Joe would have followed suit and decamped, but he couldn't get back into his room because Anna was lying smack-dab across the middle of his doorway. There was no way to close his door, not without moving her.

He scowled, trying to convince himself that now Anna was out of immediate danger, he had every right to prop her against the wall and then retreat to the sanctuary of his room. He tried hard, but he wasn't quite able to abandon her. What if she'd been badly injured? The police might arrive any minute. On the other hand, they could take an hour. More than long enough for Dreadlocks to regain consciousness and create all kinds of havoc.

Letting rip with a string of curses, Joe swung around and knelt beside Anna's unmoving body. Shit! Why the hell did she have to get herself in trouble right outside his door? He took possession of her gun so that Dreadlocks couldn't steal it, then touched his fingertips to the pulse in her neck. He was relieved to find it strong and quite steady.

Which was a hell of a lot more than could be said for his own heartbeat when he sat back on his heels and realized her eyes were wide-open and looking straight at him.

He snatched his fingers away from contact with her bare skin, as if he'd been feeling her up, instead of attempting perfectly legitimate first aid.

''Oh,'' he mumbled. ''You're awake.'' Great. He was back in full moron mode, sounding about as smart as Jemima Puddleduck quacking out the obvious.

''Yes.'' She rubbed her throat. ''Antwan was choking me, and I passed out.''

She lifted her gaze to his and her blue eyes worked their inevitable de-braining function. ''How long was I out?''

He swallowed, moistening a mouth that had gone bone dry. ''A couple of minutes, not much more. How do you feel?''

''Woozy. My throat's sore.'' Her wandering gaze suddenly registered the gun in Joe's hand and the man still stretched out on the hallway floor. ''Oh, my God! What have you done to Antwan?''

''If Antwan is that crumpled heap on the floor, I haven't done anything much. Except haul him off you when he banged you into the wall and went for your gun. He looked angry enough to shoot you first and worry about the consequences later.''

''Yes,'' she admitted. ''He was pretty wild.''

''Here. Take your gun.'' Joe held it out to her on the flat of his hand.

She took it and sat up, recovering fast. ''Thanks.''

She checked the safety and holstered the weapon with the ease of habit. ''Weapons possession is a serious parole violation, you know, Mackenzie. But I'll overlook it this time.''

''Gee, that's real big of you. Seeing as how I only took it in order to save your life.''

She frowned. ''Antwan may have looked violent to you, but he wouldn't have shot me—''

''Sure he would. He's higher than a truckload of kites. When he attacked you, he'd passed the point of flying and moved on to full-scale hallucinations.''

''Maybe, but he wasn't going for my gun.'' She rubbed her forehead. ''I can see it might have looked that way to you, but he just wanted to take back the package of heroin I confiscated from him.'' She reached inside her jacket and extracted a plastic bag of white powder from an inner pocket. ''This is all he was after. He wouldn't have hurt me.''

Joe didn't bother to hide his incredulity. ''If you want to believe that, lady, feel free. But keep up that attitude, and your friends and family will be attending your funeral some time real soon.''

''I know Antwan. He's not violent—''

''He was today. He was more than ready to off you, and me, too, if that's what it took to get his bag of smack.'' And why the hell was he wasting his breath trying to convince her that no junkie was capable of feeling any emotion beyond desire for another fix, and furious rage at anyone who stood between him and his drug supply? If she didn't know something as elementary as that, then she shouldn't be a parole officer.

Anna leaned against the wall, looking momentarily exhausted, and Joe felt a twinge of unwelcome empathy. ''You need to call for backup and I don't have a phone in my room. If the pay phone downstairs is working, do you want me to call for an ambulance?''

''No, thanks. I appreciate the offer, Mackenzie, but I'm really okay and anyway I have a cell phone.'' She looked sad. ''Unfortunately, I need to call the cops, not emergency services. Antwan's going to be heading right back to prison.''

''He's on parole? One of your cases?''

Anna nodded. ''Yes, he needed to be in a residential drug treatment program, but there were no openings. Without appropriate treatment, something like this was inevitable.''

''You sound sorry for him.'' Joe regretted the comment the moment it was made. It sounded personal, the last thing he wanted.

Anna shrugged, the gesture somewhere between resigned and angry. ''I am sorry for him. Antwan hasn't had too many chances in life, and he's obviously just blown the one he was given by the parole board. One way or another, this has been a rotten day for blown chances as far as my parolees are concerned.''

Joe didn't ask what she meant—he wasn't about to wade any further into this unwelcome conversation—and she abruptly turned away from him, as if aware that she'd confided more than she intended. She walked over to Antwan, who was beginning to stir, demonstrating surprising strength as she rolled him over onto his stomach so that she could slip on a pair of handcuffs. That done, she straightened and looked at Joe.

''Thank you for your help, Mr. Mackenzie,'' she said, reverting to the brisk manner of their afternoon interview. ''I appreciate your willingness to get involved.''

Right. He was positively a model citizen. Just call him Eager Beaver, the Handy Helper. ''You're welcome, ma'am.''

But he was only going to help out this once, Joe swore silently. From now on, he was going to make damn sure that his path never crossed with Anna Langtry's, except once a week, in her office, when he had no choice. He'd been a damn fool to come to her rescue. He should have let Antwan shoot her. At least then he'd have had a second chance at getting assigned to a parole officer who was stupid and uncaring. Not to mention a parole officer who didn't have the face of a Titian cherub perched on the body of a soft porn starlet.

Enough already. He wasn't going to devote another second to thinking about Anna Langtry. With a single curt nod, Joe went into his room and locked the door behind him.

Time to get back on track. Time to get focused on revenge.

Five

Raul, never enthusiastic about cooperating with the authorities, defied the predictions of all his doctors and refused to die. His wounded liver, nicked by the passage of two bullets, showed miraculous signs of healing, and his abused body fought off infections, fevers and the stress of various collapsing organs. By Thursday, he'd staggered out of immediate danger and onto the critical list. Calling the hospital for the latest update early on Saturday morning, Anna received the startling news that Raul's condition had once again been upgraded; the doctors were now optimistic that he would survive.

The end of the week was turning out much better than the beginning, even if Antwan Jepson was back behind bars and Stan Swann was threatening to divorce his spendthrift wife and sue for full custody of the kids. A fight, Anna had pointed out, he was likely to lose. At least Stan remained out of prison, with a fair chance of successfully completing the final two months of his parole unless he and LaToya got into another blockbuster fight. Anna considered the fact that they'd survived the week without Stan leaving town or quitting his job as cause for celebration.

The weekend brought other gifts. Ferdinand had refrained from puking hairballs and clawing holes in the furniture for five whole days and, as a bonus, the weather had also changed for the better. With the capriciousness typical of a Colorado spring, the mild sunny weather promised for Monday had arrived just in time for the weekend.

Anna would normally have taken advantage of the sunshine and joined her friends in the hiking club for a strenuous trek through eight miles of the most beautiful scenery Rocky Mountain National Park had to offer. She'd discovered in the months after leaving Alana Springs that there was nothing like physical exertion for taking her mind off her problems, and when she also realized that regular workouts meant she could eat her favorite chocolate fudge cookies without looking like the Goodyear Blimp, she'd become a devotee of climbing, skiing and walking in the rugged mountain terrain to the west of Denver.

In fact, it wasn't just the weight control aspects of aggressive exercise that Anna relished. Women in Alana Springs were supposed to be soft and plump, subservient feminine pillows always available to provide comfort for their husbands. In the wake of her escape, each new physical skill she developed became symbolic of her freedom, the satisfying equivalent of thumbing her nose at the Welks brothers and everything they stood for.

Unfortunately, there was a heavy black cloud scudding across this unexpectedly sunny weekend sky. Pete the Unfaithful Worm was a member of the hiking club—that was where they'd met—and Anna was in no mood to clamber up rocky outcroppings and admire nesting birds and cuddly bunnies with Pete in tow. There was too much danger she might brain him with the nearest boulder.

After five days of silence, Pete had come around to her condo last night, his arms loaded with red roses, along with a bottle of her favorite Merlot, and a box of imported truffles. The combination of flowers, wine and chocolate, he seemed to feel, ought to be more than enough to compensate for his minor—very minor—sexual transgression.

When Anna hadn't immediately melted into his arms and forgiven him, Pete had become angry. "Jeez, what's with you, Anna? Do you have to make such a big deal about one night of casual sex? It didn't mean anything."

"I doubt if it was one night or only one woman—"

"I swear it was." His gaze was so earnest and sincere, Anna immediately suspected him of lying. He sounded just like her parolees, who always managed to present the picture of outraged innocence when they were most guilty.

"Anyway, why would you care if I had a meaningless sexual encounter with another woman?" Pete's expression formed into one of genuine incomprehension, mingled with reproach. "That's not what our relationship is about, Anna. God knows, you have no interest in sex. Admit it. You're a real prude."

"That's not true—"

"Sure it is. I feel like I'm raping a nun every time we go to bed together. It's kind of interesting the first time. After that, it gets real old, real fast."

Pete couldn't have found a better way to put her on the defensive than by accusing her of sexual inadequacy. The analytical, professionally trained part of Anna's brain understood that he was manipulating her as compensation for his own guilt. The emotional part cringed. Her stomach lurched with the worry that she was as sexually frigid as he claimed. She couldn't deny that somewhere in the depths of her subconscious, Caleb Welks, sex and suffering were still unhealthily linked. No wonder her performance in bed tended to be on the subdued side. Fifteen years since her wedding night, and she still hadn't learned how to overcome the fear that if she gave herself freely, she was cooperating in her own oppression.

Still, she clung to the knowledge that Pete was deliberately needling her, excusing his own misdeeds by blaming her supposed lack of sexual sizzle. Refusing to get sucked into his game, Anna suppressed her humiliation and retreated behind the barrier of her professional training. She didn't want them to end up hurling accusations at each other that they would both regret, so one of them had to act like a grown-up. And right now, she seemed to be the only available adult.

"Pete, let's not fight about this. I agree we didn't set off any fireworks when we went to bed together, and I'm sorry you were so…unsatisfied. But that's no excuse for what you did last weekend. We needed to have a conversation about my failure to meet your sexual needs before you decided to spend Sunday night with another woman—"

"*Failure to meet my sexual needs?* Jesus, Anna, can't you ever talk like a real woman instead of always sounding like a damn therapy manual?"

Anna was surprised to feel a flare of red-hot anger—the most intense emotion she'd experienced toward Pete in weeks. She glared at him, eyes blazing. "You know what? You bet I can talk like a real woman if I set my mind to it. Let's see. How's this for a first attempt? Get out of my condo right now, you jerk, and don't come back. We're through.''

When he didn't move, except to protest that she was overreacting, she marched to the front door and held it open. ''Having problems understanding how a *real woman* talks, Pete? Let me rephrase. You're a prick. An annoying, self-righteous prick. Get the hell out of my condo right now, and let's try hard never to see each other again, okay?''

Her reaction might have been immature, but it had been hugely satisfying to watch Pete exit the condo, blustering excuses as he groped to catch the wine, chocolates and flowers that she thrust at him on the way out. He tripped over Ferdinand, who had an unfailing ability to put himself in whatever spot promised to be most inconvenient. Pete howled in annoyance so, for good measure, the cat bit him on the ankle. All in all, a successful end to a dreary affair.

It was, however, a lot less satisfying to contemplate a sunny Saturday morning with no hike, and no other exciting plans. She could walk alone, of course, but any route challenging enough to be interesting would require a buddy for safety reasons—and all her qualified friends would be participating in the group hike. And Leila Sworski, her best friend, the one person who could always be counted on to cheer her up, was on a three-month sabbatical in Pakistan, teaching family planning techniques to illiterate peasants. Great for the women of Pakistan, but a bummer for Anna. Right now, she could really have used a dose of Leila's cheerful, no-nonsense personality.

Well, she'd already decided she needed to break out of her rut, Anna decided. Maybe this morning was the time to put her plan into action. She'd pay a quick visit to Raul in the hospital and then swing by the Cherry Creek Mall and indulge in some serious shopping. Maybe try out a new hairstyle and have herself a manicure. Or, if she and the cat could come to a polite agreement about appropriate places for puking up hairballs, she might even search for a replacement sofa cushion.

Unusually restless, even though she now had an agenda, Anna strode into her bedroom, flinging open her closet doors and scowling at the meager contents. Her wardrobe was pretty pathetic—to put it mildly—and she hadn't splurged on a new outfit since Christmas. Shopping was definitely called for. Something expensive in silk ought to improve her mood. The fact that she had no idea when she would wear a kick-ass silk outfit simply meant that she needed to work harder to lift her social life out of the deep doldrums where it currently resided.

She was really way too picky about men, she reflected twenty minutes later, taking the elevator down to the basement parking area. A couple of times, Matt Jorgenson had suggested that the two of them should go out for dinner. He was a nice guy, and she enjoyed his company on the rare occasions when they found time to share lunch or a quick coffee break. Maybe she would take him up on his offer next time. If there was a next time. Come to think of it, she didn't actually have to wait for Matt to ask. She could take a small step in the direction of the twenty-first century and ask him out herself.

Getting into her car and opening the windows to celebrate the spring sunshine, Anna decided to ignore the warning voice that pointed out that the reason she'd refused both of Matt's other invitations was because he struck even less of a sexual spark than Pete the Creep had done. So what if she didn't find Matt sexually alluring? Given that the only man who'd lit any sort of a fire in her recently was Joseph Mackenzie, she obviously couldn't use sex appeal as the basis for picking her dates. A criminal like Mackenzie, whatever sort of animal magnetism he might exert, wasn't likely to make the sort of thoughtful, considerate sexual partner that she needed to overcome her lingering hangups. Besides, she'd get fired on the spot if it was ever discovered that she'd become sexually involved with one of her parolees.

And it was insane that she was thinking about departmental regulations as if they were the only thing standing between her and a wild sexual fling with Joseph Mackenzie. Good grief, her sex life must be in a lot worse shape than she'd realized if she was reduced to fantasizing about dating a man who looked as if his definition of tender lovemaking was anything that didn't inflict visible bruises.

On Monday, she would ask Matt out to the movies, Anna decided, finding a parking spot close to the hospital entrance. She was thirty-two years old, and it was past time for her to become proactive in regard to her relationships with men. It was embarrassing that fifteen years after escaping from Alana Springs, she still couldn't get past those years of teenage indoctrination that said the only valid purpose of sexual intercourse was procreation.

In pursuit of her new come-hither attitude toward men, she flashed a huge smile at the sixty-year-old retiree in charge of the inquiry desk, and elicited the information that Raul hadn't yet been transferred out of the prison ward's intensive care unit. A nurse at the prison wing reception area assured Anna that Raul was doing fine, although she thought it would be at least another week before her patient could be removed to the hit-or-miss care of a regular prison hospital.

''That's one lucky guy,'' the nurse said, rolling her eyes. ''If you change the path of any one of those bullets by a millimeter, he's a dead man. If he'd lost an ounce more blood before the paramedics brought him in, then he's dead. If the resident surgeon on duty hadn't been the best in Denver, he's dead.'' She shook her head. ''Man, in this job you sure learn that if it's not your turn to die, then the good Lord doesn't take you.''

Anna went into Raul's room, so buoyed by the nurse's report that she was shocked to discover him still hooked to enough hardware to launch the space shuttle, with his face darkened by bruises that hadn't been apparent earlier in the week and his body looking disconcertingly shrunken.

There was no sign of Father Pat, but Raul's wife was seated by the side of his bed, her face still pale and drawn. But today there was no trace of tears, Anna saw, and Guillermina's shoulders no longer drooped in abject despair.

It struck her that she'd been unforgivably arrogant to make the judgment on Monday that Raul would be better off dead. The nurse in reception had been correct to say that Raul was lucky. While there was life, there was hope. That was such a tired, overused cliché because it was profoundly true. With good behavior and a sympathetic parole board, Raul might make it out of prison in as little as twelve years. By that point in time, his unborn child would be in middle school, while Raul himself would be in his forties. True, half a lifetime would have been wasted, and Guillermina would probably have remarried, but father and child would have plenty of years ahead in which to forge a relationship. Anna was counting hard on the fact that parents and children could develop meaningful adult relationships even if they had been separated since birth.

Guillermina rose to her feet and Anna introduced herself again, since Raul's wife had clearly been too traumatized during Monday's visit to remember her.

"I won't disturb your husband," Anna said. "He looks as if he's resting quite peacefully. But would you let him know that if he wants me to speak on his behalf at his prison hearing, I'd be willing to do that?"

"Can you help him, *señora?*" Guillermina's eyes overflowed with sudden tears, not of despair but of hope. "Can you explain to the judge that my husband is a good man at heart? He didn't want to sell the drugs, but he had no choice, I swear it. The Colombians, they threatened to kill me and our baby if he did not go along with them."

"I'll do what I can," Anna said. "But please don't expect too much, Mrs. Estevan. Raul committed these new offenses while he was on parole, and that means there won't be a new trial, simply a judicial hearing that will take place inside the prison."

"We have a good lawyer," Guillermina said, as much to herself as to Anna. "He will help us."

A good lawyer paid for with drug money, Anna thought wryly. Talk about a cockeyed system. Raul had been brought down by the power of drug money, and might yet be saved by the same thing.

"You have to be realistic," she warned Guillermina. "Don't get your hopes up too high or you'll be disappointed. Your husband tried to kill two men in a dispute over illegal drugs. The other two men will testify that he shot first—"

"It is not true that he shot first," Guillermina said quickly. "I was there and I saw. Well, I was in the kitchen and Raul, he was in the restaurant with Carlos and Miguel. Through the window in the kitchen door I saw that Carlos was the first to draw his gun. I swear it on the life of my unborn baby."

"I believe you," Anna said. "The trouble is, you're Raul's wife, and the judge may think you're just saying what will help your husband, not what's true."

Guillermina was silent for a moment, her brows pulled together in a heavy frown. "How bad is it that the fight Raul had with those men was about drugs?"

"It sure doesn't help any. I'm not a lawyer, so I'm not sure of the details, but depending on the precise circumstances, many drug offences carry mandatory sentences, with stiffer penalties than if the same offence occurred without the accompanying drug deal—" She broke off, realizing that Guillermina might not understand the terms she'd used, but when she started to explain, Guillermina waved her clarifications aside.

"I understand what is the meaning of *mandatory.*" She clasped her hands over her pregnant belly, the fingers of her left hand inscribing a restless circle as she massaged away an ache. Seemingly lost in thought, she walked over to her husband's bed and kissed him lightly on his forehead.

Reacting to the familiar touch, Raul stirred, then

groaned before opening his eyes. When he saw his wife hovering over him, his eyes lit up, although he told her sternly in Spanish that she should go home. "You've been here too long, *chica.* It's not good for you or the baby."

Guillermina ignored his comment. "Señora Langtry is here," she said, also in Spanish, gesturing to indicate that Anna was standing behind him on the other side of the bed.

Anna walked forward. "Hello, Raul. I'm very glad to see you again. I wasn't expecting to have the pleasure."

Raul turned his head with evident effort and gave a grimace that probably was meant for a smile. "Yeah, here I am. Fooled you and the priests and doctors, too. Guess it takes more than a clip of bullets to kill me." His voice rasped so badly it was painful to listen.

"Only the good die young," Anna said, resting her hand very gently on his shoulder. "Which means, obviously, that you're going to live to be a hundred."

"Maybe even 150," he croaked, his eyes gleaming with some of his old humor.

"I have to ask you something important," Guillermina said to her husband, casting a nervous sideways glance toward Anna. Then she launched into a flood of such rapid and colloquial Spanish that it was easy to conclude she didn't want Anna to understand what was being said.

"I can leave if you have personal matters to discuss," Anna interjected as soon as Guillermina paused to draw breath. "I only stopped by to wish you well, Raul. I've already told your wife that I'll speak up for you at your hearing, although I don't know how much good that will do—''

''No, don't go.'' Raul spoke the words almost at the same time as his wife. ''You tell her,'' he said to Guillermina, his eyes closing. It was clear that even though the doctors had declared him out of danger, he was still very weak and in a lot of pain.

''Tell me what?'' Anna asked.

Guillermina drew in a deep breath. ''The argument Raul had with Carlos and Miguel, it was not about drugs.'' She looked hopefully at Anna. ''You said that if they were arguing about drugs, then the judge would put Raul in prison for longer, because of those mandatory laws. Well, it wasn't about drugs, so the sentence should be shorter, no?''

''That's true,'' Anna agreed. ''But you and Raul have to face facts, Guillermina. The Denver police and the DEA have been keeping track of your husband's activities for months. They know Carlos and Miguel worked for him. They're not going to believe this was a purely social visit on Saturday night. After all, Miguel and Carlos didn't arrive until after the restaurant was officially closed—''

''Whatever the judge believes, their argument had nothing to do with drugs,'' Guillermina repeated stubbornly. ''Except that Carlos and Miguel were high, and so they spoke when they would have been smarter to keep their mouths shut tight.''

''Raul was high, too,'' Anna pointed out. ''The tests came back positive. There's no doubt that he'd been using cocaine.''

''I know.'' For a moment Guillermina's expression became despairing again. She flashed a glance at her husband, a glance that contained anger as well as love. ''He was stupid,'' she said, scowling at him. ''He betrayed his promises to me.''

''Forgive me, sweetheart,'' Raul murmured in Spanish.

''I'm trying, even though you don't deserve it. Lucky for you that you're so sick. I can't be as angry as I should.'' Guillermina drew in a shaky breath, switching back to English as she faced Anna again. ''Men!'' she muttered. ''They would cause so much less trouble if God had only chosen to give them a brain. Just a small one, you know?''

Anna was surprised by a laugh. ''Are you sure about that? I'm not. They cause enough trouble as it is. A functioning brain might make them really dangerous.''

''Tell Ms. Langtry what happened,'' Raul interjected hoarsely, cutting off the moment of levity. ''The police have only heard from Carlos and Miguel, and they're both lying.''

''Okay, I tell her. You rest,'' Guillermina said. ''It is true that Raul had used cocaine last Saturday night. That is why my husband with the so high IQ was dumb enough to lose his temper and end up shooting at Carlos and Miguel instead of finding some other way to stop them.''

She dashed her hand across her eyes, wiping away tears that now seemed more of frustration than grief. ''But he was not angry with them because of anything to do with buying and selling drugs. My husband was angry with them because they were planning to commit murder.''

''Murder?'' Anna exclaimed. If Guillermina had been hoping to shock her, she'd succeeded. ''You

mean Carlos and Miguel came to the restaurant planning all along to kill Raul?''

''No, *señora.* Raul was not the man they intended to kill. Carlos comes from the same village as my parents, and I have known him since he was born, but he has become cruel and without conscience since he left Colombia. He boasted to my husband that he and Miguel had been paid ten thousand dollars to kill a man they had never spoken to in their lives. They showed Raul three thousand dollars they'd already been paid in advance, and they showed him a picture of the man they were supposed to kill. They said when they got paid the rest of the money they were going to quit working for Raul. They were going to fly back to Colombia and enjoy a vacation with their families.''

''And the argument was because Raul tried to stop them?'' Anna asked.

''*Sí, señora.* Raul was angry that they would kill for money. Why would they murder a man who had done them no harm? He was furious.''

Anna shook her head, massaging her temples as she tried to clear her thought processes. ''I know how frustrating this must be for you, Guillermina, but you know what Carlos and Miguel will claim. They'll stick to their story that Raul shot them because they were going to quit working for him. In other words, Raul's the bad guy and they're the good guys because they were trying to stop dealing drugs.''

With evident effort, Raul twisted his head so that he could speak without his words getting muffled in the pillow. ''Guillermina left out the most important part,'' he said to Anna.

''What was that?'' she asked.

"I recognized the photo of the man they'd been paid to kill. They were going to murder a friend of mine and I told them I would warn my friend of their plans." Raul's shoulders twisted against the bed covers in a feeble imitation of a shrug. "I should have shut up, of course, but the coke was doing my thinking for me, so I made all sorts of crazy threats. I even said I would tell the police. Unfortunately, Carlos and Miguel believed me." His words ended in a spasm of hoarse coughing.

"When my husband threatened to tell the police, that is when Carlos shot him," Guillermina said, taking up the story again. "Carlos shot first, before my husband could even reach for his gun. Then Miguel shot him, too." She stroked Raul's thick black hair away from his forehead, then turned and clutched Anna's arm in a desperate plea.

"My husband was nearly killed trying to prevent a murder," she said. "He only shot Carlos and Miguel in self-defense. Is that a reason to send him back to prison for the rest of his life?"

It was a damn clever story, Anna thought cynically. About the very best one Raul could have come up with if he and his drug-money lawyer wanted to have a shot at keeping his new sentence to a minimum. She looked at Raul, refusing to allow sympathy to overwhelm her powers of judgment.

"Is any of this true?" she asked brusquely. "Or are you just being really clever at manipulating the system, Raul? And me, too."

"It's all true," he said. "Including the fact that I was too high on Saturday night to act smart."

"Can you prove any of it?"

"Probably not." Raul's voice faded again. "Carlos

and Miguel aren't about to admit that they agreed to murder a man for money.''

''I looked for the photo they showed Raul,'' Guillermina said, sighing. ''But it was three days by the time I thought of searching for it, and it was gone. I guess the police took it, but they won't know that it was the cause of the argument.''

''You said you recognized the man in the photo,'' Anna said to Raul. ''Who were Carlos and Miguel being paid to kill? What's the name of this friend of yours whose life was supposedly on the line? Is he involved in the drug trade, too?''

Raul shook his head. ''No. He doesn't do drugs. Doesn't even smoke. He's a guy I met in prison. We got to be good friends, him and me, even though he's kind of a difficult guy to get through to. I taught him Spanish. He taught me accounting. It gave us something to do, you know, during all those hours they keep you locked down. His name's Joseph Mackenzie—''

''Joseph Mackenzie?'' Anna exclaimed. ''You know Joseph Mackenzie?''

''Yes. We shared a cell.''

She shouldn't feel so shocked. After all, the two men had been in the same federal facility for several years. Why wouldn't they know one another?

''Joe saved my life in prison and so I tried to do the same for him,'' Raul said. ''You need to warn him that he's a target, Ms. Langtry. Joe needs to know that somebody wants him dead. Tell him from me that somebody wants him dead real bad.''

Six

Anna found Raul's story disturbing. For Mackenzie's sake, she hoped the whole murder plot was a figment of Raul's vivid imagination, but for Raul's sake, she wanted the story to be true. The details were chilling enough to add credibility. On the other hand, Raul had fooled her for months. Was he playing her for a sucker again? Before she went rushing off to the authorities, yelling out accusations, she needed to consider Raul's claims away from the emotional pressure of his hospital bedside.

As she made her way back to the parking lot, Anna could find plenty of reasons to doubt Raul's version of Saturday's events. He had strong personal motives for lying. Then there was the statistical fact that, outside of the movie theater and the TV screen, few murders were committed by professional hit men. And on the rare occasions when a victim *was* gunned down by hired killers, it usually turned out that the hiring had been done by an angry spouse or a spurned sexual partner looking to provide themselves with an alibi.

According to Mackenzie's file, he had never married, so no ex-spouse could be gunning for him. Unless, of course, his official prison record turned out to be wrong, which happened more often than it should. And even if Mackenzie was a genuine, lifelong bachelor, she supposed nothing in his file ruled out the possibility of his having an ex-girlfriend who might be vengeful enough to have paid a couple of street punks to take him out.

Girlfriends were rarely mentioned in prison records unless they'd been part of the crime for which the prisoner was serving time, so Mackenzie could have a long line of angry ex-lovers for all Anna knew. In fact, he struck her as a man likely to produce strong feelings in the women he'd been involved with. The combination of intense physical attraction and financial injury could be enough to push a mentally disturbed person over the top. Given that Mackenzie had conned his most vulnerable bank clients out of almost a million bucks, it wasn't much of a stretch to wonder if he'd also conned some gullible sexual partner out of her life savings. In which case, his release from prison could well have been the trigger for a new wave of hatred by some woman who felt betrayed.

All in all, Anna decided that the *never married* notation in Mackenzie's official records was no guarantee of his safety from wrathful ex-lovers. And even if there was no irate ex-girlfriend in the picture, Mackenzie might have pissed off somebody influential while he was behind bars. The Denver West facility had plenty of high-ranking drug lords among its inmates, and any one of them would have sufficient clout—not to mention money—to recruit a couple of cheap lowlifes to take out a fellow inmate who'd offended them.

Bottom line, Anna decided that Raul's story couldn't be ignored, even until Monday. Someone needed to warn Joseph Mackenzie that he might be the target of hired killers, and Carlos and Miguel needed to answer some tough questions. Preferably before they had time to consult lawyers and amend their stories to accommodate the fact that Raul had survived and could now dispute their previous sworn statements. In addition, she needed to alert the cops to go through any physical evidence they'd collected from the crime scene. If it turned out that a photo of Joseph Mackenzie had been found at the restaurant, it would provide some slight confirmation of Raul's version of events. After all, why else would a picture of Mackenzie be there?

Leaning against the hood of her car, Anna pulled out her cell phone and turned her face to the sun. Even for Denver, the change from Monday's snow and freezing temperatures was spectacular, and she unfastened the top button of her sweater to soak up the welcome heat. Watching two squirrels chase each other up a lonely fir tree at the edge of the lot, she dialed the number for Bob Gifford, the cop who'd arrested Raul the previous Saturday. His voice mail informed her he was off duty until 8:00 a.m. on Monday. She was invited to leave a message or speak with his partner, Ed Barber, if she had urgent business.

With no other options readily available, Anna chose to make a full report of what Raul had told her to Gifford's partner. Detective Gifford had struck her as a sharp and hardworking cop. By contrast, his partner sounded old, tired and not the brightest bulb in the six-pack. Barely polite, it was obvious Ed Barber didn't see any special urgency in the situation Anna outlined. As far as he was concerned, Miguel and Carlos were behind bars and Raul would be heading back to prison as soon as he was given a medical release from the hospital. All three guys were going to serve a chunk of time, and the only real question was exactly how much. That being the case, Detective Barber saw no reason to worry about anything Anna had told him until his partner came back on duty and he wasn't so damn swamped with work.

"You might want to worry about the fact that Joseph Mackenzie is apparently the target of hired killers," Anna snapped.

"Not any more he isn't." Detective Barber sounded smug. "Even if he ever was."

"What does that mean exactly?"

"Carlos Inez and Miguel Ortega are in custody, remember? They aren't going to be gunning anyone down from their jail cell. Besides, do you really think there's a word of truth in that story Raul Estevan just conned you with?"

"Yes, obviously I do. That's why I called your partner. That's why I'm spending time on my day off making a report to you."

"Yeah, well, you probably haven't encountered as many scumsuckers as I have. Trust me on this. They all lie, all the time."

"I'm a parole officer, not a kindergarten teacher, Detective. I understand the concept of scumsucker. The term doesn't apply to Mr. Estevan."

"Huh, that's not my take on the guy. Listen, I booked Raul the last time he was arrested. I helped the D.A.'s office build a case against him. That man's ass-deep in drugs and corruption. He's got strings tied to each and every toe and finger, and the strings lead right back to the Medellin cartel in Colombia. Raul don't sneeze without permission from his handlers in Bogotá. So he's a certified, bottom-feeding, scumsucker in my book. Plus he's a wily son of a bitch.

Smart enough to invent whatever lying story is most likely to make you and the judge sympathetic—''

''I don't agree—''

''Yeah, well that proves my point. Raul's suckered you, hasn't he? Reeled you right in. He spun you a fancy pack of lies, and you fell for it.''

Anna had just spent fifteen minutes worrying about the precise same thing, but the less interest Detective Barber expressed in Raul's story, the more convinced she became that he'd told her the truth. Not only did that make the attempted murder charges against him unfair, it also meant that Joseph Mackenzie could be in imminent danger, a fact that seemed to be troubling Ed Barber not one whit.

''Raul's wife isn't a criminal, and she's corroborated everything he said,'' Anna pointed out. ''That's two people who claim Joseph Mackenzie is at risk of taking a bullet.''

The detective snorted. ''Raul's wife isn't going to say her hubby's a lying piece of shit, is she? Stands to reason she'd back up his story. Anyway, you've got no worries, even if Raul happens to be telling the truth for once. Like I said, the two supposed triggermen are locked up in the county jail, unable to make bail. So your ex-con is safe from any murderous intentions they might have.''

''But Miguel and Carlos aren't the problem any more,'' Anna said. ''It's their employer we have to worry about. Unless you question Miguel and Carlos right away, we've no idea who hired them. So their employer is free to hire another murderer any time he or she pleases.''

''Yeah, I guess that's right in theory. Always providing you believe somebody out there really did hire

Carlos and Miguel as hit men. But I've been in law enforcement twenty-four years, and I can promise you Denver doesn't have too many professional assassins.'' Detective Barber sounded wearily patient at having to explain the obvious. ''You can't just look 'em up in the Yellow Pages, you know.''

''I'm sure Denver has at least one person other than Carlos and Miguel who's willing to kill for money. It only takes one, and Mackenzie's dead. On my watch.'' Anna clamped her teeth together to prevent herself saying anything more. Informing Ed Barber that he was a stupid, incompetent prick probably wasn't going to advance her cause any.

''Yeah, I guess you're right about it only taking one. And, God knows, we wouldn't want to lose a fine, upstanding citizen like Joseph Mackenzie. Society might never recover from the loss.''

''He's served his time. He's abiding by the terms of his parole. He's entitled to the full protection of the law.''

''Sure he is. Excuse me if I'm not rushing right out to put my butt on the line for him.''

''I don't want your butt on the line, Detective. I just want you to take a nice safe car ride and warn Mackenzie that he could be in danger from a hired killer.''

Barber sighed gustily. ''All right. Since you're so anxious, I'll go warn Mackenzie as soon as I can take an hour away from this desk. Mind, I don't think the guy is in a lick of real danger. Damn nuisance he doesn't have a phone.''

''That's because he's on parole and has no money. He didn't refuse phone service just to make things difficult.'' Anna spoke through teeth still gritted tight. Oh, boy, did she ever wish there was some effective way to file an official complaint about Detective Barber, but she knew better than to try. The police department considered parole officers more as pesky social workers than as a branch of law enforcement. In the opinion of many street cops, parole officers were far too willing to put the well-being of their clients ahead of the safety of society. Anna knew departmental relations with the cops were already tense enough to cause on-going problems, without her throwing in an official protest to season the simmering pot.

"You'll warn Mackenzie today?" she reiterated.

"I'll try. Or, if you're that worried, I guess you could always go warn him yourself. Find out if he has any idea who might want to take him out and let me know what he says. After all, he's your parolee, isn't he? He's much more likely to tell you the truth than he is me. You know what ex-cons are like around cops."

Wary, Anna thought. And with damn good cause if the cop was carrying around as much baggage as Ed Barber. "You're right, Detective. Mackenzie is my parolee and my responsibility. I'll go and see him myself, as you recommend. Thanks a bunch for all your help."

Her sarcasm passed right over Barber's head. "You're welcome. Always glad to help out a colleague."

So much for cooperation between the various branches of law enforcement. It obviously required two functioning brains before that concept could work. Anna banged her cell phone shut, scowling in the alluring direction of Cherry Creek Mall. She'd been looking forward to her day of shopping and now she had no legitimate choice other than to go chasing off to warn Joseph Mackenzie that somebody might want him dead.

Oh, well. Unlocking the car door, she gave a quick shrug. What the heck. It wasn't as if she had a hot date tonight, or any night in the near future. She could shop tomorrow just as easily as today, with the added advantage that her conscience would be clear once she'd delivered her warning to Joseph Mackenzie.

She wondered if he looked any less…feral…after six days of freedom. Probably not. It usually took prisoners at least a month to adapt even marginally to the norms of life on the outside. Anyway, it was a matter of complete indifference to her how Mackenzie looked, as long as he exhibited no signs of being drunk, high or otherwise violating the terms of his parole.

Ignoring an odd little stir of anticipation in the pit of her stomach, Anna slid behind the wheel of her sensible, five-year-old Subaru and headed east along Colfax Avenue toward the Algonquin Hotel.

Seven

Joe's shift in the Westwood Hotel kitchens started at midnight and finished at nine each morning, at the end of the breakfast rush. Sundays and Wednesdays he was scheduled to be off, but the sous-chef had offered him $13.50 an hour to work this past Wednesday and Joe had jumped at the chance to earn an extra ninety bucks in take-home pay. He needed the money even more than he needed time off to pursue his research.

Today, though, he'd turned down the offer of yet more overtime for tomorrow, determined to get started on some serious investigation. When his shift ended, he ate the free meal to which he was entitled—a good way to cut down on living expenses—and walked back to the Algonquin, enjoying the sunshine, the brilliant blue sky and the fact that he could take whatever route he pleased, stop whenever he wanted and even loiter to stare in a shop window without a guard thwacking his legs with a nightstick and yelling at him to move on.

Back in the blissful solitude of his room, he showered, packed his week's dirty laundry into the zippered case from his pillow, and spent an hour at the laundromat washing clothes, filling the time while he waited for them to dry by reading a six-week-old *People* magazine.

He was surprised by how many of the featured celebrities were unknown to him. It jolted him to be presented with yet more evidence that the world he'd known four years ago didn't exist anymore, on a multitude of levels. On the other hand, it was also surprising how many of the stories remained the same, even though the faces in the accompanying pictures had changed.

A human interest feature article detailed twenty-four hours in the life of a mother of quadruplets. A movie star had just given birth to a baby boy and was refusing to identify the father. Joe could have sworn he'd read two identical stories in the dentist's waiting room right before he was arrested.

The cover spread concerned a fifty-five-year-old married congressman, whose election slogan had been Return to Family Decency. The congressman was being sued by three former interns, who claimed he'd forced them to participate in group sex. The magazine, under the guise of assessing the opposing claims, obligingly provided readers with copious titillating details of the alleged office orgies. They seemed to have been quite something.

Joe's initial reaction was contempt for the congressman and mild bewilderment that the interns had apparently never considered telling their boss to keep his fly zippered and his hands to himself. His second reaction, distinctly belated, was to wonder if the accusations were true, and to feel a surge of empathy for the congressman if by any remote chance they happened to be false.

What if the congressman's political enemies had

found this clever way to set him up? What if he had a vindictive wife who wanted to make a fortune in the divorce settlement? Whatever the outcome of the court case, the congressman's career was over. His guilt or innocence was irrelevant to public opinion, and Joe knew exactly what that felt like.

Folding his laundry, Joe felt his mouth curve into a wry grin. Here was yet another totally unexpected consequence of spending four years in the pen. He was actually feeling sympathetic toward a politician. Now there was an event to write up in the record books.

He walked home again along streets bright with midday sunshine, his face cooled by a breeze fresh with mountain snow. Stacking his small pile of laundered clothes in his chest of drawers, he realized that today, for the first time in four years, he actually felt clean. And a damn fine feeling it was, too. In fact, when he stopped to think about it, he was almost…happy. The sensation was so novel that he hadn't recognized it until now.

Joe considered his unfamiliar mood from all angles, then smiled. Hell, why shouldn't he be happy? He had a job with a paycheck plus overtime due next Friday. He had a room to live in, clean clothes to wear, not to mention an excellent ham-and-cheese omelette in his belly. His sex life remained the equivalent of a desert in high drought, but he'd gotten almost accustomed to that. Besides, hope sprang eternal. If he could find an obliging woman who was willing to enjoy a little no-strings sex some time in the next few weeks, he'd be pretty much in hog heaven.

When he thought about having sex, a vivid image

of Anna Langtry flashed into his mind. Joe pushed the picture aside so fast that he could almost pretend it had never formed. He'd been doing an excellent job the past several days convincing himself that he didn't find his parole officer in the least bit attractive and he intended to keep up the good work.

Joe mentally changed the subject far away from the hazards of sex. Maybe this was how the bastards who'd set him up expected to get away with it, he thought, shaking his pillow back into its cover. Had they assumed that by the time he got out of prison he'd be so beaten down, and so grateful for the return of freedom, that he'd forget about wreaking revenge on the people who'd arranged to have him locked away?

If so, they were about to find out they were seriously mistaken. Four years in prison had taught him to appreciate the small comforts and pleasures of life. That was why he was enjoying this sunny Saturday. Four years in prison had also taught him how to hate as he'd never expected to hate again, once he escaped from his father's brutal household.

Putting aside the dark memories of adolescence with the ease of long practice, Joe headed out again, making for the Denver Public Library and its bank of public access computers. He needed information, lots of it, and his lack of money made research difficult. Not for the first time, he wished he could get his hands on some of the million dollars he was supposed to have stolen. His life would sure be a lot simpler if he really did have thousands of dollars squirreled away in an offshore bank account waiting to be accessed.

Nevertheless, despite the difficulty of having no

money, not to mention the fact that he had no right to travel outside the Denver metro area, Joe was confident he would eventually discover who had set him up four years earlier. Not least because he wasn't willing to consider the possibility of failure. He'd been hauled off to jail because his investigation of certain accounts at the bank had scared the shit out of somebody. Now he was back, ready to pick up his investigation where it had left off. But this time he intended to be discreet, so that nobody would get scared off before he had the information he needed. He sure didn't intend to give anyone a reason to set him up a second time, especially since it would be so easy to get him sent back to prison now that he was an ex-con. Plant some drugs on him, call the cops, and he'd be locked up in his cell again before he could whistle "Dixie."

Four years ago, he'd been naive. Correct that. Four years ago he'd been stupider than a horse's ass. Even after his arrest, he'd assumed that all he needed to do was explain carefully to his lawyer about the huge sums of cash slithering through the bank's accounting systems and a thorough investigation would immediately begin. As a result of which he, Joseph Mackenzie, would be exonerated, of course.

He'd been astonished—paralyzed by disbelief—when the FBI investigators reported that nobody else could find any record of the mysterious sums of money he was talking about.

Increasingly panicked, Joe insisted that he could show the bank's internal auditors phantom accounts that had been used to process monthly sums as large as half a million dollars. That he'd made printouts of some of the most dubious transactions and kept them locked in a safety deposit box at the bank. That the key to the box was in his desk drawer and they could check out what he was claiming for themselves.

Nobody took him seriously. Neither the FBI nor the management of the bank would let him go back to the office. What was the point of allowing an arrested embezzler back on bank premises, when a careful internal audit had turned up no irregularities except the shortfall in Joe's own accounts? Access to the bank's computer systems was denied him. A search of his desk revealed no key to a safety deposit box, and no printouts of any dubious transactions, although the detectives did find a bundle of fifty-dollar bills, about two thousand bucks in total.

The fact that Joe had been scrupulous about not making accusations until he had solid proof turned out to be his downfall. If he'd been aware of irregularities for some time, the FBI agents asked him, why hadn't he reported the problem? Why hadn't he said anything to anyone, not even to his good friend, Franklin Saunders? Why had he never breathed a word about the shortfall to his fiancée, the lovely Sophie Bartlett, whose father was a prominent businessman and might well have been able to give him solid advice about how to proceed?

Those were damn good questions, Joe realized, but only in retrospect. He hadn't confided in Frank because his friend was no more capable of keeping a secret than a tabloid newspaper in possession of a scoop about Jon-Benet Ramsey's murder. As for his lovely fiancée, he had tried to talk to Sophie about the situation at the bank, but she'd expressed no interest whatsoever and he'd given up when he realized one night in bed, that, far from listening with intense interest to his explanation, she'd actually fallen asleep instead.

Perhaps that ought to have worried him in terms of what it said about their relationship, but it hadn't. He worked long hours at the bank, determined to pay his grandparents back for all the money they'd invested in his college education, and he'd been more than content to put work aside when he was with Sophie. She was a woman who specialized in having fun, a frivolous commodity that had been in short supply most of Joe's life. To his surprise, he discovered that when he was in Sophie's company, he could party with the best of 'em. It had been a liberating experience.

Although he'd enjoyed every playful hour he spent in his fiancée's company—especially the hours they spent in bed—Joe had always realized that their relationship lacked closeness. Which was his fault, of course. He just didn't do intimacy well. He'd never wanted to marry a woman who demanded that he share the secrets of his inner soul, so Sophie suited him just fine. Even before he spent four years in prison, Joe had been pretty sure that his inner soul was a dark object, better kept safely buried.

So when Agent Varek asked him why he hadn't confided in Sophie about the problems at the bank, he kind of ignored the question and explained yet again that he'd been on the brink of making a full report to the president of the bank when Varek had rung the doorbell, bringing the shocking news that there was a $923,000 shortfall in the retirement accounts Joe managed.

Joe had been first hurt, then angry, then finally scared witless when he realized that nobody, absolutely nobody, believed his claim that the real problem wasn't in his retirement accounts, but in another area of the bank altogether. His protests that he was merely the fall guy dropped onto stone-deaf ears.

In retrospect, his trust—his sheer idiotic faith in the power of the legal system to protect the innocent—was almost funny. At least he'd now wised up to the point where he understood that any mention of the words *conspiracy* or *setup* was likely to land his sorry ass back in prison before he had time to pack a toothbrush and beg for a consultation with his lawyer.

Prison had rammed home the lesson that it was a waste of time trying to provide sufficient proof to convince the official forces of law and order to take action. Consequently, his current plan was simple. He'd find out who was responsible for putting him away, and then he'd take care of the bastard. Personally. Without reference to cops or lawyers.

His modest first step toward that goal was to find out where his former colleagues at the bank were now working and living. This was a task that might be time-consuming, but it shouldn't be too difficult and, God knew, time was one thing he had in liberal supply.

Joe sat down, automatically positioning himself at a computer that was out of the line of sight of the reference librarian. In 1997, the Durango branch of the Bank of Trade and Commerce had employed only nine people. Since he wasn't guilty of embezzlement, it seemed safe to work on the theory that one of the eight remaining employees was. Identifying one out of eight as the son of a bitch who'd set him up didn't seem like an overwhelmingly difficult task.

In a way, it was a bonus that the agents from the

FBI fraud squad had conducted such a piss-poor investigation, Joe reflected, reading the instructions on the computer screen in front of him. Agent Varek, the senior FBI agent on the case, had decided within hours of arriving in Durango that Joe was a thief and a liar. Hell, he'd probably made up his mind even before he arrived in Durango. Convinced of Joe's guilt, Varek had never attempted to dig into the bank's accounting systems.

The reaction of senior bank managers had mirrored the FBI's. As far as Joe could tell, the audit ordered by headquarters' management examined every aspect of his clients' accounts, but paid little attention to anything else. Besides, the auditors had their attention firmly fixed on illegal withdrawals. Nobody had shown the slightest interest in the substantial deposits that were made each month into accounts that Joe was convinced belonged to phantom corporations.

He hoped he wasn't being overoptimistic in concluding that the real embezzler might have gotten careless. Hell, the frame-up of dumbass Joe Mackenzie had been such a resounding success that even the most cautious criminal might be tempted to push his luck a little. In which case, the original illegal activity might still be going on. Or at the very least, evidence of the old fraud might still be out there, waiting to be tracked down.

Joe logged on to the Internet, using the name and library card number of the teenage girl sitting at the computer next to him when the program requested an ID. The speed of connecting had more than tripled during his imprisonment, even on this relative clunker of a machine, and Web sites had proliferated to an amazing extent, but his computer skills had been broad and deep enough that his years inside had little impact on the ease with which he found his way around cyberspace.

A search engine soon took him to the official Web site for the Colorado Bank of Trade and Commerce. A guide on the home page directed him to a handy-dandy reference guide that listed all the full-time employees of the bank, along with their job titles and the branches where they were currently located. The site had been updated only three weeks earlier, so the information was current.

Joe had assumed it would take some skill, not to mention subterfuge, to run even a superficial check on the current whereabouts of the people who'd been working with him at the time he was arrested. The bank's Web site made his task almost absurdly easy, and he mentally tipped his hat in gratitude to the folks in the bank's PR department.

He started his check with Franklin Saunders, who had been the loan officer for the Durango branch of the bank during the entire eighteen months Joe worked there. Frank was a year older than Joe, and the sort of outgoing, good-natured guy who was liked by all his colleagues. Joe, by contrast, had never acquired the knack of easy friendship, which was presumably why everyone found it so easy to believe Frank's version of events and to discount Joe's.

Single, from a Boston family steeped in New England tradition and money, Frank was a barely competent banker and a talented skier who jokingly complained that the hours spent working in the office were a serious intrusion into time that could have been much better spent swooping down the ski slopes of nearby Telluride.

Joe hadn't been in the same league as Frank in terms of skiing ability, but he'd been better at picking up women, so he'd taught Frank how to get himself a date, and Frank had taught him how to tackle the moguls on a double-black run. Joe had been well satisfied with the exchange of skills. As far as he could tell, Frank had always been satisfied, too.

According to the Web site, Frank was still employed by the Bank of Trade and Commerce, but he was no longer located in Durango. He had been promoted within weeks of Joe's conviction, and was now Vice President for Customer Service at the flagship office in downtown Denver. No doubt a reward for having discovered the missing funds, Joe reflected cynically, because for sure it wasn't a reflection of Frank's other work skills. The fact that Frank had discovered the shortfall, as opposed to an external auditor, made it easier for the bank to prevent news of the loss turning into a public relations disaster.

Frank would be delighted with his promotion, Joe guessed. He'd always hated being stuck in the relative backwater of a small town in a remote area of the state, and he was bored out of his mind making loans to farmers and small business owners. Denver and the big city lights were much more his style.

One way and another, Frank had contributed a lot to the case that the FBI had built against Joe. In addition to being the person who'd first raised the alarm about the missing funds in the retirement accounts, Frank had been the prosecution's star witness at the trial. His eager admission on the witness stand that Joe was his best friend had given his damning evidence all the more weight. In the wake of that admission, his stumbling protests that Joe couldn't possibly be responsible for stealing from his own clients had sounded like feeble rationalizations instead of a ringing defense of Joe's integrity.

Even at the time, when Joe had been cocooned inside a daze of disbelief that charges had been leveled against him—that he was standing trial, for God's sake!—he had recognized that Frank couldn't have done much more damage with the jury if he'd come right out and accused his ''best buddy'' of embezzlement.

Still, Joe resisted the temptation to assume that Franklin Saunders had cold-bloodedly set him up to take the fall for a crime Frank himself had committed. So many flaming arrows seemed to point in the direction of Frank's guilt that Joe was suspicious. The signposting was too clear, almost as if Frank himself were the victim of a setup, this one intended to convince Joe that his former friend couldn't be trusted. The fact that Frank had never visited him in prison didn't mean much of anything. Joe hadn't written to him, either. Frank was probably too embarrassed, just as Joe was too proud.

Bottom line, Joe wasn't about to make assumptions or leap to conclusions concerning Frank's role. Leaping to conclusions was how he'd operated in the old days, when he'd had the arrogant self-confidence of a man who'd overcome the disadvantages of a miserable childhood and blithely assumed that Fate would throw him no more curve balls.

The new Joe Mackenzie might not be improved by most people's standards, but he sure as hell was a lot harder to take advantage of. Now he understood that there were no limits to the extent that Fate could choose to fuck with you. For some people, that realization might lead to a more reckless approach to life. With very little left to lose, why not throw caution to the winds? In Joe's case, he'd become more cautious. Be damned if he was going to let himself go under, just because Fate had decided to screw him. He was going to keep his cool—and fight back hot and dirty.

Not wanting to leave a paper trail, Joe committed the relevant details about Frank's current whereabouts to memory before turning his attention to Caleb Welks. Welks had already been president of the Durango branch of the Bank of Trade and Commerce for several years when Joe was first assigned there. Apparently, Caleb still held the exact same position, so the bank's senior management in Denver must have decided that he deserved neither punishment nor reward for Joe's supposed bout of embezzlement.

Since Welks was now fifty-seven, it seemed likely he would remain in Durango until he reached the bank's official retirement age in three years' time. A native of a small town in southwestern Colorado, Caleb had never seemed ambitious for promotion, so he presumably didn't care that age was creeping up on him mighty fast, leaving him little time in which to make a splash in the world of banking.

Caleb had been a competent manager, without being innovative or a charismatic leader. He had previously worked for the First Municipal State bank in Montrose, and before that he'd been assistant manager of First Municipal's Cortez branch for at least ten years.

Hired on by the Bank of Trade and Commerce in the early nineties, Caleb had earned a solid reputation in the Durango business community. He'd acted as chairperson of the United Way campaign for two years in a row, and had served on several volunteer civic boards to the satisfaction of everyone involved. Perhaps that was why the powers-that-be in Denver had chosen not to move him after the disgrace of Joe's arrest. To the bank's Durango clients, he must have appeared a reassuringly familiar face in the wake of the scandal.

There was only one part of Caleb Welks's biography that didn't fit exactly into the stereotype of a middle-class, middle-of-the-road banker, and that was his marriage. Welks was such a conservative, by-the-rules kind of a guy that Joe would have expected him to be married to his high school sweetheart, with grown children, and a neat little cluster of grandkids. Instead, proving that it was never safe to typecast people, Caleb was married to a woman some twenty-five years his junior.

The age difference wouldn't have been quite so surprising if Christine had been his second wife, but she wasn't. Welks, in a rare moment of familiarity, had confided to Joe and Frank that he'd been a bachelor until he was past forty. Then he'd met Christine at a Fourth of July picnic organized by his brother and—wham! It had been love at first sight. Caleb had been forty-three at the time and Christine had been barely out of high school. In view of the age difference, they'd waited a whole year to be married, just to be sure it was what they both wanted.

There was no indication of marital status on the bank roster, so Joe had no way of knowing if the unlikely Welks marriage had survived. Since it had already lasted nine years by the time Joe was arrested, he supposed there was no reason for it to have failed in the past four.

In matters of the heart, Joe had concluded long ago that there was no accounting for taste. Christine was pretty enough, but she wasn't very lively, and she had little to say for herself on the rare occasions when she accompanied her husband to a social event. Moreover, her younger sister, Lynette, a girl of about eighteen, had been living with her and Caleb for the entire time that Joe was in Durango. Lynette was even quieter than her sister, but she showed no sign of leaving for college or of getting herself gainful employment, and Joe had always been vaguely surprised that Caleb put up with her teenage laziness.

Joe couldn't imagine what there was about Christine that would have inspired a confirmed, middle-aged bachelor to finally succumb to the lure of matrimony, especially when she came with mooching relatives attached. Still, he didn't consider himself qualified to pass judgment on the strangeness of Caleb's romantic entanglements. Hell, no. He couldn't even understand his own.

Joe had fallen head over heels in love with Sophie Bartlett the very first time he met her. Or so he'd once believed. Now he had trouble remembering what it was that had made her appear so attractive.

He and Sophie had been engaged three months by the time he was arrested, and during those months Joe had never questioned their mutual commitment, or wondered if he was making the right choice of wife. But locked up in the county jail to await trial, denied bail as a flight risk, and with plenty of time to mull over unanswerable questions, Joe had tried to work out why he'd asked Sophie to marry him. Because they liked the same restaurants and enjoyed the same offbeat movies? Because Sophie looked really cute in ski pants? Because she had been an exciting, uninhibited lover?

What else did they actually have in common? Not an abiding faith in each other's integrity, that was for sure. Sophie had obviously considered him guilty from the moment he was arrested.

Joe wanted to believe that there had been some force binding him and Sophie together stronger than hot sex, a liking for Thai food, and a shared taste for movies where the hero was fighting wars in a galaxy far, far away. But, looking back, he could never identify an occasion when either one of them had attempted to deepen their relationship. Their weekends together were terrific, and that had apparently been enough for both of them. No way he could lay all the blame on Sophie. He'd been paddling in shallow waters every bit as much as she had.

Inevitably, once he was arrested, the superficiality of their feelings was laid bare. It became obvious within days of his arrest that Sophie wanted out of their engagement. That was bad enough. What was worse was how little the final break bothered him.

The next time he imagined he was in love, Joe decided, he was going to wait a while—like about a hundred years—before jumping into a commitment.

With a quick frown, he focused his wandering attention back on Caleb Welks. If his best buddy Frank was the most obvious candidate to have set him up, Caleb Welks had to be the second most likely. As president of the Durango branch, Welks would have had complete access to the full range of the bank's computer system. Headquarters in Denver would have exercised some control over Caleb's activities, but on the whole, he would have had virtually unlimited opportunities to set up Joe as fall guy.

But how had Caleb been blackmailed or bribed into cooperating with the criminals who were using the bank to launder their illicit profits? Joe had never seen a shred of evidence that Caleb drank, gambled, cheated on his wife, had a gay lover or indulged in any expensive vices. For that matter, the same went for all the other employees of the bank, who seemed to have been an exceptionally pure-living lot.

Even after four years of mentally chewing over the facts, trying to make all the jagged edges fit into a single neat theory, Joe still had no idea whether the embezzler had been blackmailed into cooperating, or simply been corrupted by the offer of a lot of money. Whatever the details, somebody in the bank had clearly been paid off. By Joe's reckoning, the phantom accounts had been in existence for at least three years, and possibly longer. The sums of money sloshing through the accounts were large, and they couldn't have escaped the attention of the bank's auditors for three whole years unless somebody inside the Durango branch was making sure that the accounts stayed well below the radar screen of various oversight committees.

Unfortunately, according to the FBI and the police, there was no evidence that anybody other than Joe had been living beyond his means. Joe had pointed out that just because no bank employee had gone on a spending spree didn't prove that no bank employee had been paid off. It merely proved the real embezzler had been smart enough to hide his ill-gotten gians until the heat of the FBI investigation was turned down.

His point would have had more impact if the FBI hadn't already identified a bank employee who had a gambling problem, was spending freely and living way beyond his income. Namely Joseph Alexander Mackenzie. Agent Varek saw no reason to look any further, especially since Joe was eager to toss out accusations about money laundering but, when pinned down, couldn't begin to suggest what cluster of criminal enterprises might be centered in Durango and laundering their illegal profits through the Bank of Trade and Commerce.

When news of Joe's arrest became public, most of his colleagues in the bank reacted as though he were a confirmed carrier of the Ebola virus. Their rejection of him was total. Only Frank stood by him all the way to the trial.

Caleb Welks had ended up testifying for the prosecution, but he'd appeared to have an open mind about Joe's guilt, at least in the beginning. Hurrying down to the police station, where Joe was being held for questioning, Caleb had been at pains to point out that he hoped the charges against Joe would prove to be false.

Sweating in the uncomfortably warm examination room, Caleb expressed his admiration for Joe's work and stressed that he wasn't going to make the mistake of assuming Joe was responsible for the missing funds just because Joe handled the suspect accounts and his ID had been used for the unauthorized withdrawals.

Joe had already been subjected to enough official doubt and suspicion that Caleb's words were a much needed balm on his aching pride. "Why are you giving me the benefit of the doubt?" he asked. "Nobody in the FBI believes me. And the cops all look at me as if I have a neon Guilty sign pasted across my forehead.''

''Everybody should give you the benefit of the doubt,'' Caleb said firmly. ''You're innocent until proven guilty, that's the law, which the cops and the FBI both ought to remember.''

''That's a technicality, and we both know it.''

''An important technicality, Joe. Besides, the fact that your password and employee ID was used to make illegal withdrawals doesn't prove you made the transactions. Somebody could have found out your password and used it. As for your ID number—well, I'm sure at least half of us working in the bank know it. I know it myself. The fact that your ID is on the suspect withdrawals is one of those pieces of so-called evidence that crumbles the moment you look at it more closely.''

Joe massaged the ache that had been lodged in the middle of his forehead ever since his arrest. ''I wish you'd explain that to Agent Varek.''

''I already have. I've pointed out to him that this bank only has nine full-time employees, including myself. In such a small group, it would be child's play for any of your colleagues to discover your ID. As for your password...well, that might be more difficult, but I daresay it could be done. I don't expect you change it nearly as often as you should. I know I haven't changed mine for weeks.''

Caleb took off his glasses and rubbed his eyes with hands that always struck Joe as incongruously large and beefy. ''You're an intelligent man, Joe. I'm assuming that if you were truly responsible for these shameful thefts, then you would have had the intelligence to use somebody else's ID. You're smart enough not to leave your own electronic fingerprints all over the embezzled funds.''

''Thank you, sir, for your confidence. You're right. I certainly wouldn't have laid a trail straight back to myself.''

Caleb nodded his agreement. ''However, when all's said and done, I have to put you on administrative leave, Joe. I'm sorry, but you understand the people at head office have left me no choice. But I'm working on the assumption that you'll be back on duty with us very soon.''

''I wish I shared your confidence, Caleb.''

''You should.''

''Why? The FBI has no other suspects. They're not even looking...''

''That might change quite soon. I'm urging the FBI and the police to run thorough checks on the crew that cleans our offices after hours. I learned yesterday that one of the men on the crew is a Russian immigrant who used to be a general in the Soviet army. Now there's a person who has more than enough brains and know-how to discover your password and use it for a bit of quick embezzlement. And he has motive, too. Who would want to be a cleaner when he once commanded thousands of men? I'm sure he's a very bitter and frustrated man.''

Joe allowed himself a moment of hope. Better an ex-Soviet general than him.

Caleb leaned across the dirty metal table, his expression earnest. ''Look, don't take this the wrong way, but you shouldn't rely on the police to prove your innocence. Our local cops are well-meaning, but not always as smart as they should be, and they're accusing you of tricky financial transactions that they may have trouble understanding. You need somebody who's a hundred percent on your side. Somebody who'll give the FBI an occasional kick in the pants to make sure they're headed in the right direction. In my opinion, you need to get a top-notch lawyer, just to be on the safe side."

"Yes, I'm sure you're right." Joe drew in a shaky breath. "I've already called a lawyer friend in Denver and asked him to recommend somebody. He's promised to get back to me by tomorrow morning."

"Great. And if you want someone local, I've heard that Dwight Daniels is very good. I haven't used Dwight's services myself, haven't ever had occasion to, of course, but I worked on the United Way board with him and word is he's the best defense attorney in the entire Four Corners area. Very good in a courtroom setting. You might want to give him a call. Are they letting you use the phone? I'll see to it if they're not."

With Caleb's help, Joe called his lawyer friend in Denver and asked him to run a check on Dwight Daniels. The report came back glowingly positive. "I couldn't get you anyone better," his friend said. "This Daniels guy is the best there is in southwestern Colorado."

So Joe asked Dwight Daniels to take on his case, and Daniels agreed. But Joe's relief at getting decent legal representation was short-lived. Daniels was smart, eloquent and sympathetic, but he was swamped with other cases and left most of the crucial prep work to a recently hired young woman, fresh out of law school. Who, Joe discovered later, was fired for incompetence the day Joe's trial ended.

So much for acquiring the services of the best lawyer in town.

Even if Daniels had lived up to his reputation, Joe would have had a hard time escaping conviction. The Russian ex-general was questioned and cleared of any complicity, along with the other members of the cleaning crew. The police had already questioned Sally Warner, the head teller, and the five other counter clerks before Agent Varek arrested Joe. Nothing suggested that any one of the clerks had a reason either to steal from the bank, or to set up Joe as a scapegoat.

Meanwhile, evidence against Joe continued to mount. Far and away the most damaging was the six-month spending spree he'd supposedly indulged in prior to his arrest. There was the weekend trip he'd made to Las Vegas when, according to the investigative team, he'd lost $50,000 on the slot machines and had accumulated total losses at the blackjack tables in excess of $145,000. Right there, he'd spent double his annual salary. Then there were the trips he'd made to Blackhawk, Colorado's major gambling resort, where he'd managed to lose another thirty thousand bucks playing the high-stakes poker machines.

His other presumed purchases included rare and valuable cases of wine, enough for an impressive cellar, a painting he stored in a vault in Denver, and a four-day late-winter vacation in the Bahamas when he'd supposedly entertained two professional ladies in the royal suite of the most expensive hotel on the island. His credit card bill for that little jaunt had amounted to almost seventy thousand dollars, including five thousand dollar tips to each of the "ladies."

Joe rather regretted that he hadn't actually been present for that mind-blowing expenditure, since it was this incident that Sophie used as her final excuse for breaking off their engagement. Hell, if he was going to lose his fiancée over a weekend of high-priced, tropical island sex, it was a tad frustrating not to have participated in the activities that got him into trouble.

Joe, of course, protested to Agent Varek that he hadn't vacationed in the Bahamas—he'd been visiting his grandparents in Kansas for those four days. He similarly protested that he hadn't bought any cases of vintage wine, much less a painting he didn't especially like.

The FBI agents listened with visible skepticism. His grandfather backed up Joe's story, although his grandmother was already sinking pretty deep into senile dementia, and his grandfather was forced to admit that he was so preoccupied with taking care of his wife that he didn't always keep a real good record of dates anymore. The prosecution made mincemeat out of his grandfather's testimony during the trial, making him sound almost as mentally incompetent as his wife. Another case of a friendly witness doing Joe more harm than good.

Then there was the BMW sports car he was told he stored in a garage on the west side of town. When confronted with the purchase slip for the BMW, Joe finally lost his temper. He yelled that he'd never seen the vehicle in his life, let alone driven it.

To resolve the issue, the FBI arranged a lineup at the local police station and called the owner of the garage to see if he could identify the BMW's owner. The garage owner needed all of twenty seconds to identify Joe as the person he'd seen arriving on several occasions in a blue Ford Taurus and driving away in the silver BMW.

Informed of the garage owner's sworn statement, Joe had a moment of sheer, blinding panic. Coming on top of so many other pieces of damning evidence, he had a second or two when he wondered if he might actually be some sort of Jekyll and Hyde personality who committed crimes that he didn't remember. His self-doubt lasted mere seconds, but he began to understand why Agent Varek tended to look at him as if he were something unpleasant stuck onto the sole of his shoe.

After the garage owner identified him as the owner of the BMW, Joe's life raced inexorably toward disaster. He was vaguely aware that many trials took months to move from arrest to arraignment. His own trial moved forward with relative speed. On one of his infrequent pretrial consultations with Dwight Daniels, Joe tried again to explain his theory that he was the target of a carefully planned setup. His words tumbled out higgledy-piggledy, the thread of his accusations barely coherent as he strove to get someone to pay attention to what he was saying.

Dwight Daniels did at least listen. Really listen. Then he politely asked what motive anyone might have for targeting Joe as the victim in a hugely expensive setup that would have required a minimum of six months of planning. "Why would anyone bother with such a complicated setup, Joe, when you have to figure that they ended up spending most of the money that was being embezzled just to implicate you?"

Joe responded quickly, afraid Daniels wouldn't

take him seriously. ''They didn't spend it all on setting me up. There's over nine hundred thousand dollars missing from my accounts. The FBI has found purchases and expenditures of less than half a million.''

Daniels looked significantly unimpressed. ''Half a million is all that the FBI has been able to trace, Joe. That doesn't mean it's all you spent.'' He quickly corrected himself. ''All you allegedly spent.''

''I didn't spend the money, for Chrissake! That's the whole point! Somebody else spent it!''

The lawyer winced. ''All right, I hear you. But I have to say your claim of being set up doesn't make too much sense, Joe. If somebody else stole the money, why are you the person who went on vacation? Why are you the person who bought a BMW? And where did you get the money for those expenditures? Your salary doesn't come close to paying for your recent lifestyle.''

Joe clenched his teeth so hard that they hurt. ''I didn't go on vacation. I didn't buy a sports car. Those credit card charges weren't made by me. I never even knew I owned that American Express platinum card. I'm being set up.''

Daniels ignored Joe's last sentence. ''But it's your signature on the credit card bills. The police have an expert willing to swear to that in court—''

''He can swear till he's blue in the face. I didn't sign those charge slips. They're forgeries—''

''So one of your colleagues in the bank is not only an embezzler, he's also a forger competent enough to deceive handwriting experts?'' Daniels barely concealed his skepticism.

''Yes,'' Joe said stubbornly. ''Or else the embezzler hired a forger to sign those bills. All I know is, I never opened an account with American Express. I've never been to the Bahamas. I didn't sign those receipts.''

Daniels rolled his eyes. ''A clerk from the Hotel Royale picked you out of a photo ID lineup, Joe. And you were seen driving that BMW on many occasions.''

''Eyewitness identifications are notoriously unreliable.''

Daniels sighed. ''That's true, and of course we'll hammer away at that point when we go to trial. Still, even if we concede your point and agree that the witnesses are mistaken, we're still left with the fact that the embezzler spent half the money he stole on setting you up.''

''Yes, I guess he did.''

''No jury is ever going to believe that a thief would spend more than half of his loot on setting up a fall guy.''

Joe resisted the urge to pound the table. Or the walls. Or Dwight Daniels's earnest, puzzled face. He drew in a deep breath, trying to explain one more time. ''I shouldn't have let this conversation go off at a tangent. This isn't really about the $923,000 missing from my retirement accounts. It's about hiding another, much bigger, crime. The embezzler didn't take money from my accounts to acquire spending money. He or she stole funds so that I would be arrested and thrown in jail. It's a damned effective way of stopping me investigating what's really going on at the bank, isn't it?''

Dwight Daniels sighed again, more deeply. ''Joe, speaking as your lawyer, I have to tell you that conspiracy theories don't go over too well with judges. Not to mention juries. Do you have any proof at all that somebody with connections to the bank might have some reason to want you out of the way? And can you explain how your being in prison might prevent exposure of a crime that involves even more money than the million dollars you stole?'' He caught Joe's expression. ''Allegedly stole,'' he corrected hurriedly.

So Joe had explained again, more coherently this time, about the accounts that he believed were being used to launder money. ''There's as much as a quarter of a million dollars flowing in and out of those accounts some months,'' he said. ''I estimate that in fiscal year 1997, a total of three million dollars passed through the bank. In the first quarter of 1998, I estimate another million, which means funds are moving through at an even higher rate this year than last. Those are large enough sums that it would be worth spending half a million to make sure I'm out of the picture and not causing trouble, wouldn't you say?''

Dwight Daniels managed to look both impressed and dubious all at the same time. ''How could illicit funds that large possibly go undetected?''

''They couldn't. Not without a lot of high-powered help inside the bank. That's my point. Whoever is using the bank to launder money needs help on the inside. I'm obviously causing somebody a lot of trouble because I stumbled onto what was going on, almost by chance, as it happens. That's why I'm sitting in jail right now, awaiting trial. The embezzled money was just the means of getting me here.''

''And you're claiming that you had to be taken out of the way because somebody's using the bank to launder millions of dollars each year? With help from an employee in the Durango branch of the bank?"

"Yes, precisely."

Daniels continued to look and sound dubious. Still, he was a conscientious enough lawyer that he convinced the FBI to comb through the bank's records for a second time, specifically searching for any hint of the irregularities Joe kept talking about. There was also the question of the printouts Joe insisted he'd made, which had apparently disappeared along with so much else.

The search was conducted under Dwight Daniels's watchful eye, but produced zero evidence of the sort of illegal manipulations Joe claimed to have uncovered. It was in the wake of this second fruitless search through bank records that Daniels had suggested Joe might like to consider the benefits of pleading guilty.

"If you explained that you have a gambling problem that had gotten totally out of control, it's possible I might be able to work out a deal with the D.A. We could agree to court-supervised counseling to take care of your gambling problem, and I might be able to get the D.A. to agree that you should serve no more than 18 months actual prison time. In view of the large amount of money that's missing, there's no way you're going to escape serving some time, I'm afraid. Especially since there's no possibility of you paying back the money…is there?"

Joe—brick stupid to the end—had responded with icy coldness. "There are two major problems with your suggestion, Mr. Daniels. I don't have a gambling problem, and I didn't embezzle any money from the bank. I'm being set up."

His computer screen blinked, then came back on

line again. Joe shook his head, becoming aware that he'd been staring at the same screen for over fifteen minutes. The reference librarian cast a beady-eyed glance in his direction, then looked significantly at her watch. She was soon going to come over and remind him of the thirty-minute limit the library imposed on accessing the Internet.

The last thing Joe wanted was for his visit to the library to be memorable. He quickly logged off, wandered around the stacks for ten minutes, then came back and found another bank of computers in a different section of the library. He logged on again, and searched for the remaining five employees who'd worked for the bank during his time in Durango. He discovered that three of them remained with the bank, all of them still in Durango. Doris Argyle had been promoted to the position of head teller four years ago, right after Sally Warner had resigned.

Despite the coincidence of dates, Joe didn't really believe that motherly, gossipy Sally Warner was a master criminal who'd set him up in between chauffeuring her three sons to football, soccer, basketball and baseball practice. Most likely her resignation had nothing to do with his own arrest and conviction. However, he made a mental note to find Sally so that he could make sure she hadn't suddenly ''inherited'' an unexpected fortune.

He would also have to track down Jennifer Alvarez, the other clerk who was no longer with the bank, even though Jennifer struck him as an even less likely villain than Sally Warner. She had always been friendly as a puppy, prone to giggling about her boyfriends—of which there were many—and distinctly short of wattage in the IQ department. However, Joe wasn't willing to give anyone a free pass. Maybe Jennifer was a master of disguise. Friendly but dumb would be a pretty good character for someone to adopt if she wanted to avoid suspicion. Joe decided that tracking the current addresses of Sally Warner and Jennifer Alvarez would be his first priority on his next day off.

Joe clicked away from the Bank of Trade and Commerce site, intending to shut down the computer. But the reference librarian was nowhere in sight and having access to knowledge at his fingertips proved irresistible. At the very last minute, instead of logging off, he typed in a search to see if the Durango *Daily Courier* had a Web site. It did, and Yahoo took him straight there. He provided a fictitious name and address, and the *Courier* granted him access to the paper's archives, no more questions asked.

Nowhere near as detached as he would like to have been, Joe drew a deep breath and typed in the name Sophie Bartlett.

He scored multiple hits. Not surprising, since Arthur Bartlett, Sophie's father, was president and CEO of Bartlett Nutrition, among the largest and most successful manufacturers of vitamins and health food supplements in the country, while Sophie was a leader of Durango's social elite. The entries for Sophie, he noticed, all stopped around the end of 1998. In other words, within seven months of his arrest, and less than two months after his conviction.

He wondered why. Maybe Sophie had moved, wanting to put their engagement far behind her. Joe scanned through the listings, glossing over headlines that suggested fund-raising luncheons, charitable dances, and a cluster of entries that seemed to be connected to Sophie's halfhearted pursuit of a career as the head of the PR department in her father's health food company. His cursor finally highlighted an entry headed Bartlett-Saunders Nuptials—A Celebration to Remember.

Only a newspaper in a remote country town would still refer to a wedding as ''nuptials,'' Joe thought. Even as the thought formed, he recognized that he was fixating on a minor detail because he didn't want to confront the larger issues that must be hidden behind the pompous headline.

He clicked onto the link and a photograph of Sophie—radiant in bridal white—downloaded onto his screen. He had to read through a paragraph of drivel about brilliant sunshine and a dusting of snow imparting a fairy-tale magic to the Durango Wedding of the Decade before he found confirmation of the name of the groom.

Franklin Saunders.

Well, whadda you know? It seemed that his ex-fiancée had indeed married his former best friend.

Joe could feel his features hardening into an expression of impenetrable indifference, his ultimate prison defense when he needed to protect himself against the display of the sort of emotions that made you vulnerable. He told himself that he had no rational cause to react so strongly to the news that his former fiancée had barely waited for him to be locked away before marrying his former best friend. Hadn't he just spent several minutes contemplating the fact that he and Sophie had never really been in love?

The rationalizations didn't work. As he read, Joe's initial feeling of shock coalesced into an ice-cold anger.

Supported by five longtime friends serving as groomsmen, Mr. Franklin Saunders was joyfully united in marriage with Sophie Jessica Bartlett on Christmas Eve, 1998. The groom's younger brother, Mr. Austin Saunders of Laguna Hills, California, performed the office of best man.

Ms. Bartlett, attended by her sister, Amy, who acted as maid of honor, was additionally attended by two cousins and three of her sorority friends serving as bridesmaids. The bride wore an off-the-shoulder designer gown of white silk, enhanced by a velvet hooded cape to ward off the evening chill. She carried heirloom red roses in honor of the holiday. Her attendants wore long-sleeved gowns of pine-green satin, similarly inspired by the Christmas festivities, and carried sprays of pale-pink orchids. Parents and grandparents of the bride and groom were all present for the ceremony, having traveled to Durango from as far away as Florida, Illinois and Tennessee.

Three hundred and fifty guests were later entertained at the Durango Country Club, where world-famous Chef Paul Pierre, flown in from New Orleans at the special request of the bride's mother, prepared a feast to delight the most demanding gourmet, accompanied by wines chosen from the private collection of Mr. Arthur Bartlett, the bride's father.

After dinner, the Ginger Mountain band, headed by famous lead singer Kelsey Zimmer, kept guests dancing until the wee hours.

The happy couple left on Christmas Day for a two-week honeymoon in the South Pacific island of Tahiti. Upon returning to the States, the newlyweds will reside in Cherry Hills Village, a suburb of Denver. Mr. Saunders, who has a business degree from Duke University, has worked with the Colorado Bank of Trade and Commerce for five years. He has recently been promoted to the position of vice president. The new Mrs. Franklin Saunders, who graduated from the University of Colorado with a degree in communications, plans to pursue a career in real estate.

The reporter should have added an extra paragraph, Joe thought savagely. The paper's readers would most likely have found it quite entertaining, given their near universal conviction that Joe had only gotten exactly what he deserved.

Meanwhile, back in the West Denver Federal Correctional Institute, Joseph Mackenzie, discarded fiancé of the delightful Sophie Bartlett, wore a stunning orange nylon jumpsuit as he attempted to eat his holiday dinner of turkey, lumpy gravy, and metallic-tasting cranberries, despite the inconvenience of a broken arm and three cracked ribs. Said broken arm and cracked ribs were provided courtesy of the Aryan Nation gang, who didn't like the way Mr. Mackenzie looked at one of their members during regulation exercise period on December 7.

Abruptly, Joe closed down the program and pushed his chair back from the computer desk, annoyed with his bout of self-pity. Enough already. He'd recognized four years ago that he and Sophie would have ended up miserably unhappy if they'd actually gone ahead and married. So he had no reason to feel that Sophie had betrayed him. Even less reason to feel jealous of Frank.

Joe made his way toward the library exit, keeping his head down and his expression carefully blank. The thought occurred to him that although he had no reason to be jealous of Frank, he maybe had a valid reason to be angry. He had always shied away from believing that Frank was the person who'd set him up. Not only because of their friendship, but because Frank seemed to have no motive for such a terrible betrayal. Frank's parents weren't megarich, but they were more than comfortable financially, and Frank had the indifference to money that people only seemed to acquire when they had never known the meaning of *deprivation.* In Joe's opinion, money had never seemed an adequate bait to tempt Frank into breaking the law, much less betraying a friend.

But what if Frank had been lured into framing Joe not because he was promised money, but because Joe's imprisonment would set Sophie free—and give Frank a chance to win her? Joe acknowledged that at some subliminal level he'd always known that Frank had been in love with Sophie. To an outsider, the chance for Frank to marry the woman he loved might seem like a hell of a flimsy reason to go along with massive bank fraud and the framing of a good friend. To Joe, it seemed marginally more credible than the possibility that Frank had screwed him over for the sake of money.

Either way, a trip to the Cherry Hills home of the Saunders lovebirds was definitely in order. Be damned if he was going to let another day pass without confronting the two of them and demanding some answers. They owed him. No wonder Frank had never come to visit him in prison. Yeah, that would have been cool. Arriving with a box of candy and the news that he was married to Sophie Bartlett.

Joe swung around and stormed over to the reference shelves, pulling out a Denver metro area phone directory and slapping it down on a nearby table with a satisfying thump.

There was no listing for Franklin Saunders and no listing for Sophie J. Bartlett, or any combination of the two names. Joe scowled at the directory, seething with suppressed frustration, barely resisting the urge to take the directory and throw it across the room.

After less than a minute, common sense returned and he realized just how lucky he was that Frank and Sophie either no longer lived in Cherry Hills, or had decided to leave their phone number unlisted. What the hell had he been planning to do? March up, ring the doorbell and demand that Frank confess to embezzling the money? A real smart move that would have been, and highly unlikely to achieve good results.

So much for his determination to approach this renewed investigation with extreme caution, Joe thought, once again making his way out of the library and heading for the bus stop. He'd damn near blown everything, simply because a woman he no longer cared about was married to a man he hadn't spoken to in four years.

Women could sure mess with a man's head, Joe thought, propping his back against the bus stop and squinting into the traffic to read the sign on the front of the oncoming bus. After his experiences with Sophie, he sure as hell was never going to delude himself again that he'd fallen in love. Or even in lust.

For no good reason, an image of Anna Langtry pushed itself to the front of his mind. Even more irritating, the image refused to be sent away, despite considerable effort on his part. Jeez, what was his problem? If there was one thing dumber than losing his cool over Sophie and Frank, it would have to be feeling sexually attracted to his parole officer.

After four years of dumb, it was past time for him to start concentrating on smart. Joe finally succeeded in banishing the unwanted images of Anna Langtry to the darkest corner of his dark soul, where they surely belonged.

Why had that been so difficult, he wondered. Hell, he didn't even like women with red hair. Not, of course, that Anna's hair was exactly red. More a stunning shade of darkest gold, shot through with deep russet—

Cursing silently, Joe climbed aboard the bus.

Eight

The elevator at the Algonquin was out of order again, so Joe took the stairs to the fourth floor. When he pushed open the battered fire door and turned to head toward his room, he immediately saw the woman he'd just spent an entire bus ride not thinking about. She was standing directly outside his door, scribbling something in a small, spiral-bound notebook. Her vivid auburn hair, highlighted by the caged overhead strip light, tumbled forward in a soft, shining curtain.

She looked…ravishing.

His jaw clenching, Joe reminded himself that he much preferred blondes and brunettes, but his body paid no attention to the reminder. Silently he covered the remaining few yards of hallway, careful not to notice that his *parole officer* was wearing a moss-green sweater and faded jeans that showcased her trim hips and full breasts with enticing precision. As she wrote, she frowned in concentration and the tip of her tongue appeared at the corner of her mouth.

Joe closed his eyes, fighting the predictable and infuriating symptoms of extreme lust. Why did it have to be this woman who fired up all his repressed sexual desire? Rationally, he wanted nothing to do with her. Quite apart from her official position in his life, he guessed that if he knew her better, he wouldn't like her. She seemed efficient, cool and self-possessed, with a bewildering hint of vulnerability and not a trace of the fun-loving carelessness that had made Sophie so appealing.

He wondered bleakly if prison had screwed with his mind to the point where his sexual fantasies and his need to defy authority figures now intersected in some unpleasantly sick pattern. Bottom line: whatever the messed-up psychology of his attraction to Anna Langtry, it was getting worse, not better.

"Are you looking for me?" he asked. His voice, he realized, sounded vaguely menacing. Which was better, on the whole, than having it crack with nervous sexual tension.

"Oh, Mr. Mackenzie. I'm glad I caught you. I was just writing you a note." Anna pushed impatiently at a cluster of curls, shoving them behind her ear. Joe's stomach knotted as she gave him a quick smile. "There's so much noise in this place, I didn't hear you coming."

Directing his gaze past her smile, Joe became aware of the sounds he'd automatically screened out: Eminem blasting from a tinny radio; a man and woman yelling obscenities at each other; the erratic banging of a hammer in a room across the hall; the clang of tools from the handyman working on the elevator. He felt a twinge of self-disgust that his senses had been so bludgeoned by his time in prison that he could ignore such an invasive clamor.

There was no way he would allow Anna to see his chagrin, of course. He smoothed out any trace of expression from his face and inclined his head in a slight, questioning gesture. ''Was there something you needed to say to me, ma'am?''

''Yes, Mr. Mackenzie, I have something important to discuss with you, but not where I have to yell in order to make myself heard. Could we go into your room?''

He didn't want to submit himself to the humiliation of seeing his room through her eyes. Maybe the room wasn't much, but it was his haven, and he intended to keep it that way, protected from any lingering images of her scorn. Or worse, of her sympathy. For some reason, he hated the idea of being on the receiving end of Anna Langtry's sympathy.

''There are no chairs in my room,'' he said. If anything, his voice sounded a touch more surly than before. ''We can stand, or we can sit on the bed. Those are your choices.'' He refused to get uptight about the fact that his squalid hotel room strained the limits of his ability to pay the rent. He especially refused to visualize what it would feel like to sit next to Anna on his lumpy mattress, with its tendency to roll everything toward the middle. Would they end up thigh to thigh? He looked down at the floor, disgusted by his inability to get his thoughts out of his pants.

''I've been in these rooms before. I know what they're like.'' Anna flashed him another friendly smile. He desperately wanted to smile back, so he turned his head and stared at the puke-green wall, feigning utter boredom.

''I guess the management didn't design the interior decor for gracious entertaining,'' she said.

Slowly he turned to look at her. ''No, ma'am, I guess they didn't.''

Her mouth tightened every time he said *ma'am,* Joe

had noticed. For some obscure reason, it pissed her off when he addressed her that way. For an even more obscure reason, he relished the chance to provoke her, which was why he called her *ma'am* every chance he got.

She sent him a speculative look, almost as if she knew exactly what was motivating his excess of courtesy. Why not? Probably ninety percent of her sex-starved parolees had the hots for her. With stubborn pride, Joe fixed his gaze on an ancient strip of wallpaper that hung from the ceiling, a relic of the hotel's departed glory days.

''I missed lunch and it's getting quite late,'' Anna said. ''Would you like to come and have a cup of coffee with me? I feel in the mood for something frothy and loaded with calories. How about you?''

Joe felt a surge of such intense longing that he had to take a few seconds before he could reply. It had been a while since he'd done anything as innocent and enjoyable as sharing a cup of coffee with a beautiful and sexy woman. He reminded himself for the fifth time in five minutes that, to all intents and purposes, Anna wasn't a woman. She was his parole officer, and that was a different creature entirely. Grimly, he damped down his pleasure and forced himself to look at her.

''Is that an order, ma'am?'' This time he didn't give a damn if he sounded rude. Sometimes rudeness was the only defense left to the powerless.

Her incredible blue eyes narrowed, but her gaze held his. ''Yes, Mr. Mackenzie, if you get right down to it, I guess that's an order. We need to talk. You have the choice of talking with or without the accompanying coffee.''

Joe inclined his head in ironic acknowledgment. ''Well then, ma'am, in that case I'll be delighted to come and have a cup of coffee with you. Thanks so much for the invitation.''

He shoved his hands into the pockets of his jeans. A good way of hiding the fact that they weren't entirely steady. Why would his parole officer need to speak to him in the middle of a Saturday afternoon? What the hell had he managed to do wrong since Monday? He hadn't set foot in a bar, even to order a soda. As far as he knew, his boss had expressed no complaints with his performance. What else could it be? Fear turned Joe's throat dry, the fear of a prisoner who was never quite sure what authority might demand of him next. Surely Anna wouldn't be acting this casually if she were about to revoke his parole?

He followed her down the stairs. He'd expected them to walk to the unappetizing coffee shop in the strip mall at the end of the block. Instead, when they got outside, she gestured for him to get into a gray Subaru parked in the hotel's small and debris-strewn lot. She slid into the driver's seat and a faint drift of her perfume wafted toward him. Joe quickly made a show of adjusting his seat belt and turned to stare blindly out of the window. He sat with his legs pressed together and his hands folded in his lap, determined not to let his body language betray even a fraction of what he was feeling. Better that Anna should think he was a sullen lout than a sex-starved moron.

They drove in silence, zipping through crowds of weekend traffic, until she stopped at a coffee bar with fancy striped awnings and a half-dozen wrought iron tables set outside. The entrance door was framed by two wooden tubs filled with purple crocus already in full bloom and yellow daffodils just starting to unfurl their trumpets.

It was astonishing to realize he'd once routinely stopped in places like this café without even noticing how attractive they were, Joe mused. Until he spent four years locked away, flowers had just been flowers, pretty but undifferentiated splashes of color. Was that what freedom meant, maybe? The luxury of ignoring the beautiful as well as the ugly, because you were so confident you'd encounter it again?

"I'm buying," Anna said, her first words since they got into the car. "How do you like your coffee, Mr. Mackenzie? Espresso, cappuccino, flavored or just regular?"

"A regular latte, no sugar, if you please. Ma'am."

She gave him a look that suggested she knew exactly why he'd thrown in that superfluous *ma'am.* Then she nodded. "Pick a table and sit down, Mackenzie. Unless it's too cold for you out here?"

"No, I have a jacket and I like the fresh air."

"Me, too. It's been a long winter and this sun is gorgeous. I'll be right back."

Joe automatically rose to his feet as she returned with two tall foam cups and two giant cookies on a plastic tray. "I couldn't resist," she said, tipping her head toward the cookies. "They're white chocolate macadamia nut, my favorite. I hope you like them."

"Very much." Sitting opposite this woman, Joe thought he could pretty much have eaten baked sawdust and enjoyed it. "Thank you for suggesting we should come here. It's a pleasant spot." For once he managed to express gratitude without sounding mocking.

''Mmm, it's a nice place. I often stop by when I'm at this end of town because their coffee's always fresh. Which is a bonus when you're a coffee addict like me.''

''Me, too.'' Her smile beguiled him into responding. ''I missed having a decent cup of coffee more than most things over the past few years.''

''I can imagine.'' She set the tray on the iron mesh table. ''Lots of my clients have told me it's the little things that get to you when you're locked up. The big deprivations you eventually learn to cope with.''

''That was my experience for sure.'' Joe pulled out her chair for her, then jerked away when his hands got stuck between her body and the back of the chair. He quickly sat down again.

Get with the program, moron. No more smiles. No more confidences. No more reminiscences about your time in prison. You don't want this woman to know a damn thing about you that isn't already written into your file.

Anna took a sip of her coffee, then stared at the budding daffodils for a moment before turning to meet his gaze. ''I've been trying to find a tactful way to start this conversation, but I can't, so I guess I'll just have to wade right in.''

''Yes, ma'am.''

She drew in a deep breath. ''Here goes. I learned today that two street punks have been hired to kill you. According to my informant, you're lucky to be alive, because they'd already received the advance payment for the job as long ago as last Saturday, with word to do the deed before you checked in with your parole officer on Monday. Fortunately for you, it seems the would-be assassins got diverted on their way to carry out their assignment. They got high, got into a fight, exchanged gunfire with a third party and generally messed up on their assignment. They were arrested, and since they both have a long list of priors, the judge wouldn't agree to bail. Which means they're in jail right now where they can't do you any harm.''

Anna paused for a moment, but when Joe didn't say anything, she continued speaking. ''Okay, so far I've told you the good news. The bad news is we've no idea who hired these men, so we have no way of knowing if that person will go ahead and hire somebody else to complete the job. Until we find a way to persuade one of these punks to cough up the name of their employer, you need to watch your back. And your front, too. You could be in serious danger, Mr. Mackenzie.''

At first Joe wasn't aware of having any reaction to what Anna was saying. But when she finished speaking, he realized he had jumped into an automatic state of full alert the moment she delivered her first warning sentence. Even while he listened to her, he became aware of the couple seated at the only other occupied sidewalk table. He'd ignored them before. Now, still listening to Anna, he screened their conversation for a few seconds—long enough to hear them discussing which movie they would go to that night.

Probably a harmless couple who were just what they seemed, he decided. But he continued to hold them in his peripheral vision, just in case. Prison had made him damn good at holding threats in his peripheral awareness.

Yet another part of his brain began to make a general assessment of his physical surroundings, calculating his distance from the road, and deciding which way he'd dive for the ground in order to obtain maximum protective covering. He was way too exposed, he concluded, and Anna was right in the line of fire if somebody shot at him from a passing car. Why the hell hadn't he said he wanted to sit inside the café where he'd have been in better control of his environment? How had he become so careless, so fast?

Funny, he thought bleakly. Until he went back into defensive mode, he hadn't realized how completely he'd let down his guard since he got out of prison. In one short week he'd already forgotten about the need to keep on permanent alert, constantly screening his surroundings for potential threats. At least he'd sat with his back pressed against the wall of the café, facing out toward the parking lot and the road. Some habits were too deeply ingrained after four years to be discarded without conscious effort.

Joe's mind raced, analyzing and discarding risk factors at lightning speed, but he managed to look at Anna with a pretense of indifference. Same old tiresome prison defense, hauled out for all occasions, he reflected bitterly. God, he was so tired of faking it. So tired of trusting no one. So damn tired of being on the defensive every minute of every day.

"Thank you for the warning, ma'am," he said woodenly. "I appreciate it. I'll be on my guard for sure."

"That's all you have to say, Mr. Mackenzie?" Anna sounded more frustrated than surprised by his attitude. "I tell you you're the target of a pair of hired killers and you thank me politely for the warning? Isn't that taking the macho man act a tad too far?"

He took a long swallow of coffee before replying. No point in wasting a perfectly good latte just because somebody was trying to kill him, he thought wryly. "What did you expect me to say…ma'am?"

She set down her cup with enough of a thump to splash foam onto the iron mesh tabletop. "For a start, it would be a step in the right direction if you could stop insulting me by saying *ma'am* in that snide tone of voice."

He looked at her, astonishing himself by the naked challenge he allowed to blaze in his expression. "What would you prefer me to call you? Exactly how should a convicted embezzler address his parole officer? Clue me in on the etiquette of the situation. Ma'am."

She ignored the deliberate provocation. "Ms. Langtry would be appropriate." She must have noticed the gleam in his eye because she hurried on before he could respond. "Okay, let's cut to the chase. Can you think of any reason why somebody might want to kill you, Mr. Mackenzie?"

He shrugged. "Plenty of reasons."

"Share some of them with me. Do you have any suspicions about who might have put out this contract?"

"No, not specifically." He tried to sound both puzzled and cooperative, a good way to deflect attention from what he really suspected. "I made the usual assortment of enemies during the time I was inside. Offend the leader of a powerful prison gang and you can more or less guarantee that his blood brothers will compete to see who can be first to put you in the hospital. Plus, I wasn't willing to play racial politics, so I pissed off a wide assortment of bigots with balls bigger than their brains.''

His deliberate crudity drew no reaction from her. ''But you're not aware of offending any of the other inmates to the point that they would pursue you now you're on parole?'' she asked.

He shook his head. ''Nobody I could point to. But that doesn't mean much, because for some of the guys inside there doesn't have to be a rational cause for them to hate you. There were some members of the Aryan Nation, for example, who were furious that I associated with prisoners who weren't the same race as me, and especially that I remained friendly with several Muslims after the September 11 attacks. Were they angry enough to pursue me outside the prison walls? I would have said no. Prison society is obsessively inward-looking, for obvious reasons. But maybe I underestimate the intensity of their hatred for racial and religious traitors.''

Anna brushed a cookie crumb from her fingers, her brow wrinkling in thought. ''Okay, so you made plenty of enemies, but nobody you could identify off the top of your head as hostile enough to kill you. How about friends?''

He shrugged again. ''I had some.''

''Did you know a man called Raul Estevan?'' Anna asked. ''Would you count him among the friends you made while you were inside?''

She was obviously going somewhere with this line of questioning, and Joe didn't like answering before he knew precisely where. Still, she could find out that he and Raul had been cell mates with a single phone call—probably had already made the call—so there was no point in lying.

''Yes, I knew Raul,'' Joe acknowledged, his stomach sinking. He hated to think that the man he'd considered his best friend might have betrayed him. However, Raul had been fighting a ten-year cocaine habit ever since he got out on parole. And if there was one thing you could say for sure about an addict, it was that he could always be bought. Sober, Joe would trust Raul with his life. High, he wouldn't trust him with a toenail clipping.

Anna leaned across the table. ''Mr. Mackenzie, I know the prisoner's code is never to provide a single piece of information to any government official that isn't dragged out, kicking and screaming. But I'm not conducting a police interrogation. This isn't a courtroom. It's not even a parole board hearing. Believe it or not, I'm having this conversation for one reason only. I want to help you. Could you please answer my questions?''

He'd been a little short in the helping hand department recently and the temptation to respond to Anna's generous offer of help was almost overwhelming. It was also dangerous, given his current agenda. Not sure what he could safely reveal, Joe swallowed the last of his coffee, then looked at her with deliberate blankness.

''I thought I did answer your question, Ms. Langtry. Yes, I knew Raul Estevan. We shared a cell, in fact. He got out of prison almost a year ago, though. He's written me a couple of times since then.''

''So he was a good friend of yours?'' she persisted.

Joe hesitated, then decided he needed information even more than he needed to protect his own pitiful pride. So what if Raul had betrayed him? Betrayal wouldn't exactly be a new experience for him.

''Yes,'' he said curtly. ''Raul and I were friends while we were inside.''

''That's what Raul told me,'' Anna said. ''He's in the hospital. Did you know that?''

''No, I didn't.'' Poor Guillermina, Joe thought, aware that Anna was watching him, trying to gauge his reaction to every snippet of information she dribbled out. She should give up on that, he thought cynically. Prison provided an ongoing master class in the art of inscrutability. Joe rubbed his chin, where the stubble of a twenty-four-hour beard was starting to itch.

''What happened to Raul?'' he asked Anna. ''Did he OD?''

''No. He was shot by a couple of Colombians.''

''I'm sorry. Really sorry.'' Joe gave himself a few seconds to get his voice under absolute control. ''Was he badly hurt?''

''Yes, very badly. He sustained five different bullet wounds. One nicked the liver, another got his spleen, two went into his shoulders. I understand the final one missed his left lung by less than two millimeters.''

''My God.'' Joe wasn't sure if he felt relief that Raul was alive, or fury that the stupid dick had exposed himself to such danger by refusing to stay clean.

''Yes, indeed,'' Anna said dryly. ''The wounds ought to have been fatal. In fact, a week ago, everyone thought Raul would die. Right now, though, it seems likely he's going to live. His recovery is about as close to a miracle as anyone at Denver General has seen recently.''

''I'm glad he made it. His wife must be very relieved. She's due to have a baby quite soon, isn't she?''

''She's six weeks away, I believe.''

''Do the cops know why Raul was shot?'' Joe asked. It seemed a safe enough question and provided no clue as to his own thoughts.

''The short answer is drugs. Raul and his assailants were all high. Precisely how he ended up shot depends on who's telling the story. Raul's claim is that two of his buddies came to visit him when they were high, then didn't like what he was saying, so they shot him. He fired back only in self-defense, and only after his supposed buddies started spraying bullets all around his restaurant. Naturally, the other two guys are telling a different story.''

''Naturally.'' Joe shrugged. ''For what it's worth, I spent three years with Raul in pretty close quarters, and it was my impression he always tried to avoid violence.''

''Is that so?'' Anna leaned back in her chair. ''Raul's former pals who tried to kill him are Miguel Ortega and Carlos Inez. Those names mean anything to you?''

''Not a thing,'' Joe said with perfect truth.

''Pity. Because they not only shot Raul last Saturday night, they're also the two men who were supposedly hired to kill you.''

''They were paid to take Raul out, too?'' Joe was astonished enough that he let his surprise show in his voice. Christ, maybe he'd jumped to the wrong conclusion about this hit. He'd assumed automatically that he was scheduled for elimination because of what he knew about the bank irregularities in Durango. But maybe the hit had been ordered for more mundane reasons. Maybe he and Raul really had been targeted because they had offended the wrong people in prison.

''Why are you so astonished to think that Raul might also have been a designated victim, Mr. Mackenzie?''

Anna Langtry was too damn quick on the uptake. Joe gave a tight, cynical smile, trying to deflect her curiosity. ''Raul didn't make as many enemies in prison as I did. He was better at keeping a low profile. Plus he had powerful connections of his own. They made for very effective protection.''

''Medellin connections?''

She must know the answer to that one already. ''Yes,'' he acknowledged. ''Smart prisoners don't mess with inmates who are under the protection of the Colombians. In fact, even the dumb ones learn that rule pretty fast.''

''According to Raul, Miguel and Carlos were paid ten thousand dollars to kill you. He claims he tried to talk them out of it because you're a friend of his, but they weren't willing to listen. They'd been paid three thousand bucks up front, and they were anxious to earn the rest so that they could take a vacation.''

''I appreciate Raul's efforts on my behalf,'' Joe said grimly. ''Although I guess I'm insulted that I didn't rate more than a ten thousand dollar payoff. Whoever put out the contract obviously wasn't expecting any difficulty in getting rid of me.''

''It certainly doesn't seem as if the would-be murderer was experienced at hiring contract killers,'' Anna said. ''Otherwise he'd have known not to pay two street punks with a drug habit before he had positive proof of your death.''

If the hit had been arranged by white-collar criminals operating out of Durango, presumably they didn't have too much expertise in dealing with killers for hire. Joe's suspicion intensified that this hit was connected to the money laundering in Durango, and not to any enemies he'd made in prison.

Until now, despite everything that had happened, Joe had never considered his life to be directly at risk. Whoever wanted him out of the way hadn't killed him four years ago, so why put out a contract now? He had always assumed that if they'd wanted him dead, they'd have killed him. But now he had to consider the possibility that they'd gone to all the fuss and bother of getting him sent to prison, when they really wanted him dead. Why?

Another puzzle for him to chew on when Anna Langtry's assessing gaze wasn't fixed right on him.

He'd been silent too long, and he spoke quickly, trying to cover up. "All I can say is that I'm grateful my would-be murderer made such a lousy choice of hired guns. I guess it's difficult to hire an efficient killer when you're behind bars."

"Let's not get totally hung up on the idea that this hit was ordered by an inmate," Anna said. "There are other possibilities. How about an ex-wife who is mad at you, for example? Do you have one of those?"

He shook his head. "Not possible. I've never been married."

"An ex-girlfriend? An angry fiancée?"

Joe thought about Sophie Bartlett, who had apparently taken all of five minutes to transfer her undying love to Frank Saunders. "I don't have any ex-girlfriends who care enough to flip a wet noodle in my direction, let alone hire a couple of hit men.''

He meant to sound bored, but was afraid he sounded hurt. His suspicion was confirmed when Anna directed a quick glance at him through narrowed eyes. Fortunately, she chose not to press the point. ''Okay,'' she said. ''For the time being we'll work on the assumption there are no murderous ex-wives or girlfriends out to get you. So we're not left with many choices about who arranged this hit.''

''No, we're not.''

''Your conclusion would be that Carlos and Miguel were hired by somebody you ticked off in prison, is that right?''

''It would have to be,'' Joe lied. ''Who else is there?''

''I don't know, but I suspect you do.''

After four years in prison, lying was not only real easy, it was instinctive. Joe knew his expression displayed nothing beyond puzzlement and a desire to be helpful. ''You're wrong, Ms. Langtry. I have no idea who might have ordered this hit. None.''

Anna took her napkin and stuffed it into her empty coffee cup. ''Then answer this question for me, Mr. Mackenzie. If you annoyed somebody in prison enough that they wanted to kill you, why didn't they? It would have been simple enough to arrange. A fight breaks out, two burly guys hold you down, and a third prisoner sticks a homemade knife between your ribs. Why would anyone wait until you're on the outside and much harder to take down?''

''It's only in the movies that prisoners wipe out other prisoners on a weekly basis,'' Joe said. ''In a real prison, the guards break up fights before they have dead bodies to clean up. There are so damn many forms to fill out when a prisoner dies in custody, the guards like to avoid it.''

Anna ignored his sarcasm. ''Guards don't always succeed in breaking up fights among inmates. Some prisoners die. Why not you?''

''I don't know.''

''Make some guesses.''

He frowned, considering his reply. Anna really did have an excellent point, he reflected, and for the first time he answered her as truthfully as he could. ''The guards almost always know who started the fight, and if they don't, a snitch will tell them. Maybe whoever arranged this hit realized that he'd be identified as the perpetrator if I got killed while I was inside, and he didn't want to suffer the consequences.''

''It's possible, I guess.'' Anna didn't look convinced. ''Still, an inmate who really wanted you dead ought to have been able to arrange it without incriminating himself, don't you think? He could pick a couple of lifers to help him, get witnesses to swear you started it, and that they were only acting in self-defense. Bingo, the real instigator is in the clear. For sure, it's a lot cheaper and easier to hire a killer inside prison rather than outside.''

Cheaper and easier for an inmate, but not for a white-collar criminal with no lines of communication into the prison, Joe thought. Which pretty much confirmed his suspicion that this hit had been ordered from Durango, not from inside the prison by a disgruntled leader of the Aryan Nation.

He didn't know quite how to respond to Anna. She sounded worried as well as baffled, as if she wanted to help him explore options and really get to the bottom of who was behind this murder for hire before any harm came to him. Joe could easily have resisted almost any other form of cross-examination. But it had been too long since anyone showed genuine concern for his well-being and he was a lot more vulnerable to kindness than he cared to acknowledge.

"I wouldn't have been as easy to kill as you might expect," he said finally. "I had friends inside who would have helped me—"

"Your enemies could have attacked you when you were alone, in the shower or something—"

"Prisoners aren't alone in the showers," Joe said curtly. "Besides, I could defend myself quite well even if I'd been cornered when I was alone. I could probably have held off an attack long enough to yell for help from the guards, or some of my friends."

"You could defend yourself against brutal gang members who'd trained in street fighting since they were little kids?" Not surprisingly, Anna sounded skeptical.

"I did some street fighting myself when I was a kid." He willed himself not to say anything more, but the words came out. "Besides, I have a tenth dan black belt in judo."

"You do?"

"Yeah. I needed an extra credit when I was a freshman in college and I happened to have a girlfriend at the time who was a national champion who'd competed in the Olympics. She got me interested in all forms of martial arts."

"I wouldn't have thought college judo would prove very effective against knuckle-dusters, razors and prison tempers. Much too civilized."

Joe smiled without mirth. "Yeah, the judo wasn't

much help in the beginning. But after a couple of trips to the prison hospital, I figured out that if I remembered my opponent wasn't going to bow first and stop fighting as soon as my shoulders touched the mat, then I had a much better chance of winning the argument. Besides, my girlfriend's parents were both Hollywood stunt people, and during my college vacations I worked with them on a couple of movies. They taught me a lot of dirty tricks that weren't in the official judo rule book. After my first six months inside, the other inmates didn't mess with me very often."

And that was an understatement. There were knives aplenty behind bars, but no guns and no bullets. In hand-to-hand combat, he could defend himself against the meanest and dirtiest of attackers. By the time he neared the end of his sentence, Joe's prison rep had been fearsome.

But apparently now that he was no longer behind bars, he'd forgotten the value of keeping his mouth shut. He knew exactly why he'd broken his prime rule of never giving out any extraneous information. He was so damn besotted by his parole officer that he had a sophomoric urge to dazzle her. He desperately wanted her to see him as something more than just another dreary ex-con.

His ploy worked. Anna's eyes widened. "You were employed as a Hollywood stuntman? I'm impressed. I thought there were union rules that made it nearly impossible for outsiders to get hired on."

"There are. My girlfriend's parents got me into the union."

"Lucky you!" Anna smiled, her interest well and truly caught. "What movies did you appear in?"

"The first *Die Hard* movie," he said. "And three action flicks that live on in cable land half-life."

"You were in *Die Hard?*" she breathed.

"Yep." He grinned. "Got almost four minutes of airtime that survived the cutting room floor, too."

"I love those *Die Hard* movies," she said. "Chiefly because I get to watch Bruce Willis save the world. In a ragged T-shirt, with his muscles hanging out, no less."

Joe smiled, and forgot to make it cynical. "Let me guess. You're a Bruce Willis fan."

"Big time. So loyal I've even forgiven him for making *Unbreakable.* Did you ever get to speak to him, or see him up close?"

"Real close," he said wryly. "It was only my second day on the set and I screwed up my timing. Bruce Willis tripped over my foot, which should have been six feet away, on another mark entirely. We ended up falling flat on the floor, his head buried under my shoulder. Within about ten seconds, half the production crew was on top of us, trying to find out if I'd inflicted enough damage on their star to ruin the shooting schedule."

"And had you?"

"Nah. He's a tough guy, and he knows how to fall without hurting himself. Thank God."

Anna gave an exaggerated sigh, then laughed. "It seems like a serious waste of a clinch, you and Bruce rolling around the floor together. I would have appreciated the situation so much more than you, I'm sure."

"Kayla said almost the same thing. She spent that entire summer suffering from a bad case of unrequited passion."

''Kayla?''

''My girlfriend. Well, ex-girlfriend by that time. As a twenty-year-old college kid, I offered no competition when compared to Bruce and an assorted collection of Hollywood's finest musclemen.'' He grinned. ''Still, the trade-off was definitely worth it. When I got back to school, I casually let word leak around campus that I'd been working in Hollywood as a stuntman. I have to tell you, next to being a genuine movie star in your own right, working as a stuntman has to be the best way ever invented to pick up girls.''

She laughed. ''You were never tempted to make it a full-time profession?''

''No. Doing movie stunts struck me as way too dangerous for anyone with a drop of common sense, not to mention excruciatingly boring. Hours of standing around and then five minutes of action before the director yells, 'Cut.' It sounds a little crazy to say that banking always struck me as potentially more exciting than jumping off high buildings and leaping over burning cars, but a local bank, lending money wisely, can make a huge difference in a community at the same time as it makes a decent profit for its shareholders. My grandfather—''

Joe broke off, appalled at where the conversation had taken them. One unguarded response and, before you knew it, he was halfway to telling his life history to his parole officer.

Anna seemed to share his sudden discomfort. She spoke softly. ''It's a pity you lost your idealism about what local banks are for, Mr. Mackenzie. You could have done a lot of good if you'd held true to your vision.''

It took him a moment to grasp what she was referring to. Then he realized how hypocritical he must have sounded—a convicted embezzler waxing lyrical about a bank's potential for enriching the local community. Point taken. He wouldn't forget again.

Anna stood up, sweeping their empty cups and paper cookie plates onto the tray. "We'd better get going, Mr. Mackenzie. I have a lot to do this afternoon, and I expect you need to get some sleep before your shift tonight."

"Yes." He stood up, stepping aside so that she could deposit their debris in the trash. The other couple were still sitting at their table, a newspaper listing of the movie theaters spread out between them. They demonstrated not even a twinge of interest in Joe's imminent departure.

"I'll drive you home," Anna said.

"No, thanks." Right now, he couldn't handle any more one-on-one time with Anna Langtry. "I'll walk. It's less than two miles and I could use the exercise."

She didn't attempt to persuade him. "Take care, Mr. Mackenzie. And when you go to work tonight, please take the bus. Don't walk alone down any dark alleys."

Yeah, that would keep him safe all right. "Thanks for letting me know about Carlos and Miguel," he said gruffly. "I appreciate you taking time on the weekend to warn me."

"You're welcome."

He didn't wait to see her get into her car. He didn't say goodbye. Sometimes, if you wanted to leave yourself a few tattered remnants of pride, you simply had to walk away.

Nine

Something about her recent encounter with Joseph Mackenzie was bugging her. Like a mosquito buzzing around her head, whatever it was eluded her grasp. There was something about the man that made him stand out from her other clients, but Anna couldn't for the life of her figure out what. Well, okay, so she had this weird sexual attraction to him, which was certainly a first, but there was something else. Something even more disconcerting than the fact that she had just spent an hour sitting across the table from a convicted embezzler, fantasizing about what it would be like to have sex with him.

Anna stepped on her brakes just in time to avoid rear-ending the car in front of her. Okay. This could definitely be considered a sign that it was time to stop imagining how Mackenzie would perform in bed. She was supposedly out on a shopping expedition. How about planning which store she would hit first in her quest for a new spring outfit?

Anna weighed the relative merits of a budget-busting trip to Saks or Nieman Marcus versus hitting the sale racks at Nordstrom's, but within minutes her thoughts had drifted back to Joseph Mackenzie. The wretched man knew who wanted him dead, she was sure of it, and the stupid lunkhead was going to end up playing Mr. Strong and Silent Macho Man right up until the moment when the cops scraped his dead body off the sidewalk. Damn! What was it with him, anyway? Was he afraid he'd lose his lifetime supply of testosterone if he actually trusted her with some useful information?

Stopped at a traffic light she'd actually noticed, fingers drumming on the steering wheel, Anna realized she no longer felt the slightest interest in going shopping. When her cell phone rang, she snatched it up, turning her car into a side street so that she could park while she talked.

She was honest enough to acknowledge a twinge of disappointment when Ed Barber identified himself. What had she hoped? That Knucklehead Mackenzie had been overcome by second thoughts and was suddenly going to start pouring out the secrets of his inner child?

''I went and looked through the evidence package from the Estevan shooting scene,'' the detective said, with no more preamble than stating his name. ''For what it's worth, there's a photo of a white male, early thirties, catalogued with the rest of the stuff. The photo's a bit torn up, but it's a studio shot, and you can see who it is clearly enough to make a positive identification—''

''I could drive over and take a look,'' Anna offered. ''I can confirm whether or not it's a picture of Joseph Mackenzie—''

''No need. I accessed Mackenzie's mug shot.'' Ed paused. ''The computer says it's a match, the two photos are of the same man. Which means somebody in Raul's restaurant last Saturday was flashing around a picture of your boy.'' Ed snickered. ''He's a pretty-looking fella, isn't he?''

Anna thought that *ferocious* and *dangerously sexy* would be a more accurate description, but she merely made a noncommittal murmur. Just when you were sure you had somebody neatly pigeonholed, they managed to surprise you. She would have sworn that Ed Barber would take days, if not weeks, to check through the evidence his fellow cops had collected from Raul's restaurant. Instead he'd taken only a couple of hours.

Grateful to have been proved wrong in her assessment, she thanked Ed profusely, and he volunteered the information that he would stop by Denver General hospital on Monday so that he could take a statement from Raul. If Raul made a decent case for having fired in self-defense, Ed promised that he would speak to his friend in the D.A.'s office and do his best to see that the charges of attempted murder were dropped.

''Given that Raul was hit half a dozen times, whereas all the bullets fired from his gun missed their targets, it makes sense that the other guys must have fired their weapons first,'' Ed said. He managed to sound as if he'd been convinced all along that Miguel and Carlos were lying. ''If Raul was already badly wounded when he started shooting, it would explain why he missed both of them.''

''Raul insists that's what happened,'' Anna agreed mildly. ''And, for what it's worth, his wife concurs.''

Ed grunted. ''I guess even drug-dealing slimeballs like Raul tell the truth occasionally. Of course, when you're dealing with three drug-dealing slimeballs, it's a tough choice deciding which one to believe.''

''I can see how that could be a problem.'' Anna

was so relieved that Ed had followed through and checked the evidence, she was more than willing to let him get away with designating Raul a slimeball. In their new spirit of cooperation, she gave him a brief account of her interview with Joseph Mackenzie.

She could almost see Ed's shrug when she told him that Mackenzie claimed to have no idea who might want him dead. "Well, he's been warned, that's all you can do, right? But I'll bet any money you like that he knows a hell of a lot more than he's telling."

She replied more curtly than she intended. "I'm aware of that, Detective."

"Don't let it eat at you," he said, with surprising insight. "You can't save the world, and if Mackenzie won't let you help him, that's his problem. You've done everything and more that you should, and I'll take it from here."

"Do you think Miguel and Carlos will give up the name of the person who hired them?"

"I'll give it my best shot. Trouble is, they might not know. But since you say there don't seem to be any psycho ex-wives or girlfriends in the picture, I'll put in a call to the prison and see if they have any idea who might be pissed enough to pay hard cash to get Mackenzie eliminated. If all that doesn't shake loose any leads, I'll pay Mackenzie a personal visit and see if I can scare him into sharing what he knows."

"Good luck, Detective. I don't think Mackenzie scares easily."

"Then he's probably going to end up dead some time real soon."

Anna was depressingly in agreement with that conclusion. Sighing, she thanked Ed again for his cooperation and clicked off her cell phone, easing the car back into traffic and heading toward the mall.

The purchase of a slinky black cocktail suit on sale at fifty percent off helped to improve her mood, but Anna remained restless, fighting a crazy urge to go back to Mackenzie's hotel and pound some sense into his useless male brain. Approaching her apartment building, she watched the joggers circle Cheeseman Park without really seeing them. Even the gay couple wearing lavender jogging shorts to match the hair ribbons adorning the topknots of their Afghan hounds couldn't hold her attention.

As soon as she got home, she would call a friend and suggest going out to a movie, she decided. Anything to prevent another long evening staring at the walls of her condo.

She locked her car, nodding absently to one of her neighbors. It wasn't only Mackenzie who was causing her restless mood, Anna recognized. Monday would be the first of April, and she still hadn't received her annual package from the Fords. No wonder she'd spent the past several days feeling like a reptile whose skin had begun to fit too tightly. Usually her package from the Fords arrived via the lawyer's office no later than the third week of March. What had happened this year? If she didn't hear from the Fords by Monday, she would call Derek Wu, the lawyer.

Leaving her car in the parking lot at the rear of her building, she detoured via the front entrance to pick up the day's mail. Her heart started to hammer hard and fast when she saw the padded envelope among the bills and circulars. The return address read Mr. and Mrs. Stuart Ford, in care of Wu's office.

Her birthday pictures were here.

Anna's breath caught, then raced forward in double time. She wanted privacy to view the contents of her precious package, but the wait for the elevator seemed interminable, and she had to shove one hand into the pocket of her jeans to prevent herself ripping open the envelope. Arriving on the sixth floor, she ran down the corridor to her condo, her fingers shaking so badly that she dropped her purse when she tried to unlock the front door.

Succeeding on the third try, she kicked her purse inside, too impatient to bend and pick it up. She pushed the door shut with her foot and headed for the living room sofa, scattering the rest of her mail behind her. Frantic to view the contents of the envelope, she even ignored Ferdinand. Unused to having his overtures rejected, the cat stalked away, tail in the air, thoroughly put out.

Anna didn't even notice. She tore open the flap of the envelope and sank onto the sofa, her breath coming in hard, dry pants. It was a bigger package than usual. Maybe there was more than one photo. She gave a little cry—half sob, half laugh—when she saw that this year there were at least a dozen pictures.

She tugged them out of the envelope, rifling through them so fast that she saw nothing beyond a blur of color. Forcing herself to calm down, she wiped her sweaty palms on her thighs and spread out the pictures on her coffee table.

No doubt about it, her daughter was the most beautiful person in the world. And that was a purely objective assessment, of course. Anna smiled, though her eyes were already misted with tears. She blinked and scrubbed her cheeks with a tissue, telling herself to get a grip. Dammit, she wasn't going to drip useless tears onto the pictures and ruin them before she even saw them properly.

This year, in addition to the annual studio portrait that was an obligatory part of their legal agreement, the Fords had included a dozen snapshots of Megan, along with a copy of her school report. They hadn't even blacked out the name of the school, so Anna was able to take her map of the Seattle area and pinpoint exactly where her daughter spent her days.

She had never before received such riches from Megan's adoptive parents and she feasted on the unexpected bounty. Maybe, after fourteen years, the Fords had finally decided that she could be trusted to stick to her side of the bargain and not attempt to contact Megan until her eighteenth birthday. If she wrote a grateful, begging letter via the lawyer, Anna wondered, would the Fords agree to send a video next year? It would be so wonderful to hear the sound of her daughter's voice....

Legs more than a little shaky, Anna carried the pictures to the window so that she could examine them in natural light. Scrutinizing each one intently, she searched to see how her daughter had changed since last year.

At fourteen, her daughter was beginning to look more woman than little girl. She'd slimmed down over the past twelve months, and her face had lost the last blurred softness of childhood. At the clear signs of impending maturity, Anna felt torn between gratitude that the interminable wait to see her daughter in the flesh was drawing to a close, and panic that her baby was no longer a baby.

She traced her fingers over Megan's wavy, light-brown hair, which gleamed with a captivating sheen of auburn. Luckily, Megan had inherited the elegant, toned-down version of Anna's flaming mop of curls. In the formal studio portrait, Megan's hair settled around her shoulders in a silky cloud, and her extraordinary gray-blue eyes, fringed with long dark lashes, stared into the camera with a serene confidence that spoke of a happy home life and adoptive parents who adored her.

As always, Anna could see few hints of Caleb Welks's paternity in her daughter's features. Perhaps she was swayed by her passionate wish not to credit him with any positive role in the creation of her child, but Caleb had rather bland features, except for his small ears, so it wasn't altogether irrational of her to find no trace of him in Megan. Thank God.

The snapshots showed a more casual and much more lively Megan than the studio portrait. Taken at various times throughout the past year, they provided Anna with her first-ever glimpse into her daughter's home life. Either Stuart or Jennifer Ford must be a talented amateur photographer, because the pictures were skillfully composed, with no chopped-off body parts, red eyes or fuzzy focus.

In one shot Megan knelt beside a Christmas tree, laughing into the camera, caught in the act of handing a gift-wrapped box to the person taking the pictures. Other shots captured Megan licking a wooden spoon covered with chocolate cake batter; reaching up to serve a tennis ball; diving into a swimming pool; spearing a hot dog at a backyard barbecue; and leaning against a tree, a tiny kitten in her cupped hands, while a dog of indeterminate breed snoozed at her feet.

Anna wanted to reach into that picture and scoop

her daughter out, the urge to hug her was so unbearably strong.

There was no letter from the Fords—there never was—but the school report showed her daughter getting A's for English, social studies, and Spanish, along with B's for algebra and science. A note from her guidance counselor commented on the fact that Megan was popular with teachers and classmates alike, but she needed to do a better job of getting her homework assignments in on time. Both B's were the result of downgrading for consistently failing to complete projects by the due date. The counselor suggested that Megan might need to cut back on her demanding schedule of after-school activities. Being on the debate team and playing competitive tennis might be too much to handle now that she was starting high school.

Anna fought a moment of panic that the Fords weren't helping Megan to schedule her time better, then realized she was being basically nuts. A fourteen-year-old who looked as happy as Megan, had lots of friends and was liked by her teachers wasn't exactly heading for major disaster even if she did goof off on the occasional algebra assignment.

Anna looked through the photos for almost two hours, letting her imagination roam, inventing stories to answer the questions left by the mute pictures, trying to fill the painful void left by her daughter's absence from her life.

It was ironic to contemplate how frantic she had been to escape from Caleb's household before he made her pregnant, Anna thought. It had been her desperate wish to avoid being tied to him by a baby that had given her the burst of courage needed to make her escape from Alana Springs.

If she'd known that it was already too late, that she was already carrying Caleb's child, would she have run away on their wedding night? Anna wasn't sure of the answer to that question. Education and life in a big city had so altered her view of the world that she couldn't put herself back into the mind of her cloistered, ignorant, seventeen-year-old self.

Anyway, she hadn't known she was pregnant, and she'd fled, confident that a happy future waited for her if she could just evade Caleb's clutches long enough to make it safely to Denver. With the help of the Salvation Army, she had secured a room in a house for runaway teens, found a job at Wal-Mart and enrolled in high school for the start of the new school year in September. For an entire month, life had seemed blissful.

Then she realized she was pregnant.

Scared, desperate for some way to keep her baby without returning to live under Caleb's rule, Anna had called her mother to beg for help, but Ray answered the phone and refused to let her speak with Betty Jean. Anna called again, at a time when she hoped Ray wasn't likely to be in the house.

That time Aunt Patsy answered the phone and coldly informed Anna that nobody in Ray's household would speak to her again until she returned to Alana Springs and took up her God-ordained role as Caleb's wife. When Anna had protested that she had a right to speak to her own mother, Aunt Patsy informed her she had no rights. She was lucky Ray and Caleb had decided not to notify the police and charge her with stealing Caleb's car.

Anna might have spent the six years before her ''marriage'' cut off from mainstream society, but four weeks in the real world had been enough to help her recognize that Aunt Patsy's threat was sheer bluff. Nobody in Alana Springs would have wanted to direct the attention of the authorities to a seventeen-year-old runaway who was likely to reveal that she had been coerced into becoming the third wife of a polygamist more than twenty years her senior. Besides, Anna had mailed the car keys back to Caleb, along with instructions on how to find the supermarket parking lot where she'd abandoned it. She'd done that as soon as the Salvation Army found her somewhere else to sleep.

Whatever Ray and his family had claimed, Anna had known she wasn't a thief, either legally or morally. She'd committed no crime, and there had been no way for Caleb to compel her to return. Listening to Patsy's empty threats, Anna had realized that if she went back to Alana Springs, it would only be because she chose to surrender.

Even pregnant, destitute and terrified, Anna wasn't willing to go back to a lifestyle she'd rejected and a husband she despised. Her calls to Ray's house had been a knee-jerk reaction, a final desperate plea for her mother to come to her rescue. Despite all the evidence of Betty Jean's willing subservience to the Welks brothers, Anna had hoped her mom would finally stand up to Ray and protect her.

The knowledge that Betty Jean had refused to speak to her stiffened Anna's spine and cleared her mind. Belatedly, it had dawned on Anna that her mother truly believed God wanted women to make celestial marriages, to live in western-style harems, and become unpaid servants to their husbands. Betty Jean would never have defied the community in which she'd chosen to make her life, not because she lacked the courage to rebel, but because she believed her daughter had committed a mortal sin when she ran away. Anna had realized she had been looking in entirely the wrong place when she was looking to her mom for rescue.

She had wanted to keep her baby with an intensity that had left her sleepless and sick, but not if it had to be raised as Caleb Welks's seventh child, in the suffocating, unhealthy atmosphere of Alana Springs. At seventeen, Anna didn't know much about religion and theology, apart from the creed she'd been taught by Ray and the other members of the True Life Latter Day Saints. However, she was pretty sure that in a world where God had chosen to make half of the people men and half of them women, it seemed like a pretty safe bet that he intended for one woman to marry one man, so that there would be enough of each gender to go around. She was willing to believe that God had a plan for her life, but she was positive that living in Alana Springs as third wife to Caleb Welks wasn't it.

She should have stuck a knife in Caleb's gut right before he raped her in the name of celestial duty, Anna thought savagely, returning her thoughts to the present. Her hand stroked restlessly across Ferdinand's belly, and he butted his head against her ribs, sensing that she needed comfort. Except that if she'd killed Caleb, then Megan wouldn't exist and, despite having spent the past fourteen years living with a permanent ache of grief for the loss of her child, Anna could never bring herself to wish that her beautiful, talented daughter didn't exist.

When she first realized that her mother wasn't going to help her out, Anna had spent two days immobilized by despair. Then she dragged herself back together again. Forcing herself to think of the baby she carried as Caleb's child rather than her own, she paid a visit to her local Planned Parenthood clinic, trying to convince herself that she wanted to have Caleb's seed scraped out of her. It wasn't fair that she had to face up to yet another disaster that wasn't her fault, and she was mad at the world.

Her anger only increased when the counselor she saw at the clinic talked about the possibility of adoption. What was the matter with the dumb woman? Hadn't she listened to a word Anna was saying? All she wanted was to get Caleb's baby out of her body. She wanted an abortion like yesterday.

The counselor informed Anna that she was required to wait twenty-four hours. Relieved that she had been smart enough to claim she was already a legal adult so that there would be no question of contacting her parents for permission, Anna insisted that she was absolutely sure of her decision. The counselor merely responded courteously that she still needed to wait twenty-four hours.

Anna made the earliest possible appointment for the next morning, and arrived punctually at the clinic. She'd no sooner signed in than she had to rush to the rest room to be sick. Using her sickness as an excuse, Anna sneaked back into the waiting area. After a few minutes, she told the receptionist she wasn't feeling well and she'd return the next day. The next day she'd returned—and run away again.

The third time she repeated her performance, one of the nurses grabbed her arm as she started to run and sat her down for another long talk with the counselor.

The upshot was that Anna had been put in touch with Derek Wu. Wu was a top-notch lawyer who arranged adoptions with scrupulous attention to the needs of all parties concerned. An ultrasound eventually revealed that Anna was expecting a baby girl. After extensive face-to-face interviews, Anna had chosen Jennifer and Stuart Ford from a client roster of more than a hundred financially comfortable couples all longing to become adoptive parents to a healthy baby girl.

Stuart was a pediatrician and Jennifer was a violinist with the Seattle Symphony. They'd been married six years and were both thirty-seven, younger than many of the couples trying to adopt, which was part of the reason Anna had chosen them. They had flown to Denver and spent a weekend with Anna when she was seven months pregnant. Anna had gained the impression that they were very happily married, insofar as an outsider could ever tell. The fact that they were still married fourteen years later suggested that her long-ago judgment had probably been correct.

The experiences of that first year after leaving Alana Springs had given Anna a hard-core sympathy for people struggling on the fringes of society, and imbued her with a lasting desire to see that people were given a second chance to turn their lives around after making a mistake. Her own young adult life had been filled with people trying to help her, including Megan's adoptive parents.

As part of the adoption arrangement, the Fords paid

Anna's medical expenses. In addition, they handed over ten thousand dollars—the standard payment for all birth mothers using Derek Wu's legal services. The money was supposedly intended to make sure that Anna had sufficient funds to provide herself with decent housing and nutrition while waiting for her child to be born.

Over the years, the fact that she'd accepted a ten-thousand-dollar payment had haunted Anna. When she turned eighteen, and all support from the government stopped, she'd used the Fords' money to augment her meager paychecks and enroll in community college. Community college had led to an academic scholarship to university and a new self-supporting life. But in her darkest nightmares, Anna sometimes saw herself selling her unborn baby in exchange for her college tuition.

Officially, the adoption was classified as open, with none of the birth records sealed, and with Megan able to find out the name of her biological mother any time she cared to ask for it. But Derek Wu, who had seen too many cases of disrupted adoptions where the biological mother changed her mind after giving birth, recommended that Anna should not have personal contact with Megan until she became a legal adult. He drew up an iron-clad agreement that denied Anna any access to her child, although the contract did stipulate that Megan was to be informed that she was adopted by the time she was three, so that she would never have to face the shock of discovering that her parents hadn't actually given birth to her.

There were only two concessions granted to Anna: she insisted that her daughter was to be named Megan, in honor of her father's mother; and the contract with the Fords also stipulated that they must send Anna at least one studio portrait each year on her daughter's birthday.

Anna had agreed to the stringent, no-contact terms only because she suspected in her heart of hearts that they were better for Megan. Beyond that, she hadn't allowed herself to think about the child growing inside her. With her baby's parents chosen, Anna spent the final months of her pregnancy doing her best to pretend that she wasn't pregnant. It was the only way she knew how to survive without going crazy with grief.

Practicing denial with extreme determination, she stayed in school, attending classes up until the moment she went into labor. After the birth, she insisted on spending two hours alone with her baby, even though Jennifer and Stuart had already arrived from Seattle and were waiting anxiously to meet their new daughter. When the two hours were up, Anna put her baby into Jennifer Ford's waiting arms, and returned to her hospital room without once looking back.

The Fords probably thought she was callous. Anna knew the truth: she couldn't have looked back because it required every ounce of strength she possessed to place one foot in front of the other, while simultaneously preventing herself from screaming out the depths of her grief and desolation.

One of the few advantages of giving birth at seventeen was that the physical demands on Anna's body were a lot less than they would have been ten years down the road. She was back in school a week later and graduated fifth in her class, right on schedule at the end of May. She then spent the summer fighting a depression so deep that she would probably have killed herself if she could have found the energy to do anything that proactive.

It was a school counselor, a young woman called Leila Sworski, who went way beyond the call of duty and eventually nagged and persuaded Anna back into the land of the living. After Leila's intervention, deciding to work toward a master's degree in family counseling had seemed almost inevitable.

With fourteen years of experience under her belt, Anna had learned a few tricks about coping with the annual trauma of Megan's birthday. Hard physical labor was the only thing that succeeded in keeping her even halfway sane in the twenty-four hours after she received the annual photos from the Fords. This year she had rolls of wallpaper already bought and waiting for just this moment.

She spent the rest of Saturday stripping the existing burgundy-striped paper from her bathroom, and spent most of Sunday putting up the new stuff. She'd chosen a cheerful design of colorful butterflies splashed across a creamy background. The bathroom looked a lot better for the change but, more importantly, Anna arrived at work Monday morning with her sanity intact.

For a weekend that had brought her Megan's annual pictures, that had to be considered a triumph.

Ten

"Bye, Ms. Langtry. See you next week." Stan Swann gave Anna a cheerful wave as he strolled out of her office, hands in his pockets, homeboy swagger operating at maximum wattage. He was full of the joys of spring this afternoon, his spirits buoyed by the fact that his wife had not only brought their children back from Kansas City, but had also returned in a considerably chastened mood. LaToya had endured two days of such severe scolding from her mother that Stan was confident she would think long and hard before she ran off again with his kids. In what Anna considered a wild spurt of overoptimism, Stan even believed LaToya might stop spending money they didn't have. Peace and harmony reigned in the Swann household—at least until the next blowup.

Relieved that one crisis from last week seemed to have been resolved happily, Anna buzzed through to the reception area, where she feared another crisis loomed. "Hi, Gina. Any sign yet of Joseph Mackenzie?"

"No, he still hasn't shown."

"Any message from him that didn't get routed to my voice mail?"

"No, he hasn't called. Not to leave a message, anyway. I checked with Ruth to be double sure."

"Okay. Thanks, Gina."

"You're welcome. I'm about to close up shop for the night. I'll see you tomorrow. Enjoy your evening."

"Thanks. You, too." Anna disconnected the intercom, frowning into space. Where the hell was Mackenzie? She grabbed a handful of antacid tablets, then remembered she was trying to control her stress levels by more positive methods than popping sugared calcium. Reluctantly, she tossed the pills back into their plastic tub. She tipped her chair until it hit the wall behind her and stared at a photo of Klondike and Snow, the first polar bears successfully fostered by the Denver Zoo. The sight of those chubby baby bear bellies could usually be counted on to cheer her up but today, apparently, the magic wasn't working.

She was overreacting to Mackenzie's nonappearance, Anna told herself. There could be all sorts of reasons he hadn't reported in this afternoon as scheduled. He might want to avoid a drug test. He might be drunk. He might have overslept and forgotten it was Monday, ex-cons not being known for their ability to stick to a schedule.

There were, in fact, a hundred reasons Mackenzie might have missed his appointment with his parole officer, all of them a lot more likely than the possibility that he'd been murdered. In the past she wouldn't have questioned her gut instinct that Mackenzie was far too driven—although God knew by what—to get drunk or do drugs. But her catastrophic misjudgment of Raul's situation had left her leery of trusting something as patently unreliable as her instincts.

Still, bottom line, Mackenzie hadn't shown, she

needed to find out why and staring at Klondike and Snow wasn't doing the trick. Righting her chair, Anna called first Bob Gifford and then Ed Barber at the police department, only to be switched through to their voice mail boxes. What else? The way things were going recently it would have been way too easy to find one of them at his desk.

Presumably the detectives would have notified her if Mackenzie had been gunned down, or even if they'd uncovered conclusive evidence that the hit against him was still active. On the other hand, maybe the contract had been successfully executed and they hadn't had time to call her with the news that Mackenzie was dead. Maybe they were both out even now, supervising the removal of his dead body to the morgue.

Anna chugged a mouthful of antacids and bit down with a satisfying crunch. To hell with her pathetic resolutions for clean living. Right now, she needed a crutch and calcium carbonate seemed relatively harmless, considering the alternatives.

She'd pulled Mackenzie's file anticipating his arrival for a four-thirty appointment, and the folder was the only one left on her desk. Flipping through the accumulated papers inside, she found the sheet listing the name and phone number of his boss at the Westwood Hotel.

A phone call to the kitchen manager elicited the information that Mackenzie had turned up on time for his Saturday night shift, and that he'd worked through until quitting time on Sunday morning without incident. The kitchen manager even threw in an unsolicited compliment about Mackenzie's unfailing punctuality and willingness to work hard. Since he was scheduled off on Sunday night, nobody at his workplace was expecting to see him until midnight tonight.

Anna thanked the kitchen manager and hung up. At least she now knew Mackenzie had been alive on Sunday morning. So why the heck hadn't he turned up for his appointment with her?

It was a major pain that he didn't have a phone, she thought grumpily. Dammit, how was she supposed to find out if the stupid man was alive or dead? Maybe she could try calling his hotel, for all the good that was likely to do.

She dialed the Algonquin and got through to what was laughingly termed reception—in other words, a recovering alcoholic who sat behind a steel-mesh protective grille and made no effort to help anyone with their inquiries.

As she'd expected, the receptionist had no clue if Mackenzie was in his room, and even less interest.

"Could you go take a look?" Anna asked, with no hope that he'd agree. This guy gave new meaning to the words *crabby* and *uncooperative.* "I really need to find out where Mackenzie is."

"No, I can't go take a look. I'm not a friggin' messenger service. Besides, it's against management policy for me to leave the front desk unattended."

Anna had to concede that, given the hotel's clientele, that was probably a smart decision on the part of management.

Sighing, she hung up the phone, glancing at her watch. It was already past five-thirty, and she was running out of options. She could write Mackenzie up for failure to keep a scheduled appointment, which was tantamount to signing a revocation of his parole. Or she could pay a personal visit to the Algonquin and find out if there was a valid reason he'd blown off his appointment.

Like, for example, that he was dead.

A shiver of premonition snaked down Anna's spine. Spurred into a sudden need for urgent action, she locked her desk, holstered her Glock, grabbed her coat and purse, and ran all the way to the parking lot. Her facade of irritation could no longer hide her growing panic. Whatever crimes Mackenzie had committed in the past, whoever he'd pissed off while he was incarcerated, he didn't deserve to die.

She drove along Colfax, diverting occasionally to side streets when the rush hour traffic got especially bad. Arriving at the Algonquin, she parked between a beaten-up Chevy and a taxicab, offering up her standard prayer that a drunk wouldn't rear-end her while she was inside the hotel. Fueled by frustration, she strode at high speed across the parking lot, ignoring a hooker negotiating with a john and an old man scavenging for soda cans in the overflowing Dumpster.

Crossing the tiny lobby, she flashed her badge at Oscar the Grouch in reception. "I need a key for Joseph Mackenzie's room," she said.

He blew a cloud of smoke up toward the No Smoking sign, then stubbed out his cigarette. "You got a warrant?"

"No. And you know I don't need one. I'm his parole officer, and I'm making an unannounced inspection of Mackenzie's living premises."

He sniffed. "You know his room number?"

"I think it's 312. Check your records, though." She gave him an acid smile. "You don't want me to go bursting into the wrong room or you'll get sued."

"Gee, I sure wouldn't want that. I might lose my

high-paying job.'' He checked in a dirty ledger, then took a heavy brass key out of a pigeonhole. Electronics had not yet arrived at the Algonquin. ''Here. Enjoy yourself.'' He smirked. ''That Mackenzie's a good-looking dude. If you get real lucky, he might be naked when you open the door.''

She didn't deign to reply, and merely looked straight through him. ''Is the elevator working?'' she asked.

Oscar's reply was a grunt, but he reluctantly stirred himself long enough to walk across the lobby and use his master key on the elevator doors, which were kept locked on the ground floor level as a security measure. A totally ineffective security measure, based on Anna's past experience.

As she walked down the corridor to Mackenzie's room, her sense of urgency began to dissipate and her annoyance returned. It was six-fifteen and she was getting tired of making unpaid overtime trips to this fleabag hotel just so that Mackenzie could reward her with one of his icy stares. She pounded on the door with her fist.

''Mackenzie, are you in there? It's Anna Langtry, your parole officer.''

The door remained firmly closed, but somewhere among the cacophony of noises blasting into the corridor, Anna was almost sure she had heard the sound of movement from inside Mackenzie's room.

She banged the door again. ''Open up, Mackenzie.''

Silence.

''Look, I know you're in there.'' Well, it was a reasonable chance he was in there. ''You missed your appointment this afternoon, so I'm exercising my right to conduct an unscheduled search of your living premises. I have a key, and I'm coming in.''

She drew her weapon, then inserted the old-fashioned brass key in the lock and turned it. The door cracked open a couple of inches, then stopped, held by a chain.

Door bolted on the inside means the room must be occupied.

''Mackenzie, take the chain off the door.''

No reply, and the general level of noise in the corridor made it really difficult to decide if she could detect continuing sounds of movement inside the room. Using the full force of her weight, she pushed the door open with her foot. It flew open, the chain bursting from the brackets screwed into the decrepit door frame.

At first glance, the room appeared empty. There were no drapes, no closets for anyone to hide in, but she wasn't taking any chances. Arms extended, gun held steady, she yelled out for Mackenzie to put his hands on his head before she stepped over the threshold into his room.

A faint rustle of movement suggested he might be in the bathroom. Not letting down her guard for an instant, Anna moved farther into the room. She'd never gotten herself into a situation where she had to fire her weapon in self-defense, and she didn't plan to start now. Leaving the door to the corridor open, she took yet another small step into the room.

She swung around so that she was facing the bathroom. ''Mackenzie, get out here! And keep your hands where I can see them.''

The bathroom door opened and Mackenzie walked out. His eyebrow rose slightly when he noticed the gun and he raised his hands immediately, although his gesture was so halfhearted his hands didn't get much higher than his shoulders. His expression showed nothing except, perhaps, the merest trace of amusement, as if the sight of her pointing a gun at him was faintly comic.

In fact, if he was as good at unarmed combat as he'd claimed, the gun was likely more danger to her than protection. Anna backed up a couple of paces, out of reach of any swinging kicks from Mackenzie's feet.

He was wearing jeans and a faded navy-blue YMCA T-shirt. He looked a little pale, and his hair was wet, but otherwise he appeared to be his usual arrogant, sexy self. Anna's temper spiraled a notch higher when she realized that, despite everything, her stupid, ignorant body was having its usual exuberant reaction to the sight of him. What was it about this man that sent her brain flying out the window while all her hormones started dancing?

''Did you want to talk to me?'' he asked politely, as if he'd only just realized she was there. As if he hadn't ignored her pounding on his door for the past several minutes.

She knew he was baiting her, deliberately needling her so that she would lose her fragile hold on her temper and control of the situation would pass to him.

Tough luck, Mackenzie, she thought. I'm too good at my job to allow that to happen.

She kept her gaze locked with his and made no attempt to lower her weapon. ''Don't try to play stupid games, Mackenzie, I'm not in the mood. You heard me knock at the door. Why didn't you answer?''

"I was in the shower. I thought I should get dressed before I responded."

Her gaze narrowed. "You weren't in the shower. There's no steam—"

"I was taking a cold shower." His tone became more mocking. "There's nothing like icy water for sending a man's thoughts onto a higher plane."

She refused to react to his subtle sexual provocation. "What gives, Mackenzie? I thought you were too smart to screw up your parole the first week you were out of prison. Obviously, I was wrong. You missed your scheduled appointment with me this afternoon. Why?"

He looked away for a split second, but his answer came smoothly enough. "I ate something that disagreed with me. I had violent food poisoning and I couldn't get out of bed, not even to make a phone call. I'm very sorry, Ms. Langtry. I appreciate your stopping by to check on me."

He was definitely more than a little pale. Could his story be true? He didn't appear drunk or high, and his work record showed he could keep to a schedule so it wasn't likely that he'd simply forgotten it was Monday. And yet there was something much too watchful about his eyes....

"I don't believe a word of it," Anna said. "What's really going on, Mackenzie?"

"I've told you." He pressed his right arm across his stomach, the last shreds of color draining from his cheeks. "Excuse me. I have to go—" He turned abruptly and stepped toward the bathroom, his gait not quite steady.

Had she missed something? Was he drunk or high after all? Anna caught up with him and grabbed his arm, forgetting that she ought to be keeping her distance. "Wait up, Mackenzie—"

She got no further. He collapsed against the doorjamb, blood seeping through his T-shirt and staining his arm bright red. Horrified, she pushed up his shirt and saw the makeshift bandage he'd made with a thin towel strapped to his ribs. My God, how much blood had he lost?

She grabbed another towel and shoved it against his side. The sink was full of bloody water, she saw, and there were ominously blood-drenched clothes on the floor of the shower. "God almighty! What happened, Mackenzie?"

"I was shot."

She was shocked, even though she'd been pretty sure what he would say. So Raul's story about a contract on Mackenzie had been true. "I'm calling emergency services," she said.

Mackenzie reached out and grabbed her wrist. "Don't call 911...." he pleaded. "Anna, promise me...no police."

"You need medical attention—"

"No. I'm okay." His eyes closed, and his body slowly toppled sideways, slithering down the wall to the floor.

He left behind an ominous slash of bright red blood.

Eleven

When Joe came to there was a pillow under his head and Anna was already strapping a clean washcloth over the blood seeping from the bullet wound in his side. Despite the pillow, his head ached and his stomach churned with nausea that refused to go away. In fact, he hurt everywhere, inside and out. However, since he'd been hurting like hell every minute of the past three hours, that was no change.

As soon as she noticed he was awake, Anna touched her fingers to his cheek in a brief gesture of reassurance. "Don't worry, Mackenzie. Everything's going to be all right."

Sure it was. And the Tooth Fairy collected baby teeth to build a pearl palace for her playmates. Before he could gather his wits sufficiently to stop her, Anna pulled out her cell phone and started to dial.

Joe's wandering wits came to rapid attention. He spoke through lips that felt dry and puffy. "What are you doing?"

"Calling the paramedics."

"No." Galvanized by fear, Joe grabbed her wrist, his grip tight enough to immobilize her, even though it was agony to exert that much pressure.

Anna refused to surrender the phone, and he didn't have the strength to force her, but at least she stopped dialing long enough to rebuke him. "Take your hands off me, Mackenzie. We've had this conversation before. It's an offense to assault a parole officer."

"Then don't call emergency services."

She frowned. "Why not? Would you prefer me to drive you to the emergency room? I can, if that's what you want."

"No." He was touched by her concern, and by her willingness to help, even though he didn't want to be. "Thanks for the offer," he said gruffly. "But I'll be fine after a good night's sleep."

"Right, I can see why you would say that." The glance Anna directed toward him was heavy with exasperation. "You just passed out, you can't stand up, you've a bleeding hole in your side, but you don't need medical attention. Makes perfect sense to you, maybe, but not to me."

"I can stand up," Joe said, wondering how the hell he would make good on his boast. His brain felt too big and misshapen to fit inside his skull, a condition that did nothing to aid clear thinking. But if he could just get to his feet... If he could just persuade the floor to stop swooping like a damned roller coaster, then maybe Anna would go away and leave him to take care of what had to be taken care of.

Because he had no other choice, Joe pushed against the floor with his knuckles and dragged himself into a sitting position. Willing himself not to pass out for a second time, he managed to haul himself onto his feet. Victory! Although he didn't dare to move his back away from the wall.

He hoped like hell that Anna wouldn't notice the blood oozing out of his wound and soaking into the makeshift bandage that she'd strapped around his ribs.

''See?'' he said, as soon as he could catch his breath. ''I'm fine. Really. But thanks for your help, Ms. Langtry. I appreciate it.''

Anna glared at him. In a gesture that had already become endearingly familiar, she shoved impatiently at the cluster of curls that persisted in tumbling onto her forehead. ''You have a bullet wound in your side and you've obviously lost a ton of blood. You need to be stitched up and you need antibiotics, maybe even a transfusion. Why don't you want to see a doctor? What are you trying to do, Mackenzie? Kill yourself?''

''No,'' he said, finally managing to stand without the aid of the wall. He gave her a smile that held no amusement and no warmth, but at least he answered her honestly. ''I'm trying like hell to stay alive.''

''Great, then we have the same goal. We both want you alive.'' She walked away, out of his reach. ''Which is why I'm calling emergency services right now.''

He was desperate enough to remind her of the truth. ''Hospitals have to report bullet wounds to the cops,'' he said. ''If you call emergency services, I'm going to be back in prison by this time tomorrow.''

''Why?'' She looked baffled. ''You're the victim here, Mackenzie. Why would you assume anyone is going to lock you up?''

He tried not to feel too pathetically grateful for her automatic assumption that he wasn't to blame for his injury. ''How do you know I'm the victim?'' he asked, even though he knew it would have been much smarter to remain silent. ''I might have been robbing a convenience store for all you know and been shot at by the storekeeper in self-defense. You haven't asked me a single question about how I got this wound.''

''Then I'll ask now,'' Anna said quietly. ''How did you get shot, Mr. Mackenzie?''

He hesitated for just a moment. ''I was ambushed,'' he said, which was more or less the truth.

''That's exactly what I'd assumed. Did you see the person who shot you? Could you identify him?''

''No. I was taken by surprise.'' This was definitely not the moment to tell her what he *had* seen. Joe felt the room start to spin again and he reached for the iron headboard on the bed to steady himself. ''To you, the decision to go to the ER may seem simple, but not to me. The fact that I was ambushed and unarmed doesn't make it any safer for me to go to a hospital. I'm an ex-con. In a situation like this, the cops will arrest me first and ask questions afterward.''

Anna dismissed his words with an impatient shake of her head. ''Not when you have your parole officer standing right by your side, ready to back up your story. Besides, the most important thing right now is to get your wound treated. You're in urgent need of medical attention, and I intend to see that you get it. I'll come with you to the hospital, Mackenzie, and I'll stay with you until they've stitched you up. If the ER doctors don't admit you, I'll drive you home. The cops already know there's a contract out on you and if they forget, I'll remind them. There's no reason for you to worry about being sent back to jail.''

Her faith in her ability to control the system was touchingly naive and she still hadn't asked him a single probing question about what had happened, or what collateral damage might have occurred. He sure as hell wasn't going to risk telling her. What would she say if she knew there was a dead body lying in a parking garage in downtown Denver? The dead body of a man he knew well.

She was so damn trusting—so anxious to do right by him—that Joe really hated to screw her over. But he had no choice, of course. Her fate had been sealed the moment she broke into his room. Why the hell did she have to be so diligent? Why the hell had she come to check up on him? He figured nine out of ten parole officers would simply have written him up for a violation and left it at that. If only Anna had done the same.

Joe gave a sigh that he hoped sounded resigned and defeated, shuffling so that he was in the best possible position to kick the phone out of her hand as soon as she started to dial. He reckoned he should have just enough strength left to grab her around the neck and hold her immobile while he commandeered her gun.

"All right," he said, sounding weary and submissive. "Go ahead, if you think you need to call the paramedics. To be honest, I really don't feel too good." Which, God knew, was the unfortunate truth.

"You need your jacket, Mackenzie. Can you put it on without making the wound bleed any more?"

Anna took the jacket from its wire coat hanger before he could get there and actually helped him to slip it on, easing it carefully over his wound. Then she flashed him a reassuring smile, which would have made him feel like a complete worm if he hadn't already felt several inches lower than a snake's belly.

"Don't worry, Mackenzie. Officialdom isn't so bad when you have someone on your side to steer you through the channels." Anna pulled the sides of his jacket together, zipping them up. "I'll be with you every step of the way, I promise."

If only she knew how entirely accurate that statement was. Damn it to hell, Joe thought viciously. It was bad enough that he wanted to jump her bones every time he looked at her. It was a lot worse that he was actually starting to like her. Still, he had to do what he had to do. He couldn't afford to let his feelings for her get in the way.

Joe waited until she retrieved her cell phone and began to dial emergency services. With a precision that he didn't allow to be affected by the pain of his wound, much less his feelings for Anna, he swung his left leg in a perfectly disciplined circular kick that knocked the phone out of her hand.

Anna's face froze with astonishment. In the second or two of blankness when she was still trying to comprehend exactly what had happened, he lurched behind her, wrapping his left, uninjured arm across her throat, squeezing her windpipe to immobilize her, and reaching across her chest with his right arm to take possession of her gun.

He felt a spurt of agony, followed by the sensation of blood spurting, hot and wet, from his wound. It soaked into her jacket, which was navy blue. He allowed himself to think of nothing beyond the hope that the blood would be invisible to anyone who was observing them casually. Gritting his teeth against the rising nausea, he held onto consciousness by sheer, dogged willpower. If he blacked out now, it was all over.

Better act swiftly before she realized just how vulnerable he was. Joe took off the safety on the Glock, the click sounding loud and ominous in the relative quiet of the room. Good. As a person trained in weapons management, Anna would understand what that click signified. He hoped she was intimidated by his actions, because if she struggled, he sure as hell wasn't going to fire, not even to save his sorry ass.

He poked the butt of the gun into the small of her back, afraid that if he actually pointed the nozzle, he was woozy enough that it might go off. For a moment, the only sound in the room was her breathing, ragged and scared, interspersed with his breathing, which was equally ragged and probably twice as scared.

He found his voice, none too soon. "I'm sure I don't need to remind you that I'm a violent, dangerous man, Ms. Langtry. I've got nothing to lose at this point, so if you want to stay alive, you'd better act like the smart woman you are and do exactly what I tell you."

Joe admired the coolness with which she answered him. "I'm not smart enough, obviously, or you wouldn't be holding my gun. What do you want from me, Mackenzie?"

"I want you to drive me to a doctor."

"That's precisely what I was trying to do—"

"You were trying to take me to the hospital," Joe said. "That's not where I want to go. This doctor is a personal friend of mine."

"Oh, I see. Is he a friend from prison?"

"Yes." No point in explaining that Charlie Greck had been a medic in Vietnam and was really good at stitching up torn flesh. Even less point in explaining that Charlie suffered from post-traumatic stress disorder and the chances of him being sober at this time of day were somewhere between zero and none. On the plus side, Charlie would be as anxious to stay off the police radar as Joe, since he was currently avoiding prosecution by the skin of his teeth. With a great deal of luck, Joe thought that Charlie would maybe get enough stitches into him to stop the bleeding. With even more luck, Charlie might have some antibiotics stashed away to slather over the wound, or inject into Joe's butt. Either one would help ward off the infection that currently seemed almost inevitable.

A couple of interesting purple blobs danced in front of Joe's eyes. Definitely time to get moving, before the blobs took over.

''Here's what we're going to do,'' Joe said, giving Anna's throat an extra squeeze to reinforce his words. ''We're going to ride down together in the elevator, and we're going to stay real close so that nobody can see the gun. We'll make like we're lovers who can't get enough of each other—''

She gave a scornful splutter, sucking in air so that she could speak. ''Everyone here knows I'm a parole officer. Nobody will believe that I'm...attracted...to you.''

''Then hope that nobody sees us. Because if anybody tries to stop me leaving this place, a lot of people are going to die.'' Joe gave her back another sharp poke with the butt of the gun and draped his other arm around her shoulders. ''Walk, Anna. And please don't try to be brave. I really don't want to kill you.''

He wondered if he'd gone too far. How long before Anna noticed that his dialogue owed a great deal more to the script of a very bad movie than it did to anything real people were likely to say?

Either she was accustomed to parolees who ran amok and mistook themselves for heroes in a gangster movie, or she must have been too scared to analyze his words. Whichever it was, she turned meekly and walked toward the door.

"Open it," he said.

She complied. He kicked it shut behind them and they progressed along the empty corridor toward the elevator. "Push the down button," he ordered.

The elevator clanked down from the fourth floor and the doors sputtered open, revealing Larry, the creep who took the noon-to-eight shift on the front desk.

Christ, it's all over, Joe thought. The guy was a first-rate jerk, but one word from Anna and even this pathetic specimen of humanity would surely attempt to come to her rescue. Besides, Larry, of all people, must know that Anna was a parole officer, and unlikely to be willingly waiting for the elevator arm in arm with an ex-con.

Despairingly, Joe rubbed the gun against Anna's back, hoping she would interpret the gesture as either threat or warning. Might as well carry on the charade as long as he could. "Are you going to step inside the elevator, Ms. Langtry?" he asked. "We're keeping Larry away from his desk."

To his astonishment, Anna stepped into the elevator without protest. Larry looked at the pair of them with a rheumy-eyed leer, his gaze resting with lascivious interest on the nonexistent gap between their bodies. "You found Mackenzie in his room, then," he said to Anna.

"Yes." She looked at Larry. "I thought it was against management rules for you to leave the reception area?"

''It was an emergency,'' Larry replied, none too friendly.

Anna said nothing more. Joe couldn't see her face, but if anything, her body actually felt as if it curved marginally closer to his. As if she considered him protection against Larry rather than the other way around. And if that wasn't proof that he was starting to hallucinate, he didn't know what would be.

''Mackenzie didn't give you any trouble, then?'' Larry was examining them with unabashed curiosity.

''Everything's fine,'' Anna said curtly.

Joe felt weak-kneed with relief that she'd believed his threats. Relief was immediately replaced with guilt that he'd obviously managed to terrify Anna, who'd never done anything except try to help him. He wondered despairingly why his life was so complicated that he kept finding himself in situations where his response to kindness turned out to be intimidation and betrayal.

The elevator clanged and shuddered to a halt on the ground floor. Anna stepped out, Joe glued to her side. He felt Larry's gaze boring into the back of his neck and he could almost feel the waves of suspicion radiating toward him and Anna. But Fate, after dishing out a day of unrelieved catastrophe, finally decided to toss a small crust of good fortune in Joe's direction. Two half-drunk residents chose this precise moment to punch each other out, providing just enough of a diversion for him to propel Anna down the dirty front steps without any further attention from Larry. He even managed to put the safety back into the locked position under cover of all the noise produced by the combatants. Now he didn't have to worry that Anna might attempt to free herself with some brave, cockeyed maneuver that would cause the gun to fire accidentally.

He scanned the badly lit parking lot and spotted her Subaru parked next to a battered Chevy. The parking spaces on either side were empty and there wasn't another soul anywhere on the small lot. Having fucked him totally this afternoon, Fate was apparently having some fun by pretending to be on his side for a while.

''Get your car keys out of your purse,'' he said to Anna as they approached her Subaru. He tried to sound both confident and brutal. Sheer bluff in both instances, since he knew this was the moment when it would be easiest for her to make good her escape. She might well be carrying a second gun inside her purse, in which case he'd just given her the chance she would have been waiting for to retrieve it. Even if she didn't have another gun, she could pull a trick like dropping her keys. It would be the easiest thing in the world for her to smash her head into his wounded side when she bent down to pick them up.

The way his wound was throbbing right now, Joe thought he might prefer Anna to shoot him and be done with it.

He must have been a hell of a lot more convincing in the role of murderous kidnapper than he would have guessed because, after only a few seconds of hesitation, Anna pulled a set of car keys from her purse. ''Here you are.''

He tried not to let his relief or his surprise show in his voice. ''Open the door on the driver's side and then give the car keys to me.''

Anna did as he instructed, handing the keys to him in silence. ''Get in the car,'' he said.

"Which side? Am I driving? Is that the plan?"

"Yes."

Joe waited for Anna to settle into the driver's seat before walking around and opening the door on the passenger side. Once he was inside the car, he handed her the keys with a curt instruction to drive south for a couple of blocks. He noticed that her fingers were ice-cold when she took the keys from him and her hand shook visibly as she turned on the ignition.

Joe hated that he was scaring her, but he couldn't for the life of him think what else he could do, given the circumstances. Before Anna turned up at the hotel, he'd been planning to call a taxi to take him to Charlie's house, which was only fifteen minutes away in the Capitol Hill section of town. He could still hail a cab, except he couldn't risk setting Anna free. She would call the police the second she was free, and minutes later he'd have the police crawling all over his ass.

What to do with Anna was, in fact, a major problem. Medium term as well as short. As soon as he was stitched up, he needed to get the hell out of Denver. Before the police discovered the body and tried to pin a murder rap on him. Could he leave her at Charlie's, with instructions to set her free tomorrow morning? The trouble was, he would have to tie her up, or she'd overpower Charlie for sure. And once she was tied up, could he rely on Charlie to remember to set her free? If Charlie went on a bender, Anna could be left roped to a chair for two or three days. Joe couldn't quite bring himself to subject her to that humiliation.

He saw that they'd arrived at Twelfth and he told her to turn right, heading toward Capitol Hill. Charlie lived in an old bungalow, wedged between two slightly run-down high-rise apartment buildings a couple of blocks from the community center. Fortunately, it was a neighborhood of transients, where people paid little attention to strangers. It was unlikely anyone would see them going into Charlie's house, much less pay enough attention to worry about who they were.

They'd just crossed over Clark—almost at their destination—when Joe realized that he was in seriously deep shit. His vision was blurring and the passing streetlights began to fade into a hazy streak. He closed his eyes to fight back a wave of nausea intense enough to leave him clammy with sweat.

If he could just get to Charlie's house, he could let go, surrender to the darkness that was fighting so hard to take him. God knew, the idea of letting go sounded pretty damn wonderful right now.

"Turn right onto Eastman," he said to Anna, experiencing real difficulty in getting his tongue to wrap around the complicated words. "Charlie's house is on the left. Number 1223. You can park in the driveway."

Joe closed his eyes because he couldn't keep them open. Awareness of his surroundings began to slip away and he knew that Fate had finished playing with him. She was about to spring the trap that she'd set this afternoon when—foolish to the bitter end—he'd gone to meet Franklin Saunders.

When Joe opened his eyes again, he realized that he'd blacked out for at least a few seconds. With surprising regret, he absorbed the knowledge that he'd terrorized Anna for no real purpose because he wasn't going to be able to keep hold of consciousness. Not even for the two minutes longer it would take to get into Charlie's house.

''Sorry,'' he mumbled, as the waves of rippling darkness swum nauseatingly before his eyes. ''I didn't mean to frighten you. Wouldn't...hurt... you....''

''Mackenzie, don't you dare pass out on me.'' Anna's voice penetrated the mist that was gradually creeping over him. ''You stay awake, you hear me? If you pass out, I'll drive straight to Denver General, and then the cops will have you locked up in the prison ward before you can say *not guilty.*''

A streetlight blazed, burning against his eyeballs, but Anna's voice had an odd effect on him, giving him new courage. Joe forced himself to clamber back up to consciousness, an act that required every drop of his energy and a hundred percent of his willpower. ''I feel...sick.''

''Okay, I'm sorry to hear that. But don't puke in my car, or I'll drive you to the nearest jail and lock you up myself.'' Anna slowed the car, braking to a halt. ''This is number 1223,'' she said. ''We're here.''

''Park in the driveway.'' Joe thought he might have said that before. He recognized that his command sounded about as threatening as Piglet trying to frighten the Heffalump and he wondered in some distant corner of his mind why in the world Anna had driven him here instead of to the nearest police station. Did she really believe that he'd shoot her in cold blood if she didn't obey his instructions? Couldn't she see that he was in no shape to hurt her, even if he wanted to?

As she put the gear into park, he managed to adjust

his grip on the gun and point it at Anna. ‘‘Get out of the car.’’ It was more croak than threat.

The haze in front of his eyes had thickened to the point that it seriously obscured his vision, so Joe felt the challenge in Anna’s gaze, rather than seeing it. ‘‘Why should I get out of the car?’’ she asked.

He closed his eyes to get rid of the haze. ‘‘Because I’ll shoot you if you don’t.’’

‘‘With the safety on?’’ Anna asked, her voice dry. ‘‘I don’t believe so.’’

Something about this endgame wasn’t going as it should. Joe felt a hiccup of laughter form deep inside. So what the hell else was new in his life?

The door at his side opened, letting in a gust of cold night air. He realized Anna was holding it open. ‘‘Get out of the car, Mackenzie. You’re too heavy for me to carry.’’

Obediently, he staggered to his feet, aware that a role reversal had taken place but not sure what he could do about it, much less what it meant. Anna’s arm went around his waist. He was humiliatingly aware that without her support he would never have made it out of the car, much less up the weed-strewn driveway.

It was Anna who knocked on Charlie’s battered blue door and then kept her finger on the bell until they heard the sounds of feet shuffling toward them.

Charlie opened the door a mere crack and peered at them around the corner. His wrinkled black face was set into a ferocious scowl, and the smell of Jim Beam preceded him. He grunted to acknowledge that he’d recognized Joe. ‘‘You look like shit. What do you want?’’

‘‘I need your help, Charlie.’’

"You always do. Who've you been fuckin' with this time?" Charlie opened the door wide enough for Joe to see that he was fully dressed, wearing a white shirt, with a knotted tie hanging loosely around his neck.

A promising sign, Joe thought. Charlie had apparently been to work today. Maybe they'd arrived in time to catch him before he settled down to the night's serious drinking. There was hope yet that he might get this wound stitched up before he made himself dangerously ill.

It was his last conscious thought.

Twelve

She had to be crazy, Anna thought, pacing up and down Charlie's dank basement rec room, where Joseph Mackenzie was stretched out on a billiard table that had been covered by a tattered comforter. She wasn't talking mildly nuts, but certifiably insane. Why had she brought Mackenzie here instead of taking him to Denver General, as both regulations and common sense required? What in the name of God had come over her?

Not sure whether it was more nerve-racking to watch Charlie hunched over the billiard table, or to look the other way, Anna felt as if she'd just stepped onto the movie set for the opening scene of Mel Gibson's *Payback.* Except that Mackenzie looked in much worse shape than Mel ever had.

''You mind parkin' your butt on the sofa?'' Charlie said, not looking up from his swabbing and stitching. ''You're makin' me real nervous.''

She sat down on the edge of the torn Naugahyde sofa, narrowly avoiding spearing herself on a projecting spring. ''What's taking so long?'' she asked.

''Wound's deep.'' Charlie was proving to be a man of few words. He was wearing latex gloves, which she supposed was a promising sign of desire for surgical sterility, but he kept wiping sweat from his forehead with a rag that looked as if it might last have seen the inside of a washing machine some time in the year 2000. Anna occupied a few tense minutes wondering how many germs, bugs and assorted viruses had by now floated, hopped or swum off the rag and into Mackenzie's wound. She hoped sincerely that Charlie was planning to give his patient a massive dose of antibiotics before this procedure was over.

Silence reigned for another ten minutes, the seconds marked off by the rapid beat of Anna's heart. If Mackenzie died, how was she going to live with her conscience? If Mackenzie lived, what in the world was she going to do next? Whether he lived or died, it seemed logical to conclude that her career as a parole officer was pretty much in the toilet, so she might as well concentrate on hoping he survived. At least that way one of them would be happy at the outcome of tonight's insane escapade.

''All done,'' Charlie said at last, stripping off his gloves and tossing them onto the billiard table next to Mackenzie's inert body. ''He's the same lucky bastard he always was. Bullet managed to miss everything vital and passed straight through him.''

In Anna's book, lucky meant not getting shot in the first place, rather than managing to dodge the bullet. Still, she wasn't about to quibble. Charlie didn't look like a man who tolerated dissent. ''Does that mean he's going to be all right?'' she asked.

''He's not goin' to die of his wounds, if that's what you mean. Blood loss was severe, but not life-threatening.'' Charlie snatched up the glass of Jim Beam he'd stored in one of the pockets of the billiard table and swallowed thirstily.

"Doesn't he need a shot of antibiotics to prevent infection?" Anna asked, walking up close to the billiard table and leaning over to get a better look at Mackenzie. She wished he could have a blood transfusion, or even an IV to replace the fluid and electrolytes he'd lost, but she had to admit that his color appeared pretty good, all things considered, and his breathing was a little rapid, but probably not enough to worry about.

She touched the back of her hand to Mackenzie's cheek, which felt warm, but not burning up with fever. The stubble of his beard scratched faintly against her knuckles, and she let her fingers drift gently up the side of his face, until they were nestled in his thick brown hair.

Her stomach clenched with a sensation she chose not to identify, and she laid the tips of her fingers against Mackenzie's cracked lips, letting his breath warm her. Until this moment, she hadn't registered that although Charlie had been sweating while he performed his surgery, she herself had been ice-cold with fright. But why wouldn't she be nervous? If Mackenzie had died on the operating table, heaven knew what criminal charges she would have laid herself open to.

Five minutes passed before she realized just how long she'd been standing mooning over Mackenzie's unconscious body. Anna snatched her hand away and turned quickly to see if Charlie had been watching her. He hadn't, thank goodness. Charlie was, in fact, demonstrating no interest whatsoever in her, or in anything except his bourbon, which he was sipping with loving appreciation.

"Do you have any antibiotics you could give Mackenzie?" she asked again. "Otherwise he's going to survive the bullet wound and die of secondary infections.''

Charlie glowered at her over the rim of his glass, his huge brown eyes already threaded with red. ''Quit worryin', girl. I gave him a shot already. There was a heavy-duty antibiotic in the first injection I shoved into his ass.'' He swirled his bourbon, breathing in the scent. ''Joe's got a hide like a friggin' rhino. I damn near broke the needle getting it into him.''

''I thought that shot you gave was anesthetic.'' With the amount of alcohol Charlie was knocking back, Anna decided she was justified in nagging.

''It was both.'' Charlie grunted. ''Learned how to do that in 'Nam. If you didn't give the poor bastards painkiller, they died of shock. If you didn't give them antibiotics, they died of infection. Most times, whatever you did, they died anyway.'' He upended his glass, took another healthy swig, and stared broodingly into a past full of images Anna was glad she didn't share.

''You want a drink?'' Charlie asked finally, hauling himself from his armchair and picking up the quart of Jim Beam that stood in a position of honor on top of the TV.

Anna wanted a drink badly enough that she was almost ready to risk using one of Charlie's glasses. Almost. ''No thanks,'' she said, fortifying her resolve with a glance at the filthy towel lying at Mackenzie's feet.

''Suit yourself.'' Charlie refilled his glass and returned to his chair, looking pleased when he patted around the cushion and found the TV remote. He clicked the set on, his bare-bones notions of hospitality apparently satisfied.

"Shouldn't we move Mackenzie somewhere more comfortable?" Anna asked. "That billiard table must feel very hard on his back."

"Joe's not feelin' anything right now. Besides, he's dead weight until he comes around. Without a stretcher, we'd bust our guts for sure and split open his wound into the bargain. We'll move him when he wakes up."

"When might that be, do you think?"

"Not long. Now what you gotta do is wait. That's the trouble with you young people today. You ain't got a lick of patience. Look at you, girl, you're typical. Damn near bustin' out of your skin because you have to wait a few minutes for Joe to wake up. Be patient." Having delivered his homily, Charlie turned to the TV and flicked through channels until he settled back with a satisfied murmur to watch *The Sopranos.*

Hanging around with nothing to do except watch Charlie drink while waiting for Mackenzie to regain consciousness struck Anna as a really bad idea. Hanging around gave her far too much time to wonder when and why madness had overtaken her. And if considering the sad demise of her sanity seemed too unproductive, she could always switch gears and start worrying about such related issues as whether she was merely going to get fired over tonight's happenings, or whether she was likely to find herself facing criminal prosecution for aiding and abetting a fleeing felon.

Could you be prosecuted for cooperating in your own kidnapping, Anna wondered? You wouldn't face charges if you believed your life was in danger, of course, but she hadn't believed any such thing. At least not for more than a couple of shocked minutes after Mackenzie grabbed her gun. There was a cracked mirror opposite the elevators at the Algonquin, and she'd seen that although he'd made such a big show of clicking off the safety, it was the butt of the gun he had shoved into her back, not the barrel. If the gun had gone off in a struggle, it was Mackenzie who would have taken the bullet, not her.

Still, nobody could *prove* she had cooperated in her own abduction. True, there was the unfortunate fact that she'd gotten into the elevator without attempting to enlist the aid of Oscar the Grouch. But anyone who knew Oscar would agree he was an unreliable ally, so she could always lie and claim she'd been too terrified to fight back.

Except that if she made a convincing case that she believed Mackenzie intended to shoot her, then she was automatically condemning him to spend a very long time in prison. Well, so what? He probably deserved to spend the next several years in jail.

The $64,000 question was why she, a law-abiding citizen and officer of the court, didn't want that to happen. Mackenzie was a convicted embezzler, who'd kidnapped her at gunpoint. The fact that he was desperate, and the fact that he—maybe—hadn't planned to kill her, provided no justification for what he had done, and even less for her own actions.

"You got a problem with sittin'?" Charlie asked. "You're squirmin' around on that seat like you got piles or somethin'."

"No. No, I haven't—"

"Then park your butt, for Chrissake. It's annoyin' watchin' you slide up an' down like that. Gives a man a real bad headache."

''Okay, I'll try to sit still, but I'm worried about Mackenzie.''

''Ain't no reason. Told you that already. Man's got the constitution of an ox.''

Slightly reassured, Anna settled back on the sofa, managing to avoid the potentially lethal spring, as well as a couple of areas of leaking stuffing. Two minutes was enough to convince her that following Charlie's example and watching television was impossible. She was about ready to explode with nervous tension.

Gripping the arm of the sofa to keep herself rooted, she considered simply getting up and driving away, leaving Mackenzie to Charlie's not-so-tender care. Unfortunately, Charlie was already pouring his third full glass of bourbon, and she couldn't square it with her conscience to leave Mackenzie with a man who was likely to pass out in an alcoholic stupor before the night was too much older. Not when she suspected that lack of proper nursing care could be life-threatening.

''When Mackenzie wakes up, do you think he'll be able to sit in a car long enough for me to drive him home?'' she asked Charlie.

''Sure, why not? How many ways you need me to tell you he's goin' to be okay?'' With an exaggerated sigh, Charlie muted the sound on his TV program. ''I can see you're not goin' to let me watch my favorite show. So what did you say your name was?''

''I'm Anna Langtry.''

''Anna Langtry,'' Charlie muttered, resting his glass on his belly. ''That don't sound familiar. You Joe's fiancée? The woman that never came to visit him in prison?''

"No, I'm not his fiancée," Anna said. "I'm Mr. Mackenzie's parole officer."

For a split second, Charlie stared at her bug-eyed. Then he gave a short crack of laughter, grabbing his glass when his belly shook. "Real pleased to meet you, Ms. Parole Officer. And I'm the Surgeon General of the United States. I just live in this cozy little dump here because I don't want to waste taxpayers' dollars buyin' me a fancy house in Washington, D.C."

Belatedly—when she was around Joseph Mackenzie, her brain function always seemed to kick in a little late—Anna realized that claiming to be a parole officer was probably not the smartest thing she could have done, given the situation she found herself in. Charlie had treated Joe, no questions asked, which meant that he was loyal to his friends. Still, he wasn't likely to have any excess fondness for law enforcement officials. On the contrary, he looked as if he were capable of disposing of annoying, interfering parole officers in the nearest Dumpster.

"It's an honor to meet you, Mr. Surgeon General," Anna said, deciding there was absolutely nothing to be gained by trying to convince Charlie of the unlikely truth.

"Yeah, likewise, I'm sure. So have you and Joe got a thing goin'? You his new lady?"

"No, nothing like that!" Anna realized her protest was much too vehement. "Actually, I'm just a friend of...Joe's."

"Is that so?" Charlie turned bloodshot eyes in her direction. "Didn't know Joe had any friends, outside of what he made in prison. Not friends worth countin', anyway. He never got a visitor in all the time I was in the joint, and I only got out two months ago.''

Mackenzie hadn't had a single visitor in four years? This time Anna experienced no difficulty in interpreting the emotions that knotted her stomach. They included an aching sympathy she was quite sure Mackenzie would reject, and a burst of anger that was no less fierce for being illogical.

''I didn't know Joe was doing time until he got out on parole and looked me up,'' Anna said with perfect truth. ''Maybe his other friends were in the same situation.''

Charlie shrugged, his attention turning back to his drink. ''Don't know much about Joe's background. He wasn't one to discuss his problems. That's why we got along real well. Can't abide listening to people whine.''

''The truth is, although Joe doesn't like to talk about his problems, right now he badly needs help from his friends.'' Anna leaned forward. ''He's in a load of trouble—''

Charlie rolled his eyes. ''You don't say? Guess I figured out that everything wasn't peachy keen when I was stitchin' him back together just now. The bullet hole in his side was my first clue. Me bein' a real smart dude, an' all.''

''Doesn't it worry you that somebody's trying to kill him?''

''That ain't exactly headline news. Folks been tryin' to kill Joe Mackenzie ever since I first met him.''

''But that was in prison,'' Anna said. ''Now he's on the outside, the attacks on him should have stopped.''

"Maybe. Maybe not." Even three full glasses of bourbon didn't seem to be enough to shake Charlie's tongue into providing useful information.

Anna gave up on trying to make her curiosity seem reasonable to Charlie. For that matter, she couldn't make it seem entirely reasonable even to herself. "Do you have any idea who might be trying to kill Joe?" she asked. "If we can't find out who's angry enough to plot his murder, there's no way we can hope to protect him from the danger. You were in prison with him. Who were his enemies?"

"Buncha loudmouthed racists. Mostly, Joe kept his head down, didn't talk much, avoided trouble every way he could. He didn't get real close to anyone as far as I could see."

"But he made friends with you, and with Raul Estevan."

"Yeah, well, a man's gotta have some friends inside if he's gonna survive. Even Joe."

"What do you mean—*even Joe?*"

"If you're a friend of Joe's, you must know he can protect himself better'n most. Mentally and physically."

"Because of his martial arts training?"

"Yeah. When Joe first arrived in prison, middle-class guy, sent up for a white-collar crime, he looked like a real easy mark. The bullies soon found out he was anything but. He got cut up a few times by guys who were packin' knives, but after the first three or four months, he never lost a fight."

"If he always won, why did people keep coming after him?"

Charlie shot her a look that was half amused, half pitying. "Folks inside jail aren't what you might call the best and the brightest. There were plenty of prisoners who picked fights with Joe just to prove they had balls of steel. 'Course, mostly they just proved they had brains of puffed cotton. But still, Joe got real tired of fightin'...."

No wonder Mackenzie had looked so menacing and so wary that first day in her office, Anna thought. He'd just spent four years fighting for his life. Literally. "Did you and Joe ever talk about the crimes you'd committed...er...the reasons why you were incarcerated?" she asked.

"Some. Not much." Charlie sounded bored. He was slouched deep in his chair, and the fourth glass of bourbon he was working on finally seemed to be taking its toll.

"Did Joe ever suggest to you that he was innocent?" Anna asked. She wondered if Joe had stuck to the same stubborn claim of innocence with his fellow inmates, the ones he considered friends, as he had with the parole board.

Charlie yawned, poking his fingers through the buttons on his shirt to scratch. "Yeah, I guess he did."

"Did you believe him?"

"Everybody's innocent in prison," Charlie said, his voice rich with self-mockery. "The cops set us up, and if they aren't to blame, then our lawyers screwed us over."

"Which one did Joe Mackenzie claim? That the cops set him up, or that his lawyers screwed him?"

"Both." Charlie sat up straighter, energized by the memory of Joe's stupidity. "Crazy bastard went to his first parole hearing and told the interviewing officer he was innocent. Came back shell-shocked when he had his appearance before the full board and they told him he was going to have to serve the full six-year term unless he learned to accept responsibility for the crimes he'd committed.''

''Looking back, taking into account everything you know about Joe, doesn't it seem to you that maybe he really was innocent?'' Anna could hardly believe what she heard herself saying.

''I got too much sense to waste good thinkin' time wonderin' which of my cell mates is innocent and which ones are guilty. Besides, *innocent* and *guilty* are words that don't mean as much to me as they do to some folks.''

''Doesn't it strike you as odd that somebody as smart as Joe made such an elementary mistake with the parole board? I mean, anyone who's ever watched a lawyer show on TV knows that you have to admit you're guilty and tell the board how sorry you are.''

''What are you tryin' to say, girl? Spit it out.''

''Well, I was wondering...I wondered if maybe Joe was so angry about being unjustly convicted that he couldn't bring himself to admit guilt, not even to the parole board.''

''Then he wasn't smart. He was a fool.'' Bitterness entered Charlie's voice for the first time. ''Folks on the parole board don't care about guilt or innocence. They want to see you lick ass. So, unless you plan to serve out your full sentence, you grovel. You tell them you're real sorry, that you're a changed man, that you'll never do it again. If you don't want to tell 'em that Jesus saved you, then you sure as hell better tell 'em that you've been to group therapy and you've learned how to cope with whatever problem the prison authorities wrote up in your files as the cause of your—quote—antisocial behavior.''

"What do the authorities claim is the cause of your antisocial behavior, Charlie?" Sometimes, Anna realized, she couldn't stop her training in family counseling from taking over the conversation, even when she'd do much better to keep her mouth shut.

"They claim I'm an alcoholic." He shrugged. "What else?"

"Do you agree that alcohol is a problem for you, Charlie?"

"Hell, no. Alcohol's my solution. The jungles in Vietnam and what I saw there, that's my problem."

Before Anna could reply, or ask another question, Joe gave a faint groan. Anna shot off the sofa, followed with unexpected swiftness by Charlie, who returned his glass to the billiard table pocket, wrapping his none-too-steady hand around Joe's wrist and taking his pulse.

"Humph," Charlie said, squinting at his wristwatch. "Looks like you're gonna live."

"You could have fooled me," Joe said, his voice thready. "From where I'm lying, it feels like I'm already dead."

"Nah. I guess the devil was too busy stokin' his barbecue to open the gates and let you in. You'll soon be on your feet again. Hell, with my excellent surgery, you'll be fightin' fit by tomorrow mornin'."

"I'm grateful, Charlie. You saved my life."

"Yeah, that's what they all say. What I want to know is when you goin' to learn to keep your sorry ass out of the line of fire."

"From now on. I promise."

"Hah! Wish I had a dollar for every time I've heard that." Charlie gave Joe's hand a surprisingly gentle squeeze. "Your lady's been drivin' me crazy.

She wants to take you home. I don't think she approves of my housekeepin'. You think you can sit up?''

''My lady?'' Mackenzie rolled his head to the other side of the table and his gaze encountered Anna. They stared at each other in silence for what seemed a very long time.

Anna cleared her throat. ''Charlie managed to remove the bullet without much difficulty, although you needed quite a few stitches. I'm glad to hear it didn't hit any vital organs.''

''Me, too.'' Joe kept his gaze locked with hers, not trying to hide his puzzlement. ''Why didn't you take me to Denver General when I passed out?'' he asked finally.

Because he'd begged her not to. Because she was afraid that he'd end up in prison if she did. Anna wasn't ready to give him either of those answers. She sneaked a glance at Charlie, who'd wandered back to the TV and was demonstrating his customary lack of interest in anything beyond his bourbon.

''I brought you here because you had a gun pointed at my back and this is where you ordered me to drive you,'' she said. An answer that wasn't exactly a lie, but wasn't the truth, either.

''Not true. I passed out. You could have taken the gun.''

''By the time you passed out, we were already here,'' Anna said. ''I was afraid you might die of blood loss if we drove all the way back to Denver General.''

Even woozy from the after-effects of the anesthetic, Joe clearly managed to figure out that her responses raised as many questions as they answered. For a man who'd just had a six-inch wound in his side sewn back together, he held her gaze with disconcerting intensity. "What are you planning to do now I'm awake?" he asked.

"Take you home to my condo. At least for tonight." Anna hadn't been sure she was going to commit this final act of utter folly until she actually spoke.

Joe's eyes widened in astonishment. For a second, hope blazed across his face, but he quickly controlled that momentary betrayal of vulnerability, and his expression returned to careful blankness.

"Thanks," he said stiffly. "I appreciate your offer, but it would be better for everyone if I stayed here."

"Maybe not," Charlie said, alarming Anna with the indication that perhaps he was listening to their conversation after all. "I got business to conduct tonight, Joe. This isn't a good place for you to be."

Anna pretended she hadn't heard that. It was much too easy to guess what sort of business needed the attention of an alcoholic ex-con in the middle of the night. "Don't worry, Charlie, we're leaving right now. Do you have a jacket you could lend Joe?"

Charlie muttered something affirmative. He went upstairs, his gait less than steady, and returned not only carrying a sweatshirt and a fleeced cotton jacket with a zippered front closure, but also a bottle of water and some paper cups.

"Here, have a sip." He poured water into one of the cups, handing the other to Anna. "You look like you could use a drink yourself."

"Thanks." Anna hadn't realized just how thirsty she was until she drank the water. The fact that Charlie brought the paper cups suggested to her that he was alarmingly more observant than she'd supposed and realized she didn't want to use his glasses. If the cops ever questioned him about tonight's activities, she could kiss goodbye the notion of claiming that she'd come here under extreme duress.

Charlie allowed Joe to take only a few small sips before he took away the water. "Don't want you throwing up." He held out the shirt. "This will be easy to put on, Joe. I'm goin' to burn your jacket and T-shirt, okay?"

"Yes. Good idea. Thanks."

Charlie buttoned the shirt carefully over the pad of bandages, then put on the jacket and fastened the zipper. Joe turned white as he swung his feet onto the ground, but after leaning against the side of the billiard table to get his bearings, his color came back and he was able to walk to the basement stairs with only minimal help.

The stairs themselves took longer to negotiate, but once on the ground floor, Joe drew in a deep breath that sounded fairly steady. "Thanks again for everything, Charlie. If I hadn't been able to come here, I don't know what I'd have done tonight."

"Yeah, well I got better things to do with my time than sew you up. Next time you see a bullet comin' at you, jump out of the way, okay?"

"You can count on it."

"Or better yet, find out who's aiming bullets at you and tell the police so the culprits can be arrested," Anna said.

Joe stared at her as if the lamppost had spoken, while Charlie smacked his forehead with the heel of his hand. "Jeez, what a dumbass I am. How come I never thought of that?"

"I can't imagine," Joe said. "Do you think it's

because the cops always seem to arrest us ex-cons first and listen to what we're saying afterwards?''

''Couldn't be that,'' Charlie said. ''The police never go after ex-cons just for the hell of it. Not those fine upstandin' guardians of the law.''

''You can quit with the comedy routine,'' Anna said. ''It isn't funny.''

''You're so right,'' Joe said. ''Especially if you're one of the ex-cons in question.''

''Can you walk to the car, or do you need my help?'' she asked, deciding a change of subject was definitely called for.

''I can walk.''

Charlie didn't come out of the house with them. He handed Anna a vial of pills. ''Antibiotics,'' he mumbled. ''Only five days' supply, but it's better than nothing.''

''Thanks, Charlie. For everything.''

He grunted, then stood in the doorway long enough to see Joe settled into the passenger seat before turning inside without waiting to see them drive away. His ''business'' or his bourbon were apparently calling, probably both.

When Anna leaned forward to turn on the ignition, Joe put his hand out to stop her. ''I don't know whether to thank you for what you've done tonight, or tell you that you're crazy,'' he said.

''I already know I'm crazy so don't waste your breath.''

''Then—thank you. But I can't come home with you, Anna. There are limits to how many risks I can let you take on my behalf, and we crossed over those the moment you followed me into Charlie's house.''

"So where do you plan to go if not home with me?"

"Back to the hotel." Joe's hesitation was slight, but she noticed it.

"You're not fit—"

"I will be soon. Charlie was right. All I need is a good night's sleep and I'll be fine. Don't get any more involved than you have to, Anna. Trust me, you're already way out of your depth."

He was lying about going back to the hotel, Anna was almost sure of it. Why did Joe want to ditch her? Because of a desire to protect her, or because he was up to no good? What exactly had happened tonight that caused Joe to end up with a bullet in his side? She'd assumed all along that he'd somehow managed to evade an assassin's bullet. There were, unfortunately, lots of other ways that an ex-con might have acquired a bullet wound in his side.

Her cell phone rang before she could decide whether to question Joe before or after she got him home. She answered the phone simply because it gave her an excuse to delay making a decision. "This is Anna Langtry."

"Detective Bob Gifford here, Anna. It's good to hear your voice. Sorry to bother you at this hour of night, but I wanted to be sure you were all right."

"Yes, I'm fine, thanks, Bob." Anna suppressed a quiver of foreboding. "Why wouldn't I be?"

"Larry Hochstein, the desk clerk at the Algonquin, reported that he'd seen you with Joseph Mackenzie tonight. You and Mackenzie got into the elevator together. Larry thought you might have been under duress."

Anna turned so that she was looking out of the car

window into the darkness of the street. Somehow it was easier to lie when she wasn't looking right at Joe. "Under duress? Oh, no. Not at all. How did Larry come up with that idea, I wonder?"

Bob Gifford didn't speculate. Anna had noticed many times before that real cops, as opposed to the TV variety, avoided theorizing. "But Larry is correct in stating you were at the Algonquin tonight, right?" the detective persisted.

"Yes, absolutely."

"And you saw Joseph Mackenzie while you were there?"

"Yes, I did." Anna had no idea what Bob Gifford was leading up to but she had a suspicion that, whatever it was, she wasn't going to like it. "Mackenzie has a room at the Algonquin, and I went to check on him." About to mention that Joe hadn't turned up for a scheduled parole appointment earlier in the afternoon, she realized she'd be a lot smarter to keep her answers short. In view of the number of crimes and misdemeanors she'd committed during the past few hours, there was no point in providing Gifford with a single scrap of information he hadn't asked for.

How quickly she was beginning not only to act like a criminal, but to think like one, too, Anna reflected ruefully.

"Larry Hochstein states that you got into the elevator with Joseph Mackenzie at 6:35 p.m. this evening," Gifford said. "Is that correct?"

Anna had a gloomy suspicion that she was wading deeper and deeper into trouble with every reply she gave. "I couldn't swear to the exact time," she said. "But six-thirty or so sounds in the ballpark. And, yes,

Larry is right about Mackenzie taking the elevator to the ground floor at the same time as I did.''

``Did you actually go inside Mackenzie's room at the Algonquin?''

How the hell should she answer that? ``Well, yes. I just stepped inside.''

``You didn't observe anything unusual about the room?'' Gifford persisted.

``No. Unusual in what way? What's this all about, Bob?''

Gifford didn't respond to her question. ``How did Mackenzie behave during your interview with him?''

``The way most ex-cons react when their parole officer pays an unscheduled visit. Wary. Uncommunicative.'' That, at least, was the truth.

``But in your professional opinion, there was nothing especially unusual or nervous about his behavior?''

``No. As I just explained, he behaved pretty much exactly as I would have expected.''

``Did Mackenzie tell you where he was planning on going when he came down in the elevator with you?''

``To get something from the drugstore on the corner of the block.'' Anna was now hip deep in alligators, and sinking fast into the swamp. Time to haul herself out of the mud. ``What's this all about, Detective? Why the sudden interest in Joseph Mackenzie's activities this evening?''

``We found bloody towels in the bathroom and blood splatters all over the wall of Mackenzie's hotel room. Not to mention blood-soaked clothes in the shower stall.''

``My God! You mean he's dead?'' Anna's stomach

had been swooping like a roller coaster for the last five minutes. Now it took a dive off the edge of a very steep cliff. Detective Gifford was an officer of the law, attempting to do his duty, and she was deliberately misleading him.

''We don't know. There's enough blood that we can be sure he or somebody else was badly wounded. We were afraid you might be the somebody else.''

''No, I'm fine. Just fine. Thank you for calling to check. Damn, this is terrible news.'' Anna drew in a shaky breath. She was ashamed of misleading a hardworking public servant, but not ashamed enough, apparently, to tell the truth. ''This is shocking. I can't understand it. Mackenzie gave no indication of being in trouble when I saw him. You say there's a lot of blood in his room?''

''Enough that you couldn't have missed seeing it, so that must mean the room was clean at six-thirty.'' Detective Gifford sounded puzzled. ''That doesn't fit the time frame we're looking at.''

''The time frame for what?'' Anna asked.

''Murder.'' Bob Gifford's voice was hard with anger. ''We want to question Joseph Mackenzie about an acquaintance of his who was killed this afternoon.''

''Somebody was killed? In Mackenzie's room?'' Anna was shaking so hard that she had to steady her cell phone against the car window.

''No. The victim is a man by the name of Franklin Saunders. According to his assistant at the bank where he worked, Mr. Saunders had arranged to meet with Mackenzie at two-thirty this afternoon. Their meeting was scheduled to take place in the Café Renoir, which is only a few yards from the parking garage where Mr. Saunders's body was eventually found.''

Anna slowly turned so that she was facing Joe, wondering why in the world she wasn't running from the car, screaming in terror. Her heart was pounding and her throat was so constricted that it was almost impossible to speak. But it wasn't fear *of* Joe that was taking her breath, she realized. It was fear *for* him.

''How did this Franklin Saunders person die?'' she asked.

''We're waiting for the medical examiner's report, but he took at least four bullets and it wasn't pretty. One shot just about blew off the top of his head. There was a lot of blood spattered around. Not to mention brain tissue and pieces of skull. A hell of a mess, in fact.''

Anna swallowed on a wave of nausea. ''It sounds...gruesome.''

''Gruesome doesn't begin to describe it. Saunders was a young man, too. Only thirty-five. Hell of a thing for his wife and family. The wife passed clean out when we told her what had happened.''

If Anna had thought Joe's expression was difficult to read in the past, now it was a study in rock-hard impenetrability. He could hear every word of her side of the conversation and probably some of what the detective was saying, too. He couldn't be in any doubt as to precisely what she was discussing, and yet his face betrayed not the slightest clue as to what he was thinking.

''Do you believe Mackenzie is on the run, or do you think he's dead?''

''Since you're not hurt, the most logical explanation for the blood in Mackenzie's room would be that he himself is injured—''

''If Mackenzie is wounded, wouldn't it suggest that he and Saunders were both targets, rather than that Mackenzie killed Saunders? Remember, we already had word that there's a contract out on Mackenzie.''

''It's possible, I guess. But if a professional killer was paid to take out both Mackenzie and Saunders, why didn't he succeed?''

''How do we know he didn't succeed?'' Anna asked. ''How do we know Mackenzie is still alive?''

''Because you and Larry both saw him hours after the murder took place,'' Gifford explained patiently. ''And you said he gave no sign of being injured when you were with him.''

''Oh, of course. Sorry, I'm not thinking straight. I guess Mackenzie must have fought with somebody after I left. Maybe the killer came back and tried to finish off his assignment.''

''Could be. We've taken samples of the blood so we'll soon find out if it's Mackenzie's or not. His DNA is on record.'' Gifford yawned. ''Sorry, it's been a very long day. Anyway, you're alive, that's the important thing. And if Mackenzie is also still alive, then we have to assume he's running.''

''If he's injured badly enough to have left blood all over his room, won't he need to get medical attention?''

''We've already posted his picture in all the area hospitals and warned the ER staff to be on the lookout for him, but so far we've heard nothing.''

Anna had to swallow several times before she could respond. ''Mackenzie is a smart man. All the prison IQ tests show that, and it's my assessment of him, too. My bet is that he's stolen a car and is heading out of state as fast as he can."

"Yeah, that's probably right. We have an APB in force already. Anyway, I wanted to let you know a warrant has been issued for Mackenzie's arrest on suspicion of murder. I don't suppose he's going to come anywhere near you, much less your offices, but if he does, don't try to do anything brave. Just call 911 as soon as you see him. This is a desperate man, with every reason to kill, and no reason not to."

So now she was harboring a criminal who was the object of a statewide manhunt. "I certainly will be careful, you can count on it." Anna hoped the reception on her cell phone was bad enough that Gifford wouldn't hear the tremor in her voice. "Thanks for calling, Bob. I really appreciate it. Go home and get some rest. You sound as if you could use a good night's sleep."

Anna closed her phone before Detective Gifford could ask her to come in to the police station and give a sworn statement. She looked at Joe. His face and body language still betrayed no emotion, and yet she was sure she could feel the intensity of his plea for her understanding, along with despair at the impossibility of anyone ever believing in his innocence.

For a moment, her conviction of his innocence was overwhelming. But only seconds later, she found herself wondering if that was part of his criminal power. Probably each of Ted Bundy's victims had been convinced she was the only woman to understand him—right before he raped, tortured and murdered her.

"Don't," Joe said tightly. "Don't look at me like that, Anna. For God's sake, I'm not going to hurt you. I swear, whatever that detective said, you're safe with me.'' He pressed the button to unlock the car door. ''I'll go now, before you get into serious trouble. Even more serious trouble than you're in already. Thank you again for bringing me to Charlie's house. And if…when…the police question you again, tell them I had a gun pointed at you just now, and that you had to lie because I was threatening to kill you.''

She clicked the lock into place, thwarting his attempt to leave the car. ''You have nowhere to go, Mackenzie.''

''Not true. Charlie will take me in—''

''Detective Gifford's smart and he's tenacious. It isn't going to take him long to discover that you knew Charlie in jail and that he has the rep of providing medical services to folks who don't want to attract the attention of the cops. Trust me, Gifford will be calling on Charlie. Do you want to repay your friend by putting him at even more risk than you already have?''

Mackenzie's mouth tightened. ''Okay, so I'll head out of state—''

''How do you propose to do that? Flap your wings and fly?''

''I have bus fare.''

''There's an APB issued. Everyone at the bus station will be looking for you.''

''Okay, so I'll find a car.''

''Steal one, you mean? That's a really smart move.''

''I have no other options,'' he said, his voice low.

''Yes, you do.'' Anna heard her own next words with a sensation of numb disbelief. ''You're injured, Mackenzie, and you need to rest. I'm taking you home with me, which is what we planned all along.''

He turned to her, his gaze finally revealing his puzzlement. "Why are you helping me, Anna? Franklin Saunders is dead. I didn't kill him, but I was there when he died. You heard what Gifford said. Frank's head was blown off. So how the hell can you trust me?"

"I don't know." At this moment, the only thing Anna understood less than what had really happened to Franklin Saunders this afternoon was what had happened to her tonight. "I guess because you've had plenty of chances to hurt me over the past few hours, and you haven't."

"That seems a pretty flimsy foundation on which to risk your life." He sounded almost angry with her for being so foolish.

She looked straight at him. "Did you kill Franklin Saunders?"

"No."

"Is there any way to prove to me or to anyone else that you didn't kill him?"

"No."

"Any reason you can think of why I should believe you're innocent?"

He gave a harsh laugh. "Not a single one."

Anna stared at a nearby streetlight without actually seeing it. She could sit here and ask a hundred questions, but Joseph Mackenzie was a very smart man. Smart enough to invent a hundred answers that might or might not be true. Ultimately, however many questions she asked, she would have nothing to go on except her gut instincts.

And she knew how unreliable those instincts were. They were the same ones that had left her confident

Raul Estevan was trying to reform. The same instincts that had told her Pete the Creep was a faithful lover.

But she hadn't really cared enough about Pete the Creep to analyze their relationship, Anna reflected. And Raul, despite his failure to kick his coke habit, had genuinely wanted to reform. In fact, she still harbored the stubborn hope that the next time he got out of prison, Raul would become the man and the father she knew he was capable of being. Maybe her instincts weren't so lousy after all. She'd better pray they were great, because she was going to run with them one more time.

"I won't turn you in to the cops on one condition," she said to Mackenzie.

"I accept."

"You don't know the condition."

"I know it's a hell of a lot better than being turned over to the cops."

"Okay, here it is. When we get back to my place, you have to tell me what's really going on in your life, and what happened this afternoon with Franklin Saunders. And I need the truth, Joe. The whole truth, and nothing but."

Joe was silent for a long, tense minute. "It's a deal," he said finally. "The whole truth and nothing but."

Thirteen

Joe's side felt as if red-hot slivers of steel were jabbing in and out of his flesh, and his brain was functioning with all the efficiency of a ten-year-old computer. Gritting his teeth against the pain, he tried desperately to focus. He urgently needed to concoct some tissue of credible lies that would satisfy Anna and enable him to get a few hours of sleep before he made his escape to Durango. Unfortunately, his weary brain refused to produce any story that approached coherence, let alone credibility.

Where did Anna live, he wondered. How much time did he have to get his act together? The rundown streets of Charlie's neighborhood were fast giving way to the yuppie renovations of the Cheeseman Park area, and when Anna turned into the parking lot of a freshly painted, eight-story apartment building on Race Street, Joe realized that his window of opportunity was closing fast. What the hell was the matter with him, anyway? Inventing lies had become one of his major skills over the past couple of years, ever since he took his head out of his ass and realized what he needed to do to work the system. He couldn't understand why that skill had deserted him now.

Fear swept away the fuzziness in his brain, leaving behind not clarity but utter blankness. What in the name of God was he going to say to her? His future, and maybe his life, were on the line here. Why couldn't he *think?*

Anna turned the car into a parking space in a small, underground garage. His time had finally run out, Joe realized with fatalistic calm, watching as she unbuckled her seat belt and twisted on the seat to face him. The neon lighting was glaringly harsh but not very efficient, leaving the interior of the car in a pool of semidarkness. She didn't smile, but even in the dubious lighting, Joe could see that her expression displayed concern for him rather than fear for her own safety.

Her trust unnerved him. It was a wonder she'd survived her first six months on the job, he thought, striving for cynicism. Dammit, didn't she have any clue as to the sort of physical violence ex-cons were capable of? Hadn't she listened when he explained about his skill in unarmed combat? Even with the wound in his side, he was more than capable of disabling her, probably breaking several of her bones in the process. She was crazy even to consider taking him into her home.

Joe wasn't sure whether to feel abject gratitude or major frustration that she seemed so oblivious to the threat he posed to her safety. The fact that she was absolutely correct in her belief that he wouldn't hurt her left him with no leverage and no way to manipulate her. He was more than willing to threaten violence, but he hadn't quite sunk to the point where he was willing to inflict serious injury on a woman whose only offence was that she'd gone out on a slender, dangerous limb to help him.

"My designated parking space is directly opposite

the elevator so you won't have far to walk,'' Anna said. ''I'll help you out. You don't want to twist around on the car seat and tear your stitches. By the time we left Charlie's place, he didn't look as if he was in a fit state to do a repair job.''

Anna's soft, musical voice was one of the first things Joe had noticed about her. Now the softness was warmed by a hint of rueful laughter, as if she already understood enough about Charlie to admire his strengths and forgive his weaknesses. Could she really be that perceptive? That...kind?

Looking at her, the hard knot of bitterness that had been lodged in the center of Joe's gut for the past four years twisted apart, leaving him acutely vulnerable, but free of a burden that had become almost intolerable. The incredible thought flashed across his mind that instead of lying, maybe he could just tell Anna the truth about what had happened this afternoon.

He could tell her the truth, and trust her to believe him.

Joe shot out of the car as if the hounds of hell already had their bloody fangs clamped into his flesh. Entirely by good luck, none of his stitches popped as he jumped. He strode over to the elevator—and then had to prop his aching body against the cinder block wall to stop himself keeling over.

Anna locked the car doors and scrambled after him, punching the elevator call button with excessive force. ''For heaven's sake, Mackenzie, will you quit playing King of the Macho Dung Heap? There's nobody here to impress except me.''

''I wasn't trying to impress you.''

''Good. Then you succeeded beyond your wildest

hopes.'' Anna stepped into the elevator and shoved her index finger against the button for the sixth floor.

Joe stepped in after her, staring at their reflections in the smoked glass interior. He looked gaunt, weary and menacing enough to scare small children. Anna looked—beautiful. Her skin, always pale, was almost translucent with fatigue, or more likely from stress, given what he'd put her through in the past few hours. Her hair was held back by two combs that were no longer doing an efficient job of keeping clusters of curls from falling across her forehead and into her eyes. The tumbled curls gave her the erotic appearance of a woman just roused from making love. As he watched, she tugged impatiently at one of the combs, grabbing a handful of hair and scraping it into temporary subjugation, shoving the comb back into place without even a glance toward the mirror.

Joe switched his gaze from Anna's reflection to the floor, battling a fierce desire to rip out both combs so that he could rake his fingers through her hair. Which would be a ten-second prelude to tearing off her clothes and running his hands all over her naked body. Followed in less than twenty seconds by mind-blowing sex, and to hell with rupturing his damn stitches.

Joe leaned against the elevator wall, closing his eyes. Anna was the sexiest woman he'd ever met, and he was pretty sure that wasn't four-plus years of celibacy talking. No wonder he was having such a hard time persuading his brain to function tonight. What little energy he had left was all channeled into fantasizing about having sex with Anna. Wild, hot, passionate, indescribable sex…

She touched his arm and he jerked to attention,

heart pounding, fully aroused. "Are you okay, Mackenzie? You looked as if you'd passed out on your feet."

He cleared his throat, searching for his voice. "I'm okay."

The elevator doors glided open. "This is my floor," Anna said. "My condo's just two doors down. Not far to go, and then you can relax."

Yeah, right. Relaxation was exactly what he could look forward to at this point in his life. Between wanting sex and dodging murder, he had a really laid-back attitude right now. Joe trailed Anna along the spacious hallway, his gaze fixed on the back of her head as opposed to other, dangerously seductive portions of her anatomy. While she unlocked the door to her condo, he concentrated his thoughts on Franklin Saunders, which turned out to be a damn fine way of getting rid of his erection, but didn't do much for his peace of mind.

Since his release from prison, Joe had become sensitive to smells, and the first thing he noticed as they walked into her apartment was the scent of fresh flowers, mingled with the heavier, more pungent scent of dried eucalyptus leaves. The second thing he noticed was the intriguing contrast between stark white walls and big, overstuffed furniture, upholstered in bright fall colors. Combined with drapes and carpeting in a muted shade of moss green, the overall impression was of uncluttered comfort that was at once eye-catching and welcoming. Anna's apartment suited her personality very well, Joe reflected.

It was the first time in four and a half years that he had been inside anyone's home, and he felt as out of place as a pimp in a convent. Standing gingerly in the entrance, he tried to be amused by his own reluctance to walk any farther inside. After a couple of days of feeling clean again, he now felt dirty from the inside out, as if contact with the home of a regular person exposed his underlying state of contamination. Logically, he knew that any blood on the soles of his sneakers must have dried hours ago. But at some level, deep down in the place where he still felt like a convicted felon, he was afraid that if he walked into Anna's apartment, he would leave bloodstained footprints on the pristine carpeting of her living room.

"Do you need help taking off your jacket?" Anna asked, unfastening her own blazer and revealing her shoulder holster, once again containing her Glock .45.

"I can manage, thank you." Joe eased out of Charlie's jacket, debating whether to make another grab for her gun. Once Anna was disarmed, he wouldn't have to hurt her in order to subdue her. And this time, with his wound stitched and the blood loss stopped, he ought to be able to make good his escape without passing out.

Anna followed the direction of his gaze and smiled tightly. "Don't get any stupid ideas, Mackenzie. This time I'm forewarned and I don't make the same mistake twice."

"If I wanted to take your gun, I could." Joe had a humiliating suspicion that he sounded stupidly boastful rather than coolly confident.

Anna shrugged. "Don't count on it. Besides, what would you do when you had the gun? Shoot me? I don't think so."

"I could handcuff you to the bed," Joe said. "I could escape." *I could maybe prevent you getting em-*

broiled in the god-awful mess that currently passes for my life.

"Why all the melodrama?" Anna asked, opening the hall closet so that she could stash the gun and its holster in a small safe. She dialed the lock closed and straightened to meet his gaze. "You're not a prisoner, Mackenzie. Feel free to walk out of here if you think that's a smart choice. The door's behind you. Open it. Walk through. I'm not going to stop you. The police will pick you up before morning and you'll be back in jail as fast as they can book you."

She'd called his bluff, Joe realized. He could no longer pretend, even to himself, that he wanted to get away from her. Hell, what he really wanted was to crawl into her bed and stay there for the next decade or so. But some lingering sense of honor instilled by his grandparents forced him to point out what she didn't seem to have realized. "Obviously it's to my advantage to stay here, at least for tonight. But for your sake, I ought to walk out and never look back."

"I appreciate your concern, Mackenzie, but I can take care of myself."

"You could sure have fooled me. Have you any clue how much trouble you'll be in if you continue to help me?"

Anna's gaze narrowed. "I know most of what I'm risking. I can guess the rest."

"You could lose your job—"

She smiled without mirth. "That's the least of it, Mackenzie. If I'm lucky, I'll lose my job. If I'm unlucky, I could face criminal prosecution."

Joe shook his head. "I don't get it. You seem to understand just how much you have to lose, but you've still brought me to your home. Why?"

"Because you don't deserve to die. And without my help, I'm guessing you'll be dead quite soon. If the cops don't get you, whoever hired Miguel and Carlos will." Anna sounded almost impatient, as if her motives should have been obvious to him.

"I'm a criminal, convicted of stealing the life savings of hardworking senior citizens." Joe pressed his arm against his rib cage, where his wound had started to throb. "If I'm killed, plenty of people would say I'm only getting what I deserve."

"But *I* wouldn't say that and, right now, I'm the person who counts. I'm a parole officer because I believe in second chances and I take it personally when people try to murder one of my parolees. Somebody tried to kill you this afternoon, Mackenzie. Fortunately, they failed, and I intend to make sure they don't finish the job tomorrow or the day after."

This was the first time Joe had encountered anyone connected with law enforcement who acted as though he might be a valuable human being, a man who was worth salvaging. For a moment, he didn't know how to respond, and then he realized that there was only one possible reply. "Thank you for your help, Anna. I'm truly…grateful."

"You're welcome, and you'd better make damn sure I don't regret saying that, Mackenzie." Not looking to see if Joe was following, Anna walked into her living room. A large cat, who bore a startling resemblance to Garfield, right down to the grouchy expression, jumped down from the oversize armchair where it had been snoozing and stalked over to brush itself against her legs. She bent to stroke it.

"Hey, Ferdinand, you have a guilty look. What's

up? Let me guess. You've been chewing the sofa cushions again.''

The cat delivered a scornful flick of its tail, then sat down on top of her feet and stared at Joe with reproachful yellow eyes, as if Joe were the person causing his mistress to make such unflattering accusations.

''You'd better come over here and be introduced to Ferdinand,'' Anna said. ''He likes to give his royal nod of approval before strangers are allowed to move freely around his empire. You're not allergic to cats, are you?''

''No. Animals and I usually get along pretty well.'' Joe ventured onto the plush carpet, and knelt between Anna and the cat. Ferdinand eyed him warily, but permitted Joe to scratch a spot between his ears. After a couple of minutes, Joe was rewarded with a deep purr and a friendly nuzzle, suggesting Ferdinand's fierceness might be more show than substance.

Stroking the cat was a bittersweet pleasure, reminding Joe of Warf, the black Lab his grandfather had given him when he graduated from business school. After his arrest, Joe had been forced to find a new home for the dog in a hurry. Sophie had volunteered to take him in, and Joe had accepted with real gratitude, but Warf had never adjusted to the separation. He'd lost so much weight that he'd developed sores from malnutrition. Only days after the guilty verdict, Sophie sent word through his lawyer that she was going to have Warf put down. Even at the time, when he was numb with the shock of entering the federal prison system, Joe had realized that his grief over losing his dog far exceeded his grief over losing his fiancée. A sorry commentary on his inability to form effective relationships with women, he realized now.

Sophie hadn't been lucky in her choice of men, Joe reflected. First her fiancé got sent to prison, and now her husband had been murdered. He could only hope that her marriage to Franklin Saunders had been blissfully happy for the four years it lasted. Strange to think that Sophie was probably looking back tonight over four years of marriage that she considered painfully short, whereas he considered the same period of time brutally long.

"I'm suddenly feeling hungry," Anna said, getting up and walking toward the kitchen, a pleasant area separated from the main living room only by a long, granite-topped counter. "How about you, Mackenzie?"

"I'm not very hungry, thanks. I'm thirsty, but whatever drug cocktail Charlie pumped into me seems to have killed my appetite."

"How about a bowl of soup? Just so that you don't wake up starving in the middle of the night."

"Soup sounds good," Joe said, following her into the kitchen, with Ferdinand weaving in and out of his legs.

Anna poured fresh water and kibble for the cat, then opened a cupboard and read off the labels from a set of cans. "I have chicken noodle, beef vegetable, clam chowder, and tomato bisque. Your choice."

"Clam chowder would be great."

"Okay, you've got it. What would you like to drink? I have diet sodas, and milk in the fridge."

"Thanks, but I'd prefer ice water."

"Me, too. It was thirsty work watching Charlie sew you up." Anna took two tall glasses down from a cupboard, then pulled a wry face. "I think I'm going to scrub my hands before I start cooking. After sitting on Charlie's sofa, I wouldn't be surprised to discover I'm incubating bubonic plague."

Joe gave a rueful grin. "Yeah. I guess he's not going to win the Martha Stewart Award for Fine Housekeeping. But Charlie's a good guy. Even when he's been drinking, he wouldn't hurt a fly."

Anna stopped swishing soap over her hands and turned to look at him. "I realize he's your friend, and I admit I couldn't help liking him, but there's no point in glossing over the truth. Which is that Charlie doesn't have to beat people up to harm them. Every time he sells an illegal drug he hurts people, whether he's physically violent or not."

Joe took her place at the sink to wash his hands. "Charlie would agree with you. He doesn't deal in illegal drugs, and the only drug he uses himself is legal. Namely bourbon."

Anna frowned. "Are you sure Charlie doesn't deal? He said he was expecting visitors and that he had business to handle tonight. If he wasn't involved in something illegal, then why was he so anxious to get rid of us?"

"Because he wanted you to take responsibility for looking after me tonight," Joe said. "Charlie doesn't believe in facing the night sober if he can avoid it."

"So why didn't he admit that, instead of deliberately hinting he was involved in illegal drug trafficking?"

Joe shrugged. "He didn't tell you that he wanted to drink himself into a stupor because, for all his bluster, Charlie's ashamed of his alcoholism."

"He sounds like a man in serious need of substance

abuse counseling,'' Anna muttered. ''Any chance he'd consider enrolling in group therapy if I recommended an effective program?''

''Voluntarily? None.''

Anna sighed, but she handed Joe the glass of ice water he'd asked for without further comment. Joe took it from her with care, avoiding any chance of accidentally touching her. He wondered if she'd figured out by now that this was the first meal since his arrest that he'd eaten in someone's home. His senses were on maximum overload and the self-control he'd spent four years acquiring seemed to have gone into hiding, although he wasn't sure whether that was caused by the lingering effects of Charlie's anesthetic, or from being in such close proximity to Anna. Until tonight, he'd never realized that watching a woman putter around the kitchen could be so erotic.

Joe offered to help with the preparations for their meal, but Anna told him to sit and rest. Absorbed by the illusion of domestic intimacy, he sat with his back pressed against the wall, watching as she poured the can of soup into a saucepan, adding milk and stirring. That done, she set the small kitchen table with two painted wooden place mats, paper napkins and cutlery, adding a basket of corn muffins that she'd warmed in the microwave as the centerpiece.

Most likely, Anna thought of her preparations as no-frills basic. To Joe, they looked like the epitome of gracious living.

By the time she had finished laying the table, the soup was hot. She carried over brightly painted pottery bowls, filled with steaming chowder, and set them on the matching plates. Joe thanked her politely and put off the moment when he would have to start explaining about Franklin Saunders's murder by making small talk.

''Your condo is very nice,'' he said. Man, small talk couldn't get much smaller than that. ''How long have you lived here?''

''Just over a year. I could never have afforded to buy it in normal circumstances, but the previous owners had to move in a hurry and the real estate market was just sliding into a mini slump after the terrorist attacks on the World Trade Center and the Pentagon, so I got a very good deal. There's more than eighteen hundred square feet of living space in total, which is really generous for one person.''

''It sure is. Prison cells at West Denver are eight-by-twelve, making a grand total of ninety-six square feet, usually shared by two people.'' Joe cursed silently as soon as he realized what he'd said. ''I'm sorry. Sometimes it seems that the more I try not to fixate on the time I spent behind bars, the more I keep bringing it up.''

''Don't apologize. Going to prison must be an overwhelming experience for anyone. Especially if they're innocent.''

Joe felt a spark of hope. Was Anna suggesting that she believed he might be innocent? He looked down at his plate, warning himself not to let the hope show. ''Prison is hell, whether you're innocent or guilty,'' he said.

Anna took a corn muffin and offered the basket to him. Joe took one, his appetite having revived somewhat as he ate. ''How did you get through four years of incarceration without going insane?'' Anna asked, spreading butter on her muffin.

Joe wasn't sure that he had. While he was inside,

the need for revenge had served as a lodestone that kept him oriented away from madness. But since his release, he'd begun to wonder if his overwhelming need for revenge might not itself be a form of prison-induced psychosis.

"I worked out in the gym as much as I could," he said, answering Anna's question about prison life with the practical truth rather than the emotional one. "Physical exercise helped to relieve the stress of being confined so many hours a day. And I read voraciously."

"What did you read? Books, magazines, newspapers?"

"All of the above. Anything I could get my hands on. Not surprisingly, the books in the library were slanted toward education and moral uplift, so I ended up reading a lot of so-called works of great literature."

Anna tilted her head inquiringly. "So-called?"

Joe put down his spoon. "Yeah, you know the sort of stuff I mean. The worthy, seven-hundred-page tomes you swear you're going to get around to reading one day but never do when you're on the outside and busy with normal life."

Anna rolled her eyes. "Let me guess. *Moby Dick*? *War and Peace*? *Middlemarch*?"

"All three. And *Crime and Punishment,* too. Not to mention *The Scarlet Letter, Vanity Fair* and *A Tale of Two Cities.* Somehow I managed to avoid every one of those in high school and college."

"Lucky you. I think I hit most of them one semester or another." Anna leaned back in the chair, smiling. "Did you know that a researcher from the University of Pennsylvania took a poll among college students nationwide and *Middlemarch* came out at the top of the list of Most Boring Books Ever. I think *Moby Dick* was second.''

Joe surprised himself by laughing. ''I didn't think *Middlemarch* was that bad. I guess gloomy descriptions of provincial towns and dense paragraphs reflecting on the meaning of life are easier to digest when you're locked up, trying to find a way to fill the hours. Still, I'd campaign to get bleak Victorian novels banned from high school literature classes. Life is tough enough when you're a teenager. You don't need Dostoyevsky and Nathaniel Hawthorne to add another layer of gloom to your misery.''

''Actually, teenagers often seem to enjoy reading about other people's misery. Makes them feel they're not alone in their conviction that they're living with the meanest parents in the entire history of the universe.''

''Is that the way you felt about your parents when you were growing up?'' Joe asked, trying to visualize the solid, middle-class background that Anna undoubtedly came from.

''Of course.'' Anna smiled pleasantly as she stacked their bowls and plates into the dishwasher and set a pot of coffee to brew. ''Would you like some ice cream for dessert?''

Joe wondered if he was just imagining the swiftness with which Anna had changed the subject away from her parents. Perhaps her parents hadn't been quite the paragons he'd imagined. ''No ice cream, thanks,'' he said. ''The soup and muffin will do it for me.''

She took a scoop of chocolate ice cream for herself and brought it back to the table. Savoring a mouthful, she sighed with pleasure. ''Next to a box of imported Belgian truffles, there's absolutely nothing in the world like ice cream to make the world seem a happier place.''

Joe grinned. ''Do I get thrown out of your apartment if I admit that I don't like chocolate? And I'm not all that wild about ice cream.''

''Not like chocolate? Not like ice cream?'' Anna stared at him in feigned outrage. ''Good grief, what are you, Mackenzie? A pod person?''

''It gets worse. Vegetables are my favorite part of a meal.''

Anna pulled a face, shaking her head. ''Definitely a pod person,'' she said. ''At the very least, liking vegetables is seriously un-American.''

Her smile reached deep inside him, flooding him with warmth, and Joe acted before he thought. He reached out and touched his knuckles to her cheek, so lightly that they were barely in contact with her skin. She went absolutely still, but as he traced the back of his hand along the curve of her jaw, she reached up and rested her fingertips against his mouth. He responded reflexively, parting his lips and running his tongue along her fingers. He could feel the stubble of his beard pricking against the palm of her hand, and he found the sensation unbearably erotic. Of course, right at this moment, given his state of combined arousal and infatuation, he would probably have found bumping elbows with Anna unbearably erotic.

At the touch of his tongue, her breath stumbled and her gaze locked with his, but she didn't recoil, and her fingertips remained pressed against his lips. Her eyes were so blue it was like looking at the sky on a perfect Colorado spring day, when you could believe the mountain peaks soared all the way to heaven. Amazingly, Joe would have sworn that what he saw mirrored in Anna's gaze was a reflection of his own heated desire.

If he'd stopped to make a conscious decision, he would have stayed sitting right where he was, even if he had to glue his butt to the chair. But he acted on instinct, propelled by a need to hold her that overwhelmed what frayed shreds of common sense prison had left him. He walked around the table, dragging her to her feet, and covering her lips in a kiss that started out hot and fierce, and escalated to ravenously demanding in about five seconds.

At some deep level of his subconscious, Joe expected Anna to push him away, but she didn't. Instead, she linked her hands behind his neck and tipped back her head, opening her mouth beneath his. Desire, sharp as an illegal prison blade, sliced away what was left of the control he'd built so painstakingly during his years behind bars. Stripped of that hard-won protection, he was left in the grip of a hunger as powerful as it was elemental. Passion, dark and barbaric, enveloped him, but he felt reckless enough not to care. He'd spent the past several days warning himself that the desire Anna aroused in him had nowhere to go. Friendship between them was difficult enough; a sexual relationship was outside the bounds of possibility. But right now, Joe didn't give a damn about reality. He was sick and tired of dealing with reality. For a few more minutes he wanted to indulge his fantasy that Anna shared his desires. All of them.

And it was so easy to let the fantasy take hold. Her mouth was open and eager beneath his, her body pliant in his arms. Her breathing was jagged and she gave a quick, soft moan when he pushed up her shirt and cupped his hands over her breasts. Only seconds later, he felt her reaching beneath Charlie's oversize sweatshirt, and a shudder of sheer physical exhilaration coursed down his spine as her fingers scraped across his chest. He was vaguely aware of pain shooting out from his wounded side, but the flick of her tongue against his, and her murmurs of pleasure, anesthetized the hurt.

Joe tightened his hold, pulling her even closer, his legs twining with hers. Their kisses stripped his mind clean of thought, leaving behind only sensation. He was consumed by the smell of her, the taste, the unique way her softness melded to the hard angles of his body. He wanted her beneath him, open to him, accepting him. He wanted her *now*.

Her voice came as an intrusion he wasn't willing to acknowledge. "Joe, I'm sorry. We have to stop. This is crazy. We can't do this. Not here, not now."

He barely heard her. He certainly didn't absorb the meaning of the words she'd spoken. For reply, he simply drew in another breath and slanted his mouth across hers, cutting off her protests.

For a second or two longer he was able to pretend everything was okay, but his brain soon registered the unwelcome information that Anna was no longer responding. She had become stiff and unyielding in his arms, and her mouth was closed tightly against his. Moments later, he realized that she wasn't just failing to cooperate, she was actively struggling to be free.

Joe felt desolate. Desolation was swiftly replaced by anger. Anna had no right to change her mind, dammit! She'd responded right from the minute he first touched her and that wasn't wishful thinking on his part, it was fact. She'd aroused him beyond the point that was bearable, and now he needed her, desperately.

What's more, he was powerful enough to take her, whether she wanted him or not.

Appalled, Joe stopped in his tracks as he registered what he was actually contemplating. Jesus, had prison reduced him to this? With an effort that broke sweat, he dropped his arms and managed to step back from her, but that was all he could manage. An apology was beyond his capabilities, even though he guessed that the only reason she hadn't elbowed him in the gut or kneed him in the groin was that she didn't want to reopen his wound. With bitter self-reproach, he wondered if he deserved her consideration.

Avoiding his eyes, Anna occupied herself with pushing her shirt back into the waistband of her slacks. She combed her fingers through her hair in a totally unsuccessful effort to restore a semblance of order to the tumbled riot of curls. She even took a sip of water from her glass on the table.

While she fixed herself up, Joe remained mute. Not from choice, but because his throat was still so constricted with desire that he couldn't speak. He followed Anna's example and took a long swallow of water. It didn't help much.

She finally broke the charged silence. "I'm sorry," she said. "I wasn't prepared...I didn't expect things to get so out of control so fast."

"It wasn't your fault, it was mine." Joe had recovered just enough command of himself to acknowledge the truth. His mouth twisted in bitter self-reproach. "Although you should probably have known better than to invite a sex-starved ex-convict into your home—''

''Don't do that!'' Anna said angrily. ''God, I hate it when you do that!''

''Do what?''

''Keep referring to yourself as an ex-con—''

''It's the truth—''

''Part of it. Only part. For heaven's sake, isn't there anything else to your self-image beyond the fact that you spent some time in prison?''

''Not much,'' Joe said wearily. He felt dizzy and sat down abruptly on the nearest chair.

''What's the matter?'' Anna asked, her voice softening with concern.

''Nothing—''

''You're bleeding!'' She knelt alongside the chair and hastily pushed up his borrowed sweatshirt. ''Damn! I hope we didn't rupture one of your stitches.''

''Even if we did, I'll probably live,'' Joe said. He supposed he ought to be worried about the potential dangers of opening his wound, but right now, he considered it more likely that he would die of frustrated sexual desire than secondary infection from his bullet wound.

''Stay there.'' Anna sounded stern, like Mrs. Robards, his third-grade teacher. Joe realized his thoughts were getting hazy and he forced himself to focus. He'd done more than enough passing out for one day.

''I'm going to change your dressing,'' Anna said. ''This pad Charlie put on is soaked through with blood. I'll be right back.''

She returned and cleaned him up, knitting the torn

flesh together with a tiny strip of sterile tape and covering his bruised, swollen wound with a fresh, nonstick sterile pad. Fortunately—he assumed that was the word to use—the procedure was so uncomfortable that his desire to have sex with her faded to manageable levels. By the time she finished putting him back together, he was in control of himself again. Sort of. More or less.

Joe supposed that was some kind of an achievement. It wasn't one he felt in the mood to celebrate.

Fourteen

Anna had never been short of aspiring lovers. There had been men in her life who'd wooed her with sonnets and sapphires, and men who'd promised her riches and adventures. None of them had stirred her the way Joe managed to stir her just by letting his gaze rest on her mouth.

Her nerves raw with frustrated desire, Anna discarded the bloodstained gauze pad from Joe's wound into the kitchen trash. She hadn't wanted to call a halt to what had been happening between the two of them, she acknowledged silently, but a belated instinct for self-protection had compelled her to test Joe's willingness to back off.

A few seconds before the situation spiraled totally out of control, she had realized that her behavior over the past few hours was not only outside everything in her past experience, it was flat-out dangerous. Joe was tall, strong, prison-toughened, and a master of unarmed combat. She weighed fifty pounds less than he did, and her skill at self-defense was limited to a beginner's course that she'd taken at the Y. If Joe stepped seriously out of line, her only defense would be to ram her elbow into his wound, causing major bodily injury. Since she didn't want to go that route if she could avoid it, she had needed to find out if she could trust him to stop for no other reason than the fact that she asked him to.

Given that this realization dawned when the pair of them were locked in a passionate embrace, it was safe to say that she had been a little late in deciding to conduct a test of whether Joseph Mackenzie was willing to respond to a polite request to cease and desist. A smart woman would have investigated Joe's trustworthiness considerably in advance of finding herself in his arms, on the verge of having frenzied sex. No, correct that. A woman with the brains of a mentally challenged chipmunk would have paid more attention to her personal safety than she had done thus far.

In retrospect, Anna had to admit she'd been crazy to invite Joseph Mackenzie into her home when the only hard facts she knew about him came from a prison file detailing his criminal record. Not exactly the ideal character reference for a prospective house guest, and a truly scary one for a prospective lover. What's more, she had nothing to counterbalance the unpleasant data contained in Joe's prison record beyond her gut instinct that he might, just possibly, be the first parolee she'd supervised who wasn't guilty of the crime for which he'd been sentenced.

Which meant that it was past time to cut to the chase where Joseph Mackenzie was concerned, Anna decided. At some point this afternoon, Joe had been shot and Franklin Saunders had been murdered. A few hours ago, Joe had kidnapped her at gunpoint. Those were facts. Almost everything else was speculation or wishful thinking on her part. Right now, her need for answers surely outweighed Joe's need for rest. She was entitled to find out just how crazy she had been to risk her career—her entire future—

on the belief that Joseph Mackenzie might actually be one of the world's good guys.

"We need to talk about what happened this afternoon," she said, sitting down across the table and not allowing herself to feel sympathy when she observed the lines of fatigue and pain etched into Joe's face. "Explain to me how this man…this Franklin Saunders….ended up dead. And I need the truth, Joe. The whole truth and nothing but. You promised."

"I remember." His mouth twisted into a wry grimace that wasn't a smile. "Give me a moment here. You have to keep in mind that the last time I told a law enforcement official the truth, it earned me two to six in federal detention."

"Then you'd better hope you have more luck this time, with me." Anna worked hard on not succumbing either to instant sympathy, or to the powerful tug of sexual attraction she felt building once again. She had no idea why her usual hang-ups and inhibitions didn't work around this man. She knew only that when she was in Joe's company, the sexual scars inflicted by Caleb Welks seemed too old to be either painful or relevant.

"Start with the victim in today's shooting," she said, her voice cool because she was working hard not to act like a total pushover, ready to believe whatever lies Joe spun. "Detective Gifford implied that you knew Franklin Saunders."

"Yes, I knew Frank well," Joe said, after only a moment's hesitation. "Or at least I thought I did. Before I was arrested, we both worked at the Bank of Trade and Commerce in Durango. We were about the same age. We were single, and since Durango is a small town with limited entertainment options, it isn't surprising that we spent a lot of our free time together. We became good friends."

But not good enough friends for Franklin Saunders to visit you in prison, Anna thought.

"After I got out of prison, I discovered Frank had been transferred from Durango to the headquarters of the Bank of Trade and Commerce here in Denver." Joe took a sip of water. "I went into the bank first thing this morning on the off chance of being able to talk to him."

"Were you planning a social visit, or did you have business to discuss?" Anna asked.

"Mostly business. I could have called first, but I figured there was more chance of getting Frank's co-operation if I actually went to the bank. It's not as easy to blow off an unwanted visitor in person as it is by phone."

"Why did you expect Frank to blow you off? I thought you said you were friends."

Joe shot her an incredulous look. "We *were* friends. Past tense. Frank is now a vice president of the same corporation where I was accused of embezzling almost a million dollars. It's unrealistic to expect him to be friends with me nowadays."

Anna considered that debatable. "But he did agree to speak with you?" she said, keeping her opinion of Frank's friendship to herself.

"Yes. He was in his office, and willing to see me, but he was already late to confer with a client, plus an assistant was hovering, trying to pass along messages. Frank and I spoke just long enough to arrange a two-thirty meeting for the afternoon."

"At the Café Renoir?" Anna recalled the name from Detective Gifford's phone call.

''Yes, and his assistant heard us make the arrangement. For the record, if I'd been planning to kill Frank, you can be sure I would have been smart enough not to arrange our meeting in front of somebody who would be guaranteed to remember me and the plans we'd made.''

Anna didn't say anything, and Joe gave a small, tight smile. ''You don't think that's much of an alibi, do you?''

''Not much,'' Anna agreed quietly. ''Personally, I would be surprised if you made such an obvious mistake in planning a murder. But cops expect murderers to make stupid mistakes, so it most likely won't carry any weight as an alibi with them. Criminals tend to be arrogant, overconfident, and nowhere near as smart as they believe they are, which is how they get caught a lot of the time.''

''Yeah, that's what I figured.''

''Let's not get hung up on your alibi at this point. Tell me what happened when you and Frank got to the café.''

''Nothing very exciting,'' Joe said. ''We ordered espressos. We both felt awkward at first. Truth be told, I guess I'm still furious that Frank was supposed to be a witness for the defense at my trial, but his testimony just about made the prosecution's case for them. On Frank's part, he was probably on edge because of the fact that a month after I was sent to prison, he married Sophie Bartlett—''

''Why would Frank's marriage be a problem for either of you?''

''Sophie Bartlett had once been my fiancée.'' Joe's voice was carefully neutral. ''She broke off our engagement a few weeks after I was arrested.''

''Oh, my God.'' Anna swallowed hard.

''Yeah, I'd say that about sums it up.'' The bleakness of Joe's expression belied the nonchalance of his words. ''If the police decide to pin this murder on me, they aren't going to have to dig very deep for a motive, are they?''

At the very least, you would have to say that Joseph Mackenzie had a knack for finding himself in incriminating situations, Anna reflected. She drew in a breath that was distinctly shaky. ''Let's take this step by step. Given that Franklin Saunders helped get you convicted and then married your fiancée, why did you even want to meet with him?''

''Other than to murder him, you mean?''

''Sarcasm isn't going to make these questions go away, Joe.''

''I know. I'm sorry.'' He rubbed his forehead, the gesture heavy with weariness. ''I went to see Frank because I wanted to ask him two questions—who had cleaned out my desk at the bank after I was arrested, and whether he knew the current addresses of the other seven people who were working at the bank at the time of my arrest. I also hoped that if we talked face-to-face about Sophie and the trial, then I would get a feel as to whether or not Frank had deliberately set me up to take the fall for his own crimes.''

''And what did you conclude?''

Joe spread his hands. ''That it's a lot harder to make judgments about guilt and innocence in real life than it is in the movies. That I'm not as objective about Frank as I need to be. That even though I know Sophie and I weren't really suited, it still pisses me off that she and Frank were married practically before the prison gates had a chance to clang shut behind me.''

''Angry ex-con gets out of jail and murders the former friend who married his woman,'' Anna murmured. ''I can already see the headline. I don't like to be the bearer of bad news, Joe, but everything you've told me so far is damn near making Detective Gifford's case for him.''

Joe pushed his chair back from the table with barely controlled force. ''I can't believe this is happening,'' he said, getting to his feet and pacing angrily. ''The first time around, when the cops pinned the bank embezzlement on me, I swore I would never again be naive enough to get caught in the same trap. I came out of prison convinced that I'd at least learned to work the system well enough to protect myself. And yet here I am, eight days later, and the cops are getting ready to accuse me of murder.'' He ran his hand over his buzz-cropped prison haircut. ''What the hell did I do wrong in my previous life? Steal food from starving widows and orphans? Torture people in Nazi extermination camps?''

''My hotline to God is currently experiencing technical difficulties,'' Anna said. ''So I recommend you stick to questions there's a chance we can answer. Like, for example, since you and Frank met in a coffee shop, why did Frank end up getting killed in a parking garage?''

''When I asked Frank for the addresses of my former colleagues, he wanted to know why I needed them. I said that ought to be obvious. Since I hadn't embezzled any money from my clients' accounts, that meant somebody else had. Almost certainly, that *somebody else* had worked in the bank, which made a potential pool of eight suspects. Frank pointed out that having gotten away with the crime for almost five years, the guilty party was hardly likely to confess just because I contacted him. Or her. I agreed, but asked him to give me the addresses anyway.''

''How did Frank react to the news that you included him on your list of suspects?'' Anna asked.

''He didn't have much of a reaction. Chiefly because he was anxious to tell me that Sally Warner—previously the head teller at the bank—had taken her three sons and disappeared from Durango not more than a month after I went to prison. Apparently she left overnight, without telling anyone she was moving, which caused quite a bit of gossip at the time. Then Frank heard, just a few weeks ago, that Sally was living in Dallas, in a brand-new million-dollar home that she'd paid for with money she supposedly inherited from her grandmother.''

''Supposedly?''

''Frank's word. He admitted that he'd more or less forgotten about Sally's disappearance until he heard about her fabulous new house. He clearly thought that if I was going to suspect anyone of having embezzled money, Sally Warner was the woman to choose. One minute she's a divorced mom, always in need of extra cash, the next minute she's living in luxury.''

''It seems worth checking out,'' Anna agreed.

''Yes, one more name to push up toward the top of my suspect list. Anyway, Frank said he could give me Sally's address, as well as a couple of others for ex-colleagues who'd moved, so we paid for our coffees and walked next door to the underground parking garage, where Frank leaves his car during working hours.''

Anna's forehead wrinkled. ''Why did you need to go to his car to get the addresses?''

''Because Frank said he had his personal address book in the glove compartment.''

''That's a strange place for him to keep his address book, isn't it?''

''Frank explained that he'd mailed a couple of packages on Saturday morning, and he'd forgotten to take his address book out of the car.'' Joe shrugged. ''I didn't question it at the time. In retrospect, I realize Frank must have made up the story about mailing the packages as an excuse to get me into the parking garage.''

''Are you saying that Frank set you up to be killed?'' Given what little she knew of him, Anna had no particular liking for the absent Frank. Nevertheless, she still felt a quiver of shock at the implications.

''I can't think of any other explanation for a gunman to be waiting in that parking garage, can you?'' Joe asked.

Anna thought for a moment. ''Maybe if you were being followed?''

''But only Frank knew we'd be going into the garage enough in advance to arrange to have the shooter already in place.'' Joe shook his head. ''Besides, I'm willing to swear nobody's been following me. I've been paying extra careful attention since your warning on Saturday.''

''So okay, there was probably no tail on you. On the other hand, if Frank was involved in setting you up, how could he possibly know that you were going to ask him for those addresses?''

''He couldn't. But presumably if I hadn't asked for the addresses, he'd have made some other excuse to get me down into the parking garage.'' Joe's expression became bleak. ''I guess it's possible that he'd agreed to take me to his car, but didn't know a gunman was waiting to kill me. Maybe he thought I was just going to be roughed up a little. Warned off from investigating what really happened at the bank in Durango. Who knows what he'd been told? Obviously he didn't expect to be walking to his own death, which means he wasn't fully informed about what was planned. Somebody else was ultimately in charge of setting me up, not just Frank.''

''What's your best guess?'' Anna asked. ''Do you think Frank knew you were going to be the target for an assassination attempt?''

''I think he was duped.'' Joe gave a grim smile. ''But ask me again in five minutes, and I'll most likely tell you I'm convinced he knew what was going down.''

''From where I'm sitting, it sure looks as if your ex-friend Frank knew what was going to happen,'' Anna said.

Joe gave an impatient grunt, the impatience directed at himself. ''I can't believe Frank's that good at deception. Looking back, his whole attitude while we were in the café struck me as way too casual for a man who knew somebody was about to gun me down.'' He gave a frustrated sigh. ''That's the trouble with every single damn thing Frank has done and said since the day I was first arrested. There are always two ways to interpret his actions.''

To Anna, it seemed that Joe was shedding his habitual mask of impenetrable control more and more swiftly as he confided what had happened that afternoon. She was intrigued by the tantalizing glimpses of the dynamic, spirited man Joe might once have been before he imposed a rigid control over his feelings that left him taut, wary and unapproachable.

"Let's try to lessen the ambiguity," she suggested. "Tell me *exactly* what happened when you left the café. I'm not as caught up in the situation as you are. Maybe it will be easier for me to ignore the individual trees and make out the shape of the forest."

"Okay. Here's the blow-by-blow." Joe started to pace as he talked. "Frank had an incoming call on his cell phone while we were waiting to pay the bill. I don't know who it was from, but he cut the caller off, saying it wasn't convenient to talk and that he would call back in fifteen minutes."

"That could have been a signal to the gunman," Anna said. "Or *from* the gunman."

"Yeah, it sure could." Joe let out an exasperated breath. "Or it might have been an incoming call that Frank preferred to return later, just as he claimed. Anyway, in the for-what-it's-worth department, it took us less than five minutes after the phone call—not fifteen—until the moment we stepped out of the elevator into the parking garage in the basement beneath the bank building. I had no idea where Frank's car was parked, of course, so I was following half a step behind him as we crossed the various aisles—"

"Which means he was in command of the situation and in a good position to set you up as a target," Anna pointed out. "You know, this might be a really good moment to rethink how well you actually knew Frank."

"I've been rethinking that for almost five years. It's true that when we worked together, I took our relationship at face value. But when we met today, I wasn't taking anything at face value, past or present. Which is why I can't believe I sat across the table from Frank for forty minutes and failed to sense even a hint of danger from a man who was planning to lead me to my death.''

Joe was making the mistake of assuming that Frank would feel guilty about what was planned, and therefore give off tense vibrations. Not necessarily the case, as Anna knew all too well from numerous case histories of her parolees.

''I guess in one sense, the true extent of Frank's involvement is irrelevant right at this moment,'' she said. ''The important conclusion is that we're obviously dealing with a ruthless killer, whether Frank was a willing helper or a misguided dupe. Tell me what happened next. You're following Frank, with no suspicion that you might be heading into trouble—''

''That's not quite true,'' Joe said. ''I didn't suspect Frank of setting me up, but I'm always on the lookout for trouble these days, especially since your warning last Saturday. As I walked, I was checking out the surroundings, even though at that point I simply thought I was going down to the parking garage to pick up an address book.''

''The gunman was taking a huge chance that nobody else would be there, wasn't he?''

''Not really. That level of the parking facility is strictly for bank employees, so you could pretty much count on the fact that nobody would be down there at three in the afternoon. And I guess if, by sheer chance, somebody else had arrived at just the wrong moment, then the gunman wouldn't have carried on with his plans. Or he'd have shot the witnesses.''

Anna shivered at that possibility and the images it evoked. ''Where was the gunman hiding?''

''He stayed in his car, which was parked behind one of those concrete-and-steel support pylons you always get in parking garages. I didn't see him until he started shooting, but the back of my neck had started to prick the moment we stepped out of the elevator. The exact same feeling I used to get just before some psycho inmate would rush up and try to stick a knife in my ribs. The sensation of being watched was so intense that I actually stopped for a second to look behind me. That primal warning of danger probably saved my life, because Frank chose the same moment I stopped to press the remote on his car keys. I heard the locks on a car pop open and as I started to swing around to face Frank again, I saw this blur of movement out of the corner of my eye—''

Joe stopped, correcting himself. ''No, I didn't so much *see* movement as sense it on the edges of my consciousness. I reacted long before I thought. Hell, I've not only watched this scene in the movies, I've played in it. I took a running dive to the far side of the car nearest to where I was standing. It was all reflexes and no planning on my part, but it saved my life. I heard the sound of a rifle firing as I rolled off the hood, but I didn't realize I'd been hit for another couple of minutes. In retrospect, I think a bird may have flown up into the rafters, and that may have sent the shooter's aim off, just slightly.''

''If you were shot, you must have left blood on the hood of the car.''

''Not that I saw. But if the police searched the crime scene thoroughly, they're certain to find enough of my blood to do a DNA match. If not on the car, then on the floor.'' Joe grimaced. ''They'll have no trouble proving I was at the scene.''

Anna didn't attempt to reassure him by pretending that a DNA blood match wouldn't matter, and he was grateful for her honesty. ''What did Frank do when the shooting started?'' she asked. ''Did you see?''

''I could only see his feet. They didn't move. He just stood there—''

''As if he was confident he wouldn't be hit?''

''There's no way for me to know. Maybe that. Or maybe he was just too stunned—too scared—to move. The next thing I knew, there was another burst of gunfire and Frank collapsed on the concrete floor. He fell about five feet away from where I was crouching, his head pointing away from me, out into the aisle, otherwise I'd have been splattered from top to toe with his blood.''

Anna spoke quickly to distract Joe's attention from a memory that was obviously grisly and much too vivid. ''Given the way Frank fell, could you tell right away that he was dead?''

''From the crack of his skull against the pavement, I'd say that if he wasn't already dead from the bullets, he was dead the moment he hit the ground. I never even considered the possibility that he was still alive. I was trying to decide how the hell I could prevent myself becoming the body that took the next round of bullets, when I heard the sound of a car engine being turned on and I realized the killer must be planning to drive over and make sure he'd taken care of both of us before leaving.''

''He couldn't see you, of course?''

''No. From where the gunman was parked, he had

no way of knowing whether I was alive or dead. Maybe, from the way I rolled off the car, he assumed I was dead.''

''I guess it's silly to ask if you could describe what the shooter looked like?''

Joe shook his head. ''I couldn't even say if he was black, white or brown. In fact, I don't know for sure it was a he. I don't even know if it was one person acting alone. There could have been half a dozen people in the car for all I know.''

''I'm surprised the sound of the gunshots didn't attract anyone's attention,'' Anna said.

''Maybe they did. But it's taking me a lot longer to explain what happened than the actual events took in real life. I'm guessing not much more than thirty seconds passed between the time I sensed that suspicious blur of movement and the moment when Frank collapsed onto the concrete, dead. It had probably been less than two minutes since we got off the elevator. Plus, it would take a while for anyone out on the sidewalk to identify where the shots were coming from, even if they could hear anything, which is doubtful, given the volume and roar of general traffic in that area. Remember, there are two levels of parking underneath the bank. The upper one, for members of the general public visiting the bank, has access at sidewalk level. The lower one for bank employees, where we were, is completely below ground. The sounds of gunfire ricocheted around the basement, but they may not have traveled up and out to where there were people.''

''Quite a good place to commit murder, in fact,'' Anna commented.

''Yes, the setup was well planned. The hit looked

professional to me.'' Joe helped himself to more water. ''Did the police tell you who found Frank's body?''

''No. Detective Gifford was too busy warning me how dangerous you are to provide many details about the crime.''

''I *am* dangerous,'' Joe said harshly. ''Look what a mess you're in just because you've tried to help me.''

''We've been over that ground before,'' Anna said. ''It's boring, so let's move on. How did you escape from the gunman in the end? From the scenario you've described, it would seem impossible.''

''Basically, I got lucky. The gunman couldn't drive directly to the place where Frank had fallen. He had to drive around one of those concrete-and-steel support pylons, which slowed him down. Slowing down being a relative term, of course. I realized I had a thirty-second window of opportunity maximum to make a getaway. Earlier, while we were walking to Frank's car, I'd noticed that there was an exit door marked Stairs and it was located at a forty-five degree angle behind where I was hiding. That was damn lucky for me, because I'd be moving away from the gunman's car if I ran toward the door. What's more, he wouldn't be able to follow me through the door without abandoning the car and coming after me on foot—''

''That wouldn't have been too much of a problem if there was more than one person in the car.''

''Fortunately, I didn't think of that at the time, or I might have hesitated long enough to blow my chance. Since no other more brilliant plan sprang to mind, I decided to go for it. I kept low and dodged toward the Exit sign, using the parked cars as a screen. I made it to within ten feet of the door with nobody shooting at me, although I could hear a car still driving around. Which meant, I profoundly hoped, that the gunman didn't know where I was, and couldn't see me. At this point, my escape plan disintegrated into trusting in luck. The rows of cars stopped, so I had no cover for the last few feet of my escape. If the gunman was in the wrong position and spotted me, I'd be dead. But since I'd be dead anyway if I stayed in the garage, I decided to play the odds and run across those unprotected ten feet.'' Joe shrugged. ''I guess you could say I won.''

Anna smiled. ''You're alive, and not too badly wounded. I'd definitely say you won.''

Her final word was punctuated by the sound of the front doorbell ringing. Heart thumping, she stared at Joe. He stared back, equally silent and equally horrified. In less fraught circumstances, Anna thought their frozen positions might have been comic.

The doorbell rang again. Her mouth so dry that her teeth felt as if they were sticking together, Anna spoke. ''It's almost midnight. There's a security guard on duty downstairs at this time of night. He's supposed to buzz me before he lets anyone up.''

''It must be the cops,'' Joe said, and his voice was once again drained of all expression. ''They're the only people a security guard would let in without warning.''

''We don't have to let the cops in.'' Anna paced up and down the kitchen. ''We'll ignore them.''

''If they have a search warrant, they can get the keys. Or break down the door.'' Joe walked over to the counter and quickly selected the largest and sharpest butcher knife from the wooden block by the stove.

Anna grabbed his arm. "Put it back, Joe! Don't be crazy. You can't fight off the cops with a carving knife—"

Joe shook off her hand. "I'll come with you to the door," he said, as if she hadn't spoken. "I'll hold the knife to your throat, so for God's sake don't move quickly or unexpectedly. I'll have to press the blade close to your skin to make it look convincing. We'll tell the cops I took you hostage—"

"No, we won't," Anna said. "Good grief, will you stop playing the self-sacrificing hero for five seconds? Why can't we tell the cops the truth?"

Joe looked at her in blank astonishment, then gave a harsh laugh. "There's a great idea, Ms. Parole Officer. Wonder why I didn't come up with it? Must be because I don't want to see you arrested."

The person at the door gave up ringing the bell and instead banged loudly with his closed fist. A slightly slurred voice bellowed through the heavy panels. "Annie, I know you're in there. You're always home on Monday nights. Let me in. It's Peter."

Anna let out a breath she hadn't even known she was holding and Joe set down the knife. His hand, she noticed, was not entirely steady but his gaze was sardonic as he turned to look at her. "Is Peter a client or a friend?" he asked.

"Neither. He's an extremely annoying ex-boyfriend." Fear vanished in a body-shaking tremor of rage. "I suppose I have to go talk to him," she said, her jaw clenched so tight she could barely get the words out. "We don't want my neighbors to report a disturbance and bring the cops down on us after all. Don't worry, Joe. I won't let him in."

The hammering on the door increased to ear-shattering volume and Joe gave a faint grin. "Just taking a wild guess here, but your extremely annoying ex-boyfriend doesn't sound as if he's in the mood to take no for an answer."

Too irate to respond, Anna marched to the front door and saw to her dismay that it was already open and Pete the Creep was leaning in drunken satisfaction against the wall of her little entrance hall. Damn and double damn!

"How did you get in?" she demanded.

For answer, Peter grinned and held up a set of keys. Anna cursed silently. In her haste to get the jerk out of her condo last week, she'd neglected to demand the return of her door keys. Which she had given him in what could only be termed one of her more appalling lapses of good judgment.

"Annie, my love, you look gorgeous! I've missed you this week." One hand clasping a bottle of champagne, Pete the Creep swept her into his arms before she had the wit to step out of reach. Fumes of alcohol washed over her. She would have elbowed him hard in the stomach, except that with the quantity of booze he'd already consumed, there was a serious danger he'd throw up all over her. So she stood still, neither speaking nor responding, and waited for him to stop pawing her.

It seemed a disgustingly long time before he got the message. He stepped back, and surveyed her with a pout. "Come on, Annie, lighten up, for Chrissake. You know you're pleased to see me."

She wouldn't deign to respond to that piece of idiocy. ''Give me back the keys to my condo, Peter, or I'll call security and have you thrown out.''

He squinted at her, grinning the lopsided grin she'd once considered cute. ''You know you don't mean that, Annie.''

''Try me.''

Eyes narrowing, he held the keys over his head. ''If you want them, come and get them.''

''Oh, for heaven's sake.'' Anna gave an impatient swipe at the keys. She should have paid closer attention to her aim. Pete, with surprising coordination given his drunken condition, jerked them out of reach, then quickly shoved them down the front of his pants. Since nothing landed on the floor, he'd presumably stuffed them into his underpants.

''Come and get them,'' he said again, his smile degenerating into an angry smirk. ''Bitch.''

Looking at him, Anna tried to remember what in the world it was that had ever attracted her to Peter. Did she really expect so little from her lovers that she'd been content to spend four months dating this pathetic excuse for a man?

Joe came out of the kitchen and stood beside her. Ferdinand followed, tail high, then sat down on Joe's feet, a sign of extreme favor. With a sense of finally acknowledging the inevitable, Anna turned to Joe and smiled, not bothering to hold back what she was feeling: sheer relief that he was there. It might be crazy, but she felt more threatened by Pete the Creep than she had ever felt by Joe.

Joe's gaze lingered for a moment on her smile. Then he turned toward Peter. ''Is there a problem here?'' he asked, his voice perilously quiet.

''Who's he?'' Peter demanded. ''What's he doing here at this hour of night?''

Joe and Anna both ignored his questions. ''Peter doesn't seem to understand that I want the keys to my condo back,'' Anna said.

Gently disentangling his feet from Ferdinand, Joe turned to face Peter once again. ''Please give Anna back her keys,'' he said with deceptive courtesy.

Peter, too drunk to recognize danger until it bit him on the ass, puffed up his chest and squared off in front of Joe. ''Make me.''

Joe gave a tight, hard smile. ''My pleasure.'' With movements too quick for Anna to follow, Joe stepped forward and, in a single fluid motion, pinned Peter to the wall with his arm across Peter's throat, cutting off his air supply. Not even marginally winded, Joe spoke to Anna over his shoulder.

''Where did he put your keys, do you know?''

''Down the front of his pants.''

''How...unappetizing.'' Joe moved slightly to one side, keeping Peter immobilized by the pressure of his arm against Peter's windpipe.

''Find the keys,'' he ordered. ''Give them back to Anna.''

Peter spluttered something barely audible, indicating that he couldn't reach them.

''Try harder,'' Joe said. ''You have until I count to three. One...two...''

With a snarl, Peter threw the keys onto the floor.

Anna picked them up and shoved them into the pocket of her slacks. She sent him a look of acute disdain. ''Go home, Peter, and I'll pretend this incident never happened.''

''Are you sure you wouldn't like me to teach him some manners?'' Joe asked.

''No. He's too slow a learner. Let's just get him out of here.''

''Done.'' With another impossibly swift movement, Joe grabbed Peter by the wrist and twisted his arm in a half nelson behind his back. ''Okay, Peter, time to go home. Let me escort you to the elevator.''

''I'll go by myself.'' Not surprisingly, Peter sounded beyond surly. He jerked his head around to stare at Joe. ''Who are you, anyway? I've seen you before.''

Joe's gaze barely flickered. ''I don't think so,'' he said, opening the door. ''We've never met.''

Watching his seemingly effortless control of the situation, Anna could hardly credit that Joe was actually wounded, even though she'd stood next to the table while Charlie stitched up the hole in his side. Displaying no hint of either physical weakness or alarm, Joe frog-marched Peter down the corridor, Anna following behind so that she could summon the elevator.

''Don't come back,'' she said, when Joe shoved Peter into the elevator. ''Even you must realize by now that our relationship is over.''

''There's not a chance in hell I'd ever come anywhere near you again,'' he spat out.

''That's the best news I've had today,'' Anna said. The elevator doors started to close. ''Goodbye, Peter.''

''Go to hell. Bitch.''

Fifteen

Jiggling her keys, Anna fought back laughter as she walked with Joe along the corridor to her apartment. Okay, so she was being immature and shallow, but it had been immensely satisfying to watch Peter's ego get cut down to size. Not to mention the adolescent pleasure she'd derived from watching Joe stuff him into the elevator like an unwanted package. Nothing about her tepid relationship with Peter had been intense enough to explain his sudden determination to win her back. She could only assume he was attracted to her precisely because she'd made it clear she no longer wanted him.

She high-fived Joe as they stepped into her apartment, giddy with relief that the pounding on her door had only been Peter and not the cops. Joe gave her one of his too rare smiles as she closed, locked and bolted the door behind them, but once safely inside, his smile faded.

''Peter recognized me,'' he said quietly. ''He couldn't pin a name on me, but he'll get there sooner or later.''

''I know.'' Reality pierced Anna's bubble of euphoria, and she tossed the spare keys onto the hall table, sighing with regret for the hot shower and hours of sleep she was obviously not going to get. Peter's visit made it even more urgent for them to leave Denver as soon as they could, before the police learned that their prime suspect in the Franklin Saunders murder case was being harbored by his parole officer. Until now, the major factor protecting her and Joe from discovery was the sheer unlikeliness of their situation, but Peter had the power to destroy that paper-thin veneer of protection.

"The cops must have released a picture of you to the media," she said. "We should have anticipated that."

Joe muttered a curse. "Sophie and Frank are both from wealthy families, and they were active in Denver's social circles, so he makes for an interesting victim. The murder of Franklin Saunders was probably the lead item on the local TV news tonight. Right along with the information that the police have issued a warrant for my arrest."

"Peter had been drinking before he arrived here." Anna tried to sound hopeful. "Maybe he won't remember where it was he'd seen you before."

Joe's expression indicated that he knew better than to count on such a frail hope. "Peter was tipsy, not really drunk, and we pissed him off enough that he'll mentally rerun what happened tonight over and over. Eventually, he'll work out why I looked familiar. And if by a miracle Peter doesn't recognize me, then for sure some other helpful citizen will. The bottom line is that every hour I stay here puts you more at risk—"

She interrupted before he could launch into his standard offer to leave in order to protect her. "Don't say it, Mackenzie! If you dare to suggest one more time that you're going to run away and save me from myself, I'll scream."

"How did you know I was about to suggest that?"

"I'm a trained psychologist. Besides, you're boringly predictable on occasion."

"Maybe I'm boringly predictable, but that's better than being willfully blind," Joe said heatedly. "You're determined to ignore the risks, Anna. Unfortunately, refusing to accept what's right under your nose doesn't change a damn thing. In this case, it simply increases the danger you're in."

"Are you through yet?" Anna gave an exaggerated yawn, then headed toward the kitchen.

"Yes, I'm through," Joe snapped, following her. "And if you have any better ideas about what I should do other than get the hell out of your life before I totally screw it up, then let's hear them."

"Okay, here's my suggestion. You didn't murder Franklin Saunders, so somebody else did. We need to focus on that fact, keeping in mind that the most likely suspect is the same person who hired Miguel and Carlos to kill you—"

"I agree. The police, however, don't see eye to eye with us. They've already identified their chief suspect in the Franklin Saunders murder case, and it's me. Which brings this discussion right back to where it started."

"Not really. Since the police are mistaken, we need to find out who the real killer is—"

"Golly gee, let's do that." Joe's voice dripped irony. "Shall we solve the murder right now, in the comfort of your home, or wait until tomorrow morning and wrap up the investigation at your office? A couple of hours should take care of all the loose ends, don't you think?''

Anna glared at him. ''You're very annoying when you adopt that sarcastic tone of voice, Mackenzie. I realize it's going to be a challenge to find out who killed Franklin Saunders, but I'm sure you have several excellent suggestions as to where we should start looking. Right from the moment I first warned you about Miguel and Carlos, you had a definite idea about who might want to kill you. And in case you're planning to palm off more of your bullshit about prison gangs on me, let's agree that the hit ordered on you had nothing to do with inmates you'd offended while you were behind bars. You're in this mess because of something that happened in Durango five years ago. Somebody wants to prevent you poking around in the bank records. They don't want the embezzlement case reopened, and they're willing to kill to make sure that it isn't. Obviously, there's a lot at stake here for somebody.''

''There sure is. At least we can agree that there's much more at stake than the million bucks I supposedly embezzled. In fact, Franklin's death suggests that whatever they're hiding is enough for them to kill anyone who gets in their way. And you know what? The fact that you're cute as a button isn't going to protect you.''

Cute as a button? *Cute as a button?* Is that how he thought of her, for heaven's sake? God, she hated cute. ''Are you done insulting me?'' Anna turned away, reaching to open a cupboard, which seemed a more mature choice than taking a swing at him. Joe wheeled her back around to face him. Eyes blazing, his gaze locked with hers. Whatever he'd intended to say died unspoken as they stared at each other in a silence fraught with the sexual tension that never quite left them, but which neither of them was ready to deal with.

The silence set Anna's pulse jumping. It was a measure of how far and fast her infatuation had developed that even now, when they were about to embark on a venture that left her at serious risk of criminal prosecution, she responded to Joe's nearness with a compulsive rush of sexual yearning. He only had to touch her—he didn't need to take her into his arms, much less kiss her—and she wanted to forget about killers hired to murder him and cops about to arrest the pair of them. As for Caleb Welks and her celestial marriage, the event that usually had such an inhibiting effect on her relationships with men might as well have taken place in another lifetime. After years of dominating her subconscious, Anna realized that the trauma of her wedding night had lost its power to intimidate her since she met Joe.

"What are you thinking about?" He framed her face, combing her hair out of her eyes, tucking a cluster of curls behind her ear. With Peter, she'd often felt that her hair was an untamed mess in need of better styling. With Joe, her rioting curls felt lush and flamboyantly sensual.

She didn't answer him right away, just studied him, wondering whether it was the uncompromising hardness of his features or the occasional flicker of vulnerability in his eyes that made desire coil with such intensity in the pit of her stomach. Despite that desire, she had no intention of letting down her guard and telling Joe what she had been thinking. She couldn't imagine explaining about Caleb or her marriage or the years she'd spent growing up in Ray Welks's strange household. She had never confided about her family background to anyone except Leila Sworski and that had been fourteen years ago, when the two of them made arrangements for Megan's adoption. Even then, she'd refused to actually name the father of her child. That way, Leila wasn't obligated to contact Caleb prior to the adoption, and Anna could maintain the fiction that her daughter had been created by a whim of nature, without any sordid intervention from her so-called husband.

In view of her habit of concealment, it was surprising—almost frightening—that the idea of telling Joe part of the truth even flickered across her mind. Disconcerted, Anna buried the alien impulse to confide in him somewhere deep and dark, where it belonged.

''I was thinking about something that used to be important but isn't anymore,'' she said, tilting her head back and looking up at him. Well, that was more or less the truth, wasn't it? Escaping from her own thoughts, she cradled Joe's cheek with her hand and scraped her fingers slowly along the line of his jaw, relishing the rough sensation of his beard stubble pricking against her palm. Heat, insidious and flagrantly sexual, moved up from her toes, flushing her skin, making her cheeks flame. Why now, she wondered. And why did these feelings come only in response to this man? She had never before understood how sexual desire could be a force powerful enough to enslave emperors, lure hermits away from celibacy and alter the course of history. Now she understood all too well.

''You're so beautiful, Anna.'' Joe's voice was

husky. ''And so goddamned sexy it hurts to look at you.''

She always thought of her appearance as being cheerleader perky rather than anything more seductive, and she positively despised perky. But when Joe's voice deepened, and when he looked at her with eyes that turned smoky with desire, she could actually believe that she was beautiful, and even a little bit sexy. She smiled wistfully at the crazy thought.

''I'm afraid of you when you smile.'' Joe ran his thumb across her lips. ''Afraid of what you do to me, and how you can make me feel.''

''Then we're even,'' she said, her voice husky. ''Because you scare the hell out of me, Mackenzie, and not just when you smile.''

He kept his gaze fixed on her mouth. ''Mutual intimidation seems like an interesting basis for a relationship. Our personal updated version of the Cold War.''

She laughed, because she found the comparison ridiculous and oddly sexy. No surprise there. She was beginning to realize that Joe could recite the alphabet and she would find the recitation sexy.

Joe held her gaze for a moment, then swiftly bent his head, stopping her laughter with a kiss that set her heart leaping and her body aching. Within seconds, Anna realized that she was facing a stark choice: she could be sensible and resist, or she could abandon sanity and allow herself to be consumed. With Joe, she was ruefully aware that there would be no path open to her other than total rejection or total surrender.

She pulled away, an automatic denial prompted by years of training herself never to succumb to any emotion that threatened to become too deep or too important. Experience had taught her that deep emotions brought unbearable pain. She'd learned that lesson when her father died and when her mother failed to protect her from Caleb Welks. The lesson had been rammed home with bitter intensity when Megan was born.

But Joe didn't take the hint. Had she really imagined he would back off in response to such a half-hearted and ambivalent gesture? He simply drew her back into his arms, his mouth closing over hers with hot, urgent demand. Within seconds, Anna's protective barriers crumbled, exposing all the softness and vulnerability she struggled so hard to keep hidden.

She should have been scared by the abrupt disappearance of all her familiar psychological guardrails. Instead, she felt a heady sense of freedom, as if some repressed part of her rejoiced in the destruction of defenses that had become more of a straitjacket than a genuine protection. Pleasure shimmered over her, and each little pulse of desire seemed to heal one more emotional scar. She hadn't noticed until now—until Joe—that the scar tissue layered over the wound of her wedding night had withered after fifteen years and was ready to be excised.

Joe finally dragged his mouth away in order to draw breath and she felt her throat tighten at what she saw in his eyes. His gaze stayed locked on hers, dark and full of promises, sending a surge of longing racing through her veins. Desire burned hot and fierce. Her bones turned to mush. She wanted to laugh. She wanted to cry. She wanted to rip off his clothes and haul him into her bed.

"Joe." Her voice was low, unrecognizable in its

husky undertones. That huskiness said everything about the true state of her feelings, but the force of tired old habits compelled her to make one last protest. "We can't do this."

"Sure we can." He paused. "If it's what you want."

Was it? The moment of truth had arrived. Panic flared, fighting against desire.

"Sometimes you think too much." Joe spoke against her lips, his expression oddly tender.

"I need to be in control," she blurted out.

He raised his head so that he could look at her. He appeared almost surprised. "You are in control," he said. "Absolutely. You can set the pace. How fast we move is up to you."

"I don't need to be in control of *you,*" she muttered. "I need to be in control of myself. The problem is, when I'm with you, I feel like I'm losing track of who I am."

His smile deepened. "That's what happens when you make love, honey. Everything's going to work out just fine, Anna. Trust me."

Make love? They weren't making love, were they? This was just sex. Maybe it would be utterly fantastic sex, but nothing more. Absolutely nothing more. Anna scowled at him, covering her fear. "I make it a rule never to trust a man who tells me to trust him."

He smiled, the slow, sexy smile that always drove her mildly crazy. "But we threw out the rule book the moment I walked into your office, didn't we?"

Anna finally acknowledged that what was happening now had been inevitable from the moment they first met. "Yes," she said. "I guess we did." Shivering with the anticipation of what would come, she tilted her head back and looked straight into Joe's eyes as he slowly unfastened her shirt and tugged it from her shoulders, his mouth closing hungrily on her breast.

Eyes closed, leaning against the wall for support, she gave herself up to the delight coursing through her body. She was on fire, her legs trembling, her blood roaring in her ears. Having sex with Joe might well be the most irresponsible thing she'd contemplated doing in her entire life. The cops could arrive at any second. Right now, she didn't give a damn. She wanted to take Joe into her bed and experience everything that would follow. For the first time in her life, she wanted to know what it felt like to surrender to a man without reservation.

Despite her previously humdrum sex life, Anna had always suspected that she was a woman capable of intense passion, but she'd assumed that any lover who wanted to bring her true pleasure would have to be willing to invest in hours of patient persuasion and gentle foreplay. Joe soon blew that theory sky-high. She discovered that she didn't want slow hands and tender kisses, much less soft words and whispered compliments. After a lifetime of holding back, it turned out that she wanted exactly the fierce, demanding passion that Joe was offering her.

She spoke only once. "Your wound—"

"It's fine."

That pithy exchange drained her capacity for any thought or conversation requiring higher order brain functionality. They didn't even make it as far as her bedroom, ending up on the living room sofa in a tangle of half-discarded clothing and heaving limbs, taking what her body so violently craved and Joe was so willing to deliver. Her climax was a gasping, shuddering swell of sensation, followed by an instant of sheer, piercing joy. Then everything inside her shattered, breaking into a thousand pieces that she knew instinctively could never be reformed into the old Anna.

She lay on the sofa with the heavy, satisfying weight of him pressing against her. Joe's eyes were closed and his breath came in harsh, ragged pants. She felt the rapid rise and fall of his chest and let herself drift, replete and smugly gratified that she'd exhausted him. She remembered his injury only when she felt the taped edge of the bandage brush against her skin.

"Oh, God. Are you bleeding?" She wriggled beneath him, trying to see if there was any telltale red staining his bandages.

He shook his head, his smile tired, but as sated as her own. "You underestimate Charlie's skill as a battlefield medic."

Anna let herself float back into a blissful state of lethargy. She could allow herself just a few seconds more of lying here with Joe, she decided. She knew they ought to be hurrying to get the hell out of Dodge, but the knowledge didn't seem quite as important or as urgent as it had earlier.

After the driving intensity of their lovemaking, Joe's hands were finally gentle as they moved in a languid caress over her thighs. Anna closed her eyes, surrendering to the sybaritic pleasure of his touch. Her skin began to tingle and her spine arched in sudden tension. Only moments ago she would have sworn that it would be days—weeks—before she would even think about having sex again. Astonishingly, as

Joe's fingers inched toward her inner thigh, she felt the sharp, totally unexpected stab of renewed desire.

Her hand streaked down and found him already hard and waiting. His muscles spasmed as she touched him and she shifted her hips, taking him inside her again. He plunged deep and her body convulsed before her mind even had time to consider the amazing fact that she'd had two orgasms in as many minutes.

Her body was still rippling with aftershocks when Joe got off the sofa. His breathing remained erratic and his movements were jerky, unlike his usual sinuous coordination. Okay, so she'd wanted sex that was ravenous, quick, and fiercely demanding. But right now, in the aftermath, she badly needed Joe to reassure her that what they'd shared had been as extraordinary for him as it had been for her. She watched in silence as he gathered his clothes and pulled on his jeans, zipping them closed before coming to kneel beside her, his hands resting on her knees with a casual intimacy that both shocked and pleased her.

"Anna, I can't say I regret what just happened because I don't. Not for a second. What I would like more than anything in the world right now is to take you to bed and spend the night exploring some of the ways we could make love together. Then I'd like to share breakfast and go back to bed so that we could make love some more. But we can't do that. I'm putting you unforgivably at risk every minute I stay with you. Peter might have called the police by now. The cops could arrive at any moment, with every right to break down the door if we refuse to open it. We...I...have to get out of here."

''Yes.'' The monosyllable was all Anna could manage, even though she knew he was right. Only a short while earlier, she had been reminding herself that they were racing against a ticking clock and desperately needed to get out of Denver. Now she found herself ready to count the world well lost for love.

Forcing herself to be practical, Anna sat up and reached for her discarded clothes. It was harder than she would ever have expected to make her voice sound brisk and with the program as opposed to dreamy and aroused. ''You're right. We can't take any more time here. We need to stay focused on what's important—''

Joe took her hand, his gaze locked with hers. ''What we just shared was very important to me, Anna. But if I'm going to remain a free man long enough for us to have a chance to build on what just happened between us, I need to find out who killed Franklin Saunders. And in order to discover that, I need to be out of here before the cops come knocking on the door. You're at risk, Anna.''

''We both are.'' Anna thrust her arms into her shirt and started buttoning, careful to keep her gaze averted from Joe. It seemed that her hormones were still doing the mating dance and had little or no interest in fleeing the cops, or otherwise focusing on the essential task of self-preservation.

She drew in a decidedly shaky breath. ''Okay, let's see. The best chance for us to avoid capture would be to drive out of state, but we can't run forever and we're not going to find Franklin's murderer by heading off to Nebraska or Kansas—''

''Anna, be reasonable, this isn't a journey we can make together. God knows, I'd love to have you come with me. But this is my mess, not yours, and I don't plan to drag you into it—''

''I'm already there. Hip deep and sinking fast.''

''At least don't wade any deeper into the muck. I don't need the guilt of knowing I screwed up your life along with mine. You're a smart woman, Anna, so act that way. Right now, you still have total deniability. For God's sake, don't throw it away. If I'm arrested in your company, we're talking about the potential for you to serve some serious jail time. And trust me on this, prison is no fun—''

''I am a parole officer. I know about prisons.''

''No, you don't.'' Joe's voice was flat, uncompromising. ''After I've gone, when the police question you, and they will, insist that I kidnapped you, and everything you did and said tonight was under duress.''

''Peter is going to dispute that story.''

''His word against yours. Make sure your words sound more convincing.''

Anna made a small, impatient sound. ''All we're doing right now is wasting valuable time. If you'd just stop arguing and start making some plans, we'd have a better chance of avoiding the cops. Let me make it easy for you, Mackenzie. If you want to leave here without me, you're going to have to tie me up and steal my car keys.''

''You think I wouldn't do that?''

''I *know* you wouldn't do that. You're great at making violent threats, Mackenzie, but you're lousy at carrying them out.'' Anna gave him no chance to respond. ''Will you please pour Ferdinand an extra bowl of water and give him some more food? I have a neighbor who's always willing to check on him if

I go away for a few days, so he'll be okay while we're gone. I'll push a note under the neighbor's door as we leave.''

''If you come with me, you're not just risking arrest and prosecution. There are hired killers out to get me—''

''Don't start that again.'' Anna headed toward the kitchen. ''Just feed the damn cat, Mackenzie.''

Joe poured fresh kibble into the cat's dish. ''You could be *murdered,* for Chrissake—''

''I'll take some granola bars and a bottle of mineral water with us. That way we can avoid stopping for breakfast.'' Anna rammed a six-pack of snack bars into a grocery bag. ''Mackenzie, could you demonstrate some slight sense of urgency, do you think? At the rate we're failing to progress here, it's going to be morning before we make it to the highway.''

''Goddammit, are you listening to a word I'm saying?'' Joe slammed the cat's fresh water onto the floor, spilling half of it.

''No, I'm not. You're being repetitive and boring again. Excuse me.'' She slipped past him and opened the fridge to retrieve the mineral water and added it to the grocery bag. From the corner of her eye, she watched as Joe found paper towels and mopped up the spill, muttering profanities.

''There, all done,'' Anna said, and slammed the fridge shut, taking out her aggression where she could. ''I'm going to throw a toothbrush and a few clean clothes into a backpack. I have a couple of sweatshirts that might be big enough for you, too.''

''That's just swell.'' Joe tossed wet paper towels into the trash, his expression ferocious. ''We're doing really great here, aren't we? Ferdinand's taken care of. We have emergency rations, and you're about to provide clothes for our journey. Of course, we haven't one clue where we're going, or what we might do when we arrive there—"

"You're getting that sarcastic tone of voice again, Joe. We have no idea where we're going because we haven't had a chance to talk about it and reach an agreement. Durango seems like a good place to start, don't you think?"

"No, it sounds damned dangerous. Just where the cops would expect us to go."

"Okay. Scratch Durango. Maybe. I'm willing to entertain alternate suggestions. Why don't you come into the bedroom? We can talk while I pack. That should save some time."

For a moment Anna thought he would refuse. But in the end, his sheer need for help won out. She decided to make him do the talking so that he wouldn't have time for second thoughts.

"I can't contribute much that's useful until I know more about the crime that got you sent to prison," she said, searching through her dresser drawers for sweatshirts. "You said at one point that your plan was to track down your former colleagues at the bank where you worked in Durango—"

"It seemed like a starting point, at least," Joe acknowledged. "Nobody in law enforcement ever looked for a culprit other than me, so there may still be incriminating evidence waiting to be noticed by somebody who's paying attention. I can only hope."

"You didn't have a chance to do even a preliminary investigation before your trial?" Anna dragged her backpack down from the shelf in her closet. "You have no leads waiting to be explored?"

"None. Zero. Only theories." Joe shook his head. "I was locked behind bars from the day I was arrested. The FBI believed I was sitting on a nest egg of almost a half million embezzled dollars, so I was considered a major flight risk. Local citizens were angry, so the prosecution fought hard to get bail denied and they won. From the moment I was arrested, I never again had access to the bank, to my personal records, to my desk. Nothing."

Anna pulled a sympathetic face. "At least that leaves us some obvious questions to ask, and places to look." She frowned, pausing in her packing. "Whoever's behind this... Why didn't they kill you back then, Joe? Wouldn't it have been much better from their point of view to take care of you right then, once and for all?"

"I puzzled about that for a while. In the end, I decided they were afraid a murder investigation might trigger inquiries that dug too deep. It's one thing to frame a man who's alive. Framing a dead man makes it look just a bit too convenient. I think I was a more credible suspect alive than I would have been dead."

"But they don't need to keep you alive anymore," Anna said, thinking out loud. "If Carlos and Miguel had killed you like they were supposed to, everyone would have written off the crime as a prison-related killing."

"Yeah. And if I'd been killed this afternoon, along with Frank, they'd have assumed he was just the unlucky bystander who got killed when the hit on me was activated. As it is, whoever's behind Frank's killing is in almost as good shape as if I'd been killed. After all, I'm the prime suspect in the murder. If I'm caught, you can guarantee I'll be convicted."

"Which would put you right back in jail, where you can't cause trouble." Anna was reluctantly impressed by the tightness of the noose that had been tied around Joe's neck—almost literally. "We have to go back to what happened five years ago," she said. "Did you keep a record of the irregularities you uncovered at the bank?"

He nodded. "I kept a full printout of everything that looked suspicious."

"Where did you keep it?"

"Locked in a safety deposit box at the bank, but I've no idea what happened to the file after I was arrested."

"It would have taken a search warrant to access the box," Anna said. "Somebody in the bank must have been there when the cops executed the warrant. Do you know who?"

"My lawyer was there, along with Frank and the president of the bank. But my file of notes was nowhere to be found. Naturally the FBI agents assumed that was because the file had never existed."

Anna tossed a couple of clean T-shirts into the backpack. "Where did you keep the key to the safety deposit box?"

"In my desk drawer. And you can quit rolling your eyes. You don't have to point out that this was not exactly a foolproof security system."

If he'd been cooperating in his own setup, he couldn't have made things much easier, Anna reflected. "Obviously almost anyone in the bank could have taken the key out of your desk and accessed your safety deposit box the moment the news broke that you'd been arrested," she said. "Didn't anybody in law enforcement consider that possibility?"

Joe shook his head. ''Not as far as I know. The truth is, the FBI conducted a shoddy, half-assed investigation because everyone was convinced they already had their culprit in custody.''

''Then talking to your ex-colleagues should be a good place for us to start.'' Anna slipped her wallet into the side pocket of the backpack and zipped it up. ''They may know a lot more than anyone realizes, including themselves.''

''You're right, but talking to my ex-colleagues is easier said than done. After what happened to Frank today, it's going to be damn near impossible to interview anyone without getting arrested for murder in the process.'' Joe's expression was grim. ''And it's not just me at risk. It's you, too.''

''You need an attitude adjustment, Mackenzie. Try to look on the bright side for a change.''

''Let's see. If you cut a deal with the prosecution, your sentence as an accessory shouldn't be a day over three years. How's that for sunny optimism?''

She glared at him, stuffing toilet articles into her backpack, along with a new toothbrush and a disposable razor for Joe. It was definitely time to give their discussion a new direction. ''I'm all done here. Let's head down to the garage. I already know a bit about Franklin Saunders and Sally Warner. Describe the rest of your colleagues to me as we go. After all, they're our suspect list, so I need to understand who's involved and what they're like before we can decide who to approach first.''

''Okay,'' Joe said. He finally seemed to be resigned to the fact that she was coming with him. ''I'll start with the president of the bank and work down the list.''

"Go for it. Oh, wait. I forgot socks." She turned back to the dresser.

Joe waited for her in the doorway. "The president of the bank is a man called Caleb Welks. His title sounds impressive, but actually his executive power is quite limited. All major policy decisions for the Durango branch are made by a corporate VP at the head offices here in Denver...."

Caleb Welks. *Caleb Welks.*

The name roared in Anna's ears, blocking out all other sounds. She was vaguely aware that Joe continued to speak, but she could barely distinguish the words, let alone make sense of what he was saying.

"Caleb would be about fifty-six by now, and he's been involved in the banking business for his entire career...."

Caleb Welks.

Anna sat down on the bed, because her legs suddenly felt too weak to support her. It was fifteen years since she'd last heard his name spoken out loud. Judging by her reaction, that hadn't been anywhere near long enough to get the poison out of her system.

She stared blindly around the room, searching for a familiar sight to anchor her, but the walls were spinning, dragging her back into the cold darkness of the past. She looked down, desperate for a tether to bind her to the warmth of the present. She was holding a pair of white ankle socks and she stared at them, frantically trying to remember what she'd planned to do with them.

Caleb Welks. Caleb *Welks. Caleb Welks.*

Anna drew in a deep, shaky breath, and then another. The roaring in her ears grew louder. Her stomach heaved. She was awfully afraid she was going to throw up.

Sixteen

Anna had gone dead white, Joe realized, stopping himself in midsentence. The blood had drained from her face, leaving her blue around the lips. Christ, she was going to faint! Quickly sitting down next to her on the bed, he put his arm around her shoulders.

''What's the matter, honey?'' The endearment slipped out barely noticed, a telling symptom of his hopeless infatuation. He took her wrist, feeling for her pulse. ''Can you tell me where it hurts?''

Anna didn't answer. Gave no sign, in fact, that she was aware he'd spoken. What the hell was wrong with her? Could she be having a heart attack? Her breathing was rapid and shallow, her pulse racing. Weren't those among the symptoms?

''Why don't you lie down for a minute? You'll feel better that way.'' Joe fought to keep his voice steady. He took her hands, which were ice-cold, and chafed them between his. ''Tell me where you're hurting. Talk to me, honey, please.''

Instead of lying down, she turned to him, blind-eyed. He was relieved to see that she could at least move. ''Ca-Ca-Caleb Welks,'' she said, her voice harsh with urgency despite the stutter. ''Tell me what this bank president of yours looks like.''

''Honey, that's not important now. We can discuss Caleb later, when you're feeling better—''

''Tell me what he looks like,'' she said savagely, and her eyes blazed with sudden heat. ''Tell me *now!*''

Her forehead felt a normal temperature, but she sounded feverish, almost hysterical, which was utterly unlike the woman he'd come to know. Joe decided it might be best to humor her even though he couldn't understand why she cared what Caleb Welks looked like. Watching her carefully in case she passed out, he launched into a thumbnail sketch of the bank president, paying far more attention to Anna than to his description.

''Okay. Let's see. Caleb's about my height, kind of a big, slow-moving man. He has gray eyes, I think, or they could be hazel, I don't remember. Straight brown hair, going thin on the top and silver at the sides. Average nose, mouth, eyebrows. There's nothing really memorable about his facial features, except maybe that his ears are small. He has a definite paunch, or at least he did four years ago, but nothing out of the way for a man in his fifties.''

''What about...'' Anna swallowed. ''What about his...wife?'' she asked.

''His wife?''

''Yes. What's her name, do you know?''

Joe realized that Anna's teeth were chattering. From cold? From shock? What the hell was going on here?

''His wife,'' Anna said, grabbing his shirt. ''Tell me about his wife, dammit!''

Anything to banish that frantic, haunted look from her eyes, even if it did seem crazily irrelevant.

"Caleb's wife's name is Christine, and she seems like a pleasant woman. Kind of shy, and keeps to herself. Caleb always said that he'd been lucky enough to marry the last homebody in America. Apparently Christine really enjoyed cooking and sewing and spending time with their kids, and he was grateful for that."

An expression of stark horror swept over Anna's face. "Is she…is Christine a lot younger than…him?"

Joe could feel her hands tremble as she asked the question. Belatedly, very belatedly, it dawned on him that it was his mention of Caleb Welks that had thrown Anna for a loop, not an attack of nausea, or other physical ailment. She wasn't asking questions about Caleb to distract herself from sudden pain. Caleb was the *cause* of her distraction. Of course! If he hadn't been so worried by her sudden deathly pallor, he'd have realized sooner what was troubling her. But what in holy hell could there be about the sound of Caleb's name that was sufficient to cause Anna to damn near pass out?

"Is Christine younger than…him? Maybe in her late twenties?" Anna repeated the question through gritted teeth, and there was the same odd break in her voice as before, as if she couldn't quite bring herself to utter Caleb's name.

"Yes, she's a fair bit younger than Caleb, more than twenty years, I think."

"That figures," Anna muttered, two sudden slashes of color flaring against the stark pallor of her cheeks. She shook her head violently, as if trying to dispel images she didn't want to contemplate. "Does she…does Christine seem happy?"

Joe considered for a moment. ''Yes, I guess so. She seems to enjoy her sister's company—''

''Her sister?'' Anna gave a laugh that held not a shred of mirth. ''Of course, how perfect! Her sister. Her younger sister, I'm sure.''

Joe didn't understand where this conversation was going, but he did know that it was beginning to make him very uncomfortable. ''Lynette—that's the younger sister—moved in with Caleb and Christine when she dropped out of high school. They were both really patient with her, although she made no effort to get a job, or enroll in community college—''

''Don't tell me any more, I can't bear it.'' Anna slid off the bed, picking up her backpack, which she'd dropped onto the floor. She started to walk away, then turned as if she couldn't bring herself to leave the subject alone. ''Did you say... Do Christine and Caleb...have children?'' she asked.

Joe nodded. ''They sure do. They already had three children when I was working in Durango, and Frank mentioned that they'd had two more since then, both girls, which makes three girls and two boys. That's quite a crowd by today's standards.''

Anna looked as if she might throw up at any moment. ''We have to go.'' She marched toward the door, still pale, but suddenly energized, her entire body radiating purpose.

''No.'' Joe barred her exit from the bedroom, not even bothering to point out that they hadn't yet agreed on a destination. ''Not until you tell me why you damn near fainted when you heard Caleb Welks's name. What's up, Anna?''

She hesitated. ''Nothing.''

''Like hell, nothing. Try again, Anna. Obviously,

you recognized the name. That's why you asked me to describe Caleb, so that you could be sure he was the same man you knew. Was he?''

She hesitated again, even longer this time. ''Yes. I'm sure it's the same man. Positive, in fact.''

''I'm guessing you knew Caleb quite well, and I'm pretty sure you didn't like what you knew. Come on, Anna, talk to me. You know this is a coincidence we need to explore. I really need you to tell me what you know about the guy.''

''I don't want to talk about it. About—him.''

Joe smiled tightly. ''Obviously. You can barely bring yourself to say his name. But you're a trained mental health counselor, so you should know that it's the things we don't want to talk about that most need to be discussed.''

''Go to hell, Mackenzie.''

''I almost certainly will. But not until you tell me why the name Caleb Welks sent you over the edge.''

For a moment he was convinced she wouldn't answer him. Then she looked at him with a smile so full of pain it tore his gut. ''All right, if you must know, I was married to Caleb Welks once for about twelve hours when I was seventeen. He's the father of my child, the daughter I haven't seen for fourteen years because I was forced to give her up for adoption when she was five hours old, and it's like a knife slicing pieces off my heart to hear his name spoken out loud.''

She drew in a jagged breath, then walked away to pull a tissue from the box beside her bed. ''Oh *damn!* I hate it that the slimy, two-faced bastard still has the power to make me cry. God knows, he isn't worth it.''

Anna had been married to *Caleb Welks?* She had a daughter by him that she'd been forced to give up for adoption? Jesus Christ Almighty! Joe wasn't sure what shocked him more: the discovery that Anna's jaunty and confident surface concealed wounds that ran deep and painful, or the realization that Caleb had lied about his past. Possibilities, doubts and questions jostled for his attention but he pushed them aside as he sought for a suitable response to Anna's revelation. He could find nothing to say that seemed remotely adequate.

"I've no idea why I told you about Megan." Anna's voice was muffled by tissues. "I never tell anyone about Megan."

He took a guess. "Megan is...your daughter."

Anna nodded. "She's fourteen now and living in Seattle. I can't see her until she's eighteen. It's written into the adoption agreement that I can contact her on her eighteenth birthday." The tears flowed silently down her cheeks as she spoke, and she mopped fiercely with her sodden wad of tissues.

Joe silently handed her a pile of fresh ones, not sure whether the hot acid in the pit of his stomach was caused by sympathy for Anna's loss, or rage at Caleb Welks who had, presumably, abandoned her.

Since words weren't coming easily to either of them, he wrapped his arms around her, offering the comfort he intuitively understood she needed, even though he was sure she would never ask for it. She didn't resist, but she didn't yield, either. She simply allowed herself to be drawn against his chest, her body remaining stiff and angular. Joe had the impression she was holding herself together through sheer, dogged determination. Her hands were still icy cold, although her cheeks were flushed, and she either ignored the tremors that intermittently shook her body or she wasn't aware of them.

After he'd been holding her for a while, Joe realized he didn't have to say anything brilliant or original. He just needed to murmur whatever words of sympathy and reassurance came into his mind. Most of what he found to say barely made the level of coherent, let alone brilliant, but the sound of his voice appeared to console her, at least a little.

After a few minutes, she drew in a shuddering breath and he finally felt some of the tension leave her. "Okay?" he asked softly, tilting her chin up and using his thumbs to brush away the last few tears.

She nodded. "It was just such a shock to hear his name after all these years. But I'm fine now. Truly. You can stop looking at me as if you expect me to totally freak out any second. Freak out more than I already did, that is."

Joe gave her face a quick, light caress. "Feel free to freak. I'm here to catch the pieces."

She managed a smile, albeit a watery one. "There's no time, which is probably fortunate for both of us. It's funny. Just a little while ago I was congratulating myself on the fact that I finally had my feelings about Caleb under control. Clearly, I was underestimating the power he still has to screw with my mind. Not to mention my emotions."

A dozen possible responses occurred to Joe, each one slightly more complicated than the last. In the end, he asked a trivial question because it was one of the few that seemed likely to have a clear-cut answer. "How did you manage to be married to Caleb for just twelve hours?" he asked. "I didn't realize that Nevada or any other state granted divorces that quickly.''

''Fortunately for me, the marriage wasn't legal, so I didn't have to get a divorce.'' Anna's voice was dry, but her confidence had visibly begun to return. ''Caleb already had two other wives at the time he married me. Two wives and six children, to be precise.''

''*What?* That pudgy, balding guy had two other wives that he hadn't bothered to divorce? And six kids? Good grief! Somebody needs to take the guy aside and explain to him about the wonders of modern birth control.''

''He isn't interested in birth control. It's his duty to have as many children as God sends him. And he hadn't divorced his wives because, in law, he hadn't legally married them. Caleb is a polygamist, a member of the True Life Church of Latter Day Saints. It's part of his religious belief that God wants certain chosen men to enter into celestial marriages with more than one woman. But as far as the state is concerned, I guess he's just living in sin.''

''Caleb Welks is a *polygamist?*''

''Yep, he sure is.''

Joe realized his mouth was hanging open and snapped it shut. ''You were only seventeen,'' he said. ''What the hell were your parents thinking about, letting you marry a religious crackpot with ants in his pants?''

Anna stared at him as if he'd said something shocking, and then she suddenly laughed. ''You know, I guess that's exactly what Caleb was. A crackpot with a yen for young girls. I never thought of it in quite those terms before.''

Joe was struck by another amazing thought. ''That's why you were asking all those questions about Christine and Lynette! My God, do you suspect that they're both his *wives?*''

''I'd bet a lot of money on it. I knew Christine and Lynette a long time ago, before I was married to Caleb. They were only toddlers then, of course, but they're not sisters, they're cousins. And I'd say the chances are excellent that one or more of those five kids was born to Lynette, not to Christine.''

Joe's mouth wrinkled with distaste, as if he'd just eaten something really nasty. ''My God, Lynette couldn't have been more than sixteen or seventeen when she first came to live with Caleb and Christine. It's obscene to think of him having sex with her.''

''Yeah, it sucks, doesn't it? He's almost forty years older than she is and she probably was given no choice about staying in school, or pursuing a career. But she's over the age of legal consent, and in theory, she made a free choice, so there's probably no crime Caleb could be charged with.''

The phone rang before Anna could say anything more, the sound ominously loud.

''It's past midnight,'' Joe said. ''Much too late for a social call.''

''I won't pick up. The answering machine will take it on the fourth ring.''

The answering machine on the nightstand announced that Anna wasn't available to take calls right now and Peter's voice resonated in the bedroom, lowered to a theatrical whisper. ''Annie, are you there? Are you alone?''

Peter paused, and when she didn't reply, he lowered his voice even further. ''Annie, if you're still alive, pick up the phone, for God's sake. You need to talk to me. I've got something important to tell you. Real important. I remember where I saw that creep you had in your condo tonight."

"Damn!" Joe and Anna exchanged worried glances. She hesitated for a minute, then picked up the receiver, pressing the button for the speakerphone function. "This had better be good, Peter. I have an early morning meeting tomorrow and you just woke me—"

Peter abandoned his theatrical whisper. "You ought to be more grateful, Annie. I'm just looking out for you, but you don't seem to appreciate—"

"Goodbye, Peter."

"Don't hang up!" Peter sounded genuinely alarmed. "That man in your condo tonight. Is he still there?"

"Of course he's not here." Joe was impressed that Anna managed to make the lie sound so believable. "Not that it's any business of yours whether he's here or not—"

"Thank God. Because I've remembered where I saw him before. He was on the local news tonight. Annie, the guy is wanted for murder! He's an escaped convict who killed one of his own best friends, just this afternoon, right here in Denver. My gosh, Annie, you're lucky to be alive."

Seventeen

It took Anna five minutes of fast talking to convince Peter that he was mistaken in his identification. That the man he'd seen in her apartment was an old college friend who'd arrived from Seattle only that evening, and who had been on a plane at the time Franklin Saunders was murdered. She could only hope that Peter would remain persuaded by her lies after they hung up the phone, but she wasn't optimistic and, judging by Joe's grim expression, he wasn't either. From now on, they could count on the fact that the police knew Joe and Anna were together.

Peter's phone call spurred them out of the apartment, and shortly after midnight they were heading south on I-25, with Anna behind the wheel. The last time she'd driven with her stomach lurching and pulses racing every time she heard the distant wail of an emergency siren she'd been seventeen years old and escaping from her marriage to Caleb Welks. Now a bizarre spin of the wheel of fate was sending her back to Caleb Welks, and this time the cops really were on her tail. She was sure there was some ironic life lesson to be learned from the coincidence, but right now she wasn't in the mood for life lessons.

''Have you decided to head toward Durango after all?'' Joe asked, glancing at a highway sign posting the exits for the Air Force Academy. ''Damn!'' he muttered, hastily turning to face forward again. ''There's a police cruiser behind us, closing fast.''

Flashing lights appeared in the rearview mirror as he spoke. Anna's mind went blank as glass. Then panic washed over her, obliterating the blankness. ''What shall I do if they stop us?''

''Hope like hell it's a traffic cop.''

''But I'm not speeding.''

Joe took Anna's gun from the glove compartment and laid it on his lap, aiming it toward her. ''If they stop us, don't be a hero, Anna. Tell them I forced you into the car at gunpoint.''

''They'll put you away for life if I do that.''

His eyes met hers and held for a second. He spoke quietly. ''Barring a miracle, they're going to put me away whatever you do.''

''Miracles do happen,'' she snapped.

''Only on *Touched by an Angel.* And I heard that show got canceled.''

The ominous blur of flashing lights drew nearer, their menace emphasized by the blare of the siren. With a white-knuckle grip on the steering wheel, Anna slowed to a sedate fifty-five and moved into the right lane, praying the cop would overtake her. She gave a strangled gasp of disbelief when the police cruiser sailed past her and signaled for the truck in front of her to pull over. Presumably the driver had been speeding, but she'd been so obsessed with her own guilt that she hadn't noticed.

Joe let out a breath almost as gusty as her own, and returned the gun to the glove compartment. ''That was no fun at all. Let's hope we don't run into too many more traffic cops tonight. It makes for more excitement than I can handle.''

Anna waited for her heart to slide down out of her throat before she even attempted to speak. ''I don't think I have the right character for leading a criminal life,'' she said, when she finally stopped shaking. ''I have about as much spirit of adventure as an overcooked noodle.''

Joe stared at her in disbelieving silence for a minute, then laughed. ''You're serious, aren't you? Take it from me, honey. You and wet noodles have absolutely nothing in common.''

She was ridiculously pleased by the compliment. She'd dated a lot of men in an effort to obliterate the memory of Caleb Welks, and maybe one or two of them had looked at her as Joe did. As if she were the most fascinating and sexy woman he'd ever met. As if there were nobody he would prefer to have by his side. But it was a first for her to return the look and the feelings.

His fingers trailed lightly over her knee, the gesture as much reassuring as seductive. ''So, where are we aiming for tonight?'' he asked.

''I thought we could head about a hundred miles west of Durango to a small town called Alana Springs. The cops will never look for us there and it's a good place to start asking questions.''

''Alana Springs? I don't recognize the name.''

''There's no reason why you would, even though you lived in Durango. It's a ranching town, not very prosperous. Half the families get food stamps or some other form of public assistance. There's one gas station and the only place to buy groceries is in the animal feed store. You pick up your cans of beans and jars of Miracle Whip from the shelf right next to the kerosene and hoof picks.''

Joe grinned. ''I'm guessing you haven't chosen it for the luxury accommodations, so why did you choose it?''

''Caleb Welks used to live just outside Alana Springs and the town itself is the headquarters for the True Life Church of Latter Day Saints. There's a chance that Caleb's two original wives might still be living in the same house that he owned fifteen years ago. They might be willing to talk to us. Anyway, it's a place to start.''

''A great place to start if Caleb's ex-wives are still there,'' Joe said. ''But why would they continue living together when their husband has left town?''

''Where else would they go? Darlene and Pamela both had kids to raise, and neither one of them had any job training. Besides, one of the reasons polygamy keeps its grip from generation to generation is that the men take their family obligations seriously, so in a weird kind of way, there's security for the women of Alana Springs, provided they stick to the approved code of behavior and never involve any outsiders in their problems.''

''Are you suggesting that Caleb still supports these women, even though he was never legally married to them in the first place?''

Anna nodded. ''Caleb probably pays all their household bills, and even gives them a small allowance. Polygamy is a very expensive proposition, and a lot of families in Alana Springs live close to the poverty line. Or below it. Caleb, with his white-collar job at the bank, was always looked up to as one of the richest and most successful members of the True

Life Church. He wouldn't want to blow his reputation."

"Why would Caleb care about what the other church members think of him?" Joe asked, adjusting the seat belt, which was obviously bothering him where it rubbed against his wound. "After all, he's not living in Alana Springs anymore. Surely he cares more about being accepted by the business elite in Durango than he cares about a dusty little town run by a weird religious sect?"

"That's your perspective, not Caleb's. He's always straddled two different worlds, but I think he was a sincere believer in the teachings of the True Life Church."

"He *was* a true believer," Joe said. "Past tense. He's moved away from Alana Springs now. He's been settled in Durango for at least eight years."

"But he doesn't seem to have renounced his belief in polygamy, or he wouldn't be living with Christine and Lynette and lying about his situation to outsiders."

"Isn't it possible that he's telling the truth about his marriage?" Joe asked. "Maybe he really is married to Christine, and Lynette is just staying with them because she dropped out of school and doesn't have a job."

"Then why doesn't she have a job? And why hasn't she gone back to school? Why is she still living with them seven years later?" Anna shook her head. "That tale Caleb spun is one of the standard cover stories True Life Church members use when they want to live in a regular community and hide the fact that they have multiple young wives in their household."

''How well did you know Christine and Lynette?'' Joe asked.

Anna flexed her shoulder blades and wriggled her butt around on the seat, trying to ease muscles that were protesting it was long past bedtime. ''We weren't close friends,'' she said. ''But Christine is only three years younger than me, and everyone in Alana Springs knew everyone else, after a fashion. One thing I can tell you almost a hundred percent for sure. Neither of those two girls would have been allowed to marry Caleb if he'd renounced his membership in the True Life Church.''

''I'm having a really hard time wrapping my mind around this,'' Joe said. His whole face wrinkled in puzzlement. ''Why in the world do Christine and Lynette stay with Caleb? It's one thing to accept polygamy when you're in an isolated community and everyone else belongs to the same sect. But Christine and Lynette have been living in Durango for years now. There's absolutely nothing to stop them walking away if they're unhappy with their living arrangements.''

''That's easy.'' Anna lifted her shoulder in dismissal. ''They probably aren't unhappy.''

''They *like* sharing their husband?'' Joe sounded skeptical. ''They *like* being married to a man who's a full generation older than they are?''

''Why do you find that so hard to believe?'' Anna had come to realize over the years that it was her own flight from Caleb Welks that was extraordinary, not the fact that so many young girls stayed in marriages arranged by their parents with almost no reference to their wishes. ''Christine and Lynette are fourth-generation polygamists and they've never known another lifestyle. Their fathers are both church elders, and their great-grandfather was one of the founders of the True Life movement. He broke with the Mormon Church over the issue of polygamy after he was visited by an angel back in the early 1930s. The angel ordered him to move to Alana Springs and establish the True Life Church. There were twenty settlers in the beginning and they must have been desperately poor. It was during the Depression, and Colorado was suffering from a terrible drought. The mere fact that the community managed to survive must have seemed like an act of God, showing his approval. Anyway, from those early settlers, the sect has grown to almost six thousand active members, scattered in small settlements across America.''

''Six thousand members?'' Joe jerked forward in his astonishment, yelped when the seat belt cut into his stitches, and leaned back again. ''You're telling me there are six thousand polygamists in the United States?''

''More like twenty or thirty thousand,'' Anna said. ''There are six thousand just in the True Life Church, quite a few of them in Canada. In fact, Christine's mother came from a polygamous community in British Columbia. The True Life Church teaches that girls are the property of their fathers until they're sixteen. After that, they come under the guardianship of the church elders. Unless they marry, of course, in which case they become the property of their husbands, which means they're still not free to make their own decisions. Girls are sent back and forth between Alana Springs and British Columbia all the time in an effort to prevent too many cousins ending up marrying each other.''

"But that must mean young girls end up marrying men they've never seen before, much less had the chance to fall in love with. Not to mention the fact that they find themselves living thousands of miles away from home."

Anna could almost smile at Joe's horrified tone of voice. Almost. "If you're a member of the True Life Church, marriage isn't about falling in love. Marriage is about maximizing the number of babies a man can have."

Joe let out a long breath and rolled his shoulders. "This is America, not Afghanistan. We don't have religious police patrolling the streets and whipping women who dare to step outside the home without a man to control them. I'm having a really hard time understanding why any American women would accept that sort of life. Hell, I'm having a hard time understanding why even the men would accept it."

"There are more advantages than you might think." The truth was, that until she started high school, Anna had enjoyed her life in Ray Welks's household. Her stepbrothers happened to be younger than she was, so she didn't have adolescent males to lord it over her, and she liked having stepsisters almost her own age, with whom she could share harmless secrets. She liked having the excitement of new babies arriving, and she liked having toddlers to cuddle and tuck into bed. She liked to share mealtimes sitting around the two huge tables in the kitchen, with casserole dishes piled high with potatoes and corn bread and fried chicken and Aunt Debbie's special home-canned green tomato relish. She even enjoyed meeting her girlfriends at Wednesday evening bible class, and putting on a frilly dress made by Aunt Patsy for Sunday morning service. As for her stepfather, he had been a tyrant in his own home, but he'd been a benevolent tyrant—at least until she'd started to rebel against his edicts.

"There's a kind of perverted Norman Rockwell charm to the lifestyle," she said, answering Joe's question. "If the wives happen to get along well together, they can provide real friendship and support for one another. If you're feeling sick, there's always somebody else to clean the house and take care of your kids. If you hate to cook, there's probably another wife who enjoys it, leaving you free to spend your time sewing or planting a herb garden. As for the men—they say it isn't the sex, but I think that's a big part of it, despite all their pious denials. But it's not only the sex that keeps them in the life, that's for sure. After all, they could marry one woman and have affairs on the side like most other men in America if it was only about sex."

"So if it isn't the sex keeping men within the sect, what is it?"

"The power," she said. "It's the power that really hooks the men, and keeps them believers. They're absolute masters in their own homes, and not just of one woman, but an entire harem of women. Their word is law and when the master speaks, the whole household listens and obeys. Their children quickly realize that although there are lots of mothers around, there's only one father, and he's the person you have to please. And then there's the ultimate kicker. Heaven. The True Life Church teaches that women can only go to heaven with the consent of their husband. From the woman's point of view, that transforms her into a slave to her husband's approval, and she can never rebel, because that means she'll go to hell. From the man's point of view, on the other hand, it's the ultimate power high. You don't just control your women in this life. By golly, you control them through all eternity.''

''It's sick,'' Joe said flatly. ''Totally sick.''

''Yes. But it works for a lot of people.''

''You rebelled,'' Joe pointed out. ''You escaped.''

''I'm the exception that proves the rule. And I'm probably not a true exception. My dad died when I was in the third grade, but I led a completely normal life until my mom married Ray Welks. The years I spent in a typical suburban household before my dad died gave me a standard of comparison that most of the girls in Alana Springs don't have.''

''Ray Welks?'' Joe repeated the name, staring at her through the darkness of the car's interior. ''Is your stepfather related to Caleb Welks?''

''Yes,'' she admitted. ''Ray is Caleb's older brother, and Mom married Ray about a year after my dad died.''

''So when you were paired off with Caleb, you were actually marrying your stepuncle.'' Distaste flickered over Joe's face. ''That sounds almost incestuous.''

''Mentally and socially, perhaps, but not genetically. Relationships in Alana Springs get a lot closer than that to incestuous, despite the effort to import brides and broaden the gene pool.''

They continued to talk nonstop as the car ate up the miles. It was a strange journey they were making, Anna reflected. In driving back to Alana Springs, they were both preparing to investigate their pasts in order to free up their futures. It seemed appropriate, somehow, that they should find themselves confiding intimate details of their lives to each other as they traveled through the night.

Joe asked her about Megan, and once Anna started to talk, the floodgates of self-imposed repression burst open. She shared with him every scrap of information she'd gleaned over the years, surprised to discover how much pleasure there was, albeit bittersweet, in talking out loud about her daughter.

In exchange, Joe told her about his parents. About his mother, Heather, who, he'd been told, was as sweet and pretty as her name, but had an improperly diagnosed heart ailment and died in the process of giving birth to him. He also told her about his father who was—ironically—a guard at the federal prison in Leavenworth, Kansas. Tom Mackenzie never drank, he attended church most Sundays, and although he kept his second wife, Joe's stepmother, on a very short leash, he was never physically or verbally abusive toward her. Tom saved his brutality for his only son, perhaps because he couldn't forgive Joe for arriving in the world at the expense of his mother's life.

The brutality only got worse when Joe was tested in the fourth grade and identified as academically gifted, with a special aptitude for music. His father was no great believer in book-learning, but he positively despised music, which he considered the province of homosexuals, drug addicts and other degenerates. He was horrified when he discovered his son had been taking violin lessons. The violin, for Chrissake. That was an instrument for queers and faggots if ever Tom Mackenzie had heard of one. He forbade Joe to continue his lessons, an order Joe disobeyed until his father broke his arm to underscore his point.

From then on, Tom Mackenzie kept a suspicious eye on his son, constantly on the lookout for telltale signs that Joe's dangerously high IQ was infecting him with a multitude of undesirable characteristics. Tom's cure for any and all problems was simple: beat the crap out of his son. Joe had no choice except to tolerate the abuse until his fifteenth birthday, at which point he was an inch taller than his father, albeit forty pounds lighter. The next time his father threw a punch, Joe threw one right back. And then another. He laid his father out cold on the kitchen floor, and walked out of the house with the clothes on his back and the change in the pocket of his jeans. He hitched rides to his grandparents' farm three hundred miles away in southern Kansas, and never returned to his father's house.

After that, he'd won academic scholarships to the University of Kansas, and after a couple of years working as a bond trader in New York, he'd gone back to school and earned his MBA from the Wharton School in Philadelphia. His assignment to the relative backwater of Durango had been his own choice. It was the nineties, and the stock market was soaring. Joe had wanted to find a way to integrate small rural communities into the dazzling global economy that risked roaring right past them.

They had two other scares with sightings of police cruisers, but both proved to be false alarms, and they arrived in Alana Springs at seven in the morning, having stopped by the roadside to eat their breakfast of granola bars and drink some water while they watched the sun come up. Anna's eyes felt as if they'd been rubbed with sandpaper and, despite Joe's efforts to conceal the pain, he could no longer hide the fact that his wound was hurting like hell. He swallowed one of Charlie's antibiotics along with four over-the-counter pain pills, and claimed to feel fine.

Anna didn't believe him. She felt like death warmed over herself and saw no reason Joe would feel any better. Nevertheless, the fact that they'd made it this far without being arrested seemed cause for celebration, and her mood was unexpectedly upbeat as they drove into the familiar environs of Alana Springs.

The town had apparently prospered during the boom years of the nineties. The roads had been resurfaced, and a brand-new drugstore now stood kitty-corner from the gas station at the intersection of Main Street and First Avenue. There were four cars parked outside Maisie's Coffee Shop, the unofficial meeting place for those citizens who weren't members of the True Life Church and therefore were permitted to pollute their bodies with caffeine. Otherwise the town was almost empty of traffic as they drove down Main Street, and headed out on the bumpy county road toward Caleb's former home.

The house looked smaller than Anna remembered, but it had recently been spruced up by a coat of paint, and the porch had two big barrel tubs of magnificent tulips blooming on either side of the front door. There were also gracious stands of aspen that she didn't remember clustered at either end of the house, and a garden bed running along the perimeter of the porch that looked as if it had recently been dug over, ready for spring planting. A sleek Toyota Land Cruiser stood under the shade of the carport, sharing space with a Ford Escort, and a Dodge minivan that had seen better days was parked behind the Escort. With three cars in the driveway, Anna was optimistic that they would find Darlene and Pamela at home.

She parked her Subaru on the patch of gravel in front of the steps leading up to the porch. She'd stopped in the precise spot where Ray had parked his car on her wedding day, she realized. She had to sit in the car for a minute after she turned off the ignition so that she could control the vicious pressure in her chest and the roaring in her ears. She'd known that returning to this house would bring back painful memories. She hadn't known that her body would react as if the past fifteen years didn't exist. As if she were once again a terrified seventeen-year-old about to be subjected to ritual rape in the name of religion and celestial marriage. She still hated Caleb Welks, she realized. The hate had simply shriveled from a vast, amorphous shroud into a dense, leaden weight that was lodged permanently in the dark cave of her soul.

Joe ran his hand down the back of her arm, over hers. "Are you okay?"

"I'm fine." She was also a liar.

"What do you want to do about your gun? Leave it in the car?"

She shook her head. "That's against regulations. Makes it too easy to steal."

Joe laughed.

"What's funny?" she asked.

"You worrying about breaking departmental regulations. At this point, I think that may be a lost cause."

"Then think of it as a safety issue." She checked the safety on the gun and shoved it into the side pocket of her backpack.

Joe got out of the car and stretched, hitching the backpack over one shoulder. ''There's a woman peeking at us from behind a curtain on the second floor.''

Anna looked up in time to see the curtain twitched quickly into place. ''At least we know for sure somebody's home.''

The incident with the curtains reminded her of all the silliness and hothouse secrecy of life in Alana Springs. Irritated to the point of boldness, she marched up the porch stairs behind Joe and rang the doorbell, keeping her finger on the button.

After a short wait, the door was opened by a pink-cheeked woman of average height and build, whose skin was wrinkled into premature old age by the dry air and fierce sun of southwest Colorado. Her eyes were blue, and her mostly gray hair still contained strands of flaming auburn.

For a moment, Anna forgot how to breathe. Memories and emotions rushed in, and she had to swallow hard before she could speak. ''Mom? W-what are you doing here?''

Her mother didn't answer and she didn't smile. Anger and fear flickered in her eyes. Her gaze, dark with hostility, traveled slowly from the tip of Anna's head down to her dusty sneakers. Then she switched her gaze to Joe and subjected him to the same scrutiny. Finally she turned back to Anna. ''You made your choices fifteen years ago. Why have you come back?''

The barb winged home and hooked into her heart, cutting unexpectedly deep. Anna discovered that her throat was clogged, making it impossible to speak. Fortunately, Joe answered for her. ''We're looking for Pamela and Darlene Welks.''

''They're not available. Whoever you are, you have no business with us.'' Betty Jean turned and made to shut the door.

Joe moved while Anna was still deciding how to react. He pushed his foot inside the door and leaned his shoulder against the jamb, preventing Betty Jean from closing it. ''We have some questions to ask about Caleb Welks. They're urgent.''

''You're trespassing,'' Betty Jean hissed. ''Get out.''

''As soon as you've answered our questions. Otherwise Anna and I just might decide to pay a visit to the cops in Durango and inform them that Caleb Welks is a practicing polygamist who has, at one point or another in his life, married no less than five women. Do you really want your brother-in-law to face criminal charges? Not to mention the sort of investigation his arrest and trial might trigger into the practices of the True Life Church here in Alana Springs.''

The color drained from Betty Jean's cheeks. ''Caleb has never married anyone according to the laws of the state. He's in no danger from the likes of you.'' Her gaze swivelled sideways and grazed over Anna. ''Or her.''

''Want to bet on that?'' Joe asked, his voice rich with the gloss of prison-taught menace.

''Let them in, Betty Jean. We may as well hear what they have to say.'' A man's voice spoke from behind the concealment of the half-open door. He sounded subdued, almost weary, but Anna recognized his voice with no trouble at all. Caleb Welks. How could she forget the stuff of a thousand nightmares?

He came and stood behind Betty Jean, and the scar

tissue inside her burst open, flooding her system with festering poison from a fifteen-year-old wound. She wanted to lash out at Caleb, to scream abuse until she had given voice to all the hurt she'd never been able to express. She wanted to pound him with her fists to punish him for the physical violation she'd suffered at his hands. And she wanted most of all to run away and hide somewhere deep and dark where she wouldn't have to look at Betty Jean and see betrayal written on her mother's face for the second time.

She hadn't realized that she'd reached out to Joe until his fingers curled around her hand. They felt strong and warm and blessedly normal, anchoring her to the present, preventing her sliding too far back into the nightmare of the past.

Her mother, steeped in the role of second-class citizen, edged away from the door, leaving Caleb to confront them in solitary splendor. He was older, plumper and softer than Anna's memories. Despite his prosaic appearance, she still shuddered at the sight of him.

''Anna.'' He nodded toward her in barest acknowledgment. He blinked, shielding a start of surprise, when he recognized her companion. ''Joe. My goodness, it's Joe Mackenzie. I didn't realize you'd been released from prison.''

''Yeah. I guess it was harder to kill me than anyone expected.''

Caleb gestured for them to come inside. ''Why did you want to see me?''

Joe gave a feral smile. ''You could tell me who framed me for embezzlement. That would be a real good place to start.''

Eighteen

Betty Jean ushered them into the parlor and, looking toward Caleb for approval, suggested that she should bring tea and fresh muffins that she'd baked for breakfast. Caleb nodded his permission and Betty Jean slipped quietly away to the kitchen.

He gestured for Anna and Joe to take a seat on the high-backed sofa. "Darlene just got back from the hospital yesterday," Caleb said. "That's why you found me here. Normally I visit only on the second and fourth weekends of the month. But Darlene has had surgery for an...er...for a female complaint and Betty Jean is helping to take care of her."

"I'm sorry Darlene's not well." Anna's nerve endings were raw and she barely managed the courtesy. "Where's Pamela? Why can't she look after Darlene?"

Caleb leaned back in his chair, but his hands stroked restlessly on the lace doilies protecting the arms. "Pamela doesn't live here anymore."

Anna's head jerked up. "She's left you?"

He inclined his head in barest acknowledgment. "Pamela chose to go and live with one of her cousins in California several years ago. She took both our daughters with her. Our son had already left home to join the air force." Emotion flared in Caleb's eyes, but Anna couldn't identify which one. Anger? Resentment? Humiliation?

"You don't seem to have had much luck in keeping your wives tethered to your side," she said. "I wonder why?"

Caleb turned away, but this time he wasn't quite quick enough to hide the flash of emotion. Not anger or humiliation, Anna saw, but bitter hatred. His voice, however, was smooth and even conciliatory when he spoke. "I make no apology for my chosen way of life, to you or to anyone. The United States claims to offer freedom of religious worship, but for those of us who believe in celestial marriage, that claim is a hollow mockery." Caleb smiled thinly. "However, I've come to realize in recent years that if I want to assert my right to live according to my deeply held beliefs, then I must respect other people's right to hold different views. I regret very much that you were forced to participate in a marriage you didn't want, Anna. The coercion was entirely unintended on my part. I was under the impression that you were as eager to be my wife as I was to have you as my bride—"

"Oh please, Caleb. Don't try to rewrite history. When I said I didn't want to marry you, your brother took away my shoes and locked me in a room for three days with no food, and only water to drink. The fact that I had to be imprisoned to keep me from running should have been your first clue that I wasn't exactly longing to marry you."

Caleb's voice hardened. "I was never told of your reluctance. Never. Until I woke up and found you gone from my bed, I had no idea that you didn't wish for the marriage as much as I did."

It was a convincing performance, and Anna could see that Joe was at least partially persuaded. She, on the other hand, was buying none of it. She'd watched Caleb during the six weeks of their betrothal, watched him with all the intensity of prey in the presence of a predator, and she would swear that Caleb had known she didn't want to marry him. Had known, but had considered the fact irrelevant. What's more, he was still furious that she'd escaped his clutches so quickly and—as far as he knew—so unscathed.

Betty Jean returned carrying a laden tray. She murmured a surprised thank you when Joe took it from her and carried it over to the coffee table. "I'll leave you three to talk," she said, again looking toward Caleb for approval. "I'll join Darlene. She would probably enjoy some company while she eats her breakfast. Her appetite isn't the best."

"I'm sure she would." Caleb's smile was hearty. "Thanks so much for all your help, Betty Jean."

"You're welcome." Betty Jean appeared flustered, and she kept sneaking glances at Anna, as if she wanted to speak to her but couldn't find either the courage or the right words.

"Your mother is a good woman," Caleb said as she left the room. "She knows her duty and does it with a willing heart." He got out of the chair to offer Anna the heaped platter of muffins.

She shook her head, refusing the muffin. Her throat felt so tight with suppressed rage that eating at this point would probably choke her. "I'll just have tea, thank you. Joe, would you like me to pour you a cup as well?" She knelt beside the coffee table, reaching for one of the delicate china cups, needing to have the width of the table between her and Caleb. "It'll be a herbal brew of some sort. Members of the True Life Church avoid stimulants like caffeine.''

''Herb tea would be great,'' Joe said, taking one of the muffins but putting it onto a plate and not attempting to eat it. ''Look, Caleb, I appreciate the hospitality, but Anna and I are running out of time here, and we need to cut to the chase.''

''Of course. I must say that I'm surprised to see you two together. I had no idea you knew each other....'' Caleb's voice trailed off into a question.

''Anna is helping me investigate the circumstances surrounding my arrest and conviction,'' Joe said, which wasn't exactly an answer, although Caleb seemed to accept it.

''I guessed as much.'' With careful attention, he wiped his fingers on an embroidered cloth napkin. ''I have to admit, though, that I'm not sure how you think I could help your inquiries.''

He was smooth, Anna thought worriedly. Too smooth. She and Joe were working blind, without enough information to use as a weapon to break him. All Caleb had to do was stall. She and Joe would be left helpless, with no leads to follow, and nowhere to turn—with the police bearing down fast.

Joe, thank goodness, was betraying no outward sign of their weak position. He spoke confidently. ''When I was accused of embezzling almost a million dollars in client funds, I had one advantage over the official investigators. I knew I wasn't guilty. I also knew that the $923,000 missing from my clients' accounts wasn't really the problem.''

''Forgive me for saying so.'' Caleb's voice was mild. ''Your advantage doesn't seem to have paid off very large dividends.''

''I meant I had an advantage in terms of realizing the truth about what had really been going on at the bank,'' Joe said. ''I was arrested only hours before I planned to come to you with proof that somebody unknown inside the bank had helped to set up an elaborate system of phantom companies, with phantom payrolls, and they were using these accounts to launder money.''

Barely concealed impatience flickered across Caleb's face. ''Joe, you know we discussed the existence of these phantom accounts to death while you were waiting to go to trial—''

''Yes, we did. And you claimed not to believe me then, any more than you do now. Unfortunately for me, a man locked up in jail is expected to protest his innocence, so my stories were easy to ignore. But I'm not in jail anymore, and I'm still claiming I was framed. Those funds were embezzled to distract attention from the real problem at the bank. I had to be gotten out of the way to protect whoever it was that had set up those money-laundering accounts.''

Caleb sighed. ''Maybe you're right, Joe. All I can say is that nobody could find any trace of the illicit activity you're talking about—''

''Because one of my colleagues inside the bank made damn sure the auditors and accountants didn't look in the right places.''

''It's not that easy to fool bank auditors. You know that, Joe. Believe me, your claims weren't ignored. On the contrary, our accounts have been scrutinized and audited to death, both then and every year since. I'm sorry about those four years you spent in prison, really sorry. But you can't get those years back. I don't mean to sound heartless, Joe, but you need to move on with your life—''

Caleb broke off, gasping for breath as Joe grabbed him by the lapels of his jacket and dragged him to his feet. ''I have a real short fuse on my temper these days, Caleb. So here's some advice for you. Don't give me advice.''

Joe dropped his hands and stepped away, leaving Caleb to collapse back into his chair. He tugged his sweater into place, smoothing his hair over his bald spot. ''My goodness, Joe, there's no call for you to be so aggressive.''

''There's every reason. I served four years for a crime I didn't commit. Guess what? I plan to find the bastard responsible for putting me away and take care of him.''

Caleb looked at him with a mixture of fear and bewilderment. ''What's happened to you, Joe?''

''Prison happened to me. And if you're smart, you'll wipe your mind clear of the misconception that you're dealing with the same Joe Mackenzie you knew four years ago.''

Caleb picked up his teacup with hands that weren't quite steady. ''What do you want from me, Joe?''

''Information. While I was in prison, I kept trying to figure out who in the bank might have been helping bad guys launder their illegal profits. You were my chief suspect because you were the president of the bank, and you would have had an easier time covering your ass than anyone else. Plus there was the fact that nobody else on staff really struck me as smart enough to have set up what was a pretty complicated scheme.''

"It's ridiculous even to suggest that I might have been laundering money!" Caleb spluttered.

"Not ridiculous at all." Joe shook his head. "On the contrary, it was entirely logical. My problem was that I couldn't imagine what would motivate you to do something so dangerous. You didn't seem to lead a luxurious life, so you weren't likely to be aiding and abetting criminals for the sake of the hush money. On the other hand, you didn't seem to have any special vices, so I couldn't see how you might have been blackmailed into cooperating. Then Anna gave me a little background on you, and you moved right back up to the top of my suspect list. As a practicing polygamist, with one wife who was only sixteen when you married her, you're really vulnerable to blackmail, aren't you, Caleb?"

"Anna's information is trivial. Certainly no cause for you to suspect I'm being blackmailed. According to the laws of the state of Colorado, I didn't marry anyone. And it's legal to have sex with a consenting sixteen-year-old." Caleb gave a smug smile and, for a moment, his eyes gleamed with a light Anna remembered all too well. "Trust me, Lynette is definitely consenting."

Her stomach heaving in protest at the innuendo, Anna walked over to the window, unable to bear looking at Caleb a moment longer. Joe came and stood behind her, putting his hands on her shoulders and speaking softly into her ear. "Are you okay? Do you want me to take a break?"

"No, I'm fine. Don't stop. You need to press him for answers. We don't have time for me to get squeamish."

Caleb followed them to the window. As he approached, Anna's breath started to come quick and shallow until Joe slipped his arms down around her waist and drew her back against his body. How strange it was, she reflected, that the hard muscles of Joe's body felt protective, whereas the slightest touch from Caleb would not only make her flesh crawl, but would also feel intensely threatening.

Caleb gave Joe a hearty clap on the shoulder. "Look, in the for-what-it's-worth department, I've done some thinking of my own over the past four years and I'll admit I've wondered if society might have done you a terrible injustice. I didn't like the testimony Franklin Saunders gave at your trial, and I liked it a lot less when he turned around and got engaged to your fiancée only a couple of weeks after you were sentenced. It's no secret that Frank was madly in love with Sophie Bartlett, crazy for her, in fact. I'll admit I've wondered over the years if he deliberately gave that damaging testimony so that you would be found guilty and the path would be left clear for him to pursue Sophie."

"Obviously, he did."

"Maybe," Caleb conceded. "But it's a far cry from believing that your friend served you a real dirty turn at your trial, to believing that Frank deliberately conspired to get you framed for a crime you didn't commit."

"Sorry to interrupt, Caleb, but Darlene is asking for you." Betty Jean entered the parlor and automatically began to tidy up their plates and cups, a lifetime habit coming into play. "She's taken a painkiller and she'll be sleeping soon, but she'd like to have a word with you first, if you can spare five minutes."

"Of course. I can spare all the time she wants. It's

for Darlene's sake that I'm here.'' Caleb nodded toward Joe and, even more briefly, toward Anna. ''Make yourselves comfortable. Maybe you'd like to freshen up since you've been driving all night from Denver? We have a spare bedroom and bathroom upstairs now that the children have left home, except for Darlene's youngest boy. I won't be many minutes with Darlene, I'm sure. She really isn't feeling up to long conversations right now, poor dear. Betty Jean, you'll take care of our guests, won't you? Thanks.''

Looking ill at ease, Betty Jean waited for the sound of Caleb's footsteps on the stairs to fade away. Then she straightened from her task of folding napkins and looked steadily at Anna. ''I spoke too sharply when you arrived here.'' She crossed her hands in front of her, but kept her chin high. ''The truth is, I was so shocked to see you, Anna, that I didn't know how to react.''

Anna held her mother's gaze. ''A hug would have been nice.''

''Would it?'' Betty Jean sounded surprised. ''I expected you to be much too angry with me for that. And rightly so.'' Two bright spots of color appeared on her cheeks. ''I didn't do right by you all those years ago, Anna, and I'm sorry for it.''

It was more of an apology than she'd ever expected to receive, but Anna discovered she was too full of old hurts to accept it graciously. ''I was a child,'' she said, and her voice shook just a little despite her best efforts. ''You should have been my protector. Instead, you refused even to speak to me when I called from Denver and begged for your help. I was in trouble, Mom, and you weren't there for me.''

Infuriatingly, because she very much wanted to appear strong and in charge, she had to dash her hand across her eyes to wipe away sudden tears. Betty Jean watched her anxiously, biting her lip, then turned away and rearranged the napkins that she'd already stacked, giving her daughter time to recover. Emotions on public display made folks in Alana Springs very nervous. From Betty Jean's point of view, everything about this scene could have been designed to distress her.

''I believe in celestial marriage,'' she said finally. ''After your father died, it was my salvation.''

''Fine. But it wasn't mine.''

''I realize that now, but Ray thought otherwise. He was real upset by your interest in book-learning and your talk about the teachers helping you to win a scholarship to go on to college. He believed that marrying Caleb would turn your thoughts from worldly success and show you that home and family are the best way for a woman to build up heavenly rewards. In those days, I didn't understand that submitting to the will of your husband doesn't mean that you have to do something you believe is wrong. Our church teaches that celestial marriage isn't for everyone. Folks in Alana Springs forget that sometimes. I'm your mother, and I should have recognized that it wasn't for you. I shouldn't have expected Ray to understand you as well as I did, so it was my duty to speak up.''

Anna couldn't deny something that was true. Her mother should have fought to protect her from marriage to Caleb. But she also had to admit that after her initial protests, she'd carefully pretended that she was excited to be getting married, a defense plan that had seemed quite logical to a girl who hadn't yet celebrated her seventeenth birthday, even if it seemed less than brilliant now that she was a thirty-one-year-old woman.

If she could rewrite the past, would she? Maybe. But if she'd never shared that wedding night with Caleb Welks, Megan wouldn't exist. A loving couple in Seattle might never have become parents, and she wouldn't have the bittersweet joy of anticipating her reunion with her daughter in four years' time. She would never have taken graduate courses in counseling, and she would never have become a parole officer. She wouldn't have met Joe. And, of course, right now she wouldn't be running from the law.

That final thought produced a rueful smile and, after a moment's further hesitation, Anna crossed the room to her mother's side. "Don't beat yourself up over choices that have been made and can't be changed, Mom. I always knew you loved me and you did the best you could within the boundaries you'd set for yourself."

"But I made life impossibly difficult for you."

"Not impossibly. I coped."

"No thanks to me."

Anna shrugged. "Being a teenager is always difficult, whoever you are, whatever your circumstances. I had a rough few years in the beginning, but I'm happy with my life now, and proud of what I've achieved."

"Thank you for that." Betty Jean pushed a strand of gray-and-auburn hair back into the bun she wore at her nape and Anna felt a sharp pang as she recognized the gesture, not only from memories of her mother, but also from her own daily life. She had inherited her thick, uncontrollable curls from her mother, a reminder of how close the links were between her and Betty Jean.

She gave her mother a quick, hard hug. Betty Jean returned the hug almost surreptitiously, then turned away and blew her nose on a linen handkerchief. "If you two will come with me, I'll show you upstairs to the spare bedroom. There are clean towels already out. If you'd like to take a shower, why don't you? Since you've been up all night driving, you probably need a pick-me-up right about now, and there's nothing like a shower when you're feeling tired and dusty."

Still chattering, she showed them into what must once have been Pamela's bedroom, fussing as she produced a fresh bar of soap and showed them towels and clean washcloths.

"I'm going to take a shower since it's on offer," Anna said, as soon as she and Joe were alone. "A dose of really hot water might restore some small part of my brain function. At first it seemed like such a great bonus that Caleb was actually here. Now I'm not so sure. I don't believe he's telling us the truth. On the other hand, I have no idea how we can pressure him into talking. He's not a stupid man. He must realize that if he just keeps his mouth shut, there isn't a damn thing we can do."

"We can blow off his kneecaps," Joe said.

Anna stared at him, appalled, and he grinned, then dropped a brief kiss on her open mouth. "See. Even you believed me. Let's hope Caleb is equally easy to threaten. Go take your shower. When you're through, I'll wash up at the sink. I'd better not risk getting this darn bandage wet."

Anna took the shower and changed into clean

clothes from the backpack, pulling out one of her oversize sweatshirts for Joe. She was lying on the bed, her bare feet dangling off the end, trying to convince herself that she wasn't exhausted, when Joe came out of the bathroom, holding the extra sterile pad that she'd packed for his wound. He was stripped to the waist and droplets of water gleamed on the spiked ends of his hair. Anna felt a rush of raw desire that was increased rather than diminished by the sight of the knotted scar that slashed across his upper chest, counterbalancing the bullet wound on the left side of his rib cage.

"I admit defeat," he said, his smile wry. "Could you put on this new dressing? It turns out that I can't twist and tape at the same time."

"Sure." She slid off the bed and covered the wound with the clean pad, relieved to see that Charlie's stitches were all holding and a scab was beginning to form. She stepped back, about to make some silly, joking remark, but what she saw in his gray, once-cold eyes took away her power to speak. He took her face in his hands and his eyes never left hers as he drew her closer and his mouth covered hers.

Each time she and Joe kissed, it seemed that she lost herself sooner, and fell more deeply. This time, although the passion was swifter and more intense than ever, there was something new amidst the passion. Beneath the pounding pressure of sexual desire lurked a fragile awareness that her feelings for Joe had already changed and become something much more than lust. She was so absorbed by the extraordinary combination of sensations that it took her a moment to realize the noise she heard wasn't blood roaring in her ears but the muffled thud of feet climbing the stairs.

Joe must have come to a similar realization at almost the same moment. They broke apart, and Joe grabbed the sweatshirt from the bed, pulling it over his head just as Caleb burst into the room, followed by a man in uniform.

My God, it's Sheriff Betz, Anna thought, freezing into stillness. Caleb set us up! *He called the damn sheriff.*

Gun aimed squarely at Joe's midriff, the sheriff walked into the bedroom. He was in his fifties now and had a lot less hair than Anna remembered, but it was the same man who'd held the position fifteen years ago. A member of the True Life Church, he nevertheless only had one wife as a concession to his status as an officer of the law.

Barely able to conceal his glee, Caleb hovered to one side, his gaze darting back and forth between Anna and Joe, hungry for signs of their dismay.

Sheriff Betz cleared his throat. "Joseph Mackenzie, I'm arresting you for the murder of Franklin Saunders. Anna Langtry, I'm arresting you as an accessory after the fact in the murder of Franklin Saunders, also aiding and abetting in the flight of a known felon...."

The sheriff started to read them their rights, but he got no further than the fact that they both had the right to remain silent. Joe delivered a swinging kick, knocking the gun out of the sheriff's hand. He followed up with a swift, sideways chop to the man's neck. The sheriff dropped to the floor.

"You've killed him!" Caleb squeaked, hand clasped to his chest.

"No. Not yet." Joe picked up the gun, and aimed

it at Caleb. ''What would you like me to do with him?'' he asked Anna. His tone of voice was casual, as if he wanted to know whether she preferred the garbage dumped in a trash can or in the recycling bin.

''Nothing,'' Anna said. ''I'll take care of him myself.''

She'd only completed one course in self-defense, but she remembered enough to know exactly where she had to land a blow in order for it to be effective. She thrust her fist into Caleb's pudgy, overfed midsection with the pent-up force of fifteen years. Then she grabbed a handful of his hair and pulled his head back so that she could deliver a hearty sock to his jaw.

Her knuckles stung like crazy, but Caleb's eyes crossed with satisfying swiftness. She punched him one more time for good luck. He gave a groan and slid down the wall to the floor.

Joe shook his head, fighting back a laugh. ''Violence is no answer to anything.''

''I know,'' Anna said. She grinned hugely, sucking her sore knuckles. ''Boy, did that ever feel terrific.''

Nineteen

Within a minute, Caleb was stirring. Her punches had obviously packed more gusto than punishment, Anna concluded. Conveniently, Sheriff Betz had fallen close to the bed, so they attached him to one of the bed legs with his own set of handcuffs. Anna put a pillow under the sheriff's head, causing Joe to roll his eyes.

''Get your gun,'' he said. ''Looks like we're going to need all the firepower we can get our hands on.''

Anna retrieved the backpack and found her gun, strapping on her shoulder holster. With two guns aimed at him, Caleb was easily persuaded to stumble into an adjoining bedroom, where Joe patted him down while Anna kept her gun pointed at Caleb's head. Fortunately, he seemed to believe she would use it and she had no intention of enlightening him. Joe tied him to a chair with the cord from the phone before tossing it into the corridor. Caleb glowered at them with unconcealed loathing, but didn't speak, and they returned the compliment. She had absolutely nothing left to say to him, Anna realized. It was a liberating sensation.

''We have to lock your mom into the bedroom with

Darlene,'' Joe said, once they were out in the hallway. ''Unfortunately, I don't see any way to avoid it.''

Anna winced. ''Darlene's just home from the hospital. It seems terrible to lock her up. Couldn't we just trust my mother not to call the police?''

''Maybe.'' Joe sounded less than certain. ''But that's not the point. We have to protect your mother from the charge that she helped us escape. If she's locked up and we've removed the phone from the room she's in, nobody can get mad at her for not calling the police.''

''I hadn't thought of that. At least there's an attached bathroom, so I guess she and Darlene have access to everything they might need, even if they're locked up for a couple of hours.''

''We'd better double-check Darlene has all her medications,'' Joe said. ''But presumably her condition isn't life-threatening, or she would still be in the hospital.''

Anna pushed away a flutter of panic as Joe tapped on the door of the master bedroom. This was just a room, she reminded herself. No monsters lurked inside here unless she allowed them to take shape and form. Only moments ago she'd decided that Caleb no longer retained any capacity to hurt or intimidate her. It was surely time to put the haunting sexual memories from her wedding night into the same powerless category.

Betty Jean poked her head around the door in answer to Joe's light knock. ''What's up?'' she asked, opening it wider. ''Darlene's sleeping, but I can step outside for a few minutes if you'd like to talk.'' She edged into the hallway.

''Mom, did you realize that Caleb had called the sheriff?''

Betty Jean sent her daughter a puzzled look. ''Caleb sent for John Betz? What in the world for?''

''Because Caleb wanted us safely behind bars in the county jail, out of his way.''

''In jail? But why? That's terrible. Imagine locking the pair of you up. That's outrageous. Did he accuse you of trespassing?'' Betty Jean paused for a moment, her puzzlement increasing. ''Anyway, how did he persuade John to go along with something so silly?''

Anna and Joe exchanged glances. ''Because the police in Denver have issued warrants out for our arrest,'' Anna admitted. ''Not for trespassing. For...something else.''

''For Joe? For *you?*''

''For both of us.''

''Oh, my heavens.'' Betty Jean lost color and pressed her hand to her throat. ''Oh, Anna, what have you done?''

''Nothing that justifies being arrested,'' she said, which was sort of true, at least in grand concept, if not in technical legal terms. This didn't seem like the best time to cloud the air with mention of murder and escaped felons. ''Look, Mom, we're in a really tight time crunch here and it would take at least an hour to fill you in on all the background. It's complicated, but I'm asking you to please trust me just this one time. Joe and I have done nothing wrong, I swear it, but we're pretty sure Caleb has. He's trying to get us arrested not because he believes we're guilty of any crime, but because he's trying to protect himself.''

''Where is Caleb?'' Betty Jean frowned. ''Come to

that, if the sheriff came here to arrest you, where is he?''

Joe cleared his throat. ''Sheriff Betz is...um... handcuffed to the bed in the guest room.''

Betty Jean gulped. ''Oh, my. Where's Caleb?''

''He's tied up with phone cord and locked in the other empty bedroom.''

Betty Jean astonished both of them by giving a tiny giggle, hastily suppressed. She pressed her fingers to her lips. ''Oops, that was naughty of me. But Caleb can be so...so darn smug at times.'' She looked guilty for having made even this mild criticism of a church elder and readjusted her face into stern lines. ''You know you have to set them both free right away.''

''But we can't,'' Joe said. ''And the truth is, we have to lock you up, too. I'm sorry, Mrs. Welks, but we have no choice. If we leave you free, with access to a phone, it's your duty to set Caleb and the sheriff free. The sheriff will call in backup, and before you know it, half the cops in Colorado will be on our tail. We can't let that happen.''

For the first time, Betty Jean looked frightened. ''Why can't you let that happen? Why is it so important for you to avoid the police? Tell me the truth, Anna. Have you...have you done something really bad?''

Without stopping to think, Anna reached out and hugged her mother. ''Nothing, Mom, I promise. Joe used to work in the bank where Caleb is president. He was framed for embezzling almost a million dollars, but he didn't do it. Now we're trying to find out who really stole the money.'' It was easier to explain the problem in terms of theft than of money laundering. ''We think Caleb may be involved.''

Betty Jean's face displayed no reaction to this accusation. Surely it ought to have struck her as outrageous, Anna thought.

''Even if Caleb didn't steal the money himself, we're certain he knows who was responsible,'' Joe added.

''Oh, my.'' Betty Jean's fingers worried the frilled collar of her blouse, but Anna still couldn't read what she was thinking. Betty Jean never dealt with money except on the level of buying groceries, so perhaps she hadn't understood what they were accusing Caleb of doing. Anna decided to make the point another way.

''We think Caleb has been blackmailed into cooperating with some very bad people, Mom. Whoever these people are, they're ruthless. They know Joe is closing in on them, and they're determined to stop him any way they can, up to and including murder. There are two men in jail in Denver right now, hired killers who were paid ten thousand dollars to murder Joe.''

''Hired killers are going after Joe?'' Betty Jean said faintly. ''Are you serious?''

Anna nodded. ''We're hanging on by our fingernails, Mom. One man has already died. If we don't find out the truth real soon, Joe is going to die, too.''

And she might well be in the line of fire when that happened, Anna reflected. Funny, Joe had warned her about the risks she was facing a zillion times already, but this was the first time the truth had really hit her. The fact that Caleb had been so desperate to stop them that he'd been willing to involve the sheriff spoke for itself. Sheriff Betz might be a member of the True Life Church, but that didn't mean he turned a blind eye to any crime other than polygamy.

"Caleb couldn't possibly have known about people being paid to murder Joe," Betty Jean protested. "Or if he did, that's why he called law enforcement. To keep Joe safe. And you, too, Anna."

"Trust me, Caleb has no interest in Joe's safety," Anna said. "Mom, we can't stay and persuade you that Caleb isn't the wonderful man you believe. I just wanted you to know some of the truth, before we have to lock you and Darlene up. Joe and I are really sorry, but we have no choice."

"What are you going to do once I'm locked away?"

"Persuade Caleb to tell us what he knows."

"Isn't that going to be difficult?" Betty Jean asked.

"Yeah, but we have to do it, or we're toast."

Betty Jean stepped back into Darlene's bedroom, then swung around, bumping into Joe, who was following closely behind. "Wait. Maybe I can help you."

Anna was touched by the unexpected offer. "Thanks, Mom, but I don't think you're cut out for the role of interrogator."

Betty Jean winced. "Not that," she said hurriedly. "But I have some information that you and Joe might find useful."

Time was ticking by with terrifying speed, and Anna couldn't imagine what information her mother might have that would be of even marginal usefulness. But by the standards of Alana Springs, Betty Jean had already gone way out on a limb, and Anna didn't like to cut her off too abruptly.

"If you know anything that might persuade Caleb

to cough up some information, Joe and I would be grateful to hear it,'' she said, managing to keep any trace of brusqueness out of her voice.

''You think I'm wasting your time,'' Betty Jean said, showing one of her flashes of shrewdness. ''But I don't believe I am. A few years ago—it must be right about seven, come to think of it—Ray and Caleb stopped speaking to each other for almost six months. It caused a lot of stress and strife in the church, as you can imagine. Anyway, I overheard the quarrel that started all the trouble between them, not that I ever discussed what I'd heard with anyone, of course.''

''Of course,'' Anna said dryly. Contributions from the women were not encouraged in the True Life Church, even in the interests of healing a major family rift.

If Betty Jean recognized her daughter's irony, she ignored it. ''It was a Sunday, after services,'' she said. ''Christine had brought her new baby daughter to visit us for the first time, that's how I remember it was seven years ago because Helen is seven now. Anyway, Ray was drinking a glass of iced punch out on the porch with Caleb, and the women were all in the parlor with the new baby. I was cleaning up after lunch, listening more to what the women were saying than to what Caleb and Ray were discussing. Actually, the door to the porch was shut, and until they raised their voices, I couldn't have heard anything much even if I'd been paying attention....''

Anna gritted her teeth. Her stomach was churning with impatience and she could almost feel time flying past her, while her mother plodded through her story with endless diversions.

''Mom, I'm sorry, but you have to get to the point a little bit faster. What exactly did Ray and Caleb fight about?''

''It's complicated.'' Betty Jean wasn't easy to hurry. ''Caleb told Ray that there's this man in Durango who is very rich and powerful, probably the richest and most important man in the entire Four Corners area. He has some sort of big factory there from what I gathered, and he's looked up to by everyone in the community, partly because he employs a lot of people, I expect. Caleb was explaining to Ray that this man isn't the great citizen he seems on the surface, and that he has connections to every branch of law enforcement in the Four Corners area so that he could always call in a favor when he needed it. Apparently, this man even had judges and lawyers in his pocket, not to mention that there wasn't a town council anywhere around that didn't have at least one of his people on it.''

Betty Jean had led a sheltered life, and her endearing naiveté was showing. She sounded scandalized that a rich and powerful man would engage in such corrupt practices as trading off favors with judges and police chiefs. ''Anyway, Caleb said that he was in terrible trouble because this man had found out about his membership in the True Life Church, and was threatening to reveal the truth about Caleb's marriages to the authorities. I didn't hear all the details, you understand, but I think this man was blackmailing Caleb into doing something he didn't want to do, and Ray was angry with him.''

''With the rich and powerful man?'' Joe asked, interrupting for the first time.

Betty Jean shook her head. ''No, Ray was angry

with his brother. With Caleb. Ray reminded his brother that God didn't expect us to protect our way of life by committing crimes. That Caleb should do the honorable thing, and God would take care of him, because God always protects the righteous. Caleb said that it wasn't just him who was at risk. That all the members of the True Life Church were in danger if this man wasn't stopped. That's when Ray said Caleb needed to work some on his faith. God takes care of the whole entire world, so for sure he was capable of taking care of a few hundred church members, if that was what was needed."

"That sounds like very good advice on Ray's part," Joe said. "Do you know if Caleb took it?"

"I guess he couldn't have," Betty Jean said. "Because otherwise he and Ray wouldn't have been so angry with each other, would they?"

Anna expelled a tight, nervous breath. "Did Caleb by any chance happen to mention the name of this man who was threatening him?"

"Yes." Betty Jean looked embarrassed. "The trouble is, I don't remember it. It was an ordinary, American sort of name. You know, not Russian, or Greek, or anything like that."

"How about Arthur Bartlett," Joe said. "Does that sound familiar to you?"

"Oh, my, yes, it does." Betty Jean beamed at him. "However did you guess his name so quickly?"

"It wasn't difficult. Bartlett's got the reputation of being the richest man in Durango, and it's also the headquarters of his company, Bartlett Nutrition. He's one of the most successful manufacturers and distributors of vitamins and mineral supplements in the country."

Joe sounded businesslike and yet, beneath the crisp tones, Anna detected a subtle note of something more personal. "Do you know Arthur Bartlett?" she asked.

Joe's gaze flicked toward her. "He's Sophie Bartlett's father. We've met a few times socially. I don't know him well."

Sophie Bartlett. Anna took a moment to make the connection, and then it clicked. Forcefully. Good grief, *Sophie.* Wife to Franklin Saunders and ex-fiancée to Joe. She looked toward Joe, trying to gauge his reaction, but he seemed to be avoiding her gaze.

Thanking Betty Jean profusely for her input, they checked to make sure she and Darlene were both supplied with reading glasses, cookies, and medication, before the two women were locked into the master bedroom.

Anna and Joe walked back down the hallway to the bedroom where they'd confined Caleb. Outside the door she paused and put her hands on his shoulders, sliding them down to cuff his wrists. "Just because Arthur Bartlett seems to be implicated in what's been happening to you, it doesn't mean Sophie knew anything at all about what was really going on when you were framed for embezzlement."

Joe gave one of his feral smiles, the sort she hadn't seen in several days. "She knew."

"How can you possibly say that for sure?"

"I told Sophie about the phony accounts at the bank," he said. "She was the only person I told. We'd just made love, we were lying in bed together, and I started to explain how somebody inside the bank must have helped to set up an entire series of payroll accounts that I was convinced were phony. That probably two or three million dollars a year were sloshing through those accounts and coming out at the other end nicely laundered. And when I'd finished explaining to her just what I'd uncovered, how I'd made printouts and locked them in the safety deposit box, and how I was planning to wait for the end of the quarter and just one more set of statements the following week, and then I'd report everything I'd uncovered to Caleb Welks, that's when I realized she was asleep and hadn't heard a word I'd said to her.''

''Except she probably wasn't asleep,'' Anna said.

Joe swore viciously. ''No,'' he said. ''She probably wasn't asleep. On the contrary, she was up to her cute little fanny in whatever is probably still making Daddy Bartlett several million illicit dollars a year. She was listening intently to every word I said, and when she realized I was about to blow the whistle, she must have hurried back to Daddy and warned him about what I'd discovered. Bartlett must have pulled out all the stops to get me framed and arrested so quickly. Even with his top quality connections, it takes some doing to generate that much phony evidence that fast.''

''With what my mom's already given us, do we have enough to go to the police?'' Anna asked softly.

Joe slanted her a look of sheer incredulity. ''You're joking, right? Betty Jean underestimates Arthur Bartlett's power in this part of the state. He owns fifty percent of everything that happens in this neck of the woods. We aren't going to bring him down with a rumor that maybe he isn't a nice guy after all. Caleb's going to have to give us hard, solid facts of Bartlett's participation in an indictable offense. And even then, we have to be damn sure we take the evidence to a very brave D.A.''

Anna pulled a face, knowing that Joe was right. "Then I guess this is where you pull out your gun and threaten Caleb's kneecaps. Practice your prison scowl, Mackenzie."

"The way I feel about Caleb Welks right now, I don't need to practice." Joe pulled out his gun and pushed open the door to the bedroom.

Twenty

When they entered the bedroom, Caleb was visibly sweating, although the room was quite cool. "You won't get away with this," he snarled. "If John Betz doesn't report back to base within the next half hour, there are going to be cops crawling all over this house."

"Thanks for the warning." Joe spun his gun around so that it ended up pointing straight at Caleb. He ostentatiously clicked off the safety. "That being the case, we need to make this a real quick discussion, so let's get started. How is Arthur Bartlett making all the dirty money that you launder through those phony accounts at the bank?"

Caleb gave a little start of surprise at the mention of Arthur Bartlett, then quickly closed his eyes, hiding his reaction. "I have nothing to say."

"That's not a real good decision." Joe walked over to the chair and yanked Caleb's head around. "I'm going to make this simple for you. I'm going to count to three. If you haven't started talking, I shoot your left hand. Then I count to three again, and if you still aren't talking, I shoot your right hand. After that, we start on your kneecaps. I don't know if you ever go to the movies, Caleb. But if you do, you might have seen one of those scenes where a guy gets shot in the knees. If your religion forbids you to go to the movies, let me enlighten you. Having your kneecap shot out is considered to be the single most excruciating form of pain that can be inflicted on a human being.''

He stepped back. ''Now, I'm going to ask you that question again, Caleb. How does Arthur Bartlett make his money?''

Caleb spoke through gritted teeth. ''He has a lot of diversified business interests. Real estate, a radio station and so on. But most of his money comes from Healthlife. That's the division of Bartlett Nutrition which makes vitamins and herbal supplements.''

''Another wrong answer, Caleb.'' Joe's voice acquired a hard edge of anger. ''I'm not interested in Bartlett's legal activities. I want to know how he makes his dirty money.''

''I just told you. From Healthlife.'' Caleb looked away. ''From...pills.''

Joe's gaze narrowed. ''You mean illegal drugs? My God, that's it, isn't it? Talk about hiding in plain sight! Bartlett's using that vitamin factory of his to manufacture illegal drugs. He probably has it all set up so that he can walk FDA inspectors through the place, and they'll never know what they're looking at. What's he making, Caleb? Ecstasy? LSD? Ice? PCP?''

''I don't know.''

''Well, let me guess. All of the above, I bet, and a bunch more I haven't mentioned.''

Caleb turned sheet white, clearly terrified at having hinted enough to set Joe off on the right track. ''This is sheer speculation on your part. I've no knowledge of Arthur Bartlett's affairs. I have nothing more to say.''

''Gee, that's a real shame.'' Joe turned to Anna. ''You know, I could forget about his hands and just go straight for his balls. You might like to watch that, all things considered.''

''No, Joe—''

''No?'' He shrugged. ''Okay, hands it is. One. Two...''

Anna stepped into the space between Joe and Caleb. Judging by Joe's expression, if he reached the count of three, he might actually fire the gun. ''Don't shoot,'' she said. ''Please, Joe. Let me talk to him.''

Joe hesitated, and Anna had a suspicion that the hesitation wasn't entirely faked. ''You have two minutes,'' he said, looking at his watch. ''The clock's running.''

Anna swung around to confront Caleb. ''Why are you protecting Arthur Bartlett?'' She kept her tone amicable, but her mildness failed to elicit any more of a response than Joe's ferocity. Caleb simply stared through her, his attitude suggesting that if a man like Joe Mackenzie couldn't frighten him into talking, then a woman like Anna didn't stand a chance.

She gave an exasperated sigh. ''Okay, since you're not talking, let's see if I can figure this out for myself. Maybe you're more scared of Arthur Bartlett than you are of Mackenzie. If that's the case, I can only say Mr. Bartlett must be one hell of a scary dude. Or maybe you're deluded enough to think that if you stick by your friend Arthur, he's gonna stick by you. Those are the only two possibilities I can come up with as to why you'd be dumb enough not to talk. Which one is it, Caleb?''

''Neither.'' Caleb spat out the word, but the sweat

was beginning to run down the side of his face. ''I have no information about Arthur Bartlett.''

''You know, if I were sitting where you're sitting, Caleb, with my hands tied behind my back and Mackenzie's finger twitching on the trigger of Sheriff Betz's gun, I sure wouldn't waste my time producing lies that there's no chance anyone in this room will believe.'' Anna's voice hardened. ''Let me give you a quick reality check here. First, there's no reason for you to be afraid of Arthur Bartlett because, trust me, anything he might do to you, Mackenzie will do first and worse. Second, forget about counting on Bartlett to protect you. I'm a parole officer. It's my job to work with criminals. I know the way the criminal mind works. I can guarantee you that the last two things any criminal ever does is take responsibility, or look out for his pals. When they're in trouble, criminals run. They search for an easy fix. They find someone to blame. Arthur Bartlett is a criminal, even though he lives in a fancy house and drinks cocktails with the mayor. You think Arthur Bartlett is going to risk his own skin to protect you, Caleb? Don't make me laugh. He'll offer you up on a silver platter and stick a spiced peach in your mouth to make you look more appetizing.''

''Bartlett can't turn me in without incriminating himself.'' Caleb offered the protest without much conviction.

Joe laughed. ''Sorry to interrupt, Anna, but that one's too humorous to pass up.'' He leaned over Caleb, ramming the gun into his chest. ''You're not only stupid, you're pathetic. You saw how easily Bartlett arranged to get me incarcerated once he knew I was threatening him. He tried to get me killed yesterday and murdered his own son-in-law in the process. You think a man that ruthless hasn't considered that you might get tired of dancing to his tune? Do you honestly think there's the slightest chance he's going to let you bring him down? Get real, Caleb. Bartlett has had you set up to take the fall for him from the first moment you went onto his payroll. In fact, you're so toasted, I can already smell the bread burning."

"I'm not on Bartlett's payroll." Caleb sounded offended. "I wouldn't dream of taking an illegal payoff of any sort."

"Gee, no, of course you wouldn't." Joe fought for control and barely won the fight. "You're helping a criminal to launder millions of dollars of dirty money each year. You conspired to send an innocent man to prison for four years to save your own sorry ass. But you wouldn't do anything unethical like taking a bribe. Heck, no. Of course you wouldn't. What was I thinking of?"

Anna swung around, poking her finger into Caleb's chest. "Here's how you might, just possibly, get to save that aforementioned sorry ass of yours." She followed the direction of Caleb's gaze down to her fingers and realized what she'd done. She almost smiled. What do you know? She'd touched the slimeball and her world hadn't come to an end. It hadn't even tipped slightly sideways.

Emboldened, she jabbed him again for emphasis. "Come to your office with us and download every single scrap of evidence in the bank's computer system that might help us to build a case against Arthur Bartlett. Then find yourself the best lawyer in the state—"

"How about Dwight Daniels?" Joe suggested. "Or wait! Could it be that good ole Dwight is one of the lawyers Mr. Bartlett has tied up in his pocket? Is it possible that when I believed Dwight was busting a gut to defend me, he was actually doing his damnedest to make sure the jury found me guilty?" Joe shook his head. "You know, I was so goddamn naive, I almost deserved to be put away."

"Arthur Bartlett is one of this state's most respected citizens," Caleb said, but there was doubt in his eyes as he looked at Joe. "You're a convicted felon, and now you're wanted for murder. Nobody believed you four years ago and for sure they're not going to believe you now."

"This is nothing like the situation four years ago," Anna said. "Back then, Joe was in jail, alone, with a corrupt lawyer, and nobody to fight for him. The situation couldn't be more different this time. Even if I'm arrested, I'll make bail almost immediately. And I'm not going to waste time pleading with the police or the D.A. Hell, no. I'll go to the most cutthroat investigative reporters in Denver. I'll tell them about the True Life Church, and how girls of sixteen and younger are routinely being coerced into marrying old men. I'll tell them about birth records being falsified, and women collecting welfare payments because the men can't afford to support the dozens of kids they've fathered. I'll tell them about your five wives, Caleb, and how I was one of them. And then, when the reporters are salivating at the prospect of all those eye-catching headlines about sex and polygamy, I'll tell them about Arthur Bartlett and how he's been laundering money through your bank. I won't even have to hire an honest defense lawyer. The reporters will do all the investigating for me.''

Caleb sent her a look of such loathing that goose bumps erupted under Anna's skin. ''These are your people,'' he said. ''How can you threaten them with the destruction of their way of life? Have you no fear of God's punishment?''

Anna was sure Caleb saw nothing strange about threatening her with divine retribution while ignoring the possibility that God might have a thing or two to say about Caleb's own history of lies, theft and betrayal. ''The members of the True Life Church aren't my people,'' she said quietly. ''They're yours. And you have the power to save them, just by telling us the truth about Arthur Bartlett.''

''You want revenge for what happened to you. That's what this is all about, isn't it?''

She drew in an unsteady breath. ''No, Caleb, this is about putting Arthur Bartlett behind bars, where he belongs. That, and getting delayed justice for Joe.''

Caleb shifted on the hard chair, rolling his shoulders to relieve the stiffness. ''I'm not admitting that there is any incriminating information hidden in the bank's computer system,'' he said finally. ''But, just to speculate, if it did turn out that there's some information that might be damaging to Arthur Bartlett in my possession, and if I helped you to get access to a complete printout of—let's say—all the money that might have been laundered through phony payroll accounts at the bank over the past few years, what would be in it for me? How is it going to help me stay out of jail to give you that information?''

Anna just managed to restrain herself from giving

a whoop of triumph. She and Joe exchanged covert, excited glances.

"I can't tell you what deal the district attorney's office might offer," Joe said. "But a good lawyer should be able to get you significantly reduced jail time, or even immunity from prosecution if you offered to turn state's evidence against Arthur Bartlett. After all, we're talking about a man who's ordering up contract murders and running an illegal drug empire that rakes in sufficient profit to corrupt a hefty percentage of government officials in this part of the state. In comparison to Arthur Bartlett, you're small potatoes."

Fear and resentment flickered across Caleb's pudgy features as he mulled over his options. Not surprisingly, he didn't seem to like any of them. "What's so hard to decide?" Anna said when the silence stretched out. "Face it, Caleb, you've reached the end of the road. There are no easy choices left."

"Maybe not." Caleb sounded bitter. "If I agree to take you with me to the bank and to download the information you're looking for, you have to agree that you won't contact anyone in law enforcement until I've had a chance to call my lawyer and we've discussed the best possible way for me to make a deal with the D.A.'s office."

"We'll give you time within reason," Joe said. "But keep in mind that Anna and I are both at risk of being arrested. That's a problem for you as much as it's a problem for us. If we're taken into custody, all deals are off. We have no choice but to tell the cops everything we know."

Caleb's mouth tugged down at the corners. "All

right. I guess I'm going to have to help you evade the forces of the law.''

Anna looked at him with contempt. ''I can see why that would be a serious problem for a man of high moral character like you.''

''We'll take your car,'' Joe said. ''The police must already be on the lookout for Anna's Subaru.''

''Fine. Whatever.'' Having finally conceded defeat, Caleb seemed anxious to be gone. ''Can you untie me? Let's get on the road before any deputies get here from the sheriff's office. I want this whole mess to be over.''

They decided that Caleb would drive, and Joe would sit in front, with the sheriff's gun aimed at Caleb to prevent him getting up to mischief. Although it was hard to imagine what mischief he could even contemplate, much less put into action, Anna reflected, climbing into the spacious rear section of the Land Cruiser. Once Betty Jean had identified Arthur Bartlett, Caleb had nowhere to turn. She and Joe had told the simple truth when they claimed it was in Caleb's own best interests to work with them.

It was weird how life went in circles, she mused, fastening her seat belt. Her mother had failed to help Anna avoid marriage to Caleb but now, at another crisis point in her life, Betty Jean had provided the information that made it possible to coerce Caleb's cooperation.

Caleb backed out of the carport and Anna slumped against the comfortable leather seat, finally allowing herself to notice that her muscles ached everywhere. Even her fingernails felt tired. The landscape outside the tinted windows blurred as exhaustion washed over her in a huge black wave. Hours of unrelenting tension, piled on top of the stress of meeting Caleb again, added to the surreal sensation of floating at the edge of a nightmare. She fought against sleep, as if allowing herself to slide into unconsciousness would somehow increase the danger of their situation.

Caleb, perhaps relieved to finally unburden himself, gradually became more talkative as the miles flashed past. He and Joe were soon deep in a technical discussion of exactly how the phony accounts had been set up, how taxes had been evaded, and how Caleb had concealed the flow of money from various bank oversight committees. Anna understood about one word in ten of their conversation, sinking to one word in twenty when they lapsed too far into technical financial jargon. Almost dozing, she was content to let the talk drift over her.

She perked up a little when she heard the name Franklin Saunders. For a while, Joe and Caleb dropped their jargon and spoke to each other in plain English. Frank, it seemed, had not been involved with setting up the money-laundering accounts, or even with helping to frame Joe on the embezzlement charges. However, he'd been hopelessly infatuated with Sophie Bartlett for months. The prospect of removing Joe from the picture had been too much temptation for Frank. If Joe was guilty, he could pursue Sophie with a clear conscience, so he persuaded himself that his friend had embezzled hundreds of thousands of dollars from client accounts. After that, convincing him to take the next step down the road of betrayal had been child's play. Dwight Daniels had coached him in how to deliver testimony at trial that was calculated to help put Joe away, and Frank had given a bravura courtroom performance.

Since his marriage to Sophie, as far as Caleb could judge at a distance of several hundred miles from Denver, Frank had pursued a policy of willful blindness as to what was going on in his wife's family business. Caleb, so blithely unaware of his own hypocrisy, was well aware of Frank's. Caleb professed to know nothing at all about any plans to have Joe killed, but he did say that, in his opinion, Frank was perfectly capable of arranging with Sophie to lure Joe into the underground parking garage without ever allowing himself to think about what would happen when Joe got down there.

At some point, despite all her efforts to stay awake, Anna dropped from dozing into real sleep. She jolted awake with a start of panic when she realized that the car had stopped. Glancing out of the window, she expected to see cops surrounding them, and was mightily relieved when the scene she encountered turned out to be nothing more threatening than the forecourt of a highway gas station.

''We're running on empty,'' Joe said, turning around to smile at her. He reached to touch her cheek in a light caress. ''You look tired. Hang in there, kiddo.''

Amazingly, he didn't look in the least tired. ''A bed would be great right about now,'' she admitted.

Joe grinned. ''I couldn't agree more.''

She felt her cheeks grow hot and her fatigue vanished in a momentary rush of sexual energy. ''I'm all out of cash,'' she said, trying to sound severe. ''How are we going to pay for the gas? I'm afraid to use my credit card. It's just possible the clerk might be alert enough to recognize my name.''

''I have money,'' Caleb said. ''May I open the door without getting shot?'' he asked Joe with heavy sarcasm. ''Given that your face has been on every TV screen in Colorado, you shouldn't get out of the car.''

''I can pump the gas,'' Anna suggested.

''I need to use the rest room facilities,'' Caleb said curtly. ''If I promise not to yell out that I'm being kidnapped, do you mind if I relieve myself?''

Anna couldn't see any way that Caleb was going to cause them trouble by using a gas station rest room, although her brain was fuzzy enough that she wasn't sure her judgment was reliable. ''Do you see any problems with letting him use the rest room?'' she asked Joe.

He shook his head. ''You go ahead and pump ten dollars' worth of gas. We're less than thirty miles from Durango, so that's more than we need. Caleb, stay in the car until Anna has finished pumping, then go inside with her and use the rest room while she's paying for the gas.''

Caleb scowled, irritated by the instructions. ''I don't need a watchdog,'' he said. ''I realize it's to my own disadvantage if I attract the attention of the police. You've made your point over and over. If you two are arrested, I'm in big trouble. I'm not stupid. I get it.''

Joe gave a grim smile. ''I'm glad you do, Caleb. However, in light of your past history, I'm sure you'll understand that we feel safer if we assume you're out to betray us any way and any time you can. Anna, watch him carefully.''

She didn't need the warning. Caleb's cooperation,

limited and reluctant as it was, struck her as suspicious. The convenience store was relatively crowded, but Anna could see the doors to the rest rooms even while she waited to pay for the gas. There were four people in line at the cash register ahead of her, but when she'd finished paying, there was still no sign of Caleb. The pay phones were all outside the store, or she would have suspected him of calling the police, even though that would be a sure case of cutting off his nose to spite his face.

Positioning herself in an aisle where she was concealed from the clerk, but still had a clear view of the rest room, she tried not to draw attention to herself as she waited.

It was almost three more minutes before Caleb emerged from the rest room. "Sorry to keep you," he said. "When I'm nervous, my stomach gets upset."

This was more than she needed to know about the functioning of Caleb's digestive system and she speedily marched him back to the car.

"What kept you?" Joe asked. "Was there a problem?"

She shook her head. "No, everything's fine. It was busy, but nobody paid much attention to either of us."

Caleb made a smooth reentry into the flow of traffic. "Stopping at that gas station made me realize we have a bit of a problem," he said, squinting against the sun. "There are five employees at the bank who worked with Joe and they're going to recognize him the moment he steps into the lobby. What's more, they almost certainly saw the same TV news broadcast last night as I did, which means every employee in the bank will have spent the whole morning gossiping about the fact that Joe is now wanted for the murder of Franklin Saunders. Who is, let me remind you, another one of their ex-colleagues.''

''Oh, my God,'' Joe said.

Anna's heart skipped a beat. Caleb had pointed out something that was considerably more than ''a bit of a problem.''

Caleb pursed his lips at Joe's blasphemy, but continued anyway. ''Face it, Joe. There's no way in the world that you can enter that bank without all three tellers pressing their panic buttons the first second they see you. Five minutes after we walk into the lobby, the bank is going to be swarming with cops.''

Joe stared straight ahead, his body motionless. ''Are you suggesting that we trust you to go into the bank alone, Caleb?''

''That's the most logical solution to the problem. Are you willing to go along with it?''

Not in this lifetime, Anna thought.

Caleb paused, and when neither she nor Joe responded, he continued. ''There's another possibility. I don't like it, but I'm sure you'll both prefer it. I have a computer at home that's tied into the office network. We could go to my house, which would eliminate the risk of you being identified. You could both watch me download the information about Bartlett onto a floppy disk. Then I'll call my lawyer. I admit I'd prefer to be at home to consult with him.''

''We'd prefer to go to your home,'' Joe said. ''Right, Anna?''

She nodded, scarcely able to believe that she and Joe had both overlooked the problem of his being recognized if they tried to enter the bank. Extreme fatigue was the only excuse she could come up with for such an elementary oversight. She didn't like to feel grateful to Caleb—after all, it was his own skin he was trying to save, not theirs—but in this instance she had to admit that they owed him. Big time. She wondered what else they might have overlooked. Nothing too important, she could only hope.

They passed the outskirts of Durango, where the plant for Arthur Bartlett's Healthlife company stood in the center of an acre of grass, landscaped with a pond and an aerating fountain. Profits, legal and illegal, looked to be good, Anna thought wryly.

"I have a new house since you left town," Caleb said, turning into a pleasant suburban street of expensive homes. "We outgrew the one I was living in when you were working at the bank, Joe." He drew the Land Cruiser to a halt outside a house built in typical nineties style, with a pretentious portico and huge bay windows slapped onto a basic box, the builder's attempt to justify a fifty-thousand-buck price increase. "We've made quite good time. It's only ten-thirty." He turned off the ignition, pocketing the keys.

Anna wondered if she was imagining the hint of gloating anticipation that lurked beneath his bland expression—an expression that she'd seen in church on six painful Sundays, as she waited for her wedding day to arrive. Maybe he was simply relieved to be home, about to see his children, along with his newest and youngest wives.

There was a queasy sensation in the pit of her stomach that had lingered ever since they stopped to buy gas. It wasn't caused by fatigue, or by motion sickness, or even by accumulated stress, Anna decided. It was caused by the anticipation of disaster. But what did she suspect Caleb of planning to do? If Caleb had wanted to betray them to the police, all he had to do was take them to the bank and let the inevitable happen.

"I know it's useless for me to ask you to leave your guns in the car," Caleb said. "But would you at least make sure they're completely out of sight? I'm doing the pair of you a huge favor in bringing you into my home, and I don't want my children rewarded by the sight of their father walking into the house at gunpoint."

It was an entirely reasonable request. In fact, everything Caleb had done since he got into his Land Cruiser had been entirely reasonable. That was what bothered her, Anna reflected. Caleb wasn't a reasonable man, or a gracious loser. They'd threatened him, humiliated him and forced him to confront the fact that prison quite possibly loomed in his future. Why the *hell* was he being so cooperative?

"The baby usually naps midmorning," Caleb said. "I'll take us in through the porch at the back. The kitchen door is never locked. That's one of the great things about Durango. There's no crime."

He apparently saw no irony in his remark, which didn't surprise Anna in the least. A lifetime spent in service to the True Life Church didn't make for a highly developed sense of irony.

They followed a narrow paved path along the side of the house to the porch, a pleasant screened structure filled with sophisticated wrought iron furniture, looking out over an expensively landscaped yard. A glass-topped table held a bowl of hyacinth that filled the area with fragrance.

The hairs on the back of Anna's neck started to prick.

''Honey, I'm home!'' Caleb called.

Honey. Singular.

Caleb pushed open the door connecting the porch to the kitchen and stepped inside. Anna hung back. Her gaze raked the immaculate room. Not a bib or a high chair anywhere in sight, much less a toy. Spotless tiled floor. A built-in wine rack on the wall facing her, filled with bottles of wine. The True Life Church forbade the consumption of alcohol. Gleaming countertops stood empty except for a coffeepot. The True Life Church forbade the consumption of caffeine.

''Run!'' she screamed to Joe, already fleeing back out through the porch. ''It's a trap. For God's sake, run!''

Twenty-One

It took Joe about three seconds too long to react to Anna's warning. He started to run, but before he could reach the kitchen door, Caleb swung around and thrust his elbow into Joe's rib cage, hitting him squarely in the center of his wound. Joe felt an immediate gush of blood and almost blacked out from the pain.

When he could open his eyes again, Caleb was holding Sheriff Betz's gun and Sophie Bartlett was standing in front of him, flanked by two short men with the strong, stocky appearance of Mexican laborers. Sophie, dressed in a black linen suit with a diamond pin glittering high on her shoulder, was flawlessly made up, and her blond hair framed her heart-shaped face to perfection. Her jacket was cut low enough to showcase the swell of her breasts, but not quite low enough to appear vulgar. She looked, Joe thought, like a *Vogue* model for the upscale grieving widow.

She greeted him with a smile that radiated warmth. He wondered how he had ever been deceived by it, even for a minute. ''Hello, Joe. It's been a while.''

''Sophie.'' It was all he could manage without running the risk of puking. Breathing was still difficult in the wake of Caleb's blow.

Her imperious gaze cooled and switched from him to Caleb, a queen interrogating one of her peasants. ''Where's the woman you talked about when you called me, Caleb?''

''She must have realized something was up. She was following behind....'' Caleb drew in an apologetic breath. ''She...um...got away.''

''Trust you to fuck up.'' The patrician accent contrasted oddly with the obscene language. ''What's her name, anyway? The cell phone connection wasn't good when you called and I couldn't quite catch it.''

Cell phone. Shit, Joe thought. Caleb must have had a cell phone stashed in his car. That's why he insisted he needed to use the rest room—so that he could call the Bartletts on his cell phone and get instructions.

''Anna Langtry.'' Caleb had enough sense of self-preservation not to mention that Anna had once been his wife. But the fact that he'd chosen to lead them into this trap suggested to Joe that he had only the faintest grasp of the danger he was in from the Bartletts.

Sophie turned to one of the men at her side and spoke in fluent Spanish. ''I need you to find the woman for me. Did you see her before she ran?''

''A glimpse only, *señora.*''

''She can't have gone far,'' Sophie said. ''She's driving a—'' She broke off and turned to Caleb. ''Is she driving? Does she have car keys?''

''No,'' Caleb said, holding up the keys to his Land Cruiser. ''I have them.''

Sophie didn't bother to conceal her relief. ''I guess I should be thankful for small mercies. Can you tell Jorge and Antonio what she looks like? They barely got a glimpse of her and I didn't see her at all.''

Caleb nodded. ''She has long curly hair. Auburn, I guess you'd call the color. She's tall and very athletic-looking. She's wearing jeans and a pale-yellow sweatshirt.''

Sophie turned back to the men. ''Did you understand?'' she asked in Spanish.

''If you could translate for us, *señora.* Just to be sure.''

Sophie translated Caleb's description. ''Hurry,'' she added. ''It's really important for you to find her. Once you've located her, take her back to the ski lodge in Telluride. There'll be a bonus for each of you when she's found.''

''They won't catch her,'' Joe said as the men left at a run. ''Anna's way too smart to let herself be picked up by those two.''

''Durango's a small town,'' Sophie said. ''She's on foot, and they have transportation. They'll find her.''

Joe leaned against the counter, which helped to prevent him keeling over—and also brought him within five feet of the wine rack. If he weren't already wounded, he would be able to take these two with one hand tied behind his back. As it was, he needed a weapon. ''My money's on Anna,'' he said. ''I sure hope you and Daddy have a Plan B, Sophie, because you're going to need it.''

''We don't have to listen to him,'' Caleb snarled. He aimed the gun at Joe's head. ''Why can't we kill him now?''

''Because you fucked up and Anna got away.''

Caleb waved the gun with reckless abandon. ''Why does that mean we can't kill Mackenzie?''

Sophie spoke with an exaggerated patience that only made her anger more apparent. ''Because Anna might come back here at any moment with the cops, the majority of whom aren't on my father's payroll. And even if we get lucky and the cops she brings happen to be dirty, they could hardly overlook Joe's dead body lying in the middle of my kitchen floor.''

Caleb glowered at Joe. ''We could say he invaded the house and threatened you.''

His former boss was clearly very anxious for him to die, Joe thought wryly.

''For heaven's sake, stop waving that gun,'' Sophie snapped. ''If you kill Joe, I'll be seriously pissed. And of course we can't claim he invaded the house. How is he supposed to have gotten here unless you brought him? His car is parked at your house in Alana Springs, isn't it? That's an inconvenient piece of evidence for us to account for.''

Caleb looked crestfallen, but he did finally lower his weapon. ''Anna won't go to the cops,'' he protested. ''She can't. They'll arrest her. That was the whole point of her and Mackenzie trying to force me to cooperate with them.''

''She might be willing to risk arrest,'' Sophie said. ''Or she might have some other plan that's equally annoying. We don't know what her plans might be, because you let her get away.''

''So what are we going to do?'' A note of rising panic edged into Caleb's voice. ''You told me that if I brought them here, you'd take care of everything for me.''

''I will take care of you,'' Sophie said. ''I promise.''

Caleb looked reassured by this. Joe, by contrast, decided that if he'd been in Caleb's shoes, he'd have fled for the hills without stopping to look back. Unfortunately, he and Anna needed Caleb if they were ever going to make a credible case against Bartlett. Which meant he was probably going to have to exert himself to keep the double-crossing slimebucket alive, much as he would have liked to let him meet the fate he deserved. With that in mind, Joe quietly moved another two feet closer to the wine rack.

Sophie lifted the handset from a wall phone and pressed a speed dial button. For all her bravado, her hands weren't entirely steady, Joe noticed. She wasn't a stupid woman, and she must realize that Anna's escape posed a serious threat to her father's criminal enterprises. If Sophie had managed to capture both of them, she could have killed them with impunity and had their bodies dumped in a distant canyon. With Anna on the loose, everything changed. Joe hoped to God his boast was correct and Anna wouldn't be captured. She was in superb physical condition, but she hadn't slept in over twenty-four hours. Would she be able to run fast enough and far enough to remain hidden from Sophie's henchmen?

Sophie's phone call was finally answered. ''Dad, it's me. We have Mackenzie, but the woman got away.'' She paused. ''I know. I'm sorry, but she's on foot, so she can't get very far. Her name's Anna Langtry, by the way.'' Sophie repeated Caleb's description of Anna yet again. ''Yes, she's the woman mentioned in the Denver police bulletin about Mackenzie. I already sent Jorge and Antonio in search of her, but we need everyone you can spare out looking for her, Dad. Especially any cops you can rely on. We need to comb this neighborhood and get her picked up and brought to us before she causes any trouble. She and Mackenzie both know enough to be dangerous.''

She listened while her father spoke, his part of the conversation inaudible. ''I understand. I've told the men to take her to the ski lodge in Telluride if…when…they find her. I'm going there right now, with Mackenzie. We can't risk being here if Anna comes back with the cops.''

Once again, she listened to her father. Caleb, fortunately, was hanging on her every word, wondering, perhaps, if Arthur Bartlett was going to blame him for the disaster of Anna's escape. As he listened, Caleb edged closer to Sophie, which conveniently blocked her line of sight to Joe's right hand.

If ever there was a time for action, this was it, Joe decided, sliding a bottle of wine out of the rack.

''Yes,'' Sophie said into the phone. ''I've thought of that, too. I'll check in with you in thirty minutes, as soon as we're on the road to Telluride.'' She hung up just as Joe broke his wine bottle over Caleb's head. Burgundy splattered everywhere, a deep rich crimson.

Caleb fell to the floor so heavily that Joe was afraid he might be dead. He dived down on top of him, grabbing the gun from Caleb's limp hand and pointing it up toward Sophie all in one swift movement.

Action movies, he thought, woozy with triumph and alcohol fumes. You gotta love 'em.

Caleb was breathing, thank God. There did, however, seem to be an alarming quantity of blood oozing from the cuts in his head. Joe would have been more worried if his experience with prison brawls hadn't taught him that head wounds tended to bleed a lot. Still, he'd like to get Caleb to the Emergency Room before his star witness up and died on him.

Keeping the gun aimed as best he could, Joe pushed himself into a kneeling position and then used the edge of the counter to haul himself upright. Best not to think about his wound, and what had probably happened to Charlie's stitches. No point in making himself more miserable than was absolutely necessary.

Sophie gave him a smile of such calculated charm that he felt a chasm of yearning open inside him for Anna, and her rock solid sincerity. "You know you're not going to use that gun on me, Mackenzie."

Joe's index finger squeezed the trigger before his brain had time to say no. Fortunately, some buried remnant of control warned him to aim for her shoulder. Sophie wasn't worth the black mark on his conscience that killing her would bring.

She stared at him in blank disbelief. "You shot my diamond brooch!"

Sophie couldn't have been more surprised than Joe was himself. "Yeah, well, it's damn near six inches long. It's hard to miss."

She sank down into a chair. "I'm wounded."

"Yeah, I guess you are. But your husband is dead, so you can count yourself lucky by comparison. Tell me, did you always intend to kill Frank, Sophie, or was he just unfortunate collateral damage?"

"You don't seriously expect me to answer that, do you?" She took off her jacket, indifferent to the fact that she was exposing a transparent black chiffon camisole and also that she still didn't wear a bra. She examined her wounded flesh with deep fascination. "Are you going to let me bleed to death, or are you going to help me?"

"Here." He handed her a roll of paper towels, removing the phone handset while he was in that part of the kitchen. "It's barely a scratch, Sophie. I think you'll live."

"You don't care, do you?"

"Not much."

"Pity." She looked at him through narrowed eyes. "You always were an interesting son of a bitch to hang out with."

"Is that why you agreed to marry me?" he asked, only a little curious.

"No," she said coolly. "That was because you were the best damn lover I'd ever had."

He wasn't flattered. "You seemed quite willing to trade me in for Frank. Was he the second best lover you ever had?"

"No," she said. "Not even close. Marrying Frank was strictly business."

"And murdering him was business, too?"

"I'm physically wounded, Joe, not mentally incompetent. I've already told you that I have no intention of responding to that question."

"I'm puzzled, Sophie, I admit it. I don't understand why your father started to sell illegal drugs. Healthlife has been a profitable company for years. Was the extra money that important? How many million dollars can you spend in a year, anyway?"

"It's not the money," she said. "It's the power. It's beating the bureaucrats. Having inside knowledge. Keeping secrets."

Funny, Joe reflected. Anna had said the same thing about polygamy. It wasn't the sex that kept men tied to the system. It was power, the ultimate aphrodisiac. Apparently Sophie and her father would understand what motivated the elders of the True Life Church of Latter Day Saints all too well.

Anna scrambled down the path at the side of the house and hit the sidewalk, adrenaline sending her feet flying. Joe hadn't made it out, so that meant it was up to her to thwart whatever trap Caleb had set for them both. She forgot fatigue and poured her heart into running.

She'd covered five long suburban blocks, heading first east and then north, before she realized that however fast she ran, if she didn't have a destination, she wouldn't get anywhere. She slowed her pace to a jog and took stock of her surroundings. There was an intersection about a quarter of a mile ahead. She could see the illuminated sign for a convenience store on one corner, and a public library on another. Both the library and the store would almost certainly have a phone. She could dial 911, summon the cops....

Did she want to summon the cops? Probably, she decided, jogging toward the intersection. At this point, keeping Joe alive was her first priority, and for that she needed help. Time enough after he'd been rescued to worry about his precarious legal position, not to mention her own. It might take a while to convince the cops to investigate Caleb and the Bartletts, but she was confident it would happen eventually. Oddly, after the rocky start to their relationship, she had a fair amount of faith in the integrity of Detective Ed Barber. And while she knew from firsthand experience that the criminal justice system was riddled with flaws, she saw reasons to be optimistic. She and Joe could now tell investigators exactly where to look, and what crimes to look for. She had to believe that, in the end, the two of them would be vindicated.

But only if they both lived long enough to enjoy their victory. And if that was going to happen, she needed to get off the street, Anna recognized belatedly. If Caleb had paid any attention to what she and Joe said to him, he must have realized that she was the equivalent of a lethal weapon, aimed straight at his heart. Presumably he and whoever else might have been waiting inside the house would be hell-bent on finding her.

The thought had barely taken shape when she became aware of a Jeep heading down the street toward her with ominous intent. It slowed down as it approached, and she ran across the road to avoid it, turning into a small side street.

Too late, she realized that her choice of direction had been a bad mistake. She should have run toward the intersection, where there were cars and pedestrians. Here, there wasn't a soul in sight who might help her.

The Jeep swung around in a U-turn, coming alongside her. The passenger door opened to reveal a man brandishing a knife that looked big enough and sharp enough to gut a whale, let alone a woman. Why threaten her with a knife and not a gun? Of course! He didn't want to attract attention. From his point of view it would be disastrous if he alerted homeowners to what was going on.

Well, hell, she could take care of that. Still running, from the corner of her eye Anna saw her would-be abductor jump from the Jeep. Instead of trying to outrun him, she stopped abruptly and swung around to confront him, pulling her Glock from her shoulder holster and firing at the Jeep's tires as she turned.

The Jeep swerved, suggesting she'd hit her target. She didn't take time to check. Screaming for help, she squeezed off a couple of shots aimed in the general direction of her pursuer's feet.

Her aim was seriously off—she might have expected that since her eyes seemed to have been closed when she pulled the trigger—and the shots went into the pavement. No surprise to discover that firing at real-live humans, albeit scummy ones, wasn't anything like firing her weapon at the training facility.

Her knife-wielding attacker clambered back into the lurching Jeep, and Anna got off another round of shots at the tires. Her aim was better when the target was an object rather than a person, and she hit at least two of the four. As the door of the Jeep slammed behind her pursuer, it occurred to her that just because she'd only seen a knife, it didn't mean the men didn't also have guns. Guns they would be more than willing to use now that she'd broken their self-imposed silence.

Anna's body reacted before her mind even started to analyze her best course of action. She jumped over a knee-high row of shrubs in the nearest front yard, and threw herself on the grass behind a clump of aspen just as somebody in the Jeep let off an ominous volley of shots. Jesus! What did they have for weapons? To her overstretched nerves, it sounded like cannon.

Despite the fact that she'd shot out two of their tires, the Jeep was driving away, the wheel rims grinding on the surface of the road, and there wasn't a damn thing she could do to stop it. If she stood up to take aim, she'd be dead. Anna rolled over in the grass, reaction to her brush with death combining with exhaustion to leave her virtually comatose.

At least the gun battle should have achieved her purpose, she decided, feeling her entire body start to shake. Every homeowner on the street should have placed a call to the cops by now.

Anna was still lying on the grass under the aspen trees when the first squad car rolled up three minutes later, followed in quick succession by two more. With the arrival of the cops, doors in the neighborhood began to open, and people ventured out, cautiously at first, and soon in great numbers.

It took Anna what seemed like a lifetime, but was less than ten minutes in real time, to persuade the police that before they took her to the station house for questioning, they needed to rescue Joe Mackenzie, who was being held hostage by unknown assailants, led by Caleb Welks, president of the Durango branch of the Bank of Trade and Commerce. Her cause was undoubtedly helped by the capture of her two attackers who had been foolish enough to continue driving their battered and highly noticeable Jeep, and by the reports of several neighbors, whose description of her attackers became more terrifying as the seconds passed. If she'd considered the knife whale-gutting size, Anna reflected in amusement, some of the witnesses were soon describing a weapon large enough to have taken down Godzilla.

The police drove Anna back to Harvard Street, warning her that if the situation seemed to them as threatening as she'd suggested, they would make no moves until a SWAT team arrived. But no SWAT team was needed. As the squad cars drove up, Joe greeted them at the front door.

Escorted by two policemen, Anna walked up the path to the door. Joe sent her a grin that restored life to her abused body. ''I knew I could count on you to bring the cavalry,'' he said.

''They're planning to take us all to jail,'' she said. ''Does that still count as a rescue?''

''Providing they give us adjoining cells.''

''That's touching, Mackenzie, but I prefer to work on the idea of adjoining lawyers. Highly efficient ones, who get us instant bail.''

''That, too.'' he said.

It was clear the detectives weren't going to allow them many more minutes to talk. Joe fixed his gaze on hers. ''Does this by any chance strike you as a good moment for me to tell you that I'm hopelessly in love with you?''

She stared at him, incredulous, then laughed. ''It strikes me as the perfect time, Mackenzie.''

''Great.'' The laughter fading from his eyes, Joe took her hands into his. ''I love you, Anna.''

She'd heard the words from other men, but they'd never meant very much to her, except to cause a mild regret that she couldn't return the feeling. She'd been married to Caleb before she ever had the chance to fall in love, and the trauma of giving up Megan had merely confirmed her suspicion that love was a zero sum game in which she was destined to be the perpetual loser. Ever since her daughter's birth, she'd guarded her heart so carefully that no aspiring lover had come close to breaching the blockade she'd built around her emotions. Somehow, though, Joe had distracted her attention and slipped past the barriers, leaving her desperately in love and contemplating a whole new landscape of the heart.

Anna tilted her head back and looked up at Joe. Warmth flooded her, spreading out from somewhere deep inside. ''I love you, too.''

He carried her hand to his lips and kissed her palm, before bending her fingers over and sealing in his kiss. Then he grinned and gestured to indicate that she should turn around to look across the street, where a roving TV news crew had set their cameras rolling. ''I've got that declaration on tape,'' he said, as the cops hustled him toward a waiting squad car. ''I'll hold you to it.''

She smiled at him as the cops escorted her down the steps. ''I'm counting on it, Mackenzie.''

Epilogue

September 2002

In Charlie's considered opinion, sobriety wasn't all it was cracked up to be. Especially when you were at a wedding reception and a doe-eyed woman with a silver tray and the cutest ass he'd seen in a while kept coming up and asking if you'd like a drink. What kind of a damn fool question was that? Of course he wanted a drink. Charlie sipped his ginger ale and directed a ferocious scowl at the waitress before she could come up and bother him again. The reception, thank God, was drawing to a close and he'd soon be able to go home, away from the temptation of all this damn booze. He'd been sober now for 102 days, a state of being that pretty much sucked the big one, but for some inexplicable reason he was determined to make it to day 103.

He saw Joe and Anna cross the room, heading toward him, hand in hand, both of them wearing sappy grins. Charlie had never quite understood why any sane man would want to get married. It wasn't so much the promise of eternal faithfulness that struck Charlie as unbearable; it was the prospect of having to talk to the same person every day for thirty or forty years that brought him out in a cold sweat. Still, when Anna and Joe had walked down the aisle after the ceremony, both of them damn near glowing with happiness, he had felt a twinge of envy. Hell, but Joe looked as if he'd been handed the keys to the kingdom! Charlie had a suspicion you couldn't look that pleased with life unless you were deeply in love, even if the government had just granted you a full pardon, and the bank you once worked for—fearing a lawsuit—had coughed up a cool million in compensation for the four years you'd spent in prison. The fact that Sophie and Arthur Bartlett were both facing a slew of charges couldn't hurt Joe's mood, Charlie figured. For all their fancy lawyers and friends in high places, it looked as if father and daughter were both going to be serving a chunk of time.

Couldn't happen to a more deserving couple, Charlie decided.

Joe and Anna came to a halt right in front of him. Anna leaned forward and gave him a kiss, and Charlie responded with a token growl of protest which she ignored. For some reason, Anna never had been properly intimidated by him.

She gave him a hug for good measure. Charlie glared at her, in case she should think he liked being fussed over, and her smile simply deepened. A warmth spread inside him that was almost as good as a shot of bourbon.

"Joe and I are going to leave in a couple of minutes," she said. "But I just wanted to thank you one more time. You were a terrific best man, Charlie."

"You're welcome. Any time."

Joe grinned. "This is a one-off, Charlie."

"Yeah, well I'm glad everythin' went okay." He cleared his throat. "In case I didn't say it before, I wish you both all the best. You looked…um…you look real pretty, Anna. That dress is fit for a princess." He turned away, horrified to discover a sudden lump in his throat. He swung back around and glared at her. "Cain't believe I'm congratulatin' Joe on marryin' a frickin' parole officer."

Anna laughed. "If it makes you feel better, I'm not going to be a parole officer for much longer. You're the first to hear the news, Charlie. I'm joining a group of family counselors and I'm going to work with children and teenagers who are having problems at school. I'm looking forward to the change."

"Seems like there's a lot of new beginnings for you and Joe. His new job arranging financing for excons to start their own small businesses. You workin' with kids. Settin' up in your new town house. The pair of you are goin' to be real busy."

Anna squeezed his arm. "If it weren't for you and the surgery you performed to take the bullet out of Joe's side, none of this could have happened. In fact, Joe and I probably wouldn't be here right now."

"Sure we would." Joe's eyes were warm with laughter as he looked at his new wife. "We're destined to be together. It was written in the stars."

"Oh, please." Charlie rolled his eyes. "Get the hell out of here both of you before you make me puke."

"Great advice," Joe said. "I've been suggesting the same thing for an hour now. Come on, Anna. Let's say goodbye to your mother and then we're out of here."

Joe had enjoyed today's festivities more than he'd

expected. For himself, he would have been happy to elope five months ago, but Anna's wedding to Caleb Welks had been such a sad, hole-in-corner affair that he'd understood why she needed this marriage to be celebrated in style, in a church, with friends to watch them exchange vows, and the organ booming out a triumphant recessional. In retrospect, Joe was glad that they'd waited. The memory of Anna walking down the aisle toward him in a shimmering cloud of white, her hair a deep-golden flame, was one he wouldn't soon forget.

Betty Jean was sitting at a table with two of Joe's cousins and their spouses, who had flown in from Minnesota. He was grateful to have had somebody from his family present at the wedding. It eased the sadness that his grandmother was too frail to make the trip, and anyway wouldn't have recognized him even if she'd been physically capable. Leila Sworski, who had returned from her sabbatical and had acted as Anna's maid of honor, was also sitting at the table.

Anna smiled at everyone, her gaze coming to rest on Betty Jean. "Mother, Joe and I are leaving now. We just came over to say goodbye and thank you again for coming."

There was a tiny hesitation in Anna's voice when she said *Mother,* Joe noticed. She had told Betty Jean about Megan's birth last night, and the emotions from that scene still reverberated between the two of them. Terrible guilt on the part of Betty Jean. Sadness and a lingering trace of anger on Anna's part.

Still, Joe was glad the truth was now in the open. The relationship between Betty Jean and Anna could finally grow into something less painful for both of them, even though they were never going to be truly close. The paths they had chosen were too different for real friendship to be possible, but Betty Jean was obviously trying to make up for fifteen years of bitter silence, and Anna was meeting her mother's overtures more than halfway. The fact that Betty Jean had driven up from Alana Springs to attend the wedding was a major step toward reconciliation. Until now, Betty Jean hadn't traveled farther than Cortez without her husband in the twenty-two years since she married Ray.

Maybe she'd been glad of an excuse to get away, Joe mused, as Anna completed her goodbyes. The community of Alana Springs had been thrown into turmoil by the arrest of Caleb Welks on charges of bigamy, embezzlement, fraud and conspiracy to commit murder. Ray and the other church elders lived in daily fear of being arrested for bigamy. They were right to be worried. The authorities had made it clear that if any more girls from Alana Springs dropped out of high school before they were eighteen, then prosecutions would follow.

Anna and Joe finally managed to disentangle themselves from their guests and make their way upstairs to the suite where they planned to spend their wedding night before leaving for a ten-day honeymoon in Europe. When they arrived, the lights were already turned low and a Sinatra CD was playing softly on the stereo. A magnum of iced champagne stood on the coffee table, along with a bowl of fresh strawberries. It was only as the tension drained out of her that Anna realized just how fearful she'd been of this moment. Despite the fact that making love to Joe was among the most wonderful experiences of her life, there were still a few demons to be banished in regard to her wedding night, courtesy of Caleb Welks. Apparently, though, they were about to surrender without a fight.

Joe drew her into his arms. His kiss was tender and full of promise. ''I want us to be like my grandparents,'' he said. ''The sort of people who are still madly in love when they're eighty.''

''It's less than fifty years until we're eighty,'' Anna said. ''Heck, that's going to be easy.''